**Mills & Boon are thrilled
to conclude this new family saga
from award-winning author Lucy Gordon**

THE FALCON DYNASTY

Five successful brothers looking for brides!

Amos Falcon is a proud, self-made man who
wants his legacy to live on through his five sons.
Each son is different, for they have different
mothers, but in one aspect they are the same: he
has raised them to be ruthless in business and
sensible in matters of the heart.

But one by one these high-achieving brothers
will find that when the right woman comes along
love is the greatest power of them all…

RESCUED BY THE BROODING TYCOON

MISS PRIM AND THE BILLIONAIRE

PLAIN JANE IN THE SPOTLIGHT

FALLING FOR THE REBEL FALCON

And this month the last Falcon brother's story:

THE FINAL FALCON SAYS I DO

THE FINAL FALCON SAYS I DO

BY
LUCY GORDON

MILLS & BOON®

Published in Great Britain 2014
by Mills & Boon, an imprint of Harlequin (UK) Limited,
Eton House, 18-24 Paradise Road, Richmond, Surrey, TW9 1SR

© 2014 Lucy Gordon

ISBN: 978 0 263 91249 4

23-0114

Harlequin (UK) Limited's policy is to use papers that are natural, renewable and recyclable products and made from wood grown in sustainable forests. The logging and manufacturing processes conform to the legal environmental regulations of the country of origin.

Printed and bound in Spain
by Blackprint CPI, Barcelona

Lucy Gordon cut her writing teeth on magazine journalism, interviewing many of the world's most interesting men, including Warren Beatty, Charlton Heston and Sir Roger Moore. She also camped out with lions in Africa, and had many other unusual experiences, which have often provided the background for her books. Several years ago, while staying in Venice, she met a Venetian who proposed in two days. They have been married ever since. Naturally this has affected her writing, where romantic Italian men tend to feature strongly.

Two of her books have won a Romance Writers of America RITA® Award.

You can visit her website at www.lucy-gordon.com.

To Horus, the Falcon God, whose magical powers are always there, lurking mysteriously.

CHAPTER ONE

IT WOULD BE the wedding of the year. In an elegant, luxurious church in the heart of London, crowded with wealthy, glamorous people, Amos Falcon, the financial giant whose name inspired awe and fury in equal measure, was to escort his stepdaughter down the aisle to be the bride of Dan Connor, a man of wealth and importance in the television industry.

Not that that would impress Amos Falcon. It was common knowledge that he had wanted to marry his stepdaughter to one of his own sons but had failed: one of the few times in his life when he hadn't got his own way.

The excitement level was rising. The wedding wasn't until midday, but the television cameras had been in place an hour earlier. Gossip said the entire Falcon family would be present, which meant Amos's five sons, who hailed from England, America, Russia and France. Some were famous. Some were wealthy. All were notable. And nobody wanted to miss so many fascinating arrivals.

'Travis Falcon,' sighed one young female journalist. 'Oh, I do hope he turns up. I always watch his television series and I'd love to meet him.'

'You reckon he'll really come all the way to London from Los Angeles?' queried Ken, the cameraman with her.

'Why not? He went to Moscow last month for Leonid's wedding. Hey, who's that?'

A buzz of anticipation greeted the arrival of a luxurious car, which disgorged an expensively dressed couple. But then there was a faint groan of disappointment. This man wasn't Travis.

'Marcel Falcon,' Ken mused. 'The French brother. And the one in the car just behind is Leonid.'

He focussed his camera on the two brothers as they climbed the steps to the great entrance and disappeared inside, then switched quickly back to another car from which a man and woman had emerged.

'Darius,' he said. 'English.'

'What about Jackson?' she asked. 'Surely he's English as well, and after Travis he's the best known because of those TV documentaries he does.'

'He's not a guest. He's the best man and he'll arrive with the groom. After that it'll be Amos and Freya, the bride. Ah, look who's getting out of that car! Freya's mother, the present Mrs Amos Falcon.'

Mrs Falcon was in her fifties, trim, well-dressed, but with an air of quiet reserve that made her stand out in this exotic atmosphere. She hurried up the steps, as though the spotlight made her uneasy.

Just inside the church Darius, Marcel and their wives were waiting for her. They embraced her warmly, and Darius said, 'This must be a happy day for you, Janine. Freya has finally escaped the terrible fate of being married to one of us.'

His stepmother regarded him with wry affection.

'You know very well that I'm fond of you all,' she said, 'and if Freya had really wanted to marry one of you I'd have had no problem. It was the just the way Amos— Well, you know…'

They nodded, understanding her reluctance to be candid about Amos's determination to get his own way. It had come close to bullying, but a loyal wife couldn't say so.

'How did you persuade him to give her away?' Harriet, Darius' wife, murmured. 'I should think it was the last thing he wanted to do.'

'It was,' Janine said wryly. 'I told him if he wouldn't do it, I would. When he realised I meant it he gave in. Exposing a family disagreement in public—well…'

'It would have made people laugh at him,' Harriet said. 'And he couldn't have that. You know, marrying you was the best thing that ever happened to Amos. You're the only person who can make him stop his nonsense.'

'Shh!' Janine put a finger to her lips. 'Never tell him I told you.'

'It's a promise.'

A cheer from outside put them all on alert.

'Travis,' Harriet said at once. 'When you hear them cheering you know it's Travis. I'll bet he's blowing kisses to them, putting his arms around girls in the crowd.'

'Not if Charlene's with him,' Janine observed. 'He's almost paranoid about considering her feelings.'

'And the joke is that it doesn't bother her,' Darius observed. 'He can do as he likes because Charlene knows she's got him just where she wants him.'

'Sounds the perfect arrangement to me,' said his wife.

'And you should know,' he said, smiling at her. 'You snap your fingers and I jump to attention, don't I?'

The look they shared seemed to sum up the air of joyful contentment that permeated the whole family these days. One by one the sons had found wives who were perfect for them.

Darius had turned his back on the society women who would gladly have been his to marry Harriet, a girl from the island he owned. Marcel had rediscovered love with Cassie, a woman he'd once known and lost. Travis had sought Charlene's protection against an intrusive press, only to find that his need of her went further and deeper than he could have dreamed. And Leonid's love for Perdita had survived quarrels and misunderstandings because their union had been fated from the moment they met.

Only one son was left: Jackson, who had introduced Freya to Dan Connor, the man she would marry today.

'Does anyone know anything about the groom?' Harriet asked.

'He owns a big television production company,' Travis explained. 'His documentaries made Jackson a star.'

'It's nearly time for things to start happening,' Janine said.

'Yes,' Travis agreed. 'We ought to take our places. I thought Dan and Jackson would have been here by now. I wonder what's keeping them.'

'Aren't you ready yet?' Jackson called through the half-open door of the bedroom. 'The car's downstairs.'

'I'm here,' Dan said, appearing. 'Just a few last-minute things to get right.'

The mirror threw back a reflection of two men in their thirties, both tall and handsome, both dressed for a wedding.

Jackson was the better looking, with a quick, teasing smile that could transform him. Observers sometimes said that of all Amos Falcon's sons he most resembled him. His lean face and firm features came from the same mould as his father. Amos's white hair had once been light brown, as Jackson's still was, and their eyes were an identical deep blue.

The differences between them were subtle. A lifetime

of demanding his own way and usually getting it had given Amos's face a harsh, set look, as though it rested on stone. The same features in Jackson were gentler, as perhaps his father's had been many years ago. Only the future would determine how much closer the resemblance would one day grow.

'Do I look all right?' Dan demanded, studying himself in the mirror.

'You look fine to me,' Jackson said, grinning. 'The perfect picture of a deliriously happy groom.'

Dan threw him a withering look. 'Just shut it, will you? There's no such thing as a deliriously happy groom. We're all shaking with nerves at the plunge we're about to take.'

'Come to think of it, you're right,' Jackson mused. 'My brothers were all on edge at their weddings—at least until they got their brides safely riveted. Then they relaxed.'

But even as he said it he knew there was something more behind Dan's tension. Dan was in his prime, wealthy, and with a streak of confidence that seemed to infuse his whole life. It had helped him build up Connor Productions, known for its colourful documentaries. It had also carried him through many affairs of the heart, which he'd survived by being wary of commitment.

But when Jackson had introduced him to Freya that wariness had begun to desert him, until suddenly, without warning, he'd made a determined and forceful proposal. Jackson knew that because he'd been sitting two tables away in the same restaurant, and had clearly heard Dan say, 'That's it! My mind's made up. You've simply got to marry me.'

Freya had given the rich chuckle that was one of her attractions, and teased, 'Oh, I've got to, have I?'

'Definitely. It's all settled. You're going to be Mrs Connor.' He'd slipped a hand behind her head, drawing her close for a kiss, untroubled by the crowd of other diners who'd laughed and applauded. The next day he'd bought her a diamond ring, and celebrations had commenced.

Jackson was glad for both of them. Freya had been his stepsister for six years. Their relationship might be called 'jumpy'. Sometimes they were cordial, and sometimes she challenged him.

'Who are you to give me orders?' she'd demanded once.

'I wasn't—'

'Yes, you were. You don't even know you're doing it. You're just like your father.'

'That's a terrible thing to say!'

'Why? I thought you admired him.'

'Some of the time,' he'd replied wryly. 'I don't like his way of giving orders without even realising he's doing it. But that doesn't mean I'm like him, and don't you dare say I am.'

'Oh, yeah?'

'Yeah.'

'*Yeah?*'

'*Yeah!*'

And their sparring had ended in laughter, as it so often did.

He thought fondly of her now—a sensible girl with brains enough to have passed her nursing degree with top marks, who could yet enjoy a squabble and give as good as she got. She would never be a great beauty, but her looks were agreeable. Dan had chosen well, he reckoned.

Almost at once after their engagement he'd had to leave to film a documentary on the other side of the world. He'd returned a week before the wedding and seen that his friend was on edge. He'd attached little importance to this, considering it standard bridegroom stuff. Even Dan's heavy drinking on his stag night had not alarmed him. It had merely underlined his duty to get Dan safely through the ceremony.

'Come on,' he said, opening the front door. 'Time to go.'

'Just a moment,' Dan said quickly. 'There's something—'

'Stop panicking. I've got it.'

'Got—?'

'The ring. Look.' Jackson reached into his pocket for a small box, which he opened to reveal a gold ring. 'That's what you were getting worked up about, wasn't it?'

'Of course. Of course.'

The tension in Dan's voice made Jackson regard him kindly and clap him on the shoulder. 'Everything's all right,' he said. 'Nothing can go wrong now. Time to go.'

In moments they were downstairs, greeting the chauffeur, settling into the back seat of the car.

It wasn't a long journey to the church but the traffic was heavy that morning. As they crawled along at a snail's pace Jackson gave a sigh of frustration.

'Come on,' he groaned. 'If it takes any longer, Dad and Freya will turn up before we do.'

'Is Amos really giving her away? I can't get my head round that.'

'Why shouldn't he? Oh, you mean because he wanted her to marry one of his own sons? When Leonid married Perdita there was only me left, and I told him to forget it. I like Freya, but not in that way.'

'I guess that's why you introduced me to her? Hoping I'd do what you wouldn't?'

'It wasn't like that,' Jackson said, shocked. 'Of course I was glad for her to know as many other guys as possible, but I wasn't making secret plans.'

'Aw, come on. You were hoping the old man would

admit defeat. No way. He moved heaven and earth to stop this wedding.'

'What the devil do you mean by that?'

'When I was going out with Freya he came to see me. He wanted to warn me off. Said I should leave her alone, and if I didn't—well, there were a few hints about the damage he could do to me financially.'

'But you told him to get stuffed?'

'I didn't say anything. No chance. He said his piece and walked out, slamming the door. I guess he just took it for granted that I'd do as he said.'

'Yes,' Jackson murmured. 'He has a way of doing that. He scares people. But not you. You stood up to him and proposed to her. Good for you. She's a lucky girl to have a guy who loves her so much.'

'But I'm not in love with her,' Dan said explosively. 'I lost my temper, that's all. I'm damned if I'll let any man give me orders. Sorry, I know he's your father—'

'That's all right,' Jackson said hastily. 'But are you telling me you only proposed to Freya because you were angry? I don't believe it.'

'Believe it. I just saw red. But then suddenly we were engaged and—hell, I don't know. She's a nice girl, but I'm not in love, and if Amos hadn't tried to scare me out of proposing I'd never have done it.'

'I don't believe this,' Jackson said frantically. 'I was there at your engagement party, and if ever I saw two people in love—'

'Yes, I played the devoted lover—and you know why? Because Amos was there, looking fit to do murder. Oh, brother, did I enjoy that!'

'But he's giving her away.'

'I reckon his wife twisted his arm. Freya's her daughter and she wouldn't want him making trouble.'

Jackson tore at his hair.

'Let me understand this,' he said, aghast. 'You've let things get this far, and you're really saying you're not in love with the girl you're about to marry?'

'That's right. I'm not. But what can I do? She's obviously in love with me and I'm trapped. I can feel the noose tightening around my neck with every moment.'

'You should have been honest with her before this,' Jackson said furiously. 'Now you'll hurt her a lot more if you marry her without love and let her down later.'

In his agitated state Jackson spoke instinctively. Afterwards he was to curse himself for a fool, but by then it was too late.

'That's true,' Dan said, staring at him as though a light had suddenly dawned. 'And there's still time to put things right.'

As he spoke the car halted at traffic lights. Dan opened the door and began to ease himself out.

'You go on to the church,' he said. 'Explain why I'm not with you. Make them realise I had no choice.'

'*What?* Don't be daft. You've got to go through with it now.'

'I can't. You've just made me understand that.'

'Dan! Don't you dare— Come back.'

But Dan had slammed the door and begun to run.

'Wait here,' Jackson told the chauffeur, scrambling out of the car. 'Dan! Come back. *Come back.*'

But Dan was running fast, darting in and out of the traffic which had started to move again. He reached the other side of the road and vanished down an alley. Jackson raced after him as fast as he could, nearly being hit by a car. But when he reached the street it was empty.

'Dan!' he yelled. 'You can't do this. *Please!*'

There was no answer.

'Where are you?' he cried. 'Don't hide from me. Let's talk.'

He tore along the road, searching everywhere but without result.

'I didn't mean it!' he shouted. 'Not the way it came out. I spoke without thinking but I never meant— Don't do this.'

He ran up and down for a few more minutes before facing facts.

'Oh, no!' he groaned. 'This can't be happening. But it is, and I'm to blame. It'll be my fault if— Oh, what have I done? *What have I done?*'

Windows were opening above him. He made a hasty exit, returning to the car and throwing himself into the back seat. 'Go on to the church,' he growled.

At last the building came in sight, and he groaned again as he saw the excited crowds and the cameras.

'Not here,' he said hastily. 'Go around the back.'

He slid down low, hoping not to be seen, and didn't sit up again until they reached the back of the church. He paid the chauffeur, adding a generous tip and putting his finger over his lips. Then he hurried through a rear door as fast as he could.

In seven years of making documentaries Jackson had many times had to screw up his courage. He'd faced lions, swum in dangerously deep water, and talked into cameras from great heights. But none of those things had made his stomach churn as much as the thought of the next few minutes.

He tried to tell himself that Freya would cope well. She was a trained nurse and a strong, efficient, determined young woman, not a wilting violet. But a voice in his mind wouldn't let him get away with that.

You're just telling yourself what you want to believe. This is going to devastate her, and it's your fault, so stop trying to make it easy on yourself.

As he slipped quietly into the main body of the church he saw the family gathered in the front pews. Travis looked up and gestured for him to approach.

'What's up?' he asked as Jackson neared. 'Where's the groom?'

'He's not coming. He changed his mind at the last minute and dashed out of the car. I tried to follow but I lost sight of him.'

'What do you mean?' demanded Janine. 'He can't just dump my daughter with the wedding about to start.'

'I'm afraid that's what he's done. It seems he's always had doubts and suddenly they crushed him.'

Before anyone could say more the organ burst into the melody of 'Here Comes The Bride.'

'Oh, no!' Jackson groaned.

'There they are,' said Darius. 'Oh, heavens. What a disaster!'

Everyone stared to the end of the aisle, where Amos could clearly be seen with Freya on his arm. Jackson cursed himself for his clumsiness. He should have waited outside for the car and told them the truth there. Then Freya could have returned home at once, without having to make the humiliating trip down the aisle.

He thought of hurrying forward, approaching her now before she came any closer, but she was already in the spotlight. Or at least Amos was. People recognised him. Some waved to him. Some slipped into the aisle to greet him. Jackson had no choice but to wait, suffering agonies of impatience, his eyes fixed on Freya.

For a moment he almost believed that this was somebody else. The strong, sensible young woman who lived in his mind had vanished, replaced by a girl in a glamorous white satin dress. Her fair hair, normally straight, had been curled into an exotic creation and covered by a lace veil that trailed down almost to the floor.

There was a glow about her that he'd never seen before. She was smiling as though fate had brought her to a blissful destination. It made her look exactly as a happy bride ought to look, and Jackson closed his eyes, sickened by what was about to happen.

As they neared him and saw that Jackson was alone, Amos began to frown.

'Where's the groom?' he rasped. 'Why isn't he with you?'

'Shh!' Freya silenced him with a finger over her lips. 'He must have slipped away to the Gents. He'll be here in a moment.' She gave Jackson a teasing smile. 'I expect he had a bit too much to drink last night, didn't he?'

Her good nature was almost too much for him to bear. How could Dan not have wanted to marry this sweet creature?

'I'm afraid there's been a problem,' he said in a low voice. 'Dan isn't here. He's—he's not coming.'

'What do you mean?' Freya asked. 'Is he ill? Oh, heavens, I must go to him.'

'No, he's not ill,' Jackson said. 'I'm sorry, Freya, but he changed his mind at the last minute. He got out of the car and ran. I don't even know where he is now.'

'He ran?' Freya whispered. 'To get away from me? Oh, no!' She withdrew her hand from Amos's arm and faced Jackson. 'But why?'

'He lost his nerve,' Jackson said uneasily.

The words seemed to swirl in Freya's head, meaningless yet full of monstrous meaning.

'What—what do you mean—lost his nerve?' she stammered. 'It doesn't take nerve to—to—'

To marry someone you love. The words were on the

tip of her tongue, yet some power stopped her from saying them.

Jackson understood and struggled for an answer.

'It's a big occasion,' he managed. 'Some men can't cope.'

But Dan was used to big occasions, and they both knew it. Freya's look of disbelief told Jackson he'd have to do better than that.

'Why?' she said fiercely. 'What really happened?'

'He just—couldn't cope suddenly.'

Freya swung away from him, trying to cope with the feelings that stormed through her. Pain, disbelief, disillusion, humiliation all fought for supremacy. Humiliation won.

Dan had charmed her, filled her grey world with light and made her feel special—the kind of woman that other women envied. Now he was knocking her down in the eyes of the world. She clenched her hands into fists, holding them up against her eyes and emitting a soft groan.

Behind her Jackson said, 'Freya—' reaching out to touch her, but she pulled away.

'I'm all right,' she said, dropping her hands.

He didn't believe it for a moment, but he respected her determination to appear strong.

Amos was in a stew, growling, 'Just let me get my hands on him.'

It was on the tip of Jackson's tongue to hurl a bitter accusation at his father, telling him how his actions had been the trigger. With a huge effort at control he fought back the words for Freya's sake.

A murmur was rising from the congregation as they sensed trouble. The vicar drew close and spoke quietly.

'Perhaps you'd like to come into the back and talk privately?'

Amos reached out to take Freya's hand but Jackson was there first, slipping his arm around her and leading her away to where there were no curious eyes. The family followed them.

When they were safely in the back room Jackson repeated the story, keeping hold of Freya's hand, feeling the terrible stillness that had settled over her.

'Why did he do it?' she whispered. 'What did he say?'

'Only that when he came to the point—he just couldn't,' Jackson prevaricated, wishing the earth would swallow him up.

'I'll kill him,' Amos muttered.

'Join the queue,' Travis said. 'We'll all enjoy doing that.'

'No,' Freya said. 'This is for me to take care of. I must speak to him. I need a phone.'

'Not now,' Jackson said quickly.

'Yes, now,' she said.

Darius produced a cell phone. Freya reached for it but Jackson got there first, seizing her wrist and shaking his head to make his brother back off.

'Let go of me,' she said. 'Darius—'

But Darius had read the dark message in Jackson's eyes.

'He's right, Freya,' he admitted. 'Not just now. Give yourself a moment first.'

She turned furious eyes on Jackson.

'You've got a nerve. Who are you to tell me what to do?'

'I'm your stepbrother who's concerned about you,' he said firmly.

'And who thinks he can dictate to me. Give me that phone. I must talk to Dan.'

'Wait. Let me try.'

He didn't know what he was trying to achieve by speaking to Dan first. The situation was already a car wreck.

But he took out his own cell phone and dialled the number. There was only silence.

Freya lost patience, seizing the phone from him and dialling again. Still there was no response. She closed her eyes, feeling as though she was surrounded by an infinity in which there was neither light nor sound. Only nothingness. At last she gave up. Her shoulders sagged.

'He's turned his phone off,' she said bleakly. 'He really is running away from me. I've got to get out of here. How can I find a way out through the back? I can't go back down the aisle with everyone watching.'

'Come on,' Jackson said, taking her arm before anyone else in the family could do so and leading her out.

To his relief an exit soon appeared. But his relief was short-lived. His arrival without Dan had been seen and the word had already gone round, both in the congregation and the waiting press. People were gathering at the back of the church, alive with curiosity. When Freya appeared a cry went up.

'There she is! What happened? Where's the groom?'

'Get away!' Jackson yelled. 'Leave her alone.'

He got in front of her, waving his hands to force them back.

'It's all right,' he said, turning back to her. 'Freya—Freya?'

She had gone, running away down the street in a way that ironically echoed Dan's escape. For the second time that day Jackson gave chase, this time catching up easily.

'Go away,' she cried. 'Leave me alone.'

She turned and would have run again but he seized her shoulders.

'Let me go.'

'Freya, I can't do that. Heaven knows what would happen to you. I'm not taking that risk.'

'It's my risk, nobody else's,' she cried. 'Do you think I care?'

'No, but I care.'

'Let me go!'

'No! I've said no and I mean no, so stop arguing. *Taxi!*'

By great good luck one had appeared. He hustled her inside, gave the driver the address of the hotel where the family was staying, then got into the back and took her into his arms.

'Let it out,' he said. 'Cry if you want to.'

'I'm not going to cry,' she declared. *'I'm all right.'*

But as he held her he knew she was far from all right, perhaps not weeping but shaking violently. He drew her close to him, patting her shoulder but saying nothing. Words would not help now. He could only offer friendship, knowing that even that was feeble against the blow that had struck her.

At last she looked up and he saw her face, pale and devastated.

'I'm here,' he said. 'Hold onto me.'

Even as he said it he felt foolish. Yes, he was there, the person whose clumsiness had helped to bring about this disaster. But there was nothing else to say.

At last the hotel came in sight, and at once he knew he had another calamity on his hands. The front was crowded with people watching the street for interesting arrivals.

'Oh, no!' he groaned. 'The word's got out already.'

'And they're waiting for me to come crawling back,' she said. 'Look, someone's got a camera.'

'Then they're going to be disappointed,' Jackson said grimly. 'Driver, there's been a change of plan.' He gave his own address and the car swerved away.

'They'll never find us at my place,' he said. 'You can stay until you're safe.'

'Thank you,' she whispered. 'But will I ever be safe again?'

'You will be. I'll see to it. Just hold me. Everything's going to be all right.'

If only he could believe it.

CHAPTER TWO

AT LAST THEY reached the apartment block where Jackson lived, and managed to slip inside unseen. It took a few moments to go up in the elevator, and there was his front door.

'Now we're safe,' he said, closing it behind them. 'Forget them. They can't get at you here.'

Freya looked around her as though confused, but suddenly she stopped, staring at a mirror on the wall. She was still wearing her veil and the pearl tiara that held it in place. With a gasp of fury she seized them, ripping them off and hurling them to the floor. Then she seized at her hair, tearing down the elaborate coiffure until it hung untidily about her face.

'I've got to get out of this dress,' she cried.

'Come in here,' Jackson said, leading her into his bedroom and opening the wardrobe. 'Put something of mine on. My clothes will be too big for you, but they'll do for a while. I'll leave you.'

'Wait.' She turned so that her back was towards him. 'I can't undo it alone.'

There seemed to be a thousand tiny buttons to be released, and Jackson went to work. It wasn't the first time he'd helped a woman undress, but those experiences were no use to him now. Inch by inch her figure came into view, and inwardly he cursed Dan again for abandoning such delicate beauty.

'Thank you,' she said at last. 'I can manage the rest for myself.'

'I'll be outside if you want me,' he said, and hurried away.

Left alone, Freya freed herself from the dress and the slip beneath. In the wardrobe she found a pair of jeans and a shirt, which she slipped on, and then she looked at herself in the full-length mirror.

It was only a short time ago that she'd stared at herself in the glamorous dress, hardly daring to believe that the beauty gazing back was actually herself.

'And I shouldn't have believed it,' she murmured. 'This is the real me—the one I always knew I was. Dull, ordinary. Not too bad on a good day, but pretty dreary on a bad one. I guess all the days are going to be bad from now on, and if I'm wise I'll stick to working clothes.'

For several minutes she stood there, trying to get used to this other self, stranded in a bleak world.

In his office Jackson made a hurried phone call to Janine at the hotel.

'Just to let you know that Freya's all right,' he told her. 'I've brought her home with me.'

'Oh, Jackson, thank you!' she exclaimed. 'There are such rows going on. Amos is fit to do murder. So are your brothers.'

'I thought so. Freya needs to be well away from that. Don't worry, I'll keep her safe.'

'How kind you are. She's so lucky to have you!'

He gave a silent groan. If Janine knew the full story she'd be saying something very different. It was no use telling himself that he was essentially innocent. Dan had been seeking something that would trigger him into action and Jackson's thoughtless words had done the trick. Now the beautiful bride was alone and humiliated, staring into an empty future.

'Ask her to call me when she can,' Janine said. 'But as long as she's with you I know she's all right.'

He made a polite reply and hung up. For a moment he stayed tense and still, wishing he was anywhere in the universe but here. The click of the door made him look behind him to see Freya, clad in jeans and shirt, bearing no resemblance to the dazzling creature who'd come down the aisle in expectation of bliss.

'Come on,' he said. 'Let's have something to eat. There's a Chinese restaurant nearby that delivers. You like king prawns with black pepper, don't you?'

'Yes, but how did you know?'

'It was the first thing I learned about you when we met six years ago. My father and your mother were just beginning to talk about marriage and the four of us had an evening out in a restaurant. But then some of Dad's business contacts turned up and he simply forgot about the rest of us.'

'We made a run for it,' she remembered. 'There was a Chinese place a few yards away.'

'And we had a good time there,' he said. 'Lots of laughs. Right—prawns it is.'

He made the call and the food arrived a few minutes later. Briefly they were both absorbed in serving it and getting settled at the table, but then she uttered the words he'd been dreading.

'Jackson, I want you to tell me what really happened.'

'But I've told you—'

'I mean the bits you've left out. Oh, please don't pretend you didn't. What you said in the church was the polite version. It had to be, with all those people listening, but I really need to know. Dan got this far and then he suddenly backed off. There has to be a reason, and I think I know what it is, but I need to hear you say it.'

'You—know what it is?' he said cautiously.

'Are you afraid I won't be able to cope? Don't worry. I'm not going to burst into tears and weep all over you. But, however painful the truth is, knowing it is better than wondering. Was it something I did wrong?'

'No, nothing like that.'

'Then I guess I know the answer, and I can see why you don't want to tell me.'

'Can you?' he said with growing alarm.

'Well it's obvious, isn't it? Something happened to make him realise that he couldn't go through with it.'

'Don't—jump to conclusions,' he said uneasily while his mind whirled. Surely she couldn't have guessed what had really happened?

'There's only one thing it can be.' She took a deep breath. 'When you were on the way to the church you and he got talking and—and—'

'And what?' he forced himself to say, inwardly cowering.

'He told you he's in love with someone else, didn't he?'

Jackson's relief was so great that he nearly dropped his spoon. Perhaps he was going to get off more lightly than he deserved.

'I think she must have called him before he left,' Freya went on. 'And on the journey he realised that he loved her too much to marry me.'

'No, he didn't say anything like that. He just lost his nerve.'

'Oh, please, I know you're being kind, but this isn't the

moment for kindness. It's the moment for truth, however brutal. There's another woman, isn't there?'

'Not that I know about,' he said firmly. 'But if that were the answer isn't it better for you to escape him now? If you'd found out after you were married it would have been a bigger disaster.'

'Would it? Perhaps I might have seen her off. If he'd chosen me over her—'

'Freya, listen to me. If a man can act like this on the way to his wedding then he's only interested in himself and you're better off without him.'

'Maybe I'll feel like that one day.' She sighed. 'But it's hard to imagine now. I'll always remember how it felt to walk down the aisle, looking for Dan, sure that he'd be watching for me. I was so happy—and such a fool. When you came towards us I was delighted to see you. But then—there was nothing but emptiness. I was going to build my life around Dan, and suddenly there's no life to build. Oh, I'm sorry. I promised I wouldn't embarrass you.'

'I'm not embarrassed. Say anything you want to. But listen to me. One life may have vanished, but there'll be another one—and it will be better.'

She gave a slightly hysterical laugh. 'You think I should be glad this happened?'

'Not right now, but in years to come you'll see that it was for the best that you got rid of him.'

'But I didn't. He got rid of me. He threw me aside like a piece of unwanted waste.'

'You mustn't think like that. You're worth a thousand of Dan. How could you ever have thought yourself in love with him?'

'Because right from the first moment I knew he was going to be special to me. My whole life changed just because he existed. It was as though the world had suddenly opened up. And everything was different—more exciting, more wonderful. When he proposed to me I was sure I'd never be unhappy again.'

Jackson drew a long, hard breath. It would be so simple now to tell her that Dan's proposal had just been a defiance of Amos. But her heart had already been broken once, and he flinched from the thought of breaking it again.

'He let you down,' he growled. 'He's not the man you thought him.'

'And I'm not the woman he really wanted. I can't hide from that. But I'll survive—with your help. Thanks for everything today.' She made a wry face. 'Even the bits that made me mad at you.'

'Sorry I had to come on so strong. I didn't want to pull you around, but—'

'I didn't give you any choice, did I? If you'd let me run off down the road—well, where would I be now? I'll swear you're the best brother I've ever had.'

'Since you don't have *any* brothers I'm not sure how to take that.'

They laughed together, both sounding shaky.

'And just think of the price you're going to pay.' She sighed again. 'This is going to give Amos ideas again.'

'About pairing us off, you mean? I guess so, but don't worry. You have nothing to fear from me.' He took her hand and assumed a theatrical tone. 'Freya, I give you my word, nothing will ever make me marry you. Let thunderbolts and lightning descend, I will still declare: *Not her. Anyone but her.*'

'Just be sure you say it to Amos and make it convincing.'

'You too. We'll have to persuade him that we can't stand the sight of each other.'

'I'll try, but it'll be hard. Right this minute you look like the nicest man in the world.'

'That's a delusion,' he said self-consciously.

'If you say so.'

'I do say so. If you knew what a swine I really am you'd sock me in the jaw.'

'Another time. Right now I have something else to ask of you.' She slipped a hand into the jeans pocket and brought out the luscious engagement ring that she had worn until a few hours ago. 'Will you give that back to Dan, please?'

'Oh, heavens, now I remember. I've still got the other ring.'

He reached into his jacket pocket and took out the wedding ring, laying the two of them side by side on the table.

'I'll give these to him as soon as I see him.'

She didn't reply. She was gazing at the rings as though transfixed. After a moment she brushed a hand over her eyes, but not soon enough to hide the tears.

'I'm sorry, I just—'

'You've endured enough,' he said sympathetically. 'Why don't you go and lie down? I won't disturb you. The bedroom's yours. I'll sleep out here on the sofa.'

'Why are you so kind to me?' she choked.

Because I feel guilty for what I accidentally did to you.

The words thrummed through his head, almost forcing their way out. But he controlled them and escorted her into the bedroom.

'You'll find some clean pyjamas in that drawer,' he said, and hurried out before his conscience overwhelmed him.

Left alone, she sat down on the bed, staring into space, unable to find the strength for anything else. In Jackson's company, feeling his kindly care, she'd managed to cope.

But now she felt as though she was drifting through infinity, in a world in which nothing was real.

She had tried to describe how Dan had made her feel, but there were no words for the sensation of being newly alive that he had given her. For the first time in her life she'd felt valuable to someone. Her relationship with her mother was cordial, but she knew she'd never come first. Janine and her late father had adored each other with an intensity that had made Freya feel like an outsider.

She'd made a life for herself, training as a nurse and passing her exams with honours. She'd had the pleasure of knowing that her parents were proud of her—especially her father, a learned man, who had been delighted that his brains had passed to his daughter. That had to be her consolation for the feeling of having been outside the enchanted circle.

Her loneliness had been intensified when her father died. Mother and daughter had grieved, but not together. Janine had suffered mostly alone, in a place Freya had not been able to touch.

But she was a successful nurse, and life had seemed settled on a conventional path until, two years after her father's death, her mother had become engaged to the notorious Amos Falcon and she had begun to meet his five sons.

Jackson had been the first, on that evening in the restaurant that he'd mentioned earlier. Their escape to the nearby Chinese restaurant had been merry, but there had been another feeling beneath her laughter. He was handsome, charming, and she wouldn't have minded if he'd asked her out on a date.

He hadn't. She had sighed, shrugged, and returned to the young man she'd been dating, but who had suddenly seemed less interesting. They'd drifted apart.

At last there had been the wedding of Janine and Amos

in London, and a gathering of the whole family in a hotel the night before. Jackson had greeted her with a cry of, 'There's my little sister!' and enfolded her in a huge hug.

They'd moved away from the others to chat about how their lives were going. That had been before his television career, when he'd still been a newspaper journalist, with a thousand fascinating tales to tell. Freya had listened, promising herself that this time she would attract his interest. She'd already discovered how much he liked to laugh.

'Go on—tell me more,' she'd teased. 'I'm hanging on every word.'

'Hey, I really like talking to you.' He had chuckled. 'You know how to flatter a guy's vanity. Why don't we—?' He'd stopped, riveted by something he'd seen over her shoulder. 'Hey, look who's— *Karen!*'

Then he'd been gone, racing across the room to the girl who'd just appeared, seizing her in his arms, kissing her again and again.

'So she turned up after all,' a voice had said in Freya's ear. 'We all wondered if she would.'

It had been Darius, regarding his brother with good-humoured cynicism.

'Who is she?' Freya had asked casually.

'His latest light o' love.'

'Latest?'

'They come and they go. Jackson likes variety in his life, which is partly why they broke up. Now they've got back together we'll have to wait and see what happens.'

'No prizes for guessing what's about to happen now,' Freya had observed, watching the pair slip out of the room.

'He wouldn't be Jackson if he passed up the chance.'

It was a lucky escape, she'd told herself. She might have become seriously attracted to Jackson but fate had saved her.

He'd brought Karen to the wedding as his guest. She was beautiful, Freya had thought enviously. Others had thought so too, because at the reception another man hadn't been able to take his eyes from her. He'd hovered, annoying Karen, until Jackson had taken a firm grip on him and said something that had made him back off. Freya hadn't heard the words but she'd seen Jackson's face, and there had been a look of menace that had stunned her. All the charm had gone from him.

It had been over in a moment. The man had fled and Jackson had reverted to his usual pleasant self. But Freya had never forgotten what she had glimpsed. She knew that if anyone had looked at her like that she would have been terrified.

She'd expected to hear that Jackson was engaged to Karen, but nothing had happened. And why should she care? she wondered. She'd been briefly attracted to him, but rescue had come in time and it was no big deal. They'd settled for a friendship in which they teased, challenged and infuriated each other. What might have been was safely in the past.

There was still a sense of irony that of all men it should be Jackson who had come to her rescue now, taking her into his home, offering her his shoulder to cry on. But irony had always been part of their relationship.

Early in her mother's marriage she'd joined Amos and Janine at their home in Monte Carlo. A heart attack had left him vulnerable, and Janine had asked her to pay a long visit.

'He won't hear of a nurse being there night and day,' she'd said. 'But he'll have to let my daughter visit us, won't he?'

She'd made the visit reluctantly. Nothing about Amos appealed to her, especially the stories of his several wives and affairs. But Amos had taken a liking to his stepdaughter and begun plotting to marry her to one of his sons. Freya had been far from flattered.

'Was he mad when he thought of that?' she'd demanded of her mother. 'There isn't one of them I'd ever dream of— ye gods and little fishes!'

As soon as Amos's health had improved she'd left Monte Carlo, returning to England and her nursing career.

Amos had failed to marry her to Darius, Marcel, Travis or Leonid. That left only Jackson. Their friendship was strong enough for him to 'reject' her theatrically, as he'd just done. Since she felt the same there was no problem.

She'd be as mad to marry him as he'd be to marry her. Though there was no denying he was a nice enough guy—at least he was if you overlooked a few things—but he was a bit too set on having his own way. He must get that from Amos, although he'd never admit it. But he had been good to her today.

She pulled on the pyjamas he'd offered her and lay down on the bed, certain that she would be unable to sleep, but the strain of the day caught up with her suddenly and she could do nothing but close her eyes.

Jackson spent the next couple of hours quietly, so as not to disturb Freya. There was research that needed to be done for his next documentary, but somehow it was hard to imagine himself continuing to work with Dan. Professionally they had both benefited from working together, which made their relationship cordial without being an outright friendship.

He considered calling his father but decided against it. After what he'd learned this afternoon he was afraid he might speak his mind too bluntly. He had things to say to

Amos about his behaviour, but he'd rather say them face to face.

The old man's determination to make Freya his daughter-in-law had been a source of comedy and irritation in equal measure to his five sons. Their amusement had been good-natured, helped by the fact that Freya was no keener on the idea than they were.

If anything it had seemed to put the brothers and Freya off each other. There was no denying that Jackson found her a nice, attractive girl, but he'd never really thought of Freya that way, and nor had his brothers. She'd been Amos's 'tool'—an instrument for his bullying. He briefly wondered whether Freya had ever fancied *any* of them.

No way. Unless—

A faint memory came back to him: the evening in the Chinese restaurant. They had laughed and exchanged significant glances as couples did at the start, when their attraction was in the flickering, questioning stage. But the pressure from Amos had begun soon afterwards and he'd backed off, sensing with relief that Freya was doing the same. After that each had known the other was out of bounds.

But if Amos's clumsiness hadn't come between them what would have happened? Until now he'd never really wondered.

Quietly he went to the bedroom door and opened it just a crack. From inside he could hear the sound of soft breathing. He opened it a little further, enough to catch a faint glimpse of her lying on the bed.

Freya wasn't the only woman who'd slept in that bed. It was large enough for two people, and he used it for what he thought of as 'entertaining'. Many women had lain there, skimpily dressed or undressed. They'd looked at him through half-closed eyes, pretending to sleep while actually studying him, planning their next move.

But Freya's form was totally concealed by his pyjamas. Her eyes were closed and the faint sounds she made told him that she was sunk in the sleep of exhaustion. She looked like a vulnerable child. He was heart-stricken. And he was floundering, baffled about how to cope. It was a new experience—one that alarmed him.

Quietly he closed the door and went to switch on the television. Almost at once he heard the words 'Dan Connor'.

The screen was focussed on a film première. There were the stars, walking along the red carpet, and there was a luscious young female clutching the arm of her escort. Dan Connor.

'*There's* someone we didn't expect to see,' declared the presenter. 'Dan Connor, television bigshot. He should have got married today, but—hey, Dan, what happened?'

'Life happened,' Dan declared, grinning in a way that made Jackson want to commit murder. 'Apart from that— no comment.' He leered at the girl on his arm. 'Shall we go in?'

Jackson clenched his hands, silently calling Dan every name he could think of. He moved quickly to turn the set off, but it was too late. A faint sound made him look to see Freya standing in the doorway.

'So that's who she is,' Freya said quietly.

'No. Freya, you're wrong. I'll swear he's not in love with her. He must have just grabbed the first girl he met so that he could get his face onto the news. That's a PR stunt you're witnessing. You've had a lucky escape.'

She smiled at him, calm and seemingly untroubled.

'You may be right. He replaced me easily, didn't he?

At any rate it's all over now. As far as I'm concerned Dan never existed. Goodnight.'

She retreated into the bedroom, leaving Jackson wishing he could believe that she was really recovering so easily. But his heart told him she was only putting on a brave face.

Before going to bed he listened outside her door and heard something that made him clench his hands in agony. From inside came the sound of gasping sobs, telling all too clearly of the grief Freya could only release when she was alone.

Unable to endure it, he opened the door, ready to go in, take her in his arms and comfort her. But wisdom held him back. She wouldn't be glad of his comfort. She would hate it, wanting no curious eyes.

He backed out and closed the door, knowing that he wasn't wanted.

Freya awoke early the next morning. Briefly she wondered where she was, then remembered and groaned. Creeping out of the room, she searched for Jackson on the sofa, but it was empty except for a scrap of paper that read, *I'll be back soon. Don't go away.*

She thought of the hotel, where the family was staying, and knew she should return to them, but the thought made her shudder.

If only Jackson were here. She'd always considered herself a strong person, but suddenly it seemed terrible to be alone.

'That's his fault for supporting me so well,' she muttered wryly. 'Now I can't cope without him. All his fault. Oh, where is he?'

It was an hour before he returned and it seemed like for ever.

'I've been to the hotel,' he said, dumping a large suitcase on the table. 'I took the wedding dress with me and your mother's going to pack it away for you. She gave me some clothes to bring you.'

Her wedding dress had been hanging up in the bedroom, which meant he must have crept in and removed it while she was asleep. Then her attention was taken by the clothes she found in the case.

'Why did you bring this?' she asked, lifting a glittering cocktail dress.

'You can wear it tonight, when we go out.'

'Are we going out?'

'Yes. I'll take you back to your hotel at the end of the evening, but before that we need to give Dan a taste of his own medicine. He flaunted himself before the cameras, so you have to do the same. Then everyone will know you don't give a stuff about him.'

'Don't I?'

'No, you don't. You mustn't. I know what I'm doing, Freya. Trust me.'

'I do,' she said.

'But you think I'm giving you orders again, don't you? Laying down the law, acting like my father?'

'No, he never takes so much trouble about people's feelings,' she said. 'I don't mind taking a few orders from you.'

'What was that? Did I hear you right? My bolshie Freya being meek and mild? I don't believe it.'

'I can do meek and mild if there's a good reason.' She managed a smile. 'I can even say, *Yes, sir. No, sir. Three bags full, sir.*'

'This I have to see,' he said dramatically. 'It'll be a whole new experience.' Then abruptly he dropped the humorous manner. 'Don't worry. I just mean to look after you.' He took her face between his hands. 'That's all that matters now. Please believe me.'

'I do,' she said. 'It's strange how content I feel to leave everything in your hands. I didn't know it before, but there's nobody I trust like you.'

To her surprise Jackson looked uneasy, but she thought she understood. He was more used to her sparring with him than trusting him. But now those days seemed a long way off.

CHAPTER THREE

Now Freya really discovered Jackson's flair for taking charge. In the suitcase she found items of make-up and for hair care, evidently packed by her mother.

'Thank goodness,' she said. 'At least I can look my best tonight.'

But he shook his head.

'Tonight you're a star,' he said, 'and a star doesn't do those jobs herself. She employs a professional.'

'You mean a beautician? I don't know any.'

'But I do. She'll arrive this afternoon, to place herself at your service.' He hesitated before adding, 'Unless, that is, you have any objections?'

Her lips twitched. 'Don't worry. I know the proper answer to that. Yes, sir. No, sir.'

'You forgot *Three bags full, sir*. But I'll let you off this time. I've got to leave now, but I'll be back this evening.'

Naomi, the beautician, arrived at three in the afternoon. She listened politely to what Freya had to say, but clearly needed no instructions, having already received them from Jackson.

It was ironic that once Freya would have objected to the way he was directing every step. But now the sadness that consumed her made it hard to think, and it was a relief to leave the decisions to him.

She had to admit that Naomi did a magnificent job, turning her into as great a beauty as she had been as a bride. The elegant dress had a short skirt that showed off her well-shaped legs, and the expert make-up made her look delightful, the lavish hairstyle enhanced her. But when she offered to pay Naomi waved her away.

'That's all been taken care of,' she said.

'But can't I give you a tip to thank you?'

'That's been taken care of too. Mr Falcon was very insistent.'

'You mean he told you not to take a penny from me?'

Naomi smiled and shrugged. 'Mr Falcon is a very generous man.'

She hurried out.

Yes, he is, Freya thought. More than I ever knew.

Jackson was home at six o'clock, nodded approval at the sight of her, then disappeared to don his evening clothes. When he emerged she too nodded her approval.

'We'll do each other credit,' she said.

'That's the spirit. We'll show 'em.'

Downstairs, he loaded her case into his car and headed out onto the road.

'Where are we going?' she asked.

He gave her the name of a restaurant, famous for its glamour and luxury and for being a favourite home of major personalities. Within a few minutes they had arrived.

'Ready?' he asked as they headed for the entrance.

'Ready for anything,' she replied.

'Then here we go. Smile. They'll be watching.'

'Do they know we're coming?'

'I have a few friends in the press.'

Sure enough, heads turned as they entered. There were some cheerful waves, which Jackson returned.

A waiter showed them to a table, and the first few

moments were taken up with formalities. At last they were alone.

'Now, let's get down to business,' he said.

'Business?'

'You see those two over there?' he asked, nodding in the direction of a table where a young couple were holding hands and gazing rapturously into each other's eyes.

'Yes. But we're not going to do that, are we?' she asked, aghast.

'No way. Hell will freeze over before I ask you to give me *that* adoring look. They're an example of what we mustn't do. If we act like a couple in love it'll cause a scandal. People will think you were betraying Dan and that's why he headed for the hills.'

'Right. So what *do* we do?'

'We laugh. Let everyone see how light-hearted you are.'

'You've got this all worked out to the last detail, haven't you?'

'Is that a polite way of saying that I'm taking charge too precisely?'

'No, but you do seem to have a gift for organising. Perhaps nature meant you to be a film director.'

Jackson grinned. 'You're not the first person to say that, but the guy who said it first was really mad at me. He was the director of a TV show and I annoyed him by arguing all the time. "Everything's got to be done the way you say, hasn't it?" he yelled.'

'And what did you reply? *I'm glad you've realised that*?'

'You understand me far too well.'

Then the humour died from his face and he took a long breath.

'I went to see Dan today. There were a few sharp words and now I don't work for him any more.'

'Oh, no! Your career—I never meant to harm you.'

'You haven't. I was already thinking of leaving. Someone else has been in touch.'

He named a firm, high ranking in the production business.

'They've been dangling offers in front of me for a while. I didn't accept because I was OK where I was, but that's over now, so I called the man who runs this other place. He wants to do a series about ancient Egypt—myths, traditions, rituals, pyramids, that sort of thing. Once we've settled my contract I'll go out there to explore. It's a place that's always fascinated me.'

'Yes, it's got a magical reputation hasn't it? Tell me more.'

As Jackson talked she did as he'd suggested—smiling, nodding, seeming fascinated. Nobody must guess that inside she felt wretched.

She managed the pretence until Jackson finished by saying, 'So now we can both consign Dan to the past.'

She had a feeling of being punched in the stomach.

'Yes, we can, can't we?' she said bleakly.

'But I guess it won't happen all in a moment.' He looked intensely at her face. 'Perhaps I shouldn't have mentioned him.'

'No, I'm strong. I can cope.'

'I don't think you're as strong as you like to believe you are.'

'You're wrong,' she said firmly.

'I hope so. You'll get over him, Freya. You must.'

'Yes, I must,' she whispered, dismayed at hearing her voice crack on the last word. At all costs she must not weep.

Jackson took a gentle hold of her hand.

'You can't believe it now, but truly it will happen. The best of your life is still in front of you.'

'Yes—of course—it's just—I can't—' The tears were there again, refusing to be defeated.

'Come on,' Jackson said. 'Let's get out of here.'

He summoned the waiter, paid the bill and led her outside. She sat in silence on the journey. The courage and defiance that had carried her through the evening had vanished without warning, and she felt crushed.

When they reached the hotel he said, 'Shall I call your mother and tell her you're here?'

'No,' she whispered. 'I don't want to see anyone.'

'All right.' He kept his arm around her shoulders as they went up to her room, and went inside with her.

'Goodnight,' she said.

'Not yet. I don't like leaving you alone. You've been brave, and coped wonderfully, but nobody can be brave for ever.'

'They can if they have to,' she said huskily.

'But you don't have to. You've got a friend who'll always be there for you.'

'Don't,' she begged. 'I can manage—truly I can. I just need to—to—'

She tried to fight back the tears but it was hopeless. Grief devastated her.

'You need to do this,' Jackson said, taking her in his arms and drawing her close.

At once she gave up the fight for control. The warmth and sweetness of his gesture overcame her resistance and she let her head rest on his shoulder. He was right. While he was here she didn't need to be brave.

He turned his head, resting his cheek against her hair.

'Go on,' he murmured. 'Let it happen.'

She had no choice but to let it happen. Strong, controlled Freya could do nothing but yield to the despair she'd once managed to hold at bay. She could feel Jackson patting her shoulders as they shook with sobs, and for several minutes they stood quietly, leaning against each other.

She had the sensation of being in another world. It was warm, kindly, safe. She wanted to stay there for ever.

'Freya—'

His gentle voice made her look up to see his face just above hers, so close that she could feel his breath.

'Freya—' he murmured again.

There was something in his voice that she'd never heard before: uncertainty, perhaps even alarm.

'Freya—'

'Yes—'

She felt the touch of his lips against hers and drew in a soft breath. Next moment she was pressing against him, not even knowing what she did. Something deep inside her drove her on, telling her this was where she belonged. Without realising what she was doing she slipped her arms about him. She would have tightened them, but he tensed and raised his mouth from hers.

Suddenly tremors went through her body. The world had changed. She didn't know where she was. She knew only that this wasn't where she should be.

'Freya—'

'Let me go.'

The words were needless. He was already stepping back, putting distance between them.

'I'm sorry,' he said harshly. 'I didn't mean—'

'Neither did I,' she said, in a voice whose harshness matched his own. 'Please go now.'

'Freya, my dear—'

'I'm not your dear. I'm not your anything. Just because Dan dumped me, did you think I was there for the taking?'

'Of course not. I wasn't trying to make love to you. I

promise that's one thing I'll never do. You can count on that. It was meant as comfort.'

'That's one kind of comfort I don't need.'

He seemed about to say something, but then his shoulders sagged as though he realised it was useless and he turned to the door.

'I'm sorry,' he said. 'It's not what you think. Don't be angry. I only wanted to help you.'

'Not like that,' she snapped. 'Goodbye, Jackson.'

He gave her an uneasy look, then left without another word.

He left her standing alone in the middle of the room, until her legs gave way and she collapsed onto the floor, wrapping her arms about her head, burying her face as though trying to hide from herself.

How could that have happened? How could she have felt that flickering of treacherous desire for Jackson when she was still dead inside from Dan's betrayal? She'd been so sure that all feeling was over for her, yet in a moment the old attraction for Jackson had come flickering out of the shadows, confusing, threatening.

'No,' she muttered. 'No, no, *no!*'

She'd run into his arms, grateful for the safety he'd seemed to offer. But there was no safety—only more devastation. The only safety lay in escape. She must get far away from him.

Monte Carlo. Janine and Amos would be leaving soon and she would go with them. Once there, she could retreat into herself and cease to exist as far as Jackson was concerned.

Cease to exist. It had a reassuring sound. And it was the only refuge that would not betray her.

She lay down on the bed and stared into the darkness for the rest of the night. Even darkness was reassuring now.

The next morning Freya went to Janine's and Amos's room, glad to find her mother alone. Janine was delighted with her daughter's decision.

'You're coming with us? That's wonderful. If only we could convince Jackson to come too. He was here an hour ago and Amos was hoping to persuade him, but no luck. Such a pity.'

'He's starting a new job,' Freya said.

'So he said, but Amos is furious. They've had a big row. He's as stubborn as his father, so it's stalemate for the moment. But perhaps Jackson will change his mind and join us soon.'

'No,' Freya said quietly. 'I don't think he will.'

For Jackson to join them was the last thing she wanted. Nothing mattered now but to get a safe distance from him until she could cope with what had happened.

The next few days passed in a daze: the flight to Monte Carlo, the drive to Amos's magnificent house overlooking the bay, the feeling of having put trouble behind her at least for the moment.

Jackson stayed in touch, linking up via a video connection every evening, talking cheerfully to them from the screen. At first Freya watched these occasions from the sidelines, out of Jackson's sight, not joining in the conversations.

But then he noticed her before she could slip away and cried, 'Hey, there's my little sister. How's it going, sis?'

His use of the word 'sister' sounded like a message. He was telling her that their old pleasant relationship could be restored. But she doubted that could ever happen.

'It's going well,' she said.

'Glad to hear it.'

'Is everything all right with you?' she asked politely.

'I've never had such a fascinating trip. And, Dad, when I see you I've got something to tell you that'll really make you sit up…'

At last Jackson arrived at the villa. His greeting to Freya was friendly, without any tense edge. She knew a moment's resentment that he'd brushed everything aside so easily. Clearly what had happened mattered little to him and he thought it was the same with her. Yet he was right, she realised. Casual indifference was the only thing that would make each other's presence bearable.

Over a pleasant dinner Jackson told vivid tales.

'I've never regarded myself as a man susceptible to magic,' he said, 'but the magic began as soon as I arrived. I was in a hotel that looked out over the desert where the great pyramids are, and I could see one from my widow. I'll never forget standing there as dawn broke, seeing the pyramid slowly emerge from the darkness. And everywhere I went—the temples, the Valley of the Kings—there was something that would make me stare with amazement.'

'But what was it you had to tell your father?' Janine said. 'We're dying of curiosity.'

'All right. Here goes. I had to study the Egyptian gods. There are many of them, with varying degrees of power. One of the most powerful is called Horus.'

'But why should I be interested in him?' Amos wanted to know.

'Because he's known as the Falcon god. I couldn't believe it when I first heard that, but in pictures and statues he's represented as a falcon. Look.'

He reached into a bag and brought out a small statue of a bird with a cap on its head.

'That's Horus the Falcon god,' he said, handing it to Amos.

Janine burst out laughing at the sight of Amos's face as he studied the figure.

'You said it was powerful,' he murmured.

'He's the god of the sky, the sun and the moon,' Jackson explained. 'I thought you'd enjoy that.'

It was rare for Amos to smile with genuine pleasure, but now he managed a grin.

'That sounds about right,' he said.

'They knew about you all the time,' Freya teased him.

As the meal ended Jackson drew his father aside to tell him more colourful stories about Egypt.

'I'm so glad about that,' Janine told her daughter when they were alone. 'Amos is really enjoying it.'

'I wonder how powerful Horus really was,' Freya mused. 'Maybe Jackson has exaggerated a bit to please Amos.'

'Well, good for him if he has,' her mother said. 'It was nice.'

'Yes. He *is* nice, isn't he?'

The reminder of Jackson's kindly side gave Freya a feeling of relief. At last she bade them all goodnight and went to bed. There she lay, brooding, wistful, daring to hope that perhaps the wretched memory could be banished into the shadows and their friendship could be restored. At last she fell asleep.

She was awoken by sounds coming from the next room, which she knew to be Jackson's. He was talking in a sharp voice, as though annoyed. The other man's voice sounded like Dan.

Rising quickly, she slipped on a dressing gown and went out into the corridor. Jackson's door was closed but she could hear the angry voices clearly.

'You should be ashamed of what you did,' Jackson

snapped. 'And you damned well know it. Running off like that just before the wedding.'

'Don't heap all the blame on me,' came Dan's voice. 'You were the one who made it happen.'

'That's not true.'

'Yes, it is. You said it would be better to dump her then rather than later and I took your advice.'

For a moment Freya froze, then she flung open the door.

Jackson was sitting at his computer, confronting Dan, who glared back at him from the screen via a video link. Dan's face had a self-satisfied expression that she realised she had seen many times before. But it faded as he saw her come to stand behind Jackson. Just for a moment he was taken aback.

'Surprised to see me, Dan?' she asked coolly. 'After all the times you've avoided me it must come as a nasty shock.'

Jackson had also received a shock, going by his face as he looked up at her.

'Freya,' he said, almost stammering in his dismay, 'it's best if we talk later.'

'I'll talk to *you* later. I'll talk to him now.'

'There's not much to talk about,' Dan said.

'What did you mean about taking Jackson's advice?'

'I told him I wasn't keen on our marriage and he said I should dump you right away. I thought he knew best, so I did. I've got to go now, Freya. Goodbye.'

There was a click and Dan vanished from the screen.

Freya clutched her forehead.

'He's lying, isn't he?' she choked. 'Tell me he's lying. You never said anything like that.'

'He's twisted my words,' Jackson said desperately. 'He said he hadn't ever wanted to get married. He proposed because Amos tried to scare him off, not because of love.

I was appalled that he'd deceived you and let it get so far. I said he should have been honest with you from the start, that he would hurt you more if he married you without love and let you down later.'

'So you *did* say it?' she demanded, aghast.

'Not the way he made it sound. I meant that he should never have planned a wedding in the first place, not that he should back off at the last minute. But he seized on it as a way out. Don't you see? It gave him an excuse to shift the blame. All right, I was clumsy and stupid, but not malicious. Please, Freya, try to understand. I never intended it to happen the way it did.'

'What do you mean about him proposing because of Amos?'

'Oh, heavens!' He groaned. 'Amos tried to make him back off, threatened him. Dan lost his temper and—'

'And that's why he proposed to me?' she whispered. 'That's all it was?'

'Yes.'

'He never loved me at all?'

'I'm afraid not.'

'And you've known this all the time?'

'I only found out on the way to the church. If I'd known earlier I'd have warned you, but it was too late.'

'Too late to warn me, but not too late to make him run for it.'

'I told you I never meant that to happen. I spoke clumsily.'

'You've deceived me—'

'*No!*'

'I begged you to tell me why he ran, but you never told me the truth—'

'I was as honest as I could be, but I couldn't repeat all the things he said. Have you forgotten the terrible state you

were in that day? There was no way I could tell you everything. It would have finished you off, Freya. Please be fair.'

But she was too distraught to be fair.

'I trusted you,' she choked. 'Talked to you, told you
things I'd never have told anyone else. And all the time
you were laughing up your sleeve at me.'

'That isn't true. I was trying to do my best for you. I'm
sorry if I got it wrong, but I meant well. Call me an idiot,
if you like, but don't call me a deceiver.'

'I believed you,' she whispered. 'Relied on you. I
thought you were being so kind to me.'

'I felt terrible about what happened—how I helped to
bring it about. I'd have done anything to make it up to you.'

'Anything except tell me the truth. Be honest, Jackson,
if you know how. You've been enjoying watching me be
an idiot, haven't you?'

'No, I swear it. Freya. you've got to believe me.'

'How can I? When I think of some of the things I said—
how I trusted and confided in you. What a fool I must
have sounded!'

'No, I was the fool for damaging you so idiotically. But
I did my best to help you survive it—all right, it was a poor
best, but I tried. Why don't we talk later, when you've had
a chance to calm down?'

She had a feeling that a chilly bleakness had settled
over the world.

'You think I'll see sense, don't you?' she said bitterly.
'You're wrong. Nothing will change. You won't ever look
different to me from the way you do now. Mean, spiteful,
contemptible.'

'Freya—' He reached out for her hand but she snatched
it away.

'No, don't touch me. I can't bear the sight of you.'

'Please don't let this spoil our friendship.'

'There never was a friendship,' she whispered. 'There never could be.'

'Freya—'

He reached out for her again but she darted away. After a moment he heard her bedroom door shut and the key turn in the lock.

CHAPTER FOUR

ALONE IN HER room Freya slammed her fist down on the dressing table again and again. A storm had invaded her. Rage, bitterness, disillusion and misery fought for supremacy. They all won. She was trapped in their prison and inside her there was no escape.

But outside she could put distance between herself and Jackson. She hurriedly dressed, slipped quietly into the corridor, down the stairs and out of the door. She had no idea where she was going, except that a million miles away from him would not be far enough.

Once before the world had turned upside down, and she'd survived because of Jackson's comfort and support. But that had been only an illusion. Instead there was a bleak, arid desert where the rest of her life must be lived.

She lost track of time but she must have walked for hours, because when she finally turned back the dawn was breaking.

Nearing the house, she saw her mother, standing at a downstairs window. As soon as she saw Freya she came to the front door.

'Come along in,' she said. 'I saw you leave. You were running as though the fiends of hell were after you. I was worried.'

'Sorry, Mum. That was inconsiderate of me, but I was ready to murder someone.'

'Ah, yes, Jackson got Dan on a video link, didn't he? I heard his voice. You still want to murder Dan?'

'No, Jackson,' Freya growled.

'What? Did I hear that right? But Jackson's been so nice to you.'

'Jackson is a lying, scheming, deceitful louse. And, yes, you heard that right. I said it and I mean it.'

'But he can't possibly have done anything to justify that. He's a fine, decent young man.'

'I thought so too. That's why I never realised what he'd really done.'

'Whatever do you mean?'

'It was because of him that Dan ran for it. He never wanted to marry me, and when they were heading for the church Jackson urged him to dump me then rather than later. So Dan got out of the car.'

'Darling, I don't believe this. Jackson would never do such a thing.'

'He as good as admitted it. He says it was a mistake, but he doesn't deny Dan left me because of what he said.'

'Maybe that's why he's been so kind and helpful to you since then.'

'Don't try to defend him,' Freya flashed. 'He's deceived me.'

'But I don't understand. Why did Dan propose if he didn't want to marry you?'

'Because Amos forced his hand,' Freya said bitterly.

'Never! He was against that wedding. There's no way he ordered Dan to marry you.'

'Of course not. He ordered him *not* to marry me. Dan proposed just to show Amos that he couldn't be bullied. Then he regretted it, but he couldn't find a way out. When he and Jackson were in the car Dan told Jackson what had happened, and my brilliantly stupid stepbrother said the one thing that could make it worse. Dan seized his chance and vanished.'

'Amos *ordered* Dan to keep his distance from you? Surely not.'

'Why do you say that? Isn't it typical of Amos?'

'Darling, I've got no illusions about him. He goes through life doing what he wants. But he's too shrewd to do something so pathetically stupid. And he does have a nicer side. He's always been fond of you and he wanted to take you into the family—'

'No, it's more like claiming property. He doesn't have a daughter of his own, and he wanted me to "complete the set", because he can't bear not to have everything other people have. He didn't care which one of his sons he tied me to as long as he put his brand on me. When only Jackson was left he went mad because neither of us would give in.'

'This is terrible.' Janine groaned. 'But if Dan really only proposed for such a reason he'd have been a terrible husband. Jackson was stupid, but maybe he did you a favour in the long run.'

'Don't you dare stand up for him!' Freya cried. 'When I think of these last few weeks, how I've trusted and relied on him, and all the time he was hiding the truth.'

'Because the truth would have hurt you even more. How could he do that to you?'

'How could he have let me make such a fool of myself?'

'He probably wasn't thinking straight,' Janine said wryly. 'Men tend to do what they imagine will sort the problem today without realising that it might make it worse long-term. It obviously didn't occur to Amos that his threats would have exactly the opposite effect to the one he wanted.'

'I often wonder why you put up with him. Don't tell me it's for the money.'

'No, if anything his money has been a disadvantage. It looms so large in his life that it leaves no room for anything else.'

'Then why do you stay with him?'

'He needs me, my dear. He's vulnerable in ways he doesn't realise.'

'He'd never admit that.'

'No, he likes to see himself as powerful. That falcon god that Jackson brought back from Egypt has really sent him onto cloud nine. The trouble is, that's the side of him I find hardest to live with.'

'Does he know that? No, of course not. It would never occur to him that he doesn't come up to standard. I'd like to see his face when you tell him that you know what he did to Dan.'

'I'm not sure that I will tell him. And please don't you say anything.'

'All right, I'll leave it to you. How you handle your horrible husband is your affair.'

'Forget about Amos. This isn't about him. It's about Jackson. Don't condemn him too much for keeping quiet. He did it because he was feeling his way forward, moment by moment. He didn't ask himself what would happen when you found out later.'

'He never meant me to find out at all. He wanted to rule the roost all the time—just like Amos. Like father, like son. Haven't you noticed how alike they are? You don't see it at first, because Jackson can seem so charming, but every now and then you'll catch an expression on his face that makes him the image of Amos.'

'That's true,' Janine mused. 'I remember Dan telling us that producers were always getting annoyed because Jackson kept insisting that his way was best. He said it laughingly, but—yes, I can imagine.'

'So can I,' Freya said cynically. 'I don't think it ever crosses Jackson's mind that he might be wrong.'

Janine stared. 'Darling, what's got into you? You're even more upset than you were when Dan betrayed you.'

'I'm not upset, I'm furious,' Freya said quickly.

'It's more than that. This has hit you hard—even harder than Dan.'

'No! Of course it hasn't—it's just different. Please, I don't want to talk about it any more. And I think it's time I went back to London, got another job and made a new start.'

She didn't say that she wanted to delete Jackson from her life, but no words were necessary. Each knew what the other was thinking. They hugged, and then Freya left the room to head upstairs.

Neither of them saw the man standing back in the shadows, where he'd hastily retreated to avoid being discovered. Amos knew he needed time to consider everything that he'd overheard. And that perhaps all the time in the world would not be enough.

There was a flight to London later that morning and Freya secured a seat. When she appeared for breakfast she was already dressed to depart. She found Jackson at the table alone.

'We need a nice long talk,' he said to her in a low voice.

'I'm afraid not. I'm leaving in an hour.'

'What? Freya, you can't leave things like this. We have to sort it out.'

'There's nothing to sort. I've seen the truth about you

now, and I don't like it. This is where it ends. You should be glad. I won't be a nuisance to you any more.'

He turned away and strode around the room, tearing at his hair.

'No, I'm not accepting this,' he said, returning to stand before her.

'I don't care what you accept. I didn't ask your permission,' she said furiously. 'I'm returning to London and I don't want to see or talk to you again.'

'You'd do this because I made one little mistake?'

'You treated me with contempt and I don't see that as a "little mistake".'

'Why must you be so unforgiving?' he demanded. 'I was wrong, I've admitted that. Now I want to put things right.'

'But they can't be put right. Ever. And that's final.'

Jackson stared at her as though seeing her for the first time. Or as though someone else had appeared in her place.

'I can't believe this is really you,' he breathed. 'I've never known you like this before—so hard and unforgiving.'

'I'm not hard. I'm just someone who's been pushed around and manipulated enough and I'm not going to put up with it any more. You think this isn't really me? It's the me I am now. She's different to the old one. Don't mess with her.'

Jackson met her eyes, trying to look deep inside and rediscover the woman he knew. But she'd vanished into thin air, leaving behind an enemy. There was a stab of pain in his heart, but at the same time his temper began to rise.

'Right,' he said. 'Then I won't mess with her. She's cold-hearted, ill-natured—well, never mind the rest.'

'Cold-hearted?' she echoed in fury. 'You *dare* call me cold-hearted after everything that's happened? I'm the one who's been knocked down and kicked around by people I trusted. But perhaps you're right. It's time I became cold so that it can never happen again.'

'And you think you can protect yourself from pain for ever?'

'Yes, because people who feel nothing can't be hurt.'

'That's the coward's way out. I never thought I'd see it in you, but if you can't find it in your heart to forgive a mistake from someone who's truly sorry then you're not the woman I thought you were. Just who you are is something I won't stick around to find out. But I'll say this. Heaven help anyone you meet in future. Heaven help the man who's fool enough to fall in love with you. Because you'll kick him in the guts the first time he gets muddled.'

'That's all you think it was? A muddle? Oh, no! You just thought you knew better than anyone else.'

'Yes, I believed I was doing the right thing,' he shouted. 'Is that a crime?'

'It can be.'

'You're saying I was wrong to try to protect you from more pain? I failed, but I still think I was right to try.'

How like Amos he looked, with his face set and unrelenting.

'You're so sure you know best,' she challenged.

'That's why people do things. Because they think it's right at the time.'

'But some people *always* think they're right. Look, we're never going to agree. Let's leave it there.'

'Freya, why are you so determined to think the worst of me?'

'I don't have any choice.'

'Of course you do. Something's making you attack me far more than I deserve.'

'I've just reached a turning point, that's all. You said it yourself—there's another side of me coming out.'

'Then banish her fast, or she'll haunt you for ever.'

'Good. She'll keep me safe.'

'She'll destroy you.'

'That's my decision. And this time I know best. So let's get that clear and draw a line under it.'

His face grew even more tense, and she thought he was about to say something else, but the sound of Janine's voice outside startled them both and made them turn away from each other.

'There you are,' she said, entering the room. 'Have you seen Amos?'

'He's out there,' Jackson said, pointing through the window to where Amos could be seen sitting in the garden, staring out over the bay.

He was very still, unlike his normal restless self. They all watched him for a few moments, but he didn't move.

'It's time I was going to the airport,' Freya said.

'Perhaps Jackson could take you.'

'*No!*'

They both said it, speaking so swiftly and sharply that Janine was silenced.

Freya slipped away to collect her bags and went to wait in the garden. Amos was still there, still with his eyes fixed on the sea. Before approaching him she stood back, seeing him in a new, hostile light.

This was the man whose bullying had caused Dan's proposal, thus sowing the seed for the disaster that had followed. This was the man who had made Jackson what he was.

Slowly she approached him.

'I'm going back to England this morning,' she said.

'I hope you have a good journey. Is my chauffeur taking you to the airport?'

'No, I've called a taxi,' she said. She had no wish to accept favours from him. 'I'll say goodbye now.'

Reluctantly, it seemed to her, he turned his head to look up at her. But there was nothing in his eyes. They were as empty as a desert.

'Goodbye,' he said.

'Goodbye.'

When the taxi arrived mother and daughter hugged each other.

'Goodbye, Mum, I'll call you when I get home.'

'Goodbye, Freya,' Jackson said.

'Goodbye, Jackson.'

There was no hug between them. They exchanged brief nods, not letting their eyes meet. Both understood that this was goodbye in more than words.

As the taxi pulled away she didn't look back.

From now on Jackson would be out of her life and out of her mind. But still he haunted her on the flight back to London. Their last terrible quarrel thrummed inside her head, throwing up questions and possible answers.

He'd asked why she was so determined to think the worst of him. It was because she'd once thought the best, and now, from somewhere deep inside her, a protective armour was forming. It would prevent her from ever thinking the best of him again. And that was good. It would save her from a lot of pain.

On that she was resolved.

She would have to reorganise her life in more ways than one, since she had no job and nowhere to live.

As soon as she landed in London she checked into an airport hotel and called her mother.

'Are you all right?' Janine asked anxiously.

'I'm fine. Tomorrow I'm going to sign on with that private nursing agency I worked for once before.'

'The one that sends you to nurse people in their homes?'

'That's right. Then I'll solve my accommodation problem as well—at least until I've made some long-term plans. What's the atmosphere like there?'

'Very strange. Amos wants Jackson to tell him more about this falcon god, but Jackson says he hasn't time to talk. He's given him a list of websites, so Amos is glued to the computer. If I go into the room he finds an excuse to make me leave.'

'I guess he thinks he really is a god,' Freya said wryly.

'I'm afraid you may be right.'

'The best of luck in dealing with him. Bye.'

She ate alone in her room, then had an early night. Sleep came easily, but even there the questions clamoured. The bitter pain of discovering that Jackson wasn't the man she'd thought. The feeling that suddenly nothing in the world was safe, or would ever be safe again. Nothing would drive these away.

He was there in her dreams, regarding her with harsh, angry eyes, uttering cruel words. *Cold-hearted. Ill-natured.* He had actually called her those terrible names.

She gave a cry and awoke suddenly to find that tears were streaming down her face.

The next day she registered with the nursing agency, which immediately found her an assignment in London. She told herself that this was the start of a new life that would soon help her to forget the old one.

She often talked on the phone with Janine, who soon had startling news.

'You'll never guess what Amos has organised now,' she said. 'He's going to Egypt with Jackson.'

'Whatever for?'

'To play at being the falcon god, I suppose. He's even managed to get the production company on his side. They love Jackson being a Falcon, and now they've got two of them. So we can't stop him. Amos will be coming to London so that he can take the same flight as Jackson. I'll be coming too, to see him off.'

'Why don't you go to Egypt with him?'

'I would if I thought he wanted me. But things are very strange between us now. Sometimes I look up and catch him giving me an odd look.'

'What kind of odd look?'

'I can't describe it, but it's one I've never seen before. As though he wants to say something but isn't sure. I almost think he might be going to Egypt to escape from me.'

'That I don't believe. Not Amos.'

'But he's not the same Amos. He's a different Amos, and I don't know who. Now, darling, can we arrange to meet when we come to London?'

'Easily. My job's just finishing and I was about to ask for the next assignment.'

'Take a few days off and join us in the hotel so that we can have a little time together.'

Janine and Amos arrived two days later, and as soon as she met them she knew what her mother meant about Amos. It was as though a quietness had descended on him, making him totally unlike his usual self.

That night there were only the three of them at dinner. Jackson had called to say that there were last-minute affairs he must see to before he could leave the next day. Once again Freya felt herself dividing into two selves. One of them was disappointed not to see him; the other gave a sigh of relief.

She wondered if he too was relieved he could keep their

meeting short, because next morning it was late when he joined them at the airport.

'Sorry,' he said, embracing Janine. 'Lost my passport at the last minute. All right now, though. Nice to see you, Freya. Right, Dad, are you ready to go? Good, then we'll be off. Goodbye, ladies.'

Janine opened her arms to her husband. He came into them, but only for a moment, and again Freya saw the sense of unease that he seemed to carry with him these days.

She was suddenly swamped by an irrational urge to hug Jackson. Despite the hostility that still burned between them it seemed unbearable to part as enemies. Disasters could happen. She might never see him again. Summoning all her courage, she took his arm and said, 'Don't I get a hug?'

His smile had a touch of wryness. 'Are you sure you want me to hug you?'

'I'll kick your shins if you don't,' she teased, trying to reintroduce some humour into their relationship.

'That's my girl,' he said, opening his arms. His hug was brief, but fierce. 'Goodbye,' he said huskily.

'Goodbye. Jackson—'

'Gotta be going. Goodbye.'

Then it was over. The two men were walking away, and the two women watched their retreating figures with hearts that ached. At the entrance the men turned and waved one last time. Next moment they were gone.

Now Freya could really concentrate on putting her life back together. Dan was gone. Jackson was gone. She was free to make a new future.

She accepted another nursing assignment and when it was finished went out to Monte Carlo. In their phone calls something in her mother's manner had spoken of loneliness.

'Thank you for coming, darling,' she said fervently when Freya arrived. 'You can hold my hand and I can hold yours.'

Freya hugged her, but said, 'I don't need anyone to hold my hand. I'm managing just fine.'

Janine gave her a worried look, but was too wise to say anything.

'How are they doing in Egypt?' Freya asked over supper.

'Really well, apparently. Until now they've been in Giza, with the Great Pyramids and the Sphinx. But soon they're going to Edfu, where there's the temple of Horus. Amos is revelling in being a god.'

'Now, *there's* a surprise.'

The two women laughed.

'Jackson calls me sometimes, which I appreciate. It's kind of him to keep me in the picture.'

'Doesn't Amos keep you in the picture?'

'We talk, but I always feel that he's saying what he wants me to believe rather than telling me how things are.'

'And what he wants you to believe is that the world revolves around him—which, after all, is what he's used to.'

Janine gave a little sigh. 'Well, as long as it keeps him happy.'

'What about him keeping you happy? This is the twenty-first century. Men are supposed to worry about us as much as we worry about them.'

'I don't think many of them know that yet. Jackson's kind and caring, but he's still an exception.'

'Yes, well let's not talk about that.'

'You're still upset with him? When I saw you hug him at the airport—'

'That was just a sentimental moment,' Freya said hastily. 'It came and it went. I've accepted reality.'

She spoke with a bright air that warned her mother to pursue it no further. Janine had hoped to find a softening in her daughter's attitude, but there was little to ease her mind.

'Freya, darling, can't you—? Oh, dear, there's somebody at the door.'

She rose and went out into the hall.

Left alone, Freya went to the window to look out at the glorious bay, where the sun was beginning to set. It was eight o'clock here, which meant that in Egypt it would be nine. What was it like as night fell on that mystical land? Was it as beautiful as daybreak?

She remembered Jackson saying, 'I'll never forget standing there as dawn broke, seeing the pyramid slowly emerge from the darkness.'

It was almost eerie the way he still haunted her, cropping up at odd moments, forcing her to armour her mind against him.

The shrill of the telephone interrupted her thoughts.

'Can you answer that for me?' Janine called from the hall.

'All right.' She lifted the receiver. 'Hello?'

'Janine, thank goodness you're there,' said Jackson's voice.

'I—no. I'm—'

'I was afraid you might be out and I must talk to you urgently. I'm going to need your help, and I'll need Freya's help even more. It's Amos. He's started having breathless attacks and dizzy spells, but he won't admit there's anything wrong. I've told him he should go home, but he won't hear of it. He won't go to a doctor here either, so the only hope is for Freya to come to Egypt. He'll tolerate her keeping a daughterly eye on him.'

'Jackson—'

'And if Freya doesn't want to see me, tell her not to worry. I'll keep as clear of her as she pleases, just as long as she looks after Dad. That's all I'll ask of her. My word on it.'

Freya's head whirled. Since answering the phone she'd uttered only a few words, and as her voice was very like her mother's Jackson hadn't spotted the mistake.

'Do you think she'll accept my word?' Jackson persisted. 'After what happened—does she still hate me?'

At last Freya forced herself to speak.

'I don't hate you, Jackson,' she said.

There was a stunned silence. At last he spoke, sounding shocked. 'Freya?'

'Yes, it's me. I'd have told you earlier but you didn't give me the chance. If you need my help you'll have it, of course.'

'Do you—mean that?'

'Of course I mean it. Ah, here's my mother. You'd better talk to her.'

She handed the phone to Janine, who had just appeared, murmuring, 'It's Jackson. He says Amos needs us.'

While Janine listened to the bad news Freya kept a comforting arm around her mother, supporting her when she seemed about to fall.

'Oh, no!' she wept. 'I'll come at once—'

'Me too,' Freya told her, taking the phone. 'Don't worry, Mum. I'm going to take care of everything.' Assuming her most professional voice, she said, 'Jackson, can you help me with the arrangements?'

'Certainly. We're at Giza, and the nearest airport is Cairo.'

For several minutes Freya made notes.

'As soon as I know the flight times I'll call you.'

'Fine. And, Freya, thank you for this. It means so much—I was afraid—'

'You should have known better. There's nothing I wouldn't do for my mother.'

'Oh, yes—of course. Right—'

He'd got the message. She was doing this for Janine, and only for her.

As soon as she'd replaced the receiver the two women fell into each other's arms.

'Thank you, darling,' her mother said in a choking voice. 'I don't know how I'd cope without you.'

'You don't have to,' Freya assured her. 'I'm here for you and I always will be. It's going to be all right. Trust me.'

'I do, darling. You're so strong. I think you can do anything, fight any battle. As long as you're with me I know we're all safe.'

Freya smiled and said the right things, but inwardly she wished that she too could feel safe. She had no control over what would happen now, and the feeling of being helpless alarmed her. But she'd promised, and she was determined to help her suffering mother.

She would be strong to help her mother.

CHAPTER FIVE

THE NEAREST AIRPORT was close to the French town of Nice, about ten miles away. From there they could get a flight to Cairo. When the tickets were booked she called Jackson back.

'The first available seats are tomorrow afternoon. We'll land at—'

When she'd given him all the details he said, 'You'll be met there, and a car will take you to Giza.'

'Does Amos know we're coming?'

'Yes, but he thinks it's just a family visit because you're missing him.'

Freya went to help with the packing, concentrating everything on keeping her spirits up. She remembered asking Janine how she endured Amos, and her mother's answer: 'He needs me.'

That was love. Ignoring a man's displeasing ways to see only the vulnerability beneath was the very heart of love. And it was a feeling she'd never known with Dan, who'd never seemed vulnerable.

On the journey to Nice airport the next day Freya held Janine's hand, feeling that *she* was the mother now. The three hours of the flight seemed to stretch out interminably, filled with thoughts that she would rather avoid. As a distraction she buried herself in a book she'd bought about their destination.

She meant her physical destination. The other destination, the one gradually evolving inside herself, was a mystery as fathomless as ancient Egypt.

There were the pyramids, she thought, slowly turning the pages to see pictures of the great four-sided tombs that rose from huge bases to a high point.

The ancient pharaohs had ensured that the world would always remember them by creating extravagant burial temples, starting on the day they took the throne. The best known was Tutankhamun, the boy king who'd lived three and a half thousand years ago and died after a mere three-year reign aged only eighteen. His tomb was one of the smallest, but in the last century it had been excavated by explorers, and so made 'King Tut' the most famous pharaoh of them all.

Then there was the Sphinx, the huge statue of a lion with a human head, sometimes known as The Terrifying One.

Freya felt excitement growing in her at the thought of seeing this fascinating country.

At Cairo they went through the procedures of disembarking, collecting their luggage, going through Customs, searching the crowd.

'Who did he say he was sending to collect us?' Janine asked. 'Because I can't— Amos!'

She bounced up and down, waving frantically to someone. Now Freya recognised Amos, hurrying forward, gathering speed as he neared his wife until they flung themselves into each other's arms.

Freya searched the crowd for Jackson, but she could see no sign of him.

He wasn't there, she thought with a stab of disappointment. He hadn't bothered to come and meet them.

But then she saw him, standing a few feet away, looking so changed that she barely recognised him. The hot sun had tanned him, and he looked thinner, like a man who worked long hours and neglected himself. Despite the distance she could sense his tension, and she guessed he was really worried about his father and had taken a lot of trouble for him—even to the extent of seeking the help of a woman with whom he was at odds.

He looked up and she caught the exact moment when he saw her. New life came into his face and he raised a hand in greeting.

'Thank you,' he said as they met. 'It's wonderful that you're here. You can see how happy it makes Amos.'

The older couple were still hugging each other joyfully.

'I'm glad for both their sakes,' she said. 'And how are you? I nearly didn't recognise you.'

'It's been a little tiring, but I still love doing it.' He turned to his stepmother. 'Janine, lovely to see you.'

He enveloped her in a hug, then took their bags.

Freya had thought she too might have received a warm embrace from him, especially after the hug they'd shared when they parted. She thought perhaps she'd demanded that hug as a way of hinting that hostilities could now be over. She wasn't sure.

But things were different now. He'd promised to keep his distance and clearly he intended to do so. It was foolish to feel disappointed, and she wouldn't allow herself that much weakness.

Outside, a large, luxurious vehicle was awaiting them, with a chauffeur who took charge of their bags and assisted the ladies inside. With two rows of seats it was more like a bus than a car. Jackson guided the two women to sit together while he sat opposite, with his father.

'It should only take about half an hour,' he said. 'We're going to the Harbury Hotel in Pyramids Road.'

'Pyramids Road?' Janine echoed. 'Does that mean you can see pyramids from there?'

'I'll say it does,' Jackson agreed. 'You can hardly look in any direction without seeing pyramids. It's marvellous.'

They saw what he meant as soon as they reached the city. Tall buildings rose to the sky, but behind them, dominating the world, were the pointed shapes of the pyramids.

Soon they drew up outside the hotel—an immense, luxurious building. Porters took charge of their bags while Jackson escorted them to the desk to sign in.

'The whole television crew is staying here,' he said. 'They're out doing background shots at the moment, but they'll be here soon.'

Once upstairs, Amos showed Janine to his own room, which she would now share.

'Yours is just down here,' Jackson told Freya, leading the way. 'Next door to mine, so I'm on hand if you need help.'

The room was stunning, with a floor-to-ceiling window that opened out onto a balcony from which a huge pyramid could be seen. Holding her breath, Freya went out to stand there, trying to believe that so much beauty and magnificence was so close.

Turning back, she saw Jackson waiting patiently.

'Amos looks well,' she said. 'I hadn't expected to see him so vigorous.'

'He changes from moment to moment. Mostly he seems well, but then he'll go dizzy, or breathless. I make him rest when I can, but you know what it's like trying to get him to take advice.'

'You should know that better than anyone,' she pointed out. 'He's your father.'

'Yes, but I've never had to try to make him see sense before—not like this. You're the expert. If you knew what a relief it is to me to have you here.'

'You know I'll do my best to look after him.'

'That's very sweet and generous of you after everything that happened.'

'I'm not being sweet and generous,' she said at once. 'I'm being professional. Amos is my patient, even if he doesn't know it.' With a slight edge to her voice she said, 'Feelings have nothing to do with it.'

'Of course. I only meant— I don't want you to think— Well, anyway, I'm grateful.'

He stopped abruptly. The air seemed to ring with his confusion and suddenly she too was confused. It wasn't like Jackson to be lost for words.

'I'll leave you to get on with your unpacking,' he said at last. 'Tonight you'll meet the rest of the crew. It should be a cheerful party.'

'How have they felt about Amos being out here?'

'They love him. When he started talking about the falcon god I saw Larry's face light up. That's Larry Lowton—the producer of the series. He's a terrific producer and he's treated Dad well. When we get to Edfu I think he's going to find a way of including him in the show.'

'What about you?'

'I'm always there, talking to the camera.'

'But you're a Falcon too. Doesn't he want to make use of that?'

'You're surely not suggesting that anyone could mistake *me* for a god, are you, Freya?'

'I suppose not.'

'Issuing edicts? Laying down the law? Nah! I'd be sure

to make a mess of it, wouldn't I?' He regarded her with wry amusement. 'That's one thing I guess we can agree on.'

Here was dangerous territory. But she coped with ease, simply saying lightly, 'If you say so.'

'I do say so. Right, I'll be going now. I'll collect you in an hour.'

'How do you dress for dinner here?'

'Usually it's pretty casual, but not tonight. Everyone's poshing up in your honour. If you need me I'm just next door.'

He departed without waiting for a reply. Freya gave a small sigh of relief. So far it hadn't gone too badly. Humour was a good way to deal with things.

It was a little disconcerting to know that he was next door, and when she went out onto the balcony she glanced at his window, ready to retreat if he appeared. But he didn't, and she was able to breathe in the magical atmosphere undisturbed.

She'd brought a couple of elegant cocktail dresses with her. For dinner she chose one in blue silk that fitted her figure neatly without too much emphasis. Like Jackson, she was keeping her distance.

There had been that troublesome moment at the airport, when she'd feared that he had not come. But her feelings were easily explained, she assured herself. They needed him as a guide. No more. Nothing about him could bother her now. Not even the fact that he was in the next room.

After an hour he presented himself, dressed in an evening jacket.

'You look fine,' he said politely. 'Let's go and collect our parents.'

Both Amos and Janine were smartly dressed for the evening, and Freya was glad to see that the atmosphere between them was warm. Amos seemed to be enjoying himself.

Seven people were waiting for them.

'This is Larry, the boss,' Jackson said lightly. 'He gives his orders and we all jump.'

'That's Jackson's idea of a joke,' Larry said. 'I don't think he's ever taken an order in his life.'

Freya took to Larry from the start. In his early forties, he was moderately handsome, if slightly on the plump side, and he seemed to live permanently on the edge of laughter. He introduced her to Tommy, his second-in-command, a lively, feverish young man who sent her an admiring message with his eyes and started blurting out incoherent words—which Larry firmly silenced.

'He's a good lad,' he told Freya under his breath, 'but he can be exhausting.'

Jackson joined them and introduced the rest of the team, finishing with a dazzlingly pretty young woman who greeted him with a peck on the cheek.

'This is Debra—Larry's excellent secretary,' Jackson explained. 'And sometimes she deigns to act as my secretary too.'

That wasn't her only role in his life, Freya thought; not if her teasing manner towards him was anything to go by. She watched as he sat next to Debra, giving her his full attention, laughing at something she said, meeting her eyes.

When the introductions were finished Larry led Freya to a chair and pulled it out.

'Sit next to me,' he said. 'I want to know all about Jackson.'

'Surely you know plenty about him by now?' she said.

'Only the trivial things. But every time we argue he wins. That's got to stop. I want you to tell me about his weaknesses, so that I'll have him at a disadvantage instead of the other way around.'

He spoke in a loud voice, inviting everyone to share the joke.

Jackson grinned. 'He's been trying to catch me on the hop since the day we met,' he announced. 'No success so far.'

'But I can live in hope,' Larry declared. 'If this charming lady will be my co-conspirator?'

'Nothing would give me more pleasure,' Freya assured him. 'I could always tell you about the time three years ago when— Well, let's leave that until later.'

The mention of three years ago was a message to Jackson. This was a jokey conversation in which the recent past played no part. Tonight was simply for pleasure. His nod told her that he understood and agreed.

Larry was an entertaining companion, with a gift for telling anecdotes. One in particular reduced her to such a fit of laughter that everyone else at the table stared.

'I'm sorry,' she choked, bringing herself under control. 'It's the way you tell the story—were you ever an actor, by any chance?'

'Yes, I was,' he said. 'I started as an actor and gave it up to become a director. And you saw through me. Boy, you're really clever!' He took both her hands in his, gazing deeply into her eyes. 'Some time soon we must get together and you must tell me *all* about yourself.'

She wasn't fooled. This wasn't real flirting but a bit of harmless fun. And he expected her to understand it that way. His teasing glint made that clear. She had no problem in chuckling and saying with mock fervour, 'I can't wait.'

There was a cheer from the rest of the table, and cries of, 'Watch out for him, Freya. He's a dodgy character.'

'Well, I can see that,' she said. 'There's the fun.'

Tommy raised his glass, declaring, '*I'm* a dodgy character too. Don't forget me.'

'You'll have to wait,' she said. 'I only have time for one dodgy character at a time.'

The evening was a big success. Freya would gladly have stayed later, but she could see Amos trying to suppress a yawn and not succeeding. When Janine squeezed his hand he rose to follow her without protest.

'I'll come with you,' Freya said. 'Goodnight, everyone.'

'Goodnight,' Jackson said. 'Sleep well. We've got a heavy day tomorrow.'

Debra, sitting beside him, giggled and clutched his arm. Freya turned quickly away.

Upstairs, she and Janine worked at making Amos comfortable, to which he responded with the comment, 'Stop fussing, you two. I'm all right.'

'Of course you are,' Freya said. 'I'll see you in the morning.'

She kissed her mother and departed. Now she badly wanted to be alone and it was a relief to escape to her room. Once inside she didn't put on the light, but opened the glass door onto the balcony and went out into the night air.

A soft light still gleamed on the pyramids, making them glow faintly. Entranced, she stood watching, enjoying the feeling that she was witnessing a mystery that stretched back centuries. It was a sweet, magical feeling that seemed to take her back to another time, when the world itself had seemed imbued by magic.

But what folly that had been. And how quickly, how brutally it had ended.

She was swept by a strange mood; deep inside her there was a kind of anguish—not for Dan himself, but for what he had seemed to represent: hope, wonder, a belief that life could be beautiful.

For a while after the disaster of her wedding she'd been able to continue believing. Jackson had reached out to her, and while she'd been able to cling to him the world had still been a good place. The discovery of his betrayal had been a blow over the heart that had affected her as much as Dan's. Perhaps even more.

Now the comfort that Jackson had seemed to offer was gone. Gone for ever. For how could she ever believe in anyone again?

She dropped her head, covering her eyes with her hand, seeking escape, forgetfulness, while her body trembled with sobs.

'No,' she told herself sharply. 'I said I wasn't going to give in to this again. And I'm not. I'm going to have a new world that I'll build myself, without anyone's help.'

But somehow strength and resolution were no help to her now. She gazed yearningly at the pyramid, looming high and peaceful as it had done for thousands of years—as it would do for thousands more. How petty seemed human problems against that monument and the ancient wisdom it represented. How many humans had stood before its magnificence feeling their own triviality?

'If only I knew what I—' she whispered. 'If only I could tell—'

But there was only silence and the awesome, unyielding beauty that seemed to come from another universe.

At last she turned away and moved inside, where she went to bed and lay sleepless for several hours.

For several minutes after Freya went inside, the man standing on the next balcony stayed silent and motionless, relieved that she hadn't discovered him.

Jackson wasn't proud of himself for watching Freya while she hadn't known he was there, but her entrance had taken him by surprise. He remembered that day several weeks ago, when she'd discovered his innocent deception about Dan and attacked him furiously. A few hours later he'd spotted his father standing outside the door, secretly listening to Freya and her mother talking inside. Without being able to make out the words, Jackson had guessed what was being said.

Seeing his son, Amos had placed a finger over his lips and shaken his head. When Jackson had tried to make him leave he'd refused. Nor would he discuss what he'd heard.

'And don't you tell them that you saw me,' he'd demanded. 'There are things a man should keep to himself.'

Jackson had agreed, though reluctantly. Having concealed the truth from Freya once, it hurt him to deceive her by concealment a second time. It had been a relief to leave for Egypt soon afterwards. Now a malevolent fate had tricked him into spying on her. Leaving the balcony had been impossible. The door to his bedroom was too noisy to risk. He'd had no choice but to stay and see things his conscience told him he had no right to see.

Like father, like son, he thought bitterly. He always said he wasn't like Amos, but then something like this happened and—oh, hell!

The quarrel with Freya had hurt him. When he'd first tried to help her through the misery of her cancelled wedding it had been partly from kindness, partly from guilt. Gradually he'd come to enjoy their relationship. The sense that he could bring her comfort had made him feel good about himself in a way that had been new to him.

Which just went to show how conceited he could be, he told himself wryly.

The pleasure of protecting her had been real, and her fury when she'd discovered the truth had been a blow to his heart. Then she'd seen him off at the airport and demanded a hug, giving him a moment of hope. He'd dared to think next time they met the past would be forgiven, their friendship restored.

But then had come his call to England about Amos's health, and the things he'd said to Freya thinking he was speaking to Janine. He'd said nothing that could offend her, but he'd adopted a pleading tone that now embarrassed him. How foolish he must have sounded.

When they'd met again earlier that day she'd been coolly affable, full of calm good sense. No sign of hostility, but no pleasure either. It was as though the old, friendly Freya no longer existed.

But she'd returned tonight at the dinner table. Chatting with Larry, she'd burst into delighted laughter, then indulged in a bout of teasing backchat with him.

Debra, sitting beside himself, trying to lure his attention away from Freya, had murmured, 'Those two are really on each other's wavelength, aren't they?'

'Are they?' he'd responded with a fairly convincing display of indifference.

'No doubt of it. He took to her from the first moment. You've got to admit she's a looker.'

'Is she?' Freya's personality had always appealed to him more than her looks. Studying her at that moment, he'd had to admit she was at her best—much as she had been on her wedding day.

'Oh, come on!' Debra had exclaimed. 'She's really pretty, but Larry likes them best when they laugh with him.'

'Would you like some more wine?' he'd asked with a fixed smile.

He would have offered her anything to shut her up.

Now there was no doubt. The Freya he'd once known

hadn't disappeared after all. She was reappearing, as lively, jokey and fun-loving as always.

But for Larry. Not for himself.

He'd promised to keep his distance, and for his father's sake that promise had to be kept. So he'd given her only the attention that courtesy demanded. Then he'd hidden behind the shield Debra offered, flirting with her, seeming riveted by her company, to conceal the fact that his real attention was for Freya. He'd tried to be glad that she was getting on so well with Larry, but somehow he just hadn't been able to manage it.

When the meal was over he'd seen Debra to her door and bade her a courteous goodnight, pretending not to see the invitation in her eyes, or her bafflement when he ignored it. Then he'd returned to his own room.

There had been no light under Freya's door, suggesting that she hadn't returned. Where was she? he'd wondered. Alone? Or had her joke about dodgy characters being fun actually held some meaning? Was she exploring that meaning? With Larry?

No, not Freya. Not after one brief meeting.

Surely not.

But then where *was* she?

He'd gone out to look at the pyramid, looming in the darkness, and had still been standing there when she'd arrived next door. Straining his ears, he'd heard no voices and realised, with relief, that she was alone. Next moment she'd appeared on her balcony.

He'd moved forward, meaning to speak to her, then stopped. Something about her as she'd stood there, gazing up into the night, had made him pause, enjoying the air of rapture that seemed to permeate her being. But it had passed suddenly, replaced by a sigh.

He'd watched as her shoulders had sagged, hoping to

see her pleasure return. Instead she'd dropped her head in her hands and he'd been able to hear her weeping.

He'd clenched his hands, longing to reveal himself and comfort her but knowing that he didn't dare. She would never forgive him.

He'd seen the sobs convulse her, possessing her whole body with a nameless grief. Frantically he had sought for the answer. Was it the sight of himself that had hurt her after so long? Or did the pain of that terrible day still torment her, reducing everything else to nothing?

In the aftermath of her wrecked wedding, how often had he heard her declare defiantly that she wasn't going to cry? She hadn't always managed to fight back the tears, but her courage and defiance had seldom faltered. He'd known her confident, efficient at her job, ready to confront life on equal terms. But until now he hadn't known her defeated.

The sight of her yielding to despair had made him long to reach out and console her. It would have been easy to climb the low wall that separated his balcony from hers and take her in his arms, lavish her with warmth and comfort. For a moment he'd been fiercely tempted, knowing that only he could comfort her because only he knew the full extent of her hurt.

He had reached out his hand to the wall.

But then he'd stopped himself and drawn back in alarm. Once he could have consoled her as a brother, but those days were over. The physical attraction that had flickered between them might have been brief, but its memory was searing. Neither of them could forget it, and it would destroy everything he tried to do for her. Now she was alone as never before.

The sight of her tears had seemed to bring a treacherous stinging to his own eyes, and bitterly he'd cursed the malign fate that made him helpless when she needed him so much.

At last Freya had turned away and stumbled inside, leaving him distraught and asking himself for the thousandth time, *What have I done?*

CHAPTER SIX

THE RINGING OF the phone awoke Freya before dawn the next morning. It was Janine, sounding worried.

'Please come,' she said. 'He's gasping again.'

Freya pulled on her dressing gown and hurried out into the corridor. To her surprise she saw Jackson there, turning the key in his own door.

'What is it?' he asked.

'Amos. Mum's just called me to say he's gasping.'

'Let's go.'

They found Amos sitting on the side of the bed, his chest rising and falling heavily. He looked up at Freya, and nodded when she produced the stethoscope she'd taken the precaution of bringing.

'So now we have the truth,' he said caustically. 'Your visit is just another way of mollycoddling me.'

'I'm always ready in case you need me. Now hush and let me do my job.'

'Are you giving me orders?'

'Yes, I am. So do as I say and be quiet.'

'You're as big a bully as your mother.'

'Luckily for you I am.'

She listened to his heart, fearing the worst, but was pleasantly surprised to hear it beating strongly.

'That's good,' she said.

'Of course it is. There's nothing the matter with me. Why must women always make a fuss?'

'Because you mean a lot to us,' Janine said, sounding cross. 'Although I sometimes wonder why. You miserable old so-and-so.'

Amos gave a bark of ironic laughter. 'And those are the words of a woman who says I mean a lot to her. Isn't it lucky I have a sense of humour?'

'No, it's lucky you have a wife who can put up with your carry-on,' Freya said. 'Your health isn't too bad but don't overdo it.'

'If you're trying to stop me going out today, forget it. It's our last day here before we go to Edfu and I'm not going to miss it.'

'Perhaps you should,' Jackson said. 'You've seen this place. Why not stay here and rest today so that you're fit for tomorrow?'

'I'm fit for anything I say I'm fit for,' Amos said, outraged. 'Don't tell me you've started taking their orders? That any son of mine—'

'As a son of yours I'm practical,' Jackson said. 'And being practical means I'll listen to suggestions from someone who knows better than I do.' He inclined his head to Freya. 'Find the experts and pick their brains. It's the most profitable way forward. You taught me that.'

'I'm going with you,' Amos repeated.

'All right, but take it easy,' Freya told him. 'Walk as little as you have to.' She had a sudden burst of inspiration. 'After all, our next stop is Edfu, where you and Horus will confront each other. You wouldn't want to be taken ill before you get there, would you? Imagine missing him when you've come so far to meet him. He's probably laying out the red carpet for you now.'

Amos cast her a wry look, conveying that he understood exactly what she was up to. But to their relief his mood improved.

'You're right,' he said. 'Nothing must get in the way of Edfu.'

'It's still early,' Freya said. 'Try to get some more sleep.'

Amos nodded and slid down in the bed. Jackson and Freya patted Janine's shoulder, and left.

'Is he really all right?' he asked as they went along the corridor.

'Yes, his heart sounds better than I expected. But he shouldn't walk too much. It might help to have a wheel-chair on hand, just in case.'

'Gladly. You really got the better of him back there.'

'No, you did, with your talk about profiting from the advice of experts.' She put her hand over her mouth to smother a yawn.

'And you're the expert,' he said. 'You'd better get a little more sleep. You might find tomorrow tiring. Goodnight.'

'Goodnight.'

Where was he going? she wondered as he walked away. Back to Debra, perhaps.

She remembered hearing him spoken of as 'a man who likes to enjoy life, taking pleasure wherever he finds it', and she guessed the pleasures must be many. Women would be drawn to both his looks and his growing fame as a television personality. And his easygoing good nature would add to his attractions.

As for his darker side, the one that had ruined things between them, who else but her had ever discovered it?

She had no desire to sleep. She switched on the light and took out the book about the pyramids that she'd brought with her. But even this failed to calm her mind and at last she closed it, turned the light out again and went to the window that looked out over the hotel's garden.

In the faint light she could just make out the figure of a man wandering beneath the trees. Something about him caught her attention. He seemed not merely alone but strangely cut off from his fellow humans.

Then she recognised Jackson.

So he wasn't with Debra, she thought. Unless Debra was coming out to join him.

But minutes passed and he was still alone. Again she had the mysterious feeling that loneliness was natural to him.

How could that be? Nobody as popular as Jackson was ever lonely.

Yet the thought would not be banished. For all his large family, his popularity, Jackson had nobody who was completely his. His brothers were all happily married; his father had Janine. But he drifted through life in mysterious isolation. The thought had never occurred to her before, and now she wondered why.

He turned, looked up and saw her. She half expected him to turn away, but he raised his arm in a gesture that invited her to join him. Her heart leapt. She waved back, and hurried away to slip some shorts and a T-shirt on before going to meet Jackson.

He was waiting for her at the door.

'Thank you,' he said. 'I was afraid you wouldn't come.'

'But this is a lovely place. I don't wonder you like to be here.'

He took her hand and led her through the trees to where there were some seats at the end of the garden. The pyramids were more visible now, easing their way into the light, magical, magnificent, mysterious.

For a while they sat in silence, relishing the experience, his hand still holding hers. Then he said softly, 'I can't tell

you how grateful I am to you for coming to Egypt. It must
have been difficult.'

'I wouldn't just abandon Amos. I know he means the
world to you.'

'In a way.'

'In a *way*?'

'Don't misunderstand me. I love my father. But—how
do I say it?—I don't always like him. He does what suits
himself, no matter who he hurts.'

He paused and she had a vivid sense of indecision tor-
menting him. His words were heavy with a meaning he'd
never hinted at before and perhaps couldn't speak of now.

'Is there anything you want to tell me?' she asked gently.

His hand tightened on hers.

'I've never talked about it before,' he said huskily. 'But
now I— For the first few years of my life I seemed to be
part of the ideal family. There were my parents, and Darius, my brother, and everything was fine. Then my mother
found out about my brother Marcel—the son he'd had by
Claire, a Frenchwoman, five years earlier.'

'While he was still living with your mother?'

'Yes. I think that was one of the things that hurt her
most. That he'd carried on with another woman while still
playing the loving husband.'

'How could she ever believe a word he said after that?'
Freya breathed.

'She couldn't. She left him. They divorced and he married Claire. Darius and I lived with our mother until she
died a few years later. After that we had to return to Amos.'

'How old were you then?'

'Eleven. I could never be at ease with Claire. It wasn't
her fault. She was my father's victim as much as any of
us. But I blamed her for my mother's death.'

'You don't mean your mother—?'

'No, she didn't take her life. Not exactly. But she went down with an illness that she didn't have the strength to fight, and I don't think she wanted to fight it. I was with her when she died, and the last thing she said to me was, "I'm sorry." Then she closed her eyes and just let go. Meanwhile Amos was playing the field again, with Travis's mother in Los Angeles and Leonid's mother in Moscow. Claire found out and left him, taking Marcel. By then Darius was making his own career, so I was alone with Dad for much of the time.

'It was like living with two versions of the same person. There was the man who'd broken all our hearts and didn't care—a man I resented. But there was also the "Big Beast", whom the world admired and feared, and in a way I admired him too. I wanted to be like him, earn his praise. I did some really stupid things, and the stupider I was the more he approved of me.'

'But approval wasn't enough, was it?' she asked.

'No. I wanted more. I wanted—I don't know—something else.'

'Love,' she said. 'The kind that puts you first—the kind you should expect from your parents. When grown-ups are so taken up with each other they can sometimes forget what the children need.'

He stared. 'How did you know that? Surely your parents loved you?'

'Oh, yes, but they loved each other first. I got lavish presents, but somehow I always sensed something missing. One year my father paid for me to go on a really expensive school trip. I thought he was being generous, finding so much money for me to enjoy myself. But while I was gone he and my mother took a holiday together. I thought there would be another holiday, with the three of us, but there wasn't. They'd seized the chance go away without me. I know it sounds crazy and self-centred to say it like this—'

'Not to me, it doesn't,' Jackson said. 'Everything's fine on the outside, but inside there's a place that's sad, hollow.'

As he said it she could see the child Jackson, surrounded by money and success but knowing there was no one who would put him first. The father playing the field with other women…the mother more concerned with her own misery than her children's needs.

'That's it,' she said. 'I grew up knowing that I'd have to be enough for myself. Or at least pretend to be.'

'Yes.' Jackson sighed. 'Exactly like that. It can be good to be enough for yourself, as long as you know when to drop the defences. That's Dad's trouble. He never knew. Through all those love affairs he had to be the one in control.'

They looked at each other, sharing the same curious expression.

'We've known each other for six years,' he said. 'And we've never shared this before.'

'It was never the right time before,' she said.

'Yes. And when the right time comes, you know. And you have to take it because it may never come again. I think you're the only person I could ever talk to about Dad, and how tense I feel about what I've inherited of his nature.'

'You can't help what you were born with. And you're not as bad as he is.'

'Thanks. I treasure that.' He added wryly, 'And a gift for getting your own way *can* be useful. But sometimes it makes me wonder about myself. I've got a bad side.'

'So have we all,' she said. 'Don't be hard on yourself.'

'That's nice of you, but my bad side is worse than you know. And you know plenty, after the harm I did you.'

'But you didn't do it on purpose. You made an incautious remark. You couldn't predict what Dan would do. It was a mistake, but I've made plenty of those myself. Let's draw a line under it.'

He stared. 'You've really forgiven me?'

'There's nothing to forgive. You might have been a bit clumsy—'

'Clumsy, stupid, idiotic, thoughtless—' he supplied.

'If you say so. But you weren't spiteful. You're not capable of spite.'

'That's kinder than I deserve.'

His voice was heavy and she knew he was still deeply troubled—not only by their past hostility but by the burdens Amos had loaded onto him when he was too young to bear them.

He dropped his head, fixing his gaze on the ground. She knew a deep and worrying instinct to protect him. Dazzling, self-confident Jackson had never seemed in need of anyone's protection before, but this was a new man— one he'd revealed to her and perhaps to nobody else. He trusted her. He'd said so, and had proved it by showing his vulnerable side.

In another moment she would have reached out and taken him in her arms, offering him all the comfort she could, but a warning sounded in her head. That way lay danger. The faint, flickering attraction between them might revive at any time. The memory of his lips brushing hers warned her not to take the risk.

Yet who else was there to help him? His obnoxious father? The women who came and went but never seemed to get really close to his life or his heart?

She could have cursed the malign fate that had given such insight to *her*—the one person who didn't dare use it, and yet who wanted to use it with all her heart. It was alarming how much she wanted that.

She ventured to reach out and touch his shoulder.

'Jackson—'

He raised his head and their eyes met. For a brief moment she saw him defenceless, without the mask that she now realised he wore so easily.

'What is it, Freya?' he whispered.

She drew a trembling breath. Another moment and she would have thrown caution to the winds. But alarm came to her aid, forcing her to speak common sense words.

'Let's put it in the past,' she said. 'We've always been good friends and we're not going to let anything spoil it.'

'Right,' he said, and the mask was in place again. 'Good friends it is—just like always.'

'Always have been, always will be.'

They shook hands.

'Oh, look,' she said. 'It's there.'

The great pyramid loomed gloriously above them, golden in the fast growing light, full of promise for the day to come.

'Yes, it's there,' he said. 'It could be there for ever.'

'When we're not here any more—in a thousand years.'

They sat in silence for a while. At last they rose and wandered back into the hotel. It was time for the day to begin.

At breakfast Amos was in good spirits.

'I'm beginning to find Ancient Egypt fascinating,' Freya told him. 'This place we're going to today—'

'The Giza Necropolis,' Amos put in.

'Yes, the place with all those pyramids. Will I see Tutankhamun's tomb?'

'No, that's not here,' Amos said. 'He's further down the Nile, in the Valley of the Kings. But it's quite near Edfu, so you can see him when we go there.'

'So who *is* in the Giza Necropolis?' Freya asked.

'Khentkaus the First,' Amos said.

'Who was he?'

'Not he—she,' Jackson said. 'We don't know very much about her—even who she really was. There are a thousand stories that she was the daughter of one pharaoh and the wife of another—maybe two others. She might have reigned in her own right—or maybe not. Or perhaps she was the mother of two pharaohs and the regent of one. All we know for sure is that she must have been someone important for her tomb to be located here, among kings. Apart from that she's a woman of mystery.'

'I thought Cleopatra was the great woman of mystery,' Freya observed.

'In a sense,' Jackson agreed. 'But we know so much about Cleopatra that there's less mystery to enjoy. Khentkaus hides behind a fog of ambiguity.'

'Ah, yes, that sounds far more fun,' Freya agreed.

'Definitely.'

They shared a nod.

'Time we were going,' Larry said.

Of the journey out to the Giza Necropolis she gazed, entranced, out of the window.

'Where's Khentkaus?' she asked.

'Her pyramid is just a ruin,' Jackson said. 'There's very little to see. We'll do a final shoot today and bid her goodbye.'

No sooner had they arrived than Larry summoned Jackson, saying, 'We've got a problem.'

'He doesn't look pleased,' Freya observed, for Larry's

face bore signs of intense exasperation. 'Have you offended him?'

'You bet I have,' Jackson said. 'I made some changes to the script we're shooting. I often do that, and it makes him mad.'

'I shouldn't think the scriptwriter's too pleased either.'

'No, but he's a wise man. He just keeps quiet and does what the boss tells him.'

'The boss being Larry?'

'Officially…'

'And unofficially?'

Jackson grinned. 'What do you think?'

'That's the spirit,' Amos declared, delighted.

'I guess I'm not your son for nothing,' Jackson said. 'But I sometimes have to make a show of deferring to Larry, just to keep the peace. From the way he's holding up that script and thumping it, this may be one of those times.'

He went over to Larry. The others watched, fascinated to see what would happen next, but they were disappointed when both men walked away and disappeared behind some stones.

'That's a pity,' Freya said. 'It could have been fun.'

'Jackson will win,' Debra predicted. 'He always does. He likes to change the words and even direct the research. And if he doesn't get what he wants there's trouble.'

'There they are,' Freya said, pointing.

Larry and Jackson had reappeared, still arguing. The listeners could make out most of the words.

'It's just that I can't see it that way,' Larry was saying. 'The original idea—'

'The original idea was full of holes, and it's got to be put right.' Jackson jabbed at something in the script. 'I can't say that. It doesn't make sense. I've told you what I'm going to say instead.'

'If you can get Pete to agree.'

Pete was the scriptwriter.

'No, *you'll* do that. Just tell him everything's been decided.'

'And has it?'

'You know it has.' Jackson's grin made him charming, although his words were implacable. 'C'mon, we've sorted it now. I'm not going to stand up before the camera and say something I don't agree with, so that's it. It's all settled.'

Jackson returned to their side.

'Larry's agreed to the script change. I had to admit I'd been in two minds about it at first—'

'That was bad,' Amos said quickly. 'You shouldn't have admitted that.'

'Well, it didn't do any harm. He's even going to arrange some extra shots to illustrate what I'm going to say.'

'Good. You did well. Mind you, you took too long. You should have been firmer from the start. Then he'd have capitulated sooner.'

'And there would have been a lot of bad feeling,' Jackson said. 'I work with these people. I don't want bad feeling. It's better my way.'

Amos shook his head.

'You still have something to learn about standing up to people. For one thing, you should never tell them anything they might use against you. Never let them suspect a weakness. But you'll learn. Wait till you reach my age.'

'I'm not sure I'll ever reach your age. Freya will have strangled me long before that. Right—time to get to work.'

Before leaving he gave Freya a significant look that she understood at once. He was reminding her of their talk in the dawn, of how troubled he was by this side of him although he couldn't help making use of it. She offered him a smile of reassurance and he gave her a brief nod.

Everything went well after that. Despite his firm stand Jackson still managed to stay on good terms with the others. She watched him with interest, fascinated by his expertise as he led the cameras over the ruins of Khent-kaus' tomb and delivered a eulogy.

'After thousands of years,' he said, 'there are still many questions. How many of her children took the throne? How many of her descendants walk the world today? Truly she was a woman of mystery, and the mystery lingers even now. Will those questions ever be answered? Probably not. Like many a woman of mystery, she prefers to keep her secrets to herself.'

He gave the smile that had done so much to win him an audience of eager fans.

'But one day—who knows?—perhaps she will choose to open her heart to us.'

'Cut!' Larry yelled. 'That's great. All right, everyone. Time to go.'

Dinner that night was cheerful. Debra even made a jokey comment about the argument she and Freya had witnessed.

'You won, then?' she teased Jackson.

'Of course,' Jackson declared, raising his glass in Larry's direction.

'It's got something to do with him being a Falcon,' Larry said, 'and there being a falcon god. I had to make use of that.'

'I think it's a great idea,' Freya said.

'Of course. After all, your own name is an invitation all by itself.'

'My name?' she echoed, puzzled.

Larry regarded her quizzically. 'Don't say you don't know?'

'Know what?'

'That you're a goddess?'

'Oh, come on—'

'No—really. Freya comes from Norse mythology. She's associated with fertility and she rides a chariot pulled by two cats. You actually didn't know you're a goddess?'

'No, and I don't believe it. Mum—?' Freya turned to Janine. 'Surely not.'

'It's possible. Your father chose your name. He was fascinated by mythology, and he said he'd found it in a book, but that was all. It might be true.'

'There's another thing,' Larry said, clearly enjoying every moment. 'The great goddess Freya wears a cloak of falcon feathers, so in a way you're a falcon too.'

Amos gave a crack of laughter. 'How about that? You've been a Falcon all the time.'

'Hardly,' Freya said. 'I think it takes a bit more than wearing a cloak.'

'You'd better watch out, Dad,' Jackson said. 'You've met your match.' He raised his glass to Freya. 'I salute you.'

Amos immediately did the same, and everyone joined in.

'You should do a programme about her,' Amos asserted.

'And perhaps Khentkaus as well,' Larry agreed. 'I remember once hearing somebody say that the most interesting crimes were committed by women.'

More laughter—except from Freya, whose face grew suddenly darker. But nobody seemed to notice except perhaps Jackson, who became suddenly intent on clinking glasses with everyone near him. Except Freya.

When it was time to retire Freya accompanied Amos and Janine to their room and made sure Amos was comfortable. Returning to her own room, she went outside onto the balcony to take a last look at the pyramids glowing against the night.

'Are you all right?'

Jackson's voice, coming from a few feet away, startled her. She could just make him out on his own balcony, standing quietly in the darkness.

'I—I didn't know you were there,' she stammered.

'Sorry, I didn't mean to alarm you. I was just a little concerned in case you were upset. You went quiet very suddenly at dinner, and I think I knew why. It was what Larry said about women committing the most interesting crimes. I suddenly remembered Dan saying the same thing. It came out of a book he'd read.'

'Yes, he talked to me about it. It just reminded me of him. But it's nothing.'

'Nothing? It was like he'd suddenly appeared in front of you and you were shattered.'

'No, I wasn't. Just a little surprised. But he doesn't trouble me any more.'

'I'd be glad to believe that, but I worry about you.'

'Don't. Dan isn't part of my life any more.' She assumed a dramatic air. 'Freya the goddess waved her magic wand and he ceased to exist. That's how powerful she is.'

'If only life could be that simple. We all have things we'd like to wipe out as though they'd never happened, but the more we want to be rid of them the more they seem to haunt us.'

Freya shook her head firmly. 'I'm not haunted. I don't let that happen.'

'And Freya the goddess is in complete control, eh?'

'Yes. You'd be surprised how powerful she is.'

'I'm not sure that I really would be surprised. I think you keep a lot up your sleeve, Freya.'

'I do these days—now that I've discovered how much other people keep up their sleeves.'

'Was that aimed at me?'

'Not really. No, it was more aimed at Dan.'

'So he really is still there, isn't he? I wonder—'

'It's late,' she interrupted him. 'I think I'll go to bed. Goodnight, Jackson.'

'Goodnight, Freya. Sleep peacefully.'

But he knew that he himself would be denied peace that night.

After trying without success to fall asleep, he rose from his bed and switched on his computer. A few clicks and he had what he sought.

There she was, Freya the glorious goddess, a magnificent being who carried in her train not only fertility but also beauty, war and death. One artist's impression had managed to catch all those hints.

'You'd really have to be wary of *her*,' Jackson murmured aloud. 'Because there's so much more in her than you'd ever dream at first. And you'd know only what she chose to reveal.'

He stared intently at the face on the screen, wishing that it was another face and he could reach out to it.

'A true woman of mystery…' he said.

CHAPTER SEVEN

FROM GIZA TO Edfu it was nearly two hundred miles. Once the coaches had started their journey Freya spent much of the time studying a book on Horus that Amos had bought in the hotel.

One of the greatest deities of ancient Egypt, whose influence stretched over three thousand years...

He'd been born to the goddess Isis when she had rescued the dismembered body parts of her murdered husband, Osiris, and used her magical powers to conceive despite Osiris' death.

Horus was the god of the sky and incorporated both the sun and the moon in his own being: his right eye the sun and his left eye the moon. But that wasn't the full extent of his power. He was known also as the god of war and hunting. Rumour even said that the pharaohs had been incarnations of Horus in human form.

Amos was sitting beside her, glancing at the book over her shoulder.

'And I'll tell you something else,' he said. 'Horus had four sons.'

'You're kidding me!'

'Fact! It's true—isn't it, Larry?'

Larry, whose seat faced them, was enjoying this.

'True,' he said. 'It makes you think Amos must be the real thing after all.'

'But of *course* I'm the real thing,' Amos declared. 'How could you doubt it?'

There was just enough of a twinkle in his eye to show that he was joking.

Halfway through the journey they stopped for lunch. Jackson looked for Freya, meaning to sit beside her at the table, but Larry got there first, immediately engaging her in laughing conversation. To his dismay he noticed that Larry was showing signs of being a fervent admirer, which Freya seemed to enjoy. It worried him because he knew Larry was a man any sensible woman would refuse to take seriously.

When it was time to get back into the coach for the last lap Debra parked herself very firmly next to Jackson, while Larry drew Freya to sit beside himself.

'You're Jackson's sister, aren't you?' he said.

'His stepsister. My mother is married to his father. There's no blood relation between us.'

'I was wondering of you knew the truth about the story that's been whispered about him for the last few years.'

'What story?'

'Something about one of the early TV documentaries he did. It was right at the start of his career and he had an explosive row with the producer. Nobody seems to know the details, but he dug his heels in so hard that he never worked for that firm again.'

'But how come people don't know more about it?'

'Because the firm won't talk about it and Jackson won't talk about it.'

'You mean it's a scandal?'

'I've no idea, but it certainly sounds as though Jackson's grim, unyielding side was in evidence. He mostly keeps it under wraps, but sometimes he can't. It makes you wonder if there was a Horus the Younger as well as Horus the Elder. Ah, who cares? He's a huge success in front of the cameras.'

'And what else matters?'

They shook hands triumphantly. Neither of them noticed Jackson, looking back at them from a few seats away.

Soon they were all keeping watch through the windows for the first sight of Edfu, a smallish city on the left bank of the Nile.

Freya liked it as soon as they arrived. There were cars, as befitted a modern city, but the roads were also filled with carts drawn by horses, giving the place a friendly air.

They were booked into a small hotel next to the river, with rooms overlooking the water. Here too she had a balcony, but Jackson wasn't next door. Her neighbours were Amos and Janine—which, she told herself, she should be glad of.

Drifting out onto the balcony, she found Janine looking down at the street.

'I'm glad you're close to me,' Janine said. 'I really need you.'

'Is Amos being more difficult than usual?'

'You've seen how he is: he's really enjoying this. But there's something else—something I can't define.'

'Is he still giving you funny looks?'

'Yes, but there's more—a new atmosphere that's never been there before. He keeps asking me what I think about things. In the past he hardly ever asked my opinion. It's almost as though he's lost confidence.'

'Him?' Freya echoed sceptically. 'I haven't seen that.'

'No, it only happens when he's with me. Others see only the Amos who's always convinced he's right. But there's another Amos, and for some reason he's not so sure of himself. I get glimpses of him, but then he hides away again.'

'I remember you saying that he's more vulnerable than anyone suspects.'

'Hush, keep your voice down. He must never know I said that.'

'Perhaps it would be good for him to know.'

'Amos couldn't cope with the knowledge that anyone thought him vulnerable. Let's go down and have something to eat.'

Downstairs they found a stall selling books about Edfu in several languages for tourists. Amos snapped up three and plunged into them at the table.

'It says here,' he declared, 'that the Temple to Horus is the most completely preserved temple remaining in Egypt. They must have realised how much it matters.'

He switched to a page containing a photograph of the temple taken from the air.

'It's huge,' Freya breathed. 'All those sections—the Festival Hall, New Year Chapel, Hall of Offerings, Sanctuary of Horus.'

'And look at those shapes carved into the wall,' Janine said. 'What are they?'

'The one on the left is a king,' Amos explained. 'The one closest to him is Horus, and the one standing behind him is the goddess Hathor—Horus' woman. The small one is their little son, Ihy. The King is making an offering to them, to show his respect.'

'Of course,' Jackson said. 'His power was immense and his influence spread over centuries. Meeting him is going to be really something.'

'Yes,' Amos said. 'Oh, yes.'

Amos said little for the rest of the meal, but the smile stayed on his face. When Freya suggested an early night to prepare him for the demands of the following day he made no objection.

'Good idea,' Jackson said.

'What about you?' she ventured to ask.

'No chance of an early night for any of us. Too much work still to do.' He laid a hand on her shoulder. 'Get some sleep. Tomorrow will probably tire you.'

She nodded and patted his hand. They had reached their comfort zone again.

Next morning everything was forgotten except the excitement that awaited them. As soon as the coach started Amos produced one of the books he'd bought the night before and went carefully through it, noting all the places to see—especially the Hypostyle Hall, where a statue of Horus was to be found.

'I thought he was a man with a falcon's head,' Freya said, looking over Amos's shoulder at a picture in the book. 'That just looks like a bird.'

'That's how he's represented in statues,' Jackson said. 'Just as a bird—like the model I brought home, except a lot bigger. But in the temple you'll see etchings of him on the walls, and in those he's a man with a falcon's head.'

When they reached the temple they headed for the spot and found what they were looking for.

'Get a load of that!' Larry breathed, staring up at the falcon-shaped statue which loomed over them a good twenty feet.

'I hadn't expected it to be so big,' Freya murmured.

'But of course,' Amos said. 'He has to be majestic.'

They moved on to where there were pictures carved into the wall and found the one they had seen in the book, in which Horus was receiving tribute from royalty. As Jackson had said, here he was a man with a falcon's head. Behind him stood the goddess Hathor, a beautiful woman with a magnificent headdress. Around her neck she wore an elaborate necklace.

'She was known as the cow goddess,' Jackson explained. 'She has a woman's face, but those two curving horns you can see on her head are a version of cow's horns. The orb between them represents the world.'

'She too was great and glorious,' Amos observed. 'She embodied motherhood, feminine love and happiness.'

'And she was his wife?' Freya said.

'That's right,' Amos said, taking Janine's hand in his. 'The most valuable wife and goddess a deity ever had. He gave her that necklace, you know, to show how much he valued her.'

He inclined his head towards Janine. She smiled back, looking a little surprised. Amos's words might almost be described as sentimental—an unusual departure for him.

Jackson too was looking surprised, and he said, 'Actually, it's not that simple. In some legends she was his wife, but in some she was his mother.'

'I thought Isis was his mother,' Freya said.

'It depends whether you're talking about Horus the Elder or Horus the Younger.'

'There really were two?' Freya queried.

'Father and son. That's the fascinating thing about the ancient Egyptians. They could believe and understand several versions of a legend at once.'

'Good for them,' Amos said. 'There's nothing more useful than being able to manipulate the facts—without being too obvious about it, of course.'

'I don't dare ask what you mean by that,' Jackson said, grinning. 'But I'm sure the markets would be interested.'

Amos gave a cackle and slapped his son on the shoulder.

'Horus the Elder and Horus the Younger,' he said. 'What a splendid idea!'

After that he had the time of his life exploring the temple.

'It's really going well,' Jackson said, falling into step with Freya on their way back to the coach. 'Amos doesn't seem at all weak any more.'

'You're right. I think I may be able to return home soon.'

'Don't be in a rush. You should be having a good time out here.'

'No, I'm just getting in the way of your work. You'll be glad when I'm gone.'

'I'll be glad when I'm not being snubbed by you for no reason,' he said wryly. 'I thought we were friends again?'

'We are. I'm not snubbing you. I have an important reason for needing to get home.'

'I see. Should I be happy for you?'

'No,' she said vaguely. 'It's nothing like that.'

'You mean it's not another guy?'

'I mean it's nothing I'm prepared to talk about.'

'But it's important?'

'Yes.'

She hurried away, leaving Jackson staring after her, wishing he could sort his brain out one way or the other. But with Freya that was increasingly difficult.

And he was beginning to fear that it wasn't his brain that caused the problems.

For some reason Freya couldn't quite enter into the spirit of the evening when they all met downstairs for supper. She chatted with Amos, encouraging his triumphant mood at the memory of his encounter with Horus, and she reassured Janine that all was well with her husband. But as the evening drew on she knew that something was missing between them.

Tommy, Larry's irritating second-in-command, was at his liveliest and most tiresome, flirting madly with every female in the group and finally announcing his intention of kissing each of them, one by one.

The others smiled with pleasure at the thought, but Freya shied away.

'I'm leaving,' she said.

'Oh, you're not going now, are you?' Tommy said, confronting her as she rose. 'Just one little kiss.'

'Not me. Please get out of my way.'

'The others were nice about it. Why can't *you* be nice?'

'I'm not nice,' she told him coldly. 'And if you don't stand aside I'll make you regret it.'

But Tommy obviously didn't believe her. He lunged. She ducked, but not in time to avoid him. His lips brushed over hers, lightly, but enough to horrify her and to make Jackson furious.

'That's enough,' he said, seizing Tommy in a fierce grip. 'Get out before I make you sorry.'

'Ah, c'mon, it's just a joke. Freya understands—don't you, Freya? Freya? Where's she gone?'

Where Freya had stood a moment earlier there was only a space.

'She ran out through that door,' Larry said.

'I'll get you for this,' Jackson snapped at Tommy.

'OK, OK…no need to get violent.'

'There's every need. But I'll deal with you later.'

He ran out of the door, looking right and left. There was no sign of Freya, but the door to the street was half open. Frantically he dashed through it, and saw her on the far side of the road.

'Freya!' he yelled. She stopped and looked back at him. 'Come back here, *now*.'

He couldn't tell if she'd heard him above the noise of the street, but she turned away and plunged down a side street, vanishing at once. Jackson darted across the road, causing cars to stop abruptly and horns to blare. He didn't hear them. All his attention was taken up by the chase and his fear of losing her. He ran down the road she'd taken and just saw her at the other end before she vanished behind a building.

An alarming sense of *déjà vu* overtook him. Once before he'd chased someone down side streets, losing him in the distance. The result had been a catastrophe. Driven by desperation, he raced to the far end, just in time to catch a glimpse of her before she vanished again. He tore on and this time luck was with him, for she'd run into a dead end and he caught her as she turned back.

'You crazy woman!' he cried, seizing hold of her. 'Of all the daft things to do! Suppose you'd got lost in these streets? How would you have found your way back? Stupid! *Stupid!*'

'I'll come back when I'm ready,' she said. 'Just let me go!'

'Not in a million years,' he snapped, tightening his grip.

'I said, let me go.'

'And I said no. Do you want to make a fight of it here in the street?'

'If I have to.'

A noise from behind Jackson made them both freeze and turn to see a policeman. He'd plainly heard them speaking, for he addressed them in careful English.

'You don't treat a woman like that,' he said. 'I arrest you.'

Freya drew a sharp breath. 'No,' she said. 'There is no need.'

'This man attacked you.'

'No—it's a misunderstanding.'

'You do not mind that he attacked you?'

'It's not like that.'

He studied them, undecided. Jackson placed both hands on Freya's shoulders.

'We are a couple,' he said. 'We belong together.'

The policeman spoke to Freya. 'You do not wish to be rescued from this man?'

'No, he isn't dangerous,' she said. 'But I thank you for your concern.'

He nodded and backed away. They watched until he was out of sight. Then Jackson blew out his lips in relief.

'Thank you,' he said. 'That could have ended badly.'

'Oh, heavens! I'm so sorry.'

'No need for you to be sorry. Let's just get away from here.'

He hailed a horse carriage that was passing by. It stopped and he helped her aboard, calling to the driver, 'Just take us to the river.'

He got in beside her and they moved off.

'Are you all right?' he said after a while.

'Yes, it's just—oh, goodness! If only—'

'Don't try to talk just now. Let's just ride quietly.' He touched her arm. 'You're shaking,' he said.

'I know. Everything happening suddenly like that—it took me by surprise. I guess I didn't cope very well.'

'Come here.' He put both arms around her, drawing her close so that she rested her head on his shoulder.

At last there was peace, she thought, feeling the strength and comfort he had to offer.

'I'm sorry,' she said again. 'I never meant to get you into trouble.'

'Don't worry. You rescued me in time.'

'You rescued me, you mean. Do we have to go back

just yet? I can't face the way they'll all look at me. I'll bet they're laughing fit to bust.'

'Let them laugh. What do we care? We'll stay out awhile and give them time go to bed first.'

They had reached the river now, and sat quietly watching the water glide past.

'I blame myself,' he said. 'I shouldn't have let Tommy get near you. Especially when—well, when you have other interests in your life now.'

He was referring to the hint she'd dropped earlier about having an important reason to get home. She'd refused to say more but he had no doubt of her meaning. Another man had come into her life. She wasn't ready to confide in him, but perhaps he could hope to urge her a little.

When she didn't reply he sighed and continued, 'If Tommy gives you any more trouble just tell me and I'll deal with him. Promise.'

'I don't think he'll trouble me again. You really scared him.'

Yes, he thought. He'd scared Tommy because he'd meant to. He'd been driven by rage at the sight of Freya's distress. Nor had the sight of her being handled by another man improved his temper.

For a while they gazed at the river, until Jackson said, 'Let's have a stroll.'

Leaving the carriage, they walked along the bank until they came to a little café with tables in the open.

'Let's have a coffee,' he said. 'To tell the truth, you're not the only one who needs time before we go back. Tonight something really weird happened.'

She waited until they were seated comfortably before saying, 'What happened?'

'When I was chasing after you through those confusing

streets it was as though time had slipped back.' He stopped, embarrassed. 'No, you don't want to hear about that.'

'Yes, I do. Where did time slip back to?'

'Your wedding day. When Dan jumped out of the car and ran. I went after him but he vanished into side turnings until I couldn't see him any more. And then tonight—'

'I did the same,' she said with a little smile to show there were no hard feelings.

'It was eerie—like being part of a ghost story.'

She patted his hand. 'It's not like you to be afraid of ghosts.'

'I wasn't before. I think I am now. You can be like a ghost yourself.'

'You don't mean you're afraid of me?'

'Not exactly. But sometimes I think I could be. It depends on you.'

The arrival of a waiter made them fall silent. While he poured the drinks Freya mused over his words, wondering if she had the courage to pursue them further. Sadly, she realised that she didn't. Not yet, anyway.

When the waiter had departed she said lightly, 'Not all ghosts are evil. Sometimes they're friendly—like the one who's just appeared in my life.'

There it was again he thought, the glancing reference to another man. And suddenly he couldn't bear to be shut out of her confidence a moment longer.

'Is it anyone I know?' he asked.

'Oh, yes, it's someone you know, and when I tell you the name you won't believe me.'

Out of sight, he drove his nails into his palm.

'Tell me,' he said. *'Tell me who it is.'*

CHAPTER EIGHT

'ALL RIGHT, ALL RIGHT,' Freya said in a soothing voice. 'No need to get agitated.'

She didn't know it but there was every need. Agitation was growing in him with alarming speed. He hated her having another man, but most of all he hated his own reaction.

'Just tell me who it is,' he said.

'And stop giving me orders.'

'I'm not giving you orders. I'm pleading with you. Don't you recognise the difference?'

'*Is* there a difference? When a man says *please* isn't it mostly an act, to hide the fact that he's not giving you a choice?'

'Is that experience talking?'

'Yes, it is. Dan used to do it—and Amos too. I hear him talking to my mother. When he says, "Please, my dear…" there's always a slightly ironic note that means he's really saying, *stop wasting time arguing.*'

'And of course you've decided that I'm tarred with the same brush as my father?'

'Well—'

'Come on, we've discussed this before, so let's have the truth. In your eyes I'm as big a bully as he is—just a bit more cunning in how I go about it.'

'Look, I'm sorry, I—'

'Too late to be sorry. My Amos side has taken over. Tell me what I want to know or I'll do something violent.'

'Oh, yeah? Such as what?'

'Such as this,' he said, and stamped his foot hard on the ground. *'Ouch!'*

'Is that the best you can manage?'

'I'm afraid so,' he said, pulling off his shoe and rubbing his foot.

'Have you hurt yourself?'

'Yes—my ankle and further up. Ouch! *Ouch!*'

'I'm not surprised. You slammed it down so hard that the shock must have gone right up your leg. Here, let the nurse do her job.'

She took over, removing his sock and rubbing the foot while he breathed hard.

'That's better,' he said with relief. 'But could you go a bit harder on my ankle? Yes, like that. *Ahh!*'

When she'd done his ankle she moved further up his leg, massaging the calf muscle until its tension relaxed.

'Thanks,' he said at last. 'I think I'll survive now.' He pulled on his sock and shoe, saying wryly, 'Perhaps I'd better give violence a miss in future.'

'Yes, you're not very good at it, are you? I guess it just doesn't come naturally to you.'

'Oh, I don't know. In the years we've known each other I can remember a dozen times when I've wanted to thump you.'

'But you never did. Admirable self-control.'

'Self-control, nothing. I was just scared of how hard you'd thump me back.'

'You do me an injustice. I'm a nurse.'

'But a nurse would know exactly where to thump to reduce me to a shivering wreck.'

'Don't tempt me.'

'Yes, ma'am. No, ma'am. Whatever you say, ma'am,' he said, saluting vigorously. 'Why are you laughing?'

'I was thinking suppose that policeman came upon us again just now.'

'The one who thought I was attacking you?'

'Yes. Imagine how confused he'd be.'

He joined in her laughter before saying, 'I'd have to explain to him that Freya the goddess has all sorts of secret knowledge and skills that she keeps to herself, and that the rest of us had better be very careful. Including him.'

Freya regarded him fondly, relieved and happy that their old, jokey relationship was coming back.

'So, do you still want me to tell you the name of the ghost whose appearance has transformed my life?' she asked.

'I'd kind of like to know.'

'You'll never believe it.'

A sudden dread struck him. 'Oh, no! Tell me it isn't Dan. Freya, you couldn't—'

'No, of course I couldn't. It's not Dan. It's Cassie.'

He stared, astonished into silence. 'What—what did you say?'

'I said Cassie.' Freya regarded him with her head on one side, enjoying his look of stunned bafflement.

'Cassie? You mean Marcel's wife? I don't understand. How can—?'

'Before I left London Cassie called to tell me something that will make a world of difference to me. Did you know that Amos was so set on me marrying one of you that he actually gave me a large sum of money?'

'I heard a rumour, but I wasn't sure. I suppose he was hoping that one of us would marry you to get our hands on it. How did he think that would make you feel?'

'Does he worry about how people feel as long as they do what he wants?' she asked ironically. 'The odd thing is that he's not an unkind man. He does care about people's feelings—in his own way. But his way is to assume that they'll only be happy if they do what he plans for them.'

'Yes, I know. He's always been like that. So now you'll be a prosperous woman in your own right. You should go out and live the high life on the money. That would teach him.'

'Yes, I could do that now—because I'm beginning to get it back.'

'Get it back? What happened to it?'

'Marcel was having money problems at the time, and Amos thought it might make him turn to me. Instead I loaned it to Cassie, so that she could buy into Marcel's property in Paris and then confront him on equal terms. It helped clear the air between them and they ended up married. Amos was livid.'

Jackson gave a crack of laughter. 'He gave you that money so that you would marry Marcel and you actually used it to help Marcel marry Cassie? I've heard of courage, but that beats all. Dad must be pretty annoyed with you, and yet he still wants you in the family.'

'I think he puts it down to a woman's foolishness. He reckons that if I'm his daughter-in-law he can instruct me in better ways.' She chuckled. 'Or perhaps he thinks if he can make me your wife that'll be a way of punishing me. He's probably thinking, *Then she'll find out what a monster Jackson really is. That'll teach her.*'

'Then he's miscalculated,' Jackson said cheerfully. 'You already know what a monster I am.'

'I'll bet there's a lot still to find out.'

'I'll leave you guessing about that.'

'Anyway, are you saying you didn't know about me lending the money to Cassie? Amos never told anyone?'

'Tell people that you made a fool of him? Can you imagine him doing that?'

'No, you're right. But there's more. It was a good investment. The hotel's doing well and Cassie has now started repaying me with interest.'

He stared. 'So she's the ghost?' he whispered, scarcely able to speak.

'Yes, I hadn't expected to get anything back so soon, but some of the money has gone into my bank already and there's more on the way. I'm going to be a rich woman.'

He pulled himself together.

'Aha! So now you're letting me know that if I need a rich wife you're available?'

'Letting you know that I don't need a husband, and that one word out of place will make me take terrible revenge.'

He grinned. 'Nice to get that clear. Except that I already knew.'

'Well, we've always agreed that we drive each other mad.'

'And as long as it's mutual what does it matter? Have another drink.'

He spoke lightly to hide the storm inside. So she *hadn't* found another man. Just a simple misunderstanding, but it had disturbed him to an extent he didn't want to think about. The implications were too troublesome.

He drained his glass, trying to summon up the courage to say what was on his mind. At last he managed it. 'As you said, not all ghosts are evil. But some of them are. One that still haunts me, and always will, is knowing that I did you harm.'

'Jackson, stop it. We talked about this the other morning in the hotel garden. I told you that there was nothing to forgive and we agreed to put it behind us as though it had never happened.'

'But it did happen. Nothing can make it *un*happen. The effect will be with you all your life. And now I'm going to say something that will make you hate me again. I'm *glad* you didn't marry Dan. I'm not glad of the way it happened, but it's best that you didn't marry him. You wouldn't have been happy. There—now you can call me all the names you like.'

As he spoke he gave her a quizzical look.

'I think I may pass that chance up,' she said. 'I know it wasn't your fault that Dan backed off. He was just looking for an excuse and he seized it. That wasn't what I minded most—'

'I know. It was me not telling you everything about how it happened and why he proposed in the first place. But I swear to you, Freya, I was only thinking of you. You were so hurt I couldn't bear to hurt you even more. I never thought of you finding out some other way. You thought I was laughing up my sleeve at you, but I wasn't.'

'I know. I feel I know you better now, and you wouldn't do that. I shouldn't have flown at you, but suddenly everything seemed to get on top of me.'

Her voice faded and against her will she closed her eyes.

'Freya,' he said anxiously. 'You're not coping well, are you? Even all these weeks later you haven't really begun to get over it.'

'Of course I have,' she said with a bright air that didn't fool him. 'I'm managing just fine. It's like it never happened. Dan isn't worth bothering about.'

She was lying, he thought, and not just to him but, more seriously, to herself. Dan had hurt her more than she could bear, and she denied it as the only way of coping.

He thought of their meeting in the garden, when she

had seemed the strong one, offering him comfort. Now he realised that he'd believed too easily. She seemed in control but she was struggling for that strength and the fight was exhausting her.

Bitterly, he blamed himself again. Would she ever be free of that pain? Would he ever be free of his guilt?

'It's not just Dan,' he said. 'It's what I did too. You're still hurting inside but you won't admit it. You think you can hide it from the world. Well, maybe you can with others, but not from me.'

He waited for her to insist that she was all right, as she so often did, but this time her shoulders sagged.

'Tell me,' he said.

'Oh, it's just—' She sighed. 'That idiot Tommy. I wish he hadn't managed to kiss me—even that brief little kiss. Oh, yes, *you* kissed me once, soon after it happened—'

'And I got it wrong again,' he remembered. 'You thought I was taking advantage.'

'I was off my head. You were being kind. I didn't mean what I said.'

'Don't brood about Tommy, Freya. He doesn't count. I don't count. One day you'll meet a guy who knocks you for six. You'll want him, he'll want you, and you'll be so happy you'll forget Dan ever existed.'

'Oh, no! That's not what I'm planning.'

'Does life happen the way we plan?'

'It does if you've got money. I told you—I'm a prosperous woman now. I'm going to become a business tycoon, investing Amos's money where it'll make the most profit. And I won't care about anything else.'

He had a shocking vision of the cold, unfeeling creature she seemed to want to become.

'Stop it, Freya. That's not you talking'

'Really? Then who is it?'

'Someone else that you think you are—that maybe you want to be. But it won't make you happy. You'd need to be heartless, and you're not.'

'You don't know what I'm like. Even I don't know what I'm really like. But I'm going to enjoy finding out. Maybe I'll get Amos to give me some investment advice. He's always wanted me to be his daughter. I'll never be his daughter by marriage, but I can please him another way.'

'By being his daughter of the heart, you mean?' Jackson asked wryly.

'His daughter of the brain. That's the bit that counts. Neither he nor I has much of a heart.'

'Stop it!' he said fiercely. 'Don't talk like that. Don't even *think* like that. Don't you realise it'll never make you happy?'

'And what *will* make me happy? Another man? I don't think so. It's best to go my own way, keep my fate in my own hands. From now on my life is going to be governed by *my* decisions.'

'If that worked out it would make you stronger than the rest of us. Nobody's life is governed solely by their own decisions, Freya. Don't you know that by now?'

'I should do, shouldn't I? But at least I'll have some kind of control.'

'I imagine Dad thought that, when he gave you money so that you'd marry Marcel. But he was fooling himself— as you showed him.'

'Yes, I did, didn't I? My first success as a businesswoman. The world should beware.'

'Perhaps you're the one who should beware,' he said gently. 'Now, I think we should go. You need some rest.'

He drew her to her feet, supporting her, and they strolled slowly back along the river, his arm about her shoulders. He felt passionate relief that the atmosphere between them had eased and she seemed willing for them to be close again. But he saw more trouble on the horizon.

Freya was vulnerable, and all the more so because she seemed unable to understand just how vulnerable she was. But he saw it clearly, and his old protective instinct rose up again. It was about to make him do something that he knew was a risk, but he was going to do it anyway. For her sake.

Soon the hotel was in sight. He stopped and drew her into the shadows.

'Look at me,' he said.

She raised her head so that her face was illuminated by the moon. He thought he'd never seen anything lovelier.

'Freya, I'm your friend. You do believe that, don't you?'

'Yes, I believe it now.'

'Then take this as an act of friendship,' he whispered, brushing his lips against hers.

He felt her tense and drew back an inch.

'This is to make you forget about that kiss from Tommy,' he said. 'Only that. Do you understand?'

'Yes,' she murmured. 'Yes—'

He laid his lips on hers again, lightly, touching her just enough for her to feel him while keeping his inner self far back in the shadows. He didn't seek a response from her, either from her flesh or her emotions. He had no wish to intrude on her heart. He meant only to drive away the memory of the man who'd troubled her tonight.

'All right,' he said softly. 'Time to go in.'

She followed his lead into the hotel, not speaking. At the door to her room she turned a puzzled gaze on him.

'Goodnight,' he said. 'Sleep well.'

She backed into her room, still not speaking, not taking her eyes from him. When the door was closed Jackson turned away, prey to a wild confusion of thoughts and feelings.

But then, to his annoyance, he saw the last thing he wanted to see. Tommy was standing there in the corridor.

'What the hell are *you* doing here?' Jackson snapped.

'Look, I just came to apologise. I didn't mean things to happen like they did. I didn't know that you and she were—you know—a couple—'

'Shut up!' Jackson told him. 'Do you hear me? *Shut up!*'

Tommy didn't reply. One look at the murder in Jackson's eyes was enough to make him flee.

Janine came to Freya's room early next morning as she was getting dressed.

'Amos has already gone downstairs,' she said. 'He wants to look over the tourist shop again. I can tell that he's got something fixed in his mind, but he won't tell me what.'

'He really enjoyed yesterday,' Freya observed.

'Yes, I haven't seen him so cheerful for a long time. He was on the phone last night to England, I think. I didn't hear everything, but what I did hear sounded businesslike.'

'He's not still doing business, surely? Isn't he retired?'

'He still has a lot of investments, and he likes to stick his nose in. I don't know—I've just got a funny feeling.' She looked curiously at her daughter. 'Freya, are you listening?'

'Yes—yes, of course.'

'You look as if your mind was on another planet.'

'Sorry, I just got distracted.'

'Are you all right, darling?'

'I'm fine,' she said quickly. 'It's just that it's going to be a busy day and there's a lot to think of. Shall we go downstairs?'

Once downstairs she might escape her mother's all-seeing eye. To say that she was distracted was putting it mildly. She been devastated ever since she'd left Jackson the night before.

It had all seemed to go so well. They had cracked jokes with each other, just as in the past. The resentment that had once smouldered in her had faded and it had seemed that their friendship was being restored.

Then he'd kissed her and everything had changed.

The touch of his lips had sent tremors through her, making her heart beat with a force that had taken her by surprise. She'd wanted to cry out in protest. Such things no longer had a place in her life. She was resolved on that and no man was to be allowed to change it.

But the pleasure that had surged through her body couldn't be denied. It had prompted her to yearn towards him, returning the kiss, increasing her own desire and seeking to inspire it in him.

Yet he'd uttered those ominous words. *'Act of friendship.'*

She'd agreed—'Yes—yes…'—but the words had been spoken mindlessly.

When he'd released her she'd somehow kept control of herself, walking and talking like an automaton until she was in her room and the door was safely closed between them. But inside she had been shattered by what had happened to her feelings. Jackson had acted as a kind friend. He'd been careful to make that clear. But her own reaction had been everything she didn't want it to be—everything she didn't want to admit.

Had he sensed her response? The thought made her cringe with humiliation. Whatever it cost her, he must never be allowed to suspect.

It won't last, she told herself. *Just a momentary reaction. It'll pass and things will be all right.* She was still repeating this assurance to herself as she went downstairs with Janine.

The route to the breakfast room lay past the tourist shop. Through the glass door they could see Amos, talking earnestly to an assistant. He saw them, waved, and came out empty-handed.

'You didn't buy anything, then?' Janine said.

He grinned. 'Let's say I'm thinking about it. Shall we go?'

He went ahead to the breakfast room, walking with the lofty air of a man who had a victory to celebrate. Janine and Freya exchanged baffled glances before following him.

Jackson was there ahead of them, indicating for Freya to sit beside him.

'My leg's still hurting a bit,' he murmured. 'You couldn't bear to give it another rub, could you?'

'You don't need me,' she said. 'I'm sure the hotel has a good doctor.'

'Just a little rub?' he pleaded.

Once she would have agreed without question. Now the thought of touching him like that made her inner self back off. She *must* not touch him. She didn't dare.

'Sorry, Jackson, I won't have time. I've got to stay close to Amos.'

'He seems fine to me.'

'That's when I have to be most careful. I think I'll go and sit beside him.'

He clasped her hand, preventing her from leaving.

'Have I offended you?'

'Of course not. Don't be silly.'

'You're acting like you're cross with me. If it's about—'

'It's not about anything. Stop being melodramatic.' Her sense of humour came to her rescue. 'Or I shall do something violent.'

'I dare you.'

'Don't. You'll regret it. Now, let me go. I have to go to my patient.'

'But I'm your patient too.'

'You'll be a patient with singing in his ears in a minute. Let go.'

'Oh, all right.' He leaned a little closer to whisper, 'Bully.'

'Not a bully. Just a woman who can take very good care of herself and doesn't need anyone else.'

She slipped away to the next table, where Amos was sitting. But she couldn't resist glancing back at Jackson, and was both dismayed and enchanted to find him watching her with a look of confusion.

CHAPTER NINE

FOR THE REST of that day Amos's behaviour was mysterious. When the others were ready to leave he delayed them while he paid another visit to the tourist shop. Once more he emerged smiling mysteriously, refusing to tell anyone what he was up to. Plainly he was enjoying himself.

At the temple he wandered off alone, insisting that now he knew the place well enough to cope. It seemed to be true, for when Freya and Janine went looking for him she found him before the carved wall picture that they had seen on the first day.

There was Horus, the man with a falcon's head. There was his wife, Hathor. There was the King, respectfully offering them gifts. And there was Amos Falcon, regarding them all with a look of blissful self-satisfaction.

Even as they watched he burst into a laugh that was half a giggle, giving a thumbs-up sign to the wall. Something was making him almost dance with glee. Which wasn't necessarily a good sign.

His cell phone rang. He seized it.

'Yes? Yes? It's all right? You've got it? Great. Let me know when— OK…fine, fine!'

He thrust it back into his pocket, then rubbed his hands with delight and satisfaction.

'Let's go,' Freya muttered, drawing Janine away. 'I can't believe he's actually doing business deals out here.'

'It's more than that,' Janine said. 'It's not just business. He's up to something.'

'Yes, you're right. Come on, Mum. I've got other things to think about than Amos and his carry-on.'

'Lucky you!'

On their return to the hotel Amos again vanished into the tourist shop, then hurried upstairs before they could join him. When it was time for the meal he insisted on going down alone, and they next saw him seated at the table.

Janine went over, but Jackson took Freya's hand.

'What's up with him?' he murmured in her ear.

'He's your father,' she murmured back. 'Surely you know him well enough to read his mind?'

'I think Janine understands him better than anyone.' He gave a wry smile. 'That's why she sometimes gives him a hard time. She knows the best way to deal with him is to stand up to him.'

'That's the best way to deal with any man,' she said lightly.

'Ah, yes, kick him in the teeth at regular intervals, whether he deserves it or not.'

'Some men *always* deserve it,' she observed.

'Why doesn't that surprise me?'

'I can't think. I'd better go now. Amos is waving for me to go and sit with him and Mum.'

It was a cheerful meal. The trip was going well, and only a couple of days were left before they would leave.

At last Amos rose to his feet.

'Before we say goodnight I have something to say.'

They all regarded him with curiosity. Amos took a moment to be sure he had everyone's attention, then began to speak.

'Yesterday we all met Hathor, wife of the falcon god. Naturally she made a huge impact on me.' As he'd done before, he inclined his head towards Janine. 'I particularly noticed her splendid jewellery,' Amos continued. 'So appropriate for a woman of her power and magnificence. It must have been a gift from Horus. And, since he and I are undeniably connected, I felt it was only right to follow his example.'

Amos leaned down, drew a large box out from under the table, and opened it to gasps from everyone at dinner. Inside was a large necklace of gold, studded with rubies, emeralds and sapphires. One look was enough to make clear that they were genuine. The falcon god didn't waste time on imitations.

'Stand up, my dear,' Amos commanded Janine.

Dazed, she did so, and stood while he draped the necklace about her neck, then stepped back and made a flourishing gesture towards her.

'For Hathor, queen of heaven and queen of goddesses,' Amos declared. 'In tribute to her beauty and greatness. She lives by Horus' side, and it is only with her help that he can rule the world.'

Everyone applauded, and some of them cheered. Janine blushed and seemed overcome.

Amos leaned towards her and Freya could just make out that he'd murmured, 'Say something.'

She replied softly, 'In front of all these people?'

'Of course. Everyone must know how much you matter to me.'

Blushing, Janine put her arms around him and gave him a kiss. At once the others rose and crowded around her, gazing entranced at the valuable jewels.

'However did you afford those?' Larry asked, dumb-founded.

'No problem!' Amos declared loftily. 'The falcon god can do whatever he chooses.'

More applause.

Then Amos continued, 'And that's not all. There are also these.'

He produced two large earrings and a bracelet, all of them matching the fabulous necklace. There were more gasps as he draped them about his wife and stood back with a flourish.

'Thank you, my dear,' she stammered, apparently over-come. 'They are beautiful—so beautiful.'

'Take them as a tribute to the best wife in the world,' he declared loudly. 'No, not the world—the universe.' He threw out his arms. 'From Horus to Hathor, until the end of time.'

He stretched out a hand and Janine laid her own hand into it. He led her around the table so that everyone could have a good look, then swept her out of the room.

There were astonished murmurs. Most of the people around the table were very impressed. Only Jackson looked wry and thoughtful. And Freya was still a little unsure of her own feelings. She couldn't be sure of anything until she'd talked to Janine.

She slipped away. Upstairs, she went to the room shared by Amos and Janine and knocked. Amos opened the door.

'Doesn't she look wonderful?' he trumpeted, standing back to let her in.

'Marvellous,' Freya agreed as Janine paraded for her. 'Those jewels are so beautiful.'

'And worthy of Hathor,' Amos proclaimed.

Janine twisted and turned into positions that showed off the glittering stones. She was smiling, but Freya could sense something was not quite right. She offered extravagant admiration, embraced her mother, then Amos, and escaped.

It was no surprise when a knock at her door an hour later announced Janine's arrival.

'I slipped out when he'd fallen asleep,' she said. 'I hope I didn't wake you?'

'It doesn't matter. I had the feeling that you might want to talk. What an evening!'

'Yes, it was lovely. Such a wonderful, generous thing for him to do.'

'But...?' Freya queried. For there was something in Janine's voice that was more doubt than pleasure.

'But—oh, I don't know, darling. I feel guilty for not being happier about it. I'm a really ungrateful cow.'

'That's all right. Hathor is the cow goddess.'

'Yes, *she's* a cow—but I'm not Hathor. I'm Janine. And Amos isn't the falcon god. He's just my husband. If only he saw it that way.'

She spoke with a sigh that made Freya sit beside her on the bed and say, 'You didn't really enjoy it, did you? Most women would have loved being given such a magnificent gift like that in front of everyone.'

'But that's just it. *In front of everyone.* If we'd been alone, just the two of us, and he'd spoken from his heart, it would have meant so much more.'

'Perhaps he thought you'd enjoy being in the spotlight?'

'No, the spotlight was all for himself. He was making a grand gesture and he wanted everyone to know it. What you saw tonight wasn't about Hathor receiving a gift. It was about the falcon god making a splendid gesture in the eyes of the world.'

'But that doesn't mean he doesn't have feelings about

it,' Freya protested. 'It's nice that he took the trouble and spent all that money.'

'The money's nothing to him. As for trouble—the shop assistant did all the real work. That's what was going on all day.'

'Mum, why are you so determined to see this in a bad light?'

'Perhaps because I want so badly to believe he did it out of true feelings. But I know Amos too well for that.'

'Maybe there's more to him than you think. Maybe his feelings are true and this is just his way of expressing them.'

'Thank you, darling, but it's not that simple. Ever since I discovered what he did about Dan I've seen him in a different light.'

'But why? You already knew what he was like.'

'Yes, but that seemed to cast an extra cloud and I can't shake it off. It's terribly confusing. I simply never know what's going to happen next.'

'Mmm…' Freya nodded.

'Goodnight, darling. I won't keep you awake any longer.'

When Janine had gone Freya sat by the window, too restless to sleep. Her mother was right. With Amos you never knew what would happen next. Which was also true of Jackson, she reflected. Recent events had taught her *that* with a vengeance.

The next day work at the temple proceeded well, and suddenly Larry came up with a sizzling idea.

'Horus is a falcon,' he told Jackson. 'You're a Falcon. Your father is a Falcon. The viewers will see the connection between Jackson Falcon and the falcon god, so we'll have to say something. And we'll bring your father on for a quick mention. It won't take over the show, but you can interview him in front of the statue and we'll have a little innocent fun. Do you think he'll be up for it?'

'Oh, yes,' Jackson said fervently. 'I think he'll be up for it.'

As expected, Amos was enthusiastic. The scene was set up quickly, with only a slight hiccup when he tried to insist that Janine should be included.

'If Horus is there Hathor should be there too,' he declared.

Larry would have yielded, but it was Janine who killed the idea.

'You do it, darling,' she told Amos. 'I just wouldn't feel easy in front of the cameras.'

'Oh, nonsense! I'll be there to look after you. You must be part of this.'

'I said no. I don't belong in this. That's it. Finished.'

Janine walked away, leaving him thunderstruck.

'You'd think nobody had ever said no to him before,' Freya murmured from the sidelines, where she was standing with Jackson.

'They've tried, but without success,' he replied. 'Janine can mess with his head so that he doesn't know if he's coming or going. And nobody's ever done that before.'

Things calmed down enough for the project to go forward. The camera was put in place, Jackson conducted a brief, good-natured interview with his father, and everyone was pleased.

But when Freya went looking for Amos afterwards she couldn't find him. Nor was there any sight of him until it was time to leave for the hotel. As soon as he was aboard the coach he appeared to go to sleep—not with his head resting on Janine's shoulder, but turning the other way, leaning against the window.

Freya wondered how much asleep he really was.

She wished she knew what was really going on between her mother and Amos.

Back at the hotel, Amos vanished again. There was no doubt that he was avoiding everyone, but most of all he was avoiding his wife.

Freya found him at last in the garden, drinking coffee alone at a table beneath a tree.

'Can I join you?' she asked, sitting beside him without waiting for an answer.

He nodded and made an unconvincing effort at a smile.

'What's the matter?' Freya asked. 'Tell me what's troubling you, Dad?'

He sighed. 'It troubles me when you call me Dad—after what I did to you.'

'Did to you?' she asked carefully.

'Don't pretend you don't know—about Dan, how I tried to make him back off. If I'd had the sense to keep quiet and— Well, everything would be better.'

She stared, wondering if she could have heard right. Amos, famed for his bullying and self-righteousness, was actually admitting that he'd got something wrong? Impossible.

'You do know what I mean, don't you?' Amos persisted. 'Jackson told you, and you told your mother.'

'How do you know that?'

'I was just outside the door.'

'You were—?'

'I couldn't tell anyone what I'd heard, but I've wanted to tell you I'm sorry. I know how much in love with him you were, and but for me he might have proposed for the right reasons.'

'No, I don't think he would,' she said.

'Then you must really resent me for the way I've made you suffer.'

Out of the corner of her eye she saw Jackson appear and move slowly towards them, remaining in the shadows.

'But I don't resent you,' she said. 'I'm over Dan, and I've even begun to wonder if I was ever really in love with him.'

'That's kind of you, but—'

'No, I mean it. He dazzled me. Suddenly all the lights seemed to come on in my life and everything was different, more exciting. I really enjoyed that, but it's not love. It's a bit like going on an exotic holiday, but it comes to an end and you return to reality. Don't worry about me. My heart's not broken.'

'You don't know how glad it makes me to hear that. And, my dear, before we go back, I'd rather your mother didn't know that I was listening when—well, you know.'

Freya understood perfectly. Janine had spoken frankly about the doubts she sometimes had about him, and he cringed at the thought of admitting that he'd heard that.

'Don't worry,' she said. 'I won't tell her.'

'Promise?'

'Promise.'

'Word of honour?'

'Word of honour,' she repeated, struck by his intensity. 'Ah, here's Mum.'

Janine appeared, laying her hand on Amos's shoulder. 'I wondered where you'd vanished to,' she said. 'Time to go in.'

Before leaving Amos gave Freya a significant look, to remind her of the secret she'd promised to keep. She smiled and nodded. Reassured, he turned away.

When she was alone Jackson appeared from behind the tree where he had been lingering.

'I had a feeling you were there,' she said.

'I'm glad I was,' he said. 'I can hardly believe what I've just heard. He actually admitted that he could have been wrong. Who'd have thought he'd ever admit to hearing that talk you had with your mother?'

'Especially given what she said about him.'

'Why? What did she say? I knew he'd eavesdropped that night, because I saw him. But I don't know what he heard.'

'Mum told me she had some doubts about him…whether they had a future together.'

Jackson whistled.

'You mean she might be thinking of leaving him?'

'That was the hint.'

'But women don't leave Dad. He leaves them. Heaven knows he's left plenty of them over the years.'

'But not any more,' Freya observed. 'Suddenly the positions are reversed and he's the one who might be left. That's why he's seemed so different recently. It must have given him a nasty shock, but only in his pride. I doubt if his feelings were hurt.'

'I don't know. I've often wondered if he feels things more than he lets on, because he sees emotion as a weakness. Of course that's why he swore you to silence. He'd die rather than have Janine know he heard her threatening to dump him.'

'Pride again,' she mused. 'I almost feel sorry for him.'

'And that's something you must never let him suspect.'

'I know. He'd regard pity as an insult. Poor Amos. And yet—Jackson, was I wise to promise not to tell Mum? Will I be able to keep that promise?'

'Well, you know, one of the lessons Dad taught me was that wisdom sometimes lies in knowing when to break your word.'

'Yes, I can imagine him saying that.'

'There may come a day when she's entitled to know. But not just yet. For now there's something I want to say.'

He hesitated, as if unsure how to go on. She gave him a questioning look and he seemed to make up his mind. 'Thank you for being so good to him tonight. The way you told him that everything was all right, that you're not pining for Dan—that was very kind.'

'I'm fond of Amos,' she said. 'Oh, I know I get mad at him sometimes, about his habit of insisting on his own way, but it's nice that he wants me in the family—even if I can't say yes.'

'Was it true? What you told him? That you're over Dan? That maybe you never really loved him?'

'Of course it's true. I've told you before, several times.'

'Yes,' he murmured, almost to himself. 'You keep saying it.'

'I'm not weeping and wailing because a man didn't want me. I've got a life to live, and I'm living it very comfortably on my own. So if Amos ever asks you about me, you tell him that he did no harm and I'm perfectly happy.'

'Fine, I'll tell him he did no harm.'

'And that I'm happy.'

'Are you sure about that?'

'Are you doubting me? I said happy and I meant happy—especially with all that money coming my way.'

'And money equals happiness? You're beginning to sound like him.'

'Well, maybe he gets it right sometimes.'

'Don't!' he said fiercely. 'Don't talk like that. It isn't you.'

'It could be the new me. I told you, I'm exploring new

horizons and some of them are great fun. Goodnight, Jackson.'

'Goodnight,' he said as she walked away. 'Goodnight—goodbye? I wonder which…'

They were close to finishing the project. Near the end of the next day Jackson was glad to slip away for a breather.

As if drawn by magnets he wandered to the statue of Horus and stood looking up at it, recalling the first time he'd seen it. A bird elevated in such a way might have looked ridiculous, but it didn't. Rearing up to more than twice his own height, its sharp beak impressive against the sky, it suggested only power and danger.

He thought of Amos, a man with white hair and an elderly face, who carried the same aura. The grasping ferocity that had imbued his life and his career was always there, threatening in the background. In that he was undoubtedly Horus.

The light was fading. The others were almost ready to leave and soon he must join them. But first there was something he must do. Leaning back, so that he could confront the creature rearing above him, he spoke.

'I had to come here,' he said. 'You seem to call me. You're just like my father. He won't leave a fellow alone either. Even after we all grew up he could never understand that we were independent. *"Come here…" "Do that…" "Marry the woman I've chosen for you…"'*

Then marry her, whispered a voice in his head. *You know you're in love with her.*

'No way!'

Yes, you are. You've been trying not to admit it but maybe it's time to face facts. She touched your heart when she clung to you in despair.

'That was because I felt guilty.'

Was that the only reason? Maybe you just like being needed.

'Even if you're right—it's too late now, isn't it? She's still snubbing me. She does it with smiles and charm, but a snub is a snub. I'm being kept firmly on the outside. It's not just because of our quarrel. We've kind of made friends again. But more recently she's backed off since the night I kissed her. I only meant to be kind and free her from Tommy—I did, honestly. I wasn't thinking of anything more.'

Don't kid yourself.

'Well, maybe just a little. All right, more than a little. But she wouldn't look at me after everything that's happened.'

Don't give up so easily. Perhaps your moment has come.

The words were so clear he could almost swear that a real voice had spoken. Stunned, he turned around, wondering if he was going mad. Overhead Horus maintained his lofty dignity.

'Did you say something?' Jackson demanded of him. 'Let's face it, you're never short of opinions. And you're not the only one.'

This time there was only silence, but something about it made the air throb with warning. Horus was as impressive when he said and did nothing as when he exercised his power.

'All right, I'm going,' Jackson said. 'I don't know if we'll ever meet again, but I do know that you'll always be with me; haunting me, advising me, troubling me. Will I be glad of that or not? I wish I knew.'

He hurried out to the coach. Once inside he sat apart, pretending to be asleep. He wanted no contact with anyone now. The thoughts seething in his head needed to be controlled.

But they wouldn't submit to control. They whirled, end-lessly repeating.

Don't give up so easily. Perhaps your moment has come—perhaps your moment has come—your moment has come—

Shut up! he told the ghost. *I make my own decisions.*

But this is your decision.

What do you think you know about me?

What do you think you know about yourself?

To his relief the coach was slowing. They had arrived at the hotel.

Once inside, his father pounced on him.

'I've had a marvellous idea,' he said. 'That interview we did went well, didn't it? We could do some more.'

'Dad, we're leaving in a couple of days.'

'But you could persuade them to stay a little longer. We must do it now. Later will be too late. This is no time to be giving up.' He made a theatrical gesture. 'Seize the moment.'

'What—what did you say?' Jackson stammered.

'I said, seize the moment. That's the philosophy I've lived by all my life and it's made me a winner. You should know that by now.'

'But is it that simple?' Jackson asked. 'Surely you must first recognise the moment?'

'Of course. That goes without saying.'

'But can you always tell that the moment has come?'

'A strong man creates the moment.'

'Can you really do that?' he murmured. 'And risk get-ting it wrong?'

'If a man knows what he's doing, he doesn't get it wrong.'

Jackson considered this for a moment.

'That might work sometimes,' he mused. 'In business.

But life isn't all money.' Almost under his breath he added, 'Other things matter.'

'I've told you before, the rules that govern business are the same for the rest of life. It doesn't seem that way but it works out that way. A man has to stand his ground.'

'And risk getting it wrong? Risk losing the moment?'

'Then create another moment. Never admit defeat. Make things happen your way.'

Jackson didn't try to answer this. The conversation had drifted into paths he didn't want to follow. Amos's words were so close to what he had seemed to hear in the temple that it gave him an eerie feeling.

He told himself that it meant nothing. Amos often talked this way and his own mind had attributed the words to Horus. That must be the answer.

But still he couldn't quite dismiss the feeling of unease.

CHAPTER TEN

IT WAS THE last night. Tomorrow they would start the journey back to Cairo. In the restaurant everyone was celebrating. There were brief speeches of triumph and satisfaction. Somebody proposed a toast to Horus and Hathor, which made them all beam. In reply Amos raised his glass to 'My loyal subjects!' Saying it in a humorous way that made everyone laugh and cheer.

Freya looked at Jackson, sitting on the other side of the table, joining in the toasts, enjoying every moment. He was handsome, she had to admit. More handsome than any other man at the table. And others seemed to think so too, because Debra passed him by, touching his shoulder, claiming a friendly kiss before passing on.

Again Freya felt the tremor she'd known when his lips had fleetingly brushed hers. She'd banished that memory, but it refused to be dismissed, slipping back at odd moments, warning her that nothing was finally settled. Nor did she want to dismiss it. She felt herself smiling and didn't even try not to.

He glanced up, saw her watching him and answered her smile with one of his own. Did he know what she was thinking? she wondered. Was he remembering the same? Was that the meaning behind his smile?

At last it was time to say goodnight. They began to

drift out into the hall and up the stairs. But Freya, over-come by a sudden impulse, slipped out of the front door. She wanted to be alone, to walk by the river, to give her-self up to memories that she must defy yet could enjoy one last time.

There along the bank was the place where Jackson had kissed her, tenderly brushing his lips against hers as an act of kindness and friendship. How many times had she re-minded herself of that? How often had she warned herself not to hope for anything else? How often had she called herself a coward for being determined to avoid love for the rest of her life, or resist it if it couldn't be avoided?

Here was the place. Here, if nowhere else in the world, she could allow herself to remember the forbidden feel-ings and revel in them.

'*This is to get rid of Tommy,*' he'd said. '*Only that. Do you understand*?'

He'd tried to protect her from responding to him. And he'd failed.

Closing her eyes, she leaned against the rail, raising her face to the glowing moon, and allowed the tremors to run through her again.

For the last time, she promised herself. The very last time.

At last she opened her eyes.

He was there.

At first she thought he was a delusion, but then she realised that Jackson was standing there, just a few feet away, watching her.

'I guess we both had the same idea,' he said, coming towards her.

'We both—?' Her heart was beating with either hope or disbelief. Or perhaps the two of them.

'Coming out here,' Jackson said. 'I had to take a walk

along the river. I've loved this place and I'll be sorry to leave. I'm glad you feel the same. It's a pity you didn't summon me to come with you. If you say you don't want me I'll go away.'

'No, don't do that,' she said quickly. Pulling herself together, she assumed a nonchalant demeanour. 'I just thought you were tired and wanted to get to bed.'

'Meaning I'm a wimp? Thank you, ma'am. No, I wouldn't want to miss a last look here. It's a lovely place.'

Freya had command of herself now and managed to say lightly, 'It's affected us all in so many ways. Amos, my mother.... Things seem so different between them now.'

'Yes, ever since he learned that she had her doubts about him. Perhaps it explains that dramatic gift to "Hathor". She's got him worried. He won't admit it, but he's trying to bind her to him.'

'But Mum didn't marry him for his money and she isn't a woman to be impressed by grand gestures. If he's trying to win her heart again he's going the wrong way about it.'

'Yes, and he thinks he's being so clever,' Jackson mused. 'That's the trouble. It's easy to think you're being clever when you're actually making a woman despise you.'

She regarded him with her head on one side and a teasing smile on her face.

'Despise you? I shouldn't think you have much to worry about in that direction. Your fan base doubles every day, so I hear. I expect Travis is getting quite jealous.'

'Ha-ha!' he said ironically. 'Yes, I have my female fans—women who don't know me, who wouldn't give tuppence for me if they did know me. I'm talking about real relationships. I've never been brilliant at those.' He hesitated before saying, 'There was this girl—it took me too long to realise what we might be to each other, and by the time I did—well, I'd messed up.'

She too paused before speaking, wondering if she'd divined his true meaning.

'So what happened? Has she married someone else?'

'No, but I expect she will.'

'Maybe not,' she said carefully. 'She might have gone off the whole idea.'

'Blaming all men because of one useless dope? That's a bit hard, isn't it?'

'Perhaps she thinks *all* men are useless dopes,' Freya said, elaborately casual.

'She might be right. But some are less dopey than others.'

'And some are more dopey than others.' She laughed softly. 'And some are so hopelessly dopey that it's a waste of time trying to improve them.'

He considered this. 'She shouldn't judge too soon. It might be time well spent.'

'Maybe—maybe not. We might never know.'

'Oh, yes,' he said softly. 'We'll know. Perhaps we already know. But things get in the way. If we let them.'

'If we let them it's because there's no choice,' she said gently.

'Then we'll have to wait and find out.'

She nodded, meeting his eyes directly. It felt good to be here, talking in a mysterious way that might mean something or might not. That would be decided in another world.

Neither of them realised that they were being watched from a window on the second floor of the hotel. Absorbed in each other, they didn't glance up, but began to walk along the river, hand in hand, until they were out of sight.

'Oh, that's lovely,' Janine said, drawing back from the window. 'They look so right together.'

'Of course they're right together,' Amos said. 'I've always said so, but nobody would listen to me.' He gave a deep, self-satisfied sigh. 'I knew it would work.'

'Knew what would work?'

'Getting Freya out here.'

'She came out to look after you because you were unwell.'

'That's what I wanted everyone to think, but there was nothing really wrong with me. I was sure that once she was here they'd get together at last.'

'Nothing wrong with you?' Janine repeated slowly. 'All those breathless attacks—'

'They weren't difficult to stage. I did it to make you both come out here. I knew they'd have to spend a lot of time together.' He gave a rich chuckle. 'And it worked. Oh, come on, don't look at me like that. You know I occasionally bend the facts a little.'

'A *little*?' she breathed. 'This wasn't a little. It was a massive deceit.'

'But it was for a good cause. Wouldn't you like to see them married?'

'Yes—if it's what they both want. But not just because they were manipulated.'

'All I did was give them the chance to be together. Was that wrong?'

'No,' Janine said. 'But you could have confided in me. If you'd told me that your illness was only a pretence—let me be part of it—if only you'd trusted me enough to do that. But you shut me out. Do you know how I've felt since I thought you were ill again? I've lain awake at night, worrying about you. It never once crossed my mind that the whole thing was an act to get your own way.'

She seemed to pull herself up short, and a new, harder note came into her voice.

'But perhaps it should have done. As you say, I know

what you're like. I know you don't have a conscience about
how you make everyone jump to do your bidding. I even
know about how you tried to order Dan to stay away from
Freya.'

Amos raised his head to gaze at her with a mixture of
astonishment and dismay. For once in his life words did
not come easily.

'Yes,' he mumbled. 'Well—'

Janine regarded him curiously. 'Is that all you've got
to say? Did you hear what I just told you? I know about
what you did with Dan—how you tried to break him up
with Freya.'

'Let's leave that,' he said hastily.

'You don't seem surprised. Don't you wonder how I
knew?'

'I know Freya told you,' he growled.

'How?'

'I—I happened to be passing the door when she was
talking.'

'I see. You "happened" to be passing the door, and then
you "happened" to stay there and spy on us. And you
heard—?'

'Yes,' he snapped. 'I heard everything.'

Everything. The word seemed to echo in the air. 'Everything' meant he'd heard her remarks about him.

*'He likes to see himself as powerful. The trouble is,
that's the side of him I find hardest to live with.'*

He knew she'd said that. And he'd heard Freya ask why
she stayed with him, heard her reply.

*'He needs me. He's vulnerable in ways he doesn't re-
alise.'*

How he would resent her for daring to suggest that he
was vulnerable!

'I heard everything,' Amos repeated now in a harsh

voice. 'So I've known all this time that you know about me and Dan. But you never said anything to me about it.'

'What could I say?' she flung at him. 'For a while I tried not to believe it. I didn't want to think that even you would go that far. But in my heart I knew it was true, and I know it even more now that you've told me about the trick you pulled to get Freya out here.'

'I was trying to save her from pain, and I was right. Dan behaved as badly as I knew he would.'

'*You* were the cause of her pain. Dan would never have proposed in the first place if you hadn't made him angry. Don't try to play the saint, Amos. You thought of what you wanted and nothing else, and that's why Freya got hurt. And now she'll get hurt again, because you have to twist everything.'

'Why should she be hurt again? Jackson's a good man. He'll make her a fine husband.'

'Who says she'll marry him? Who says she'll marry any man? Don't you understand that now she sees your sex in a completely new light and it isn't a favourable one? And I can understand that. But you just can't see anyone else's point of view. This latest deception—'

'My dear—'

'Don't call me that. I'm not your dear. I wonder if I ever was.'

'I was only going to say that "deception" is pitching it too strong. I played a little trick, that's all.'

'One trick too many. You really are as unpleasant as people say.'

'Don't make a drama out of this. Perhaps I should have told you that I was pretending, but what would you have done? Helped me? I don't think so.'

'So anyone who dares to disagree with you is banished

out into the cold?' She gave a great sigh. 'And that includes me.'

Amos waved his hands helplessly. 'I didn't mean it like that. Look, I'm sorry. But we can put it behind us.'

'Perhaps you can. I'm not sure that I can.'

'But I've tried to show you how much you mean to me. Look at those lovely jewels I gave you.'

'Oh, Amos, you're as blind to the truth about yourself as you're blind to other people. That wasn't a gift to me. That was a parade in the spotlight for you.'

'You were in the spotlight too. Everyone said how marvellous you looked.'

'I didn't want the spotlight. It would have been nicer to be alone with you. But when we got back to our room you couldn't wait to take the jewels off me and lock them away safely.'

He gave a grumpy sigh. 'I don't know what to say to you.'

'You never did,' she told him softly. 'Let's not talk about it any more now. I need to do some thinking about the future.'

'What are you saying?' he demanded. 'We're married. That's the future.'

'Perhaps. Let me think about it first.'

'You'd do better getting some sleep. You're tired. That's what this is all about. Tomorrow none of it will matter.'

But he didn't risk looking at her as he said it. She might have seen the fear in his eyes.

'Perhaps it's time we went back,' Jackson said.

He hailed a horse-drawn carriage and helped her aboard. For a few minutes they sat enjoying the clip-clopping rhythm. He took her hand in his.

'Freya,' he said softly, 'there's something— I don't

know when I'll get the chance to— Please understand and don't hate me again.'

'Hate you for what?'

'This,' he said, taking her into his arms.

At once she knew that she'd wanted this ever since that night. One part of her mind told her she should be cautious and resist him, but everything else in her knew that she would never have forgiven him if he hadn't placed his lips on hers, tenderly but insistently.

Her response was beyond her own control, making her slip her hands up around his neck, then his head, drawing him closer so that her mouth could explore his more thoroughly. He made a soft, sighing sound and increased his fervour.

'Freya?' he whispered.

'Yes— Yes—'

Somewhere at the back of her mind a warning voice tried to say no, but she ignored it. She would be sensible another time, but for now she could only allow her feelings to take over, driving her towards him, ever closer, ever more desirous.

'I've wanted this ever since last time,' he murmured.

'But you said—friendship—'

'I know. But I was wrong. I can't help it. It's there between us and I can't make it go away. *Freya*—'

Whatever answer she might have made was silenced in the renewed pressure of his lips, moving fiercely over hers. Helplessly she abandoned all efforts at self-control and gave herself up to the pleasure that was coursing through her.

It was a kiss of discovery for both of them.

Jackson had followed her out in the hope of making this very thing happen, yet even he was caught off-guard by sensations and emotions. He'd imagined himself prepared for those feelings, but nothing could have prepared him for what was happening deep in his heart and his body.

Horus had warned him that he was falling in love, but even Horus didn't understand everything. The road that stretched ahead was one that he must negotiate by himself. Perhaps with her help.

Freya felt as though everything was whirling about her. What was happening now was exactly what she had vowed she would never allow. But she seemed to have been transported to another world, one where her determination counted for nothing.

She had enjoyed Dan's kisses, but she knew now that he'd never given her this sense of conveying a secret message from his inner self. Willing or not, she responded, moving her lips in soft caresses, sending her own message from a part of herself she'd never known before.

It was like becoming a different person with different thoughts and feelings in a different world. And she knew that she must become this new person—or refuse to become her to her own eternal regret. She must make the decision any moment now, but first she would allow herself to relish the joy that possessed her for one more moment—one more—one more...

'We've arrived,' Jackson murmured. 'Let's slip in quietly.'

They managed to cross the lobby and go up in the elevator without being seen by anyone who knew them.

At the door of her room she stood, hesitant.

'Can I come in?' Jackson whispered, moving closer.

Unable to speak, she nodded and opened the door. He followed her in, closed the door and immediately took her in his arms.

'I've wanted this,' he murmured. 'I was sure our time must come—and now it has. Don't you feel that?'

She couldn't answer, for he was kissing her again, holding her tighter than before, his eyes, his mouth, his whole body full of intent. The moment was drawing near.

Suddenly she drew a long, trembling breath.

'No. Jackson. Wait.'

'What is it?'

'I—I don't know, but I can't— I'm not ready.'

'We're both ready. This has been waiting for us.'

'No, please—'

'Freya—'

'Let me go.'

'But I—'

'Let me go, *please*.'

She felt a fierce tremor go through him and for a moment she thought he would refuse. But then he dropped his hands and stepped back. He was breathing heavily, and she had the feeling that he was fighting for control.

'I'm sorry,' she said. 'I didn't mean this to happen. But I'm not sure— I need more time.'

'All right,' he said in a rasping voice. 'Don't worry. I'm going.'

'Jackson, I'm really sorry.'

'Don't be sorry,' he said. 'There's still a lot we don't know about ourselves and each other. We'll have time to find out and then—then will be the time for you to make your decision. I'll be waiting for you, and I know you'll come to me. Goodnight.'

She was left looking at the closed door, shaking with the ferocity of her own reaction and the struggle within herself.

She had wanted what was happening. Her whole self had seemed to cry *yes*. But without warning everything had gone into reverse. *Yes* had become *no*.

And the reason, deny it as she might, was fear. Jackson

had said there was still a lot they didn't know. He was right. And one thing she didn't know was whether she could risk falling in love again after the first disaster.

Coward, she told herself scornfully. *You keep telling yourself that you weren't really in love with Dan. And you weren't. You know that now.*

But she'd believed she was at the time. The devastation had been terrible, and too little time had passed for her to recover her courage.

And courage mattered. Instinct told her that it would need every scrap of daring she could find to love Jackson. And just now she wasn't sure she wanted to take the risk.

He'd known how uncertain things were between them, but only she understood how uncertain they might always be.

'I'll be waiting for you, and I know you'll come to me.'

The memory of those words almost made her cry out in anger and frustration.

How certain he was that her decision would be the one he wanted. Before she even knew it herself.

She wouldn't allow herself to think tonight. She lay down, seeking the release of sleep, but it was denied. Her mind was in turmoil, and after tossing and turning for half an hour she sat up, realising that there were raised voices coming from Amos and Janine's room next door.

She went out. The voices were sharper, revealing that a row was going on.

She heard Amos snap, 'You're making a mountain out of a molehill.'

Then he came storming out and stomped away down the corridor without seeing Freya. Quickly she knocked on the door, which Janine opened, standing back to usher her in.

'Mum, what's happened? What are you rowing about?'

'The way he's behaved to you.'

'You mean that business with Dan? Don't worry, that's history.'

'It's not just that. You'd think he'd learn his lesson about interfering in other people's lives, but no. Not him. He's still trying to marry you off to Jackson.'

'What? Surely not?'

'That's why he got you out here.'

'But he was poorly…he needed looking after— Oh, no! Tell me what I'm thinking is wrong. He couldn't— He didn't—'

'I'm afraid he did. There was nothing wrong with him. That heavy breathing was an act. He meant you to come out here, spend a lot of time with Jackson, and—oh, well, you can guess the rest.'

Freya banged her hand against her forehead, snapping out a thoroughly unladylike word.

'I don't know why I'm surprised,' she said. 'You said he couldn't surprise me any more. He actually thought that Jackson and I—after everything that's happened—'

'Well, the two of you do seem to be getting on very well again.'

'Only as friends,' Freya said quickly. 'Nothing more. How did you learn what he'd been up to?'

'Earlier tonight we saw you wandering along the riverbank together and he was so pleased with himself that he told me what he'd done—pretending to be ill to get you out here.'

'And you were so worried…' Freya breathed. 'Didn't he understand what he was doing to you?'

'Does he ever understand anything that doesn't suit him?'

'No, never. Well, that's it. He doesn't need me, so I'm going back to England. I don't think I can endure the sight of him any more.'

'I think I'll come with you. I need to put some space between Amos and me while I try to see into the future. Don't go to England. Come to Monte Carlo and stay with me for a while.'

'All right. It'll be good to have some time alone together. Are you seriously thinking of leaving Amos?'

'I don't really know. What I do know is that things between us aren't as I hoped, and I have to mull it over. I need space and to be free of him for a while.'

'Yes,' Freya murmured. 'To be free.'

CHAPTER ELEVEN

As THEY WAITED for the coach the next morning Jackson came to stand beside Freya.

'What's up with them?' he asked, inclining his head to Amos and Janine. Although they were standing together there was an unmistakable air of frostiness.

'They've quarrelled, and this time it's serious,' Freya said. 'She found out that he never was ill. He only pretended to be short of breath.'

'But why?'

'To make me come out here and to get you and me together. He hasn't given up, and this is his latest trick.'

Jackson swore under his breath. 'I could strangle him!'

'Join the queue.'

'How did your mother find out?'

'He told her. Apparently he was so sure the trick had worked that he boasted about it.'

'I should have realised, but I can hardly believe it—even of him. Goodness knows what the atmosphere will be like between him and Janine now.'

'You don't need to worry about that. Mum's going home. She says she needs to get away from him for a while. And I'm going with her.'

'Must you?'

'I can't let her be alone now she's so unhappy.'

'I suppose not, but I wish you weren't going. Ah, well, we'll be finished in Egypt soon. Once we're all back in England things will be better. We can meet and talk.'

'I shan't be in England for a while. I'm going to Monte Carlo with her.'

'How long for?'

'I'm not sure. Certainly until Amos comes home, and maybe a while after that if I think she needs me.'

'But, Freya—'

'Oh, look, Amos is waving at you. Perhaps you should go and talk to him.'

He seemed about to protest, but then he nodded and went over to his father.

Freya joined Janine.

'You were both very quiet at breakfast.'

'I've told him I'm returning to Monte Carlo and he's furious with me. But I'm going anyway. My days of jumping to do his bidding are over.'

'It's news to me that you ever did jump to do his bidding.'

'I tried to please him as often as possible. If I had to refuse him I did it gently, lovingly. But now I have to make a stand. I'm doing what suits me, and if he doesn't like it he can take a running jump.'

'Good for you. I'll call the airport as soon as we reach Cairo.'

On the coach journey they sat together, while Jackson claimed the seat beside his father. Their words were inaudible, but Freya sensed that Jackson was trying to soothe him. She doubted that he was totally successful, but Amos's scowl faded, to be replaced by a look that might have been sadness.

When they reached the hotel in Cairo Freya went straight to the reception desk and asked for a call to be put through to the airport. What followed took only a few minutes.

'There's a plane leaving for Nice tonight,' she told Janine. 'I've booked us on it.'

She heard Amos's harsh gasp and guessed that he'd counted on having this evening to pressurise Janine into staying. But Freya knew her mother's mind was made up. Suddenly everything had changed, making her stronger. Clearly Amos had also sensed that change, but he seemed unable to cope with it. Freya actually found herself feeling sorry for him.

Jackson and Amos came with them to the airport and saw them as far as Check In. Jackson drew Freya aside.

'I wish you weren't going,' he said, his hands gentle but firm on her arms.

'You'll be better without me,' she said. 'I'm a distraction. It's your first job with this firm. You have to give it everything.'

'There's only one thing in the world that can make me want to give everything. All myself. All my heart and soul.'

'Don't.' She laid her fingertips over his mouth. 'Not yet.'

'Not yet? But perhaps some day soon?'

'I don't know,' she said desperately.

'But one thing you do know. I'm yours if you want me. Do you need to know more?'

'I need time. Sometimes things seem so clear and sometimes everything's a wild confusion. Please, Jackson.'

'All right. I guess I can be patient as long as I have some hope. But don't torture me too long. Please.'

'Jackson, I don't— I can't—'

Their boarding call came from the loudspeaker.

'I must go,' she said quickly. 'Goodbye.'

'Goodbye—until we meet again.'

Together the two women walked away through Check In and on to the Departure Lounge. At the end of the corridor they turned and saw the two men still standing there, watching them from a distance.

Freya had an eerie feeling of history repeating itself in mirror image. It was only a few weeks ago that she and Janine had stood together in an airport, watching Amos and Jackson depart. There had been desolation in her heart then, although nothing like what she felt now. It was all so different, and she no longer knew what to think about anything in the world. Including Jackson. Including her own heart.

His words should have made her spirits soar. Yet to hear his declaration of love when she was walking away from him, perhaps for ever, had sunk her in despair.

I'm mad, she thought. *Mad, crazy, stupid. And I have no idea what to do about it.*

'Are they still there?' Janine asked, straining to see.

'Yes,' Freya whispered. 'Still there.'

'Oh, yes. Look how alike they are. It almost makes you believe in Horus the Elder and Horus the Younger.'

'Don't,' Freya said with a shudder.

'You're right. Let's put them behind us.'

When they had turned the corner out of sight the two men watching them stood for a moment without moving.

At last Amos spoke. 'So that's that.'

'I wonder,' Jackson mused, 'just how often that really *is* that.'

'I know this has got you down, but don't give in to those feelings. Just because a woman goes away it doesn't mean she's abandoned you. Of course she'd like you to think so. It's a power game. You're supposed to go after her. And if you don't, she'll come back to you.'

Slowly Jackson turned his gaze on his father. 'That's what you really think, is it?'

'Just remember, don't be the one to give in. You've got to be strong. That's the rule of life and the rule of love.'

'Unless it backfires,' Jackson murmured. 'And what do you do then? Especially if *she's* playing by different rules, and you don't know what they are.'

Amos gave a snort of derisive laughter. 'Women always play by different rules, and no man ever knows what they are. All you can be sure of is that they'll trip you up if they can.'

'Then I reckon we've both been tripped up,' Jackson observed. 'It's time we were going.'

For much of the flight from Cairo to Nice Freya gazed out of the window at the clouds. By the time they got into the taxi from Nice to Monte Carlo she was ready to sleep. It was a relief to let her mind do nothing.

As the days passed she was glad she'd chosen to be with her mother. It was a long time since they had been alone together, able to talk freely and confide their troubles. It meant facing searching questions from Janine, but they forced her to confront herself and her own confusion.

'You really came with me to get away from Jackson, didn't you?' Janine asked once.

'Yes, I think I did.'

'I thought you two had made up. Have you quarrelled again?'

'No.' She sighed. 'It's not a quarrel. It's sadder than that.'

'If it's not a quarrel, what can it possibly be?'

'I don't know.'

'But it worries you. Darling, if you're falling in love with him don't fight it just to teach Amos a lesson.'

'I'm not falling in love with him.'

'Are you sure?'

'Quite sure,' she said firmly.

'It's just that when it all happened I had the strangest feeling that quarrelling with Jackson hurt you more than losing Dan.'

'Mum, will you let it go, please? I'm not falling in love with Jackson.'

If Janine thought her daughter was trying to convince herself she was too tactful to say so.

'All right, darling,' she murmured. 'Whatever you say.'

'I'm not ready to fall in love with anyone yet,' Freya asserted. 'Maybe never.'

Even to Janine she could not explain the storm of confusion that Jackson caused within her. Part of her yearned towards him, longed for his love. But part of her recoiled from the strength of her own feelings—especially for a man she did not completely trust.

He was too much like Amos—too likely to indulge in deception to achieve his ends. But his charm could make her forget the danger, and his kisses had a power that alarmed her. She missed him terribly, but she also felt safer at a distance.

On the day Amos announced that he would soon be home Freya received a call from Cassie in Paris.

'She's making another repayment to me,' she told Janine, 'and she says that since I'm getting so interested in finance I should visit them and learn some more about it. I've said yes. It'll get me out of the way when Amos arrives. I think the two of you need to be alone.'

'Good idea,' Janine agreed. 'Have a wonderful time in Paris.'

Two days later Freya was comfortably ensconced in a room at La Couronne, the luxurious Paris hotel that

Cassie and Marcel jointly owned and where they lived. She plunged into the pleasures of this new life, learning about finance and being treated as an honoured guest.

Jackson called her every day. She talked to him cheerfully, but in a way that revealed no feelings.

'I'm having a wonderful time,' she declared. 'Paris is lovely and I'm really enjoying my new life. Just you wait and see. I'm going to be the businesswoman of the year.'

'I'm sure you can be anything you want. So that's it? You've got the future all arranged?'

'Maybe. I've discovered that you don't arrange the future. It just happens and you try to turn it to your advantage.'

'Very shrewd. Right, I've got to go now. Goodbye.'

'Goodbye,' she said, hanging up. 'Goodbye…'

And it might be goodbye finally. Perhaps that was what the future held. If so, she would do her best to turn it to her advantage.

There was no lack of pleasures available to her. Marcel even had a handsome friend, Pierre, who paid her particular attention.

'I must warn you about him,' Marcel said one evening. 'He needs money, and word's got around that you could afford a few investments.'

'That's what I figured,' she replied. 'Don't worry, I'm in no danger.'

The four of them would sometimes dine together downstairs in La Couronne's restaurant, and Pierre would give a performance of devotion that might have convinced her if she'd wanted to be convinced. As it was, she merely laughed, heard his speeches with a pretence of attention and let him kiss her hand.

'Hey, look who's here.' Cassie said suddenly one evening. Turning, they saw a man standing nearby, watching them with hard eyes. His gaze was fixed on Pierre, holding Freya's hand to his lips, and a fierce glow seemed to come from him.

It was Jackson.

Marcel rose, greeting his brother cheerfully, bringing him over to the table.

'Great to see you. Why didn't you say you were coming?'

'It was a last-minute decision and I can't stay long. Freya, can we go somewhere?'

'But surely you can have something to eat first,' Cassie protested.

'Thank you, but I can't. Freya?'

'Yes,' she said.

There was no way of refusing this man's fierce intent. The moment had come. The moment that in her heart she had always known would come.

He didn't speak as she led him into the elevator and up to her room. When the door was closed she spoke in a voice that sounded tremulous even to her own ears.

'You gave me a shock, appearing out of the blue like that.'

'Are you surprised that I came here? You shouldn't be. You practically forced me.'

'I didn't force you.'

'When we speak on the phone it's like talking to a stranger. Is that what you want to be to me? A stranger?'

'No, of course not. But—'

'Whenever we've spoken I've felt that you've withdrawn a little further.'

'It's just that I'm very busy.'

'Too busy to spend time with the man who loves you? Don't look so surprised. I told you at the airport that I love you—'

'You didn't actually use the word *love*,' she mused.

'I told you I was yours, heart and soul. If that doesn't mean love, what does it mean? And you must have guessed my feelings before that.'

'I know that we both got carried away. So much has happened that we can't really see each other straight any more. Isn't it better to step back and wait a little?'

'No, it isn't better. And wait for what? For you to let me into your life? I could wait for ever for that. And I won't wait. I love you. I think I've loved you for a long time, and I'd probably have realised it sooner but for Dad. The way he kept trying to force us together just had the opposite effect. But we can't let him do that to us. I've held back, waiting for you to see that we belong with each other not because of Dad but in spite of him.'

'How do you know that we belong together?' she cried. 'Just because it's what you want?'

'No, I think it's what you want too. I feel it when I hold you in my arms. I feel it even more when I kiss you and you kiss me back. I think you love me as much as I love you.'

'You have no right to take that for granted.'

'You think I believe only what I want to believe? All right, why don't you prove me wrong?'

Before she could answer he'd taken her in his arms and was kissing her with an intensity that had a hint of desperation. The instinct to resist him flared for the briefest moment and died before the ferocity of her own feelings. Without wanting to she was kissing him back, moving her lips in ways that she knew challenged him, teased him, taunted him.

'I had to come here,' he said. 'I told myself I was going to be patient, but I can't think of anything but you. I want to marry you. I want you more than I've ever wanted anything in my life. I can't believe that it's all for nothing.

Freya, don't tell me it's all on my side. You wouldn't kiss me like that if you felt nothing for me. You're mine. You can't be anyone else's.'

But suddenly the fear was there again, making her struggle free.

"That's the sort of thing Dan said,' she cried. 'And it was all a lie. No, leave me alone.'

'But I want to marry you. I *have* to. I won't give up.'

'Do you know how much like your father you sound when you say that? He announces what he wants and everyone has to fall in line.'

'I'm not my father, and I'm not like him. I'm not doing this to please him. I think I've wanted to marry you for a long time.'

'How long? Was that in your mind on my wedding day, when you drove my groom away? Has that been the truth all the time?'

'Don't say that. Don't even think it.'

'Why shouldn't I say it? You've as good as admitted it.'

'No!'

'That's been the truth all the time, hasn't it? You wanted me so you manipulated everything to get me. I trusted you. I relied on you. I felt I could turn to you. But you've never really been the man I thought you were.'

'If that's what you truly think of me,' he said, 'then I've been wasting my time. We've both been deceived in each other.'

He drew a long, rasping breath.

'I'd better go. If I stay any longer I could start to hate you as much as I love you.'

'Yes, go—*go!*'

He stepped back to the door, opened it, and then paused to say quietly, 'I've never loved anyone in my life as much as I love you. When I understood that it was like the sun coming out in the universe. I felt that nothing could ever be the same again. And it won't be. But I didn't realise it would be like this. Goodbye, Freya. I hope that somehow you find the good life that I can't give you.'

The door closed.

Freya reached out her hands towards it, but stopped, drew back, and threw herself on the bed in a passion of sobs.

Again she had a sense of history repeating itself. After Dan's desertion she'd set herself to build a new life. Now she was rebuilding again, but she knew that Jackson had not deserted her. It was she who had deserted him.

The thought of his pain broke her heart, but she knew she'd had no choice. Something wasn't right between them, and until she understood it and dealt with it there was no way of going forward.

In her darkest moments she feared that there never would be a way.

She tried to distract herself by concentrating on business, learning something new from Marcel and Cassie every day. They both acclaimed her as a splendid pupil.

'I think life as a businesswoman might well suit you,' Marcel observed one evening. 'You've got the shrewdness and clear sight, plus a good head for figures. And you're not easily taken in.'

'You mean I saw through Pierre and the other men who thought they could seduce me and part me from my money?'

'Yes, it was wonderful watching you,' Cassie chuckled.

'They were easy to see through,' Freya said with a shrug. 'Mind you, most men are.'

'Stick with that belief,' Marcel told her. 'You'll end up as a millionaire.'

They all laughed.

He was about to refill their glasses when the phone rang.

'Who can that be at this time of night? Hello? Leonid! Good to hear from you. What's that? Congratulations! How is Perdita? Fantastic!'

'Has she had the baby?' Cassie asked eagerly.

'Yes. It's a girl. Mother and daughter are doing fine.'

'Wonderful!' Freya and Cassie exclaimed, throwing their arms around each other.

After a few more minutes Marcel hung up.

'We're all invited to the christening,' he said.

'Lovely!' Cassie cried. 'I've always wanted to see Moscow. Oh, Freya, won't that be exciting?'

'Thrilling,' she agreed.

It would be good to see Jackson. Things might never again be right between them, but she needed to see his face, watch his eyes, discover the future.

The next day she returned to Monte Carlo, to discover Janine in an edgy mood.

'I hoped things would be better between you and Amos by now,' she ventured.

'He plays the devoted husband, but I'm not fooled. You only have to look at how eager he is to go to Moscow.'

'But of course. He's going to be a grandfather,' Freya argued. 'The world's going to have another Falcon.' She struck a theatrical attitude. 'An addition to a great dynasty. He must be basking in it.'

'Oh, yes,' Janine sighed. 'And if it was just that I wouldn't mind. But I can't help thinking about Varushka, Leonid's mother.'

'I thought she was dead.'

'She is. She died six months ago, and he made a dash to Russia to be there at her bedside to say goodbye.'

'But doesn't he still have some business interests over there? He was probably visiting anyway.'

'No. We were planning a few days away, to celebrate my birthday, but he suddenly announced that he had to go to Russia urgently. He dashed off the same day and was gone nearly a week. He said it was business, but the day after he got back there was an e-mail from Leonid, thanking him for being there to say goodbye to Varushka. Of course I wasn't supposed to see it, and he doesn't know that I did. But he's never mentioned her—just told me a pack of lies.'

'But, Mum, it doesn't mean that he loved her. It was probably for Leonid's sake.'

'Yes, his sons are more important to him than anyone else,' Janine agreed wryly. 'More important than wives.'

'Did he ever make it up to you for your birthday?'

'He would claim that he did. I got a diamond necklace, but we didn't go away. Taking a trip involves time and work, but necklaces are easy.' She added ironically, 'As I have reason to know.'

'Hathor,' Freya said, remembering that night in Edfu.

'Yes, it makes you wonder if that's how Horus bought her off.' She gave a wry smile. 'I'm sure Hathor always said the right thing to keep him happy. That's what one learns to do.'

'I'm not so sure. Some of us never learn to do that.'

'You'll learn with Jackson.'

'Will I? I don't think so. I guess I'm too clumsy.'

'You just need practice. It's lucky he'll be there in Russia.'

'Yes,' Freya murmured. 'He will, won't he?'

CHAPTER TWELVE

LEONID HANDLED ALL the arrangements for their trip to Russia. First they would go to the little town of Rostov, for the christening. Then they would spend a few days in Moscow, celebrating.

The flight for Russia left from Nice Airport. Amos, Janine and Freya began the journey by staying overnight in Nice, where they were joined by Cassie and Marcel.

'Since the baby was born in Moscow, why isn't it being christened there?' Marcel wanted to know as they all shared a drink in the evening.

'Rostov was his mother's home,' Cassie said. 'He just managed to tell her about the baby before she died, and he wants to christen it in the church where she's buried.'

'Fancy Leonid being sentimental!' Marcel exclaimed.

'Hush,' Freya urged quietly. 'Don't let my mother hear you.'

'Surely she's not troubled by Varushka?' Marcel said. 'Not after all the other women our father's had?'

It was Cassie who silenced him with a finger over her lips. She drew him away with an understanding smile for Freya, who mouthed *Thank you*.

She was relieved to see that Janine was contentedly drinking coffee. She wasn't pleased about going to Rostov, but she hadn't said so to Amos. To Freya's eyes she had seemed to settle into calm resignation.

Jackson wasn't there. He was coming from London and would arrive after everyone else. She wondered how they would meet. Would he try to avoid her? Could she blame him if he did?

Next day they travelled to Rostov, where Leonid and Perdita were waiting to welcome them with open arms. That evening there was a merry party in the hotel.

Except for Jackson, everyone was now there. The Falcon brothers missed no chance to get together as a family, and this was the first occasion since Freya's aborted wedding. She recalled Jackson once saying that he felt especially close to Darius, the eldest. Of Amos's five sons they were the only two who shared a mother as well as a father.

She liked Darius, and had been enchanted by Harriet, the wife he'd met on Herringdean, the island that had become his in payment of a debt. Everyone had expected him to sell up as soon as possible and return to his life as a business magnate. But with Harriet's help he'd become enchanted by island life and now he was settled there for ever, with her and the child she had borne him.

Harriet saw her first and waved. Freya waved back and rushed to join her.

Both Harriet and Darius regarded Freya sympathetically.

'How's life treating you since the wedding?' Harriet asked gently.

'Everything's fine,' Freya said cheerfully.

'Isn't Amos making your life a misery, trying to tie you to Jackson? He's the only son left.'

'No chance. Jackson and I would never suit each other. We're both too set in our ways.'

'Set in your ways?' Marcel echoed. 'Him? You?'

'Jackson doesn't like being said no to. And I'm an awkward customer who likes saying no. Just think how miserable I'd make him.'

'You mean you think he's too like Amos?' Harriet ventured.

'I've heard people say that.'

'I know he's inherited Amos's forcefulness,' Harriet agreed. 'But there's a side of him that he doesn't show too often. He's drawn to people who need his protection.'

Freya nodded. She had reason to know that.

'And not just people,' Harriet added.

'I don't understand.'

'At one time he used to do nature documentaries. I remember him coming to Herringdean to shoot a programme about our wildlife, and there was a baby seal who'd got stranded in an awkward place. Jackson became his guardian and protector. He said the seal's mother would be looking for him, and he must be taken care of until she arrived. He settled down beside him and stayed there for two days and nights, waiting for the mother to come searching for her baby. He said he wasn't going to let her find a dead body.

'He refused to move away, even to eat. Darius and I used to take food to him, otherwise he'd have starved. And he wouldn't let anyone film them in case the baby was upset, so we had to keep the crew away as well. I remember we stayed with him one night, and he was so gentle and loving with that little creature. In the end the mother arrived and Jackson carried her baby to her.

'The boss was furious that he wouldn't let the cameras get near him. Everyone thought Jackson would seize the wonderful publicity it would give him. But all he cared about was that helpless little creature. When it was all over the boss fired him and he had to find another job. That's how he came to be working for Dan.'

'He never told me,' Freya breathed.

'He doesn't talk about that side of himself. I think he's afraid it will make him sound like a softie.'

'What's wrong with being a softie?' Freya demanded with a touch of indignation.

'Nothing. I agree. I think he's always been a bit embarrassed about having a sweet nature in case it makes Amos ashamed of him. But you could say that it's another aspect of being a bully.'

'What?'

'The instinct to take command and override any opposition. A nasty bully says, "I'm taking charge and you'll do what I say. No argument." A nice bully says, "I'm taking charge and I'm going to protect you, whatever you say, and woe betide anyone who tries to stop me. Even you."'

'Yes,' Freya murmured. 'Oh, yes….'

A scene was playing out in her memory. Suddenly she was back in the time when she'd first discovered why Dan had fled and Jackson had concealed the worst facts from her. She'd flown at him in fury and he'd tried to defend himself, pleading, 'You're saying I was wrong to try protect you from more pain? I failed, but I still think I was right to try.'

'You're so sure you know best,' she'd raged.

'That's why people do things. Because they think it's right.'

He'd taken the blame for Dan's behaviour as few men would have done. She'd attacked him, despised him, frozen him out, and he'd endured it all as the price of protecting her. When she'd relented just a little he'd offered her his love.

Was this man a bully?

Or a guardian angel?

Or both?

Another memory returned: Larry telling her about the fight Jackson had had with a production company. He'd won, but at the cost of his job, which was how he'd come to work for Dan. Nobody knew the details, but it was spoken of as proof of Jackson's toughness, his determination to impose his own will.

'But it was this,' she murmured. 'Protecting a baby seal. Who would believe it? Except me. I'd believe it, because he protected *me*.'

She'd accused him of being driven only by guilt, and he'd never denied that he was troubled about the part he'd played. But there was more. He was a man who reached out to creatures in pain because he yearned to be needed. And perhaps some of that need was rooted in the unhappy childhood about which he'd confided in her and no one else.

She had struggled to understand him and thought she'd succeeded. But she had failed. If she'd seen as deeply into his heart as she now did she would have drawn closer, perhaps close enough to be the woman he longed for and needed.

She slipped away as soon as possible. Now she needed to be alone—to think about the way the world had changed yet again.

Once in her room she paced back and forth, tormented by the knowledge that what she wanted most in life was slipping away from her—and it was her own doing. Would she ever see Jackson again?

There was a knock on her door. Reluctantly she opened it, ready to drive away whoever dared to intrude on her sadness. Then she gasped.

Stunned, she stared at Jackson, trying to believe what she was seeing. His face was tense, almost haggard. Where was the confident Jackson? Who was this man with an air of hesitancy, almost defeat?

She had a feeling that at an unfriendly word from her he would turn tail and run, and she knew an impulse to reach out and say kindly, *It's all right. I'll take care of everything.*

Instead she said simply, 'Come in.'

He hesitated, and she guessed the memory of their last meeting was still vivid in his mind. She took his hand and drew him into her room.

'Thank you,' he said. 'I won't trouble you long. There are things I must say, and then I'll go and not bother you again. But I beg you to hear me out first.'

'You don't have to beg me.'

He answered not in words but with a wry smile that reminded her of all that had happened between them.

'You don't,' she repeated. 'What can I do for you, Jackson?'

'I've come to do something for you—something I hope will make you glad.' He drew a long breath. 'Dan has been in touch with me.'

She waited for the leap of her heart that this news would once have given her. But nothing happened.

'He wants me to do a few programmes for him,' Jackson continued.

'But surely you're under contract to Larry's firm?'

'Partly, but I can still do some freelance projects. I've had a couple of meetings with Dan, but they weren't very productive about work. All he can talk about is you.'

'Tell him not to worry. I'm not coming after him with a shotgun.'

'He's not worried about that. He's more concerned about coming after you with a wedding ring.'

'That's a very bad joke.'

'It's not a joke. He keeps bringing the conversation around to you. He's realised what a big mistake he's made.'

Freya stepped back and regarded him, trying to read his face. But it was unreadable. Inside herself the reaction to Dan's name was the same as before. Nothing.

'I think that's really why he's been in touch with me,' Jackson continued. 'He wants me to talk to you on his behalf.'

'Then he's got a hell of a nerve!' she said indignantly.

'Has he? I wonder...'

'This makes no sense. If Dan wants to talk to me, why doesn't he just call me?'

'He's afraid to. He thinks you'll slam the phone down on him.'

'Which I would.'

'I don't think so. Not at first anyway. You'd hang on a few minutes for the pleasure of hearing him crawl.'

'Oh, yes, I'm known for my spite and vindictiveness.'

'No, just for your ability to stand up to a man and refuse to take any nonsense. I know all about that from my own experience. But Dan doesn't want to put a foot wrong.'

'Why not? He's put everything else wrong.'

'Yes, I told him that. He understands that he must do this the right way, and I promised to talk to you.'

'Then you're mad. I'm not in love with Dan—if I ever was. That's over—finished. I've told you this before.'

'Yes, you've told me this before—again and again. Maybe too often, as if you were trying to convince yourself.'

'Perhaps in the beginning, but not now.'

That had only been her way of coping. At last she understood the difference between the shallow feelings Dan had inspired and the passionate love that had grown in her for Jackson.

'Freya, listen to me. I've been thinking long and hard about why I never stood a chance of winning your love. And at last I know. I'd always suspected it, but I wouldn't let myself face it because I couldn't bear to. The fact is that you've never stopped loving Dan.'

'Please—'

'And he loves you. You can put the past right. Let me go back and tell him he has a chance.'

'I don't know how you can bring yourself to talk like this,' she said in a fury. '*This* is all your protestations of love for me meant? How dare you?'

At once his temper rose in response to hers.

'You stupid woman!' he snapped. 'Don't you understand that I'm doing this because I *do* love you?'

'Handing me over to another man?

'A man you love as you could never love me. A man who can give you all the happiness that I can't. I want you to have that happiness more than I've ever wanted anything in the world.'

The words were tender but his voice was harsh: the voice of a man determined to do things his way—even if he broke his own heart in the process.

Freya tried to speak, but now the tears were coming fast enough to choke her.

'Perhaps I really am stupid,' she said huskily. 'But I can't get my mind around this.'

His anger died. 'It's not your mind that needs to understand,' he said quietly.

'But my heart tells me that this is madness. Even if I believed in Dan's love, that doesn't change the kind of unreliable man he is.'

'Your love can improve him, make him want to be better.'

'And if it doesn't?'

'Then I'll always help you in any way you want. I can go back to work for Dan, and if necessary I can knock some sense into him. And if you need someone to turn to I'll always be there.'

She stared at him, stunned by the implications of what he was suggesting.

'But you can't do that,' she whispered. 'It would spoil your career, swallow up your life, leave you with nothing.'

'I have nothing now,' he said simply. 'As for my life— it's yours. You can't send me away because I won't go as long as there's even a hint that you might need me. And if I can believe that you *don't* need me, I'll just wait until it happens again.'

She couldn't believe what she was hearing. Jackson, a determined, forceful man, was putting himself at her mercy. Now the mask was tossed aside, the armour removed. What was left was the real man—vulnerable, defenceless, unprotected, and above all content for her to know it.

'Do you understand?' he asked. 'I belong to you and you can't get rid of me.' He gave a faint smile. 'You see what a bully I am.'

'Yes, the worst kind,' she murmured, moving closer to him. 'The kind who thinks he knows what's best for someone else. You won't listen when I tell you I don't love Dan. But I don't—and I'm going to force you to accept that, because I can be a bully too.'

A new look had come into his face. Confusion, mixed with hope and a little alarm, as though he feared to hope for too much.

She met his gaze, silently telling him what to believe.

'My methods are ruthless,' she said, 'and by the time I'm finished you'll have to believe me.'

'How are you going to manage that?' he whispered.

'Like this.'

Reaching up, she drew his head down far enough to rest her lips against his.

'Freya—'

'Kiss me, Jackson. That's an order. You're not the only one who likes to be obeyed. Kiss me.'

He obeyed with fervour, wrapping his arms right round her so that she couldn't have escaped if she'd wanted to. But she didn't want to. She wanted the pressure of his lips, growing fiercer with every moment. She wanted the feel of him shaking with desire against her own body, which was also shaking as never before—not for Dan, not for any other man, only for this man in her arms, where she was determined to keep him.

She had everything she wanted. He was hers as completely as she was his. His lips told her so, as did his arms, and the powerful beat of his heart that she could just hear. She wanted him with an intensity that only one thing could satisfy, and she was determined to have it.

When she drew him towards the bed he hesitated for a tiny moment, as though not daring to believe that his dreams could come true. But then doubt was swept away by desire and they fell onto the bed together, kissing, embracing, murmuring, pulling at each other's clothes until there was not a stitch left between them.

He made love to her with a mixture of tenderness and passion that left her dizzy. She responded with everything in her, and had the delight of seeing in his eyes that she had taken him by surprise.

Afterwards he held her close, her head against his chest, so that she could hear his heart again, beating more slowly now, with sweet, gentle contentment.

'I feel as though we've only just met,' he murmured.

'Yes, that's just how it is,' she said happily. 'This is a

new life for us. And there's something else as well. Thanks to Harriet, I know you better than ever before.'

'Harriet?'

'She told me about that baby seal on Herringdean, and the sacrifices you made to protect it. I'd already heard a rumour about how you quarrelled with a production firm and stormed out, but it made you sound grim and threatening.'

'Good,' he said at once. 'If my father knew the truth he'd cut me out of his life.'

'But it made me want you in my life. I began to understand how much you need me and how deeply you long to be needed in return. Not just loved, but needed.'

'Yes,' he breathed. 'Yes. I didn't realise before. Freya, is this really happening to us?'

'I don't know. I can hardly believe it. It's so beautiful. Can it be true?'

'It can be as true as we make it.'

'Yes,' she murmured. 'Oh, yes.'

'There are still questions whirling in my brain,' he murmured against her hair. 'You were so much against me. You didn't want my love. At least, you said you didn't. When I held you in my arms and kissed you I dared to hope that you wanted me a little—'

'More than a little, my darling. I've wanted you for quite a while, but I wouldn't admit it even to myself. I was afraid. After what happened with Dan I didn't want to fall in love—'

'Especially with me,' he said wryly.

'Yes. I was more afraid of getting close to you than anyone else—maybe because I knew it was inevitable. That night in Monte Carlo I resisted you because I felt caught up in something beyond my control. I know now that I was right, but I shouldn't have been afraid of it because the fate beyond my control was love.'

'Mine too. That's why I came here as Dan's spokesman. I thought it would be what you wanted.'

'You thought I'd let you spend your life watching over me?'

'*Let* me?' His voice became teasing. 'You couldn't stop me.'

'Oh, yes, I could. There's a very simple way.'

'Tell me.'

'I won't marry Dan. I'm going to marry you. That way *I'll* be *your* protector. So come on—we're getting married. That's an order.'

'Hey, I was going to say that.'

'Tough. I got in first.'

'Yes,' he said happily. 'You did. I guess I'll have to get used to you taking command.'

'You'll have to get used to me protecting you as much as you protect me.'

'Joint partnership.'

'Fifty-fifty.'

Solemnly they shook hands.

'I can hardly believe in such happiness.' She sighed blissfully. 'And it's even more lovely in this place, where so many of the family are happy too. All except—' She broke off and sighed.

'Your mother and my father,' Jackson supplied. 'Yes, it's sad, isn't it? How can we really enjoy our own happiness when things are still so wrong between them? At first I thought they'd sort it out soon and rediscover what they used to have. But it's getting worse.'

'It's because he overheard Mum say she had doubts about him and wasn't sure that they'd stay together,' Freya recalled. 'That really seemed to knock him sideways.'

'Yes, he's used to women wanting him more than he

wants them. I'm sure he could win her over if he tried, but he doesn't know how to give in, to say he's sorry.'

'He'd see it as a weakness,' Freya said. 'And he avoids that like the plague. I remember him telling you that you shouldn't let anyone know anything about you that they could see as weak and use against you.'

'Right. He's never understood that when you really love someone you're not afraid to let them know your weakness, the way you know mine.'

'Mum hated coming here to Russia. She thinks Varushka was the great love of Amos's life because of the way he rushed out here to her deathbed.'

'She's wrong. I think Janine means more to him than any other woman has, but he doesn't know how to show it. Even with her he can't risk seeming vulnerable, and it could be the worst mistake he's ever made.'

'But if they can make it right,' Freya said hesitantly, 'how will you feel? After what you told me about your mother—'

'I know. But I like Janine. She's always been pleasant to me. And she's his victim too. As for Amos, he's still my father, and I'd still like to see him find happiness in love.' He drew her closer. 'Especially now that I've found it myself.'

'Yes,' she murmured. 'Enough about them. I want to think only of you. Come to me, my darling—come to me—that's right—yes—*yes*—'

The christening was held in a little church on the edge of town. Everything went perfectly. Janine showed no sign of trouble, and Freya began to hope that all would be well.

Afterwards Leonid led the way to his mother's grave at the back, followed by the family, including Amos and Janine.

Freya tried to draw her mother away, but Janine resisted.

'I will go where my husband goes,' she said.

Varushka's marble gravestone was simple but lovely. Flowers lay around the base, put there earlier by Leonid.

'It's beautiful,' Charlene said. 'I wish I could read the Russian words.'

'They just give the date she was born and the date she died,' Leonid told her.

He said the words in English, and at once Freya sensed disaster. For the date of Varushka's death was the exact date of Janine's birthday.

She had coped with Amos's absence on that day, but now the coincidence of the dates seemed to make everything worse. Janine didn't speak, but she turned and walked away.

Freya hurried after her.

'Mum, the date's just an unlucky coincidence.'

'I spent that day in tears. It was my birthday, and we were going to have a lovely celebration holiday together. But that was the day he said goodbye to *her*—held her in his arms, kissed her, told her he loved her. The very same day.'

'He's coming over,' Freya murmured.

Amos and Jackson were approaching.

Janine turned to face Amos, who tensed.

'What's the matter?' he demanded. 'Why do you look at me like that? I was only paying my respects.'

'Drop the pretence,' Janine snapped. '*She's* the one who has your heart. I've known for months now—ever since you dumped me to rush here to her deathbed. You chose her over me.'

'No!' Amos said explosively. 'No, that wasn't what happened. I came because I had to.'

'Yes, she wanted you, so you had to. When we get home I'm leaving you.'

Amos drew a sharp breath. Freya and Jackson exchanged glances, both sensing that Amos was about to make a momentous decision.

'All right,' he said. 'Here's the truth. I didn't come here from choice. I was blackmailed.'

'Oh, Amos, please—do you expect me to believe that Leonid blackmailed you?'

'No, not him. He knew nothing about it. It was—' He stopped and a shudder went through him. 'It was Perdita.'

Janine didn't speak, but her face showed her scepticism. Amos tore at his hair.

'It's true,' he cried. 'Perdita was a journalist in those days. She found out about a slightly iffy deal I'd done. She could have caused me a lot of trouble if she'd talked. And she threatened to do exactly that if I didn't come out here to see Varushka before she died. That was why it happened so suddenly. I only had a few hours to save myself from disaster. I didn't want to come. Over the years I'd seen Varushka so rarely that I barely knew her. But I had no choice.'

He took a deep, painful breath.

'That's the truth, my dear. Please believe me.'

The word 'please' made everyone look up, alert, wondering if they'd heard properly. Amos had actually said *please* to a woman.

And Freya saw something else. There on Amos's face was the same defenceless look she'd seen on Jackson's face the previous night.

It was a look that neither man had ever worn before. She was sure of it. And it meant the same: a willingness to sacrifice everything to win the valued prize.

Horus the Elder and Horus the Younger had achieved victory at the same time. She could almost hear the cries of triumph from the Edfu temple.

Janine's gaze was fixed on Amos, who was totally still, tense with apprehension as nobody had ever seen him before. Then she gave a cry of joy and threw herself into his arms. He seized her fiercely, burying his face against her neck and saying her name in a muffled voice. By now the rest of the family had caught up, and they gave a big cheer.

'He did it!' Jackson said triumphantly to Freya. 'He told her about his weakness. He trusted her with it. That's the bit that makes all the difference.'

'Oh, yes!' she exclaimed joyfully. 'She's the one.'

Amos lifted his head. His cheeks were wet.

'I guess I still have to catch up with a few things,' he said huskily.

'Just a few,' Jackson agreed.

'And to prove to you that I've seen the light I promise to leave you two alone. I won't try to make you marry each other. That's over, for good.'

'It was over anyway,' Jackson told him. 'We got engaged this morning.'

More cheering.

The whole family rioted in delight, dancing around them, slapping them on the back.

Jackson and Freya were barely aware of them. Looking into each other's eyes, they saw only what mattered to them, what would matter for the rest of their lives.

'Let's go away,' Jackson said. 'I have a lot of things to say to you.'

'And I to you. But they don't really need saying.'

'No, but I want to say them anyway.'

They drifted off. The ground sloped gently upwards, so that after a while they could look back on where the family was still rejoicing, waving up to them. They laughed as they saw Amos give them a victory gesture.

'I guess he's got what he always wanted,' Freya said.

'Yes. Look, he's trying to placate Janine in case she makes him suffer. I guess that's how it'll always be between them from now on. Between us too, perhaps.'

'Don't worry. I won't be too hard on you,' she teased.

'Is that a promise?'

'Wait and find out.'

They shared a gentle kiss, stood for a moment contentedly resting against each other. Then they resumed their walk, leaving the others far behind—leaving the whole world behind. For they had a new world now, one in which nothing and nobody else existed.

And that was how it would always be.

EPILOGUE

THEIR WEDDING WAS a quiet affair in a church so small and so deep in the country that birdsong could be heard during the service. This was Freya's choice, and Amos had acceded to it willingly. All he'd asked was to be the man who gave her away to his son, and she'd happily agreed.

She had no fear that her groom would go missing this time. She knew that no power on earth could take Jackson from her. He'd told her so in words and actions, and she knew it on a level too deep for words.

All the Falcons were present. Nothing could have kept them away from this wedding. They smiled as Amos and Freya moved slowly down the aisle, noting how Jackson kept his eyes fixed on his bride, as though only half daring to believe that she was really there. They all enjoyed the moment when Amos handed Freya to her groom and couldn't resist giving a thumbs-up sign to celebrate his triumph.

Then he slipped away to join Janine in a pew. Together they listened as the priest began to speak the words that would unite the family as never before.

'We are gathered here to join together this man and this woman…'

This man and this woman.

Out of sight, Amos took hold of his wife's hand,

squeezed it a little, and sighed with relief when she squeezed back. Since that day in Russia when they had rediscovered each other he'd had the sense of living in a new universe, one that had yet to be explored.

The wedding service continued, with the bride and groom taking it in turn to utter their vows.

For better, for worse.

Amos murmured in Janine's ear, 'Try to forgive me for the worse.'

Smiling, she turned to meet his eyes, murmuring, 'From now on it's going to be better.'

At last it was time for the bride and groom to leave the church, ready to start their marriage. And there behind them were Amos and Janine, also making a new start that only they understood.

Perhaps Jackson and Freya came closest to perceiving the truth.

As they lay in each other's arms that night she murmured, 'There was more than one bride and groom today.'

'Yes, I thought so too,' he said with a warm chuckle. 'When you think how nearly they missed each other—'

'How nearly *we* missed each other. If you hadn't come up with that mad performance—'

'It was true. Dan really had contacted me.'

'Yes, but the rest—the things you said about watching over me, forcing him to be a good husband. Surely you couldn't really have done that?'

In the dark warmth of the bed she felt him chuckle.

'Couldn't I? I don't know. I was desperate enough to try anything that might work.'

She thumped him lightly.

'You lousy, cheating so-and-so. You just said what you knew would get you your own way.'

'That's the best reason for saying anything. I wanted

you and I didn't care what I had to do to get you. After all, I'm a Falcon.'

'So am I now, so you'd better watch out. But you couldn't *really* have lived up to that stuff about being my guardian angel even if it meant sacrificing your career. Could you?'

'I hope so, but the honest answer is that I don't know myself well enough to predict how well I'd have succeeded. I still have a lot to learn about who I am and what I can do. But I can't learn it alone. You'll have to teach me.'

'Hmm. Now, that might be interesting.'

'More than interesting…'

He drew her closer, wrapping his arms about her with an intensity that was both commanding and protective.

'Why don't we start now?' he whispered.

* * * * *

"Ready?" he asked under his breath.

When she nodded with reluctance she heard his sharp intake of breath.

"Maybe this will help."

He pulled her into his arms and found her mouth with a fierceness she wasn't prepared for, almost as if he was expecting her to fight him.

Stephanie clung to him, helpless to do anything else, and met the hunger of his kiss with an eagerness she would find embarrassing later. At last he was giving her a tender kiss, hot with desire, the one she'd been denied last night.

The way he was kissing her took her back to that unforgettable night on Grand Turk, when they'd given each other everything with a matchless joy she couldn't put into words. He pressed her against the doorjamb to get closer. One kiss after the other made her crazy with desire. Stephanie was so in love with Nikos nothing existed for her but to love him and be loved.

THE GREEK'S
TINY MIRACLE

BY
REBECCA WINTERS

Published in Great Britain 2014
by Mills & Boon, an imprint of Harlequin (UK) Limited,
Eton House, 18-24 Paradise Road, Richmond, Surrey, TW9 1SR

© 2014 Rebecca Winters

ISBN: 978 0 263 91249 4

23-0114

Rebecca Winters, whose family of four children has now swelled to include five beautiful grandchildren, lives in Salt Lake City, Utah, in the land of the Rocky Mountains. With canyons and high alpine meadows full of wildflowers, she never runs out of places to explore. They, plus her favourite vacation spots in Europe, often end up as backgrounds for her romance novels, because writing is her passion, along with her family and church.

Rebecca loves to hear from readers. If you wish to e-mail her, please visit her website: www.cleanromances.com.

To my talented daughter Dominique,
a writer for Harlequin herself, who has put up with
her *outrée* writer mom and encouraged her
through thick and thin. How lucky can I be?

CHAPTER ONE

April 27

EVERY TIME MORE hotel guests entered the beachfront resort restaurant on Grace Bay in the Turks and Caicos Islands in the Caribbean, Stephanie expected to see her black-haired Adonis appear. That was how she thought of Dev Harris.

After their fantastic ninety-foot dive to Elephant Ear Canyon that afternoon to see the huge sponges, the tall, powerfully built New Yorker, who resembled a Greek god, had whispered that he'd meet her in the dining room at eight for dinner. They'd watch the sunset *and later, each other.*

As he'd helped her out of the dive boat, giving her arm a warm squeeze, his eyes, black as jet, conveyed the words he didn't speak in front of the others in their scuba diving group. He was living for another night with her like last night.

She'd reluctantly left him to go to the beachfront condo and get ready for dinner. Her silvery-gold hair needed a shampoo. She'd decided to wear it loose from a side part. Time with the blow dryer and a brush brought out the natural curl, causing it to flow across her shoulders.

With the golden tan she'd picked up, tonight she'd chosen to wear a blue sleeveless sundress. She wanted to look beautiful for him. Last night she'd worn a filmy tangerine-colored dress and had bought a shimmering lip gloss to match. He'd told her that, in the dying rays of the sun, she'd look like a piece of golden fruit he longed to devour very slowly and thoroughly.

Her body trembled just remembering those words. While she waited for him to come, the memory of the way he'd made love to her over and over again made it difficult to breathe. It was her first intimate experience with a man, and had happened so naturally she felt as if she was living in a dream, one from which she never wanted to awaken.

In ten days' time Stephanie had fallen so deeply in love, her whole world had changed. Throughout her dating years she'd had various boyfriends. Just last week she'd gone on a date with a guy named Rob Ferris, who ran an auto parts franchise, but she knew when he took her home after dinner that she really wasn't interested in a second date.

Then she met Dev. The first time she'd seen him walking toward the boat with the dive master, her breath had caught. When their gazes collided, that was it. The feeling she'd been waiting for all her adult life.

Other relationships with past boyfriends had nothing to do with the profound kind of love she felt for the sophisticated thirty-two year-old bachelor, who'd told her he was in the international exporting business. He blew away every other man in existence.

Her three girlfriends who'd arranged their April

vacations to come on this scuba diving trip with her fully agreed he was out-of-this-world gorgeous. Melinda thought he must be one of those frogmen from the military, the way he maneuvered under the water. He was certainly built like one.

Stephanie agreed with her friends, but there was more to Dev than his physical attributes and diving skills. Much more. Everything he said and did revealed that he was well-traveled and educated, making him exceptional, and so charismatic she could hardly breathe when she thought about him.

Where was he? By now it was quarter to nine. Obviously, he'd been held up. The only thing to do was go back to her room and call him on the hotel land line. His beachfront condo, where they'd spent last night, was located on the other side of the restaurant, but she thought she should phone him first.

Stephanie was on her way out when a waiter came toward her with a florist box in his hands. "Ms. Walsh? This is for you, with Mr. Harris's compliments."

Thrilled to have received it, she went back to the table to take off the lid. He was probably on his way to her now. Inside the tissue was a corsage of gardenias with a card.

Thank you for the most memorable ten days and nights of my life, Stephanie. Your sweetness is like these gardenias and I'll never forget you. Unfortunately, I've had to leave the island because of an emergency at my work that couldn't be handled by anyone else. Enjoy the rest of your trip and be safe flying back to Crystal River. I miss you already. Dev.

Stephanie sat there and felt the blood drain from her face.

Her spring idyll was over.

He'd already driven to the airport to catch his flight to New York. *Of course* he hadn't left her a phone number or address, nor had he asked her for the same information. On purpose he hadn't given her a shred of hope that they'd ever see each other again.

She had to be the biggest fool who'd ever lived.

No, there was one other person she knew who shared that honor. Her mother, who'd died from cancer after Stephanie had graduated from college. Twenty-four years ago Ruth Walsh had made the same mistake with an irresistible man. But whoever he was hadn't stuck around once the fun was over, either. Stephanie didn't know his name and had no memories of him, only that her mother had said he was good-looking, exciting and an excellent skier.

He and Dev were two of a kind.

Stephanie closed her eyes tightly. How many females went off on vacation and supposedly met their soul mate, who swept them off their feet, only to abandon them once the excitement wore off? It had to be in the hundreds of thousands, if not the millions. Stephanie, like her mother, was one of those pathetic statistics who'd gotten caught up in the rapture.

White-hot with anger for being in her mid-twenties before learning the lesson she should have had memorized early in life, because of her birth father, Stephanie shot out of the chair. As she passed the waiter, she gave him a couple dollars and told him to get rid of the things she'd left on the table.

Stephanie didn't know about her friends, but she

couldn't possibly stay on the island for the last four days of their trip. Tomorrow morning she'd be on the first plane back to Florida. If a man was too good to be true, then shame on the woman who believed she was the first female to beat the odds.

Dev was so attractive there had to be trails of broken-hearted females around the scuba diving world who knew exactly what it was like to lie in his arms and experience paradise, only to wake up and discover he'd moved on.

He'd told her that scuba diving was his favorite form of recreation. What he hadn't mentioned was that womanizing went hand in hand with his favorite pastime. It was humiliating to think she was one of those imbeciles who didn't have the sense to take one look at him and run far away as fast as possible.

Too furious for tears, she returned to the condo, thankful her roommates were still out. They'd probably gone into town to party with some of the other tourists staying at the resort. That gave Stephanie time to change her flight reservation and pack without them asking a lot of questions.

By tomorrow afternoon she'd be back on the job. Stephanie loved her work. Right now she was planning on it saving her life.

If she let herself think about those long walks with Dev, past the palms and Casuarina trees while they were entwined in each other's arms, she'd go mad.

July 13

"Captain Vassalos?"

Nikos had just finished putting on the jacket of his

uniform—the last time he would wear it. Steadying himself with his crutches, he looked around in time to see Vice Admiral Eugenio Prokopios of the Aegean Sea Naval Command in Piraeus, Greece, enter his hospital room and shut the door. The seasoned Greek naval hero was an old friend of his father and grandfather.

"This is an honor, sir."

"Your parents are outside waiting for you. I told them I wanted to come in first to see you. After your last mission, we can be thankful the injury to your spine didn't paralyze you, after all."

Thankful?

Nikos cringed. His last covert operation with Special Forces had wiped out the target, but his best friend, Kon, had been killed. As for Nikos, his doctor told him he would never be the man he once was. His spine ought to heal in time, but he'd never be 100 percent again, and couldn't stay in the Greek military as a SEAL, not when he would probably suffer episodes of PTSD for a long time, maybe even years.

He'd been getting counseling and was taking a serotonin reuptake inhibitor to help him feel less worried and sad, but he'd had several nightmares. They left him feeling out of control and depressed.

"Now that you're being released from the hospital this morning, it won't be long before you won't need those crutches."

Nikos hated the sight of them. "I'm planning on getting rid of them as soon as possible."

"But not until you've had a good long rest after your ordeal."

"A good long rest" was code for one reality. The part

of his life that had brought challenge and purpose was finished. Only blackness remained.

"I don't expect it to take that much time, sir."

After a two and a half months' hospitalization, Nikos knew exactly why the vice admiral had shown up. This was his father's work. He'd been thwarted when Nikos had joined the military, and expected his son to return to the family business. Now that he was incapacitated, his father had sent his good friend Eugenio to wish him well with a pep talk about getting back in the family fold.

The older man eyed him solemnly. "Our navy is grateful for the heroic service you've rendered in Special Forces. You're a credit to your family and our country. Your father is anxious for you to resume your place with your brother at the head of Vassalos Shipping so he can retire."

His father would never retire.

Vice Admiral Prokopios had just let Nikos know— in the kindest way, of course—that though his military service was over, the family business was waiting to embrace him again. Of course, the older man knew nothing about Nikos's history with his father, or he would never have said what he did.

Until after Nikos was born and turned out to be a Vassalos, after all, his father hadn't believed he was his son, all because of a rumor that turned out to have no substance. The experience had turned him into a bitter, intransigent man. The damage inflicted on the Vassalos marriage carried over to the children, and had blighted Nikos's life.

The navy turned out to be his escape from an impossible situation. But ten years later it was back in triplicate.

He was thirty-two years of age, and everything was over.

Sorrow weighed him down at the loss of Kon Gregerov. Nikos's best friend from childhood, who'd come from a wonderful family on nearby Oinoussa Island, had joined the navy with him. The man had been like a brother, and had helped keep Nikos sane and grounded during those tumultuous years while he fought against his father's domination, among other things.

He and Kon had plans to go into their own business together once they'd retired from the military, but his friend had been blown up in the explosion that almost killed Nikos.

It should have been me.

"I'm sorry you were forced to leave Providenciales unexpectedly to perform your last covert operation. So when you're ready, we'll send you back there for more rest and relaxation."

Nikos's stomach muscles clenched at the mere mention of Providenciales. That experience had been like a fantastic dream, one he'd relived over and over on those nights in the hospital when he wasn't suffering flashbacks. To go back there again without *her* would kill him. After what had happened to him, there could be no Stephanie Walsh in his life. He was going in another direction entirely.

"Nikos?" the vice admiral prodded.

"Thank you for the kind offer, but I'd rather recuperate at home."

"If that's your wish."

"It is."

"Then I'll say goodbye for now. Be assured I'm mighty proud of you. Good luck."

They saluted before he left the room. Moments later one of the hospital staff entered with a wheelchair. As Nikos sat down, his parents swept into the room. They'd been constant visitors, but they hovered until he felt he would choke.

"Darling!" his mother exclaimed, and hugged him before carrying his crutches for him. "You look wonderful despite your weight loss. Once we get you home, we'll fatten you up in no time. Your grandparents are elated and your sister and Timon have already arrived with the children to welcome you back."

"This is a great day, son." His exultant father embraced him before reaching for his luggage. "Leon's eager to talk business with you."

Nikos had no intention of working in the family business like his elder brother, and his father knew it. But his dad never let up about anything, and it had driven a wedge between them that couldn't be breached. However, now wasn't the time to get into it. The three of them moved out of the room and down the corridor.

"How did it go with Eugenio?"

As if his father didn't know. "Fine."

They emerged from the main doors of the hospital under a blue sky. Once they were settled inside the limousine, his father said, "We've been waiting for this day. So has Natasa. She and her parents will be joining us tomorrow evening for a small party."

Nikos's anger flared. "Then *uninvite* them. You might as well know that after tonight, I'll be living on the *Diomedes* while I get my strength back." He was sick of visitors and hospital staff. He needed to be completely alone and didn't want anyone to know his activities. His boat would be his refuge from now on.

"You can't do that to us *or* to her!" his father thundered. "You've put this situation with Natasa on hold for long enough. A marriage between the two of you has been understood for years. She's expecting it now that you're home for good. Your mother and I want you to give us grandchildren. We've waited long enough."

Their families had been best friends for years. His sister, Gia, and Natasa Lander had always been close. It had been an impossible situation he'd been happy to get out of when he'd joined the military.

"Then that's a pity, because I never made love to her or asked her to marry me. She should have moved on years ago." She was attractive enough and would have made a good wife and mother, but he'd never been on fire for her. Thank heaven he hadn't made the mistake of sleeping with her. After meeting Stephanie, the thought of Natasa or any another woman was anathema to him. "Now that I'm out of the hospital, I need to go my own way."

"But that's absurd! She's in love with you."

"It's a moot point, since I'm not in love with her and never have been. Any hope you had for me marrying her is out of the question. I'm deadly serious about this."

His father's cheeks grew ruddy with emotion. "You don't know what you're saying!"

"But I do. Natasa is a lovely person, but not the one for me." Unless she had an agenda of her own, there was something wrong with her for waiting around for him this long. "At this point I'm afraid a marriage between the two of us is only a figment of your and her parents' imagination."

"How dare you say that!" his father muttered furiously.

"How dare *you*?" Nikos retorted back. "You'll be doing her a favor if you tell her and her family that I'm not well enough to see anyone now. Hopefully, they'll finally get the point! Don't turn this into a nightmare for me or you'll wish you hadn't!"

Nikos had suffered too many of them since the fishing vessel with all the surveillance equipment, along with Kon, had been blown out of the water by the enemy. If Nikos hadn't happened to be over the side, checking the hull for damage because of a run earlier in the day, he wouldn't still be alive.

As it was, he'd been found unconscious in the water. The doctors at the hospital hadn't given him a chance of walking again due to the damage to his lower spine, but they'd been proved wrong. He'd come out of it with deep bruising and reduced mobility. No one could say how much he would heal with time.

"We can discuss this later," his mother said, always anxious to mollify his father. For as long as Nikos could remember, she'd tried to keep peace between them. Though he loved her for it, the ugly history with his father had dictated that certain things would never change....

"There's nothing to discuss."

His military career was over. Life as he'd known it was over. Nikos was living for the moment when he could be away from everyone. Both his parents crowded him until he felt stifled, but he knew he had to endure this until tomorrow morning.

He'd already made arrangements with Yannis, who would come to the house and drive him to the marina in Nikos's car. Once on board the *Diomedes,* he intended to stay put. Drinking himself to death sounded better and better.

Silence invaded the vehicle until they reached the small airport in Athens. Nikos took a fortifying breath as he stepped out and reached for his crutches to board his father's private jet. The steward knew him well and nodded to him. "Welcome home, Nikos."

"Thank you, Jeno."

"Are you hungry?"

"No."

"Some tea?"

"How about a beer?"

The other man smiled. "Coming right up."

Nikos found a seat in the club compartment with his parents, who for once had gone quiet. He put the crutches on the floor and fastened himself in. It was a short forty-minute flight across the Aegean to Chios. From there they'd take the helicopter to Vassalos Shipping on Egnoussa, where they'd land and drive home.

He stared blindly out the window until fatigue took over, causing him to lounge back in the seat and close his eyes. The mention of marriage had triggered thoughts of a certain female in another part of the world he'd had to leave two and half months ago—so abruptly he still hadn't recovered from the pain.

Stephanie Walsh would have received the gardenias with his note. It would have sent a dagger straight to her heart. Nikos knew how it felt, because when he'd had his farewell gift delivered to the restaurant, he'd experienced gut-wrenching pain over what he'd been forced to do.

His hand formed a fist, because there hadn't been a damn thing he'd been able to do to comfort her at the time. As a navy SEAL, everything about his life was classified. Since then his whole world had been turned upside down, ensuring he would never seek her out again.

From the second he'd first met the beautiful American woman on the beach, her appeal had been so strong he couldn't find the strength to stay away from her. Knowing his leave was for only two weeks, he hadn't intended to get involved with her. Because he'd be returning shortly to join his unit, there could be no future in it.

Every day he kept telling himself he'd go to another resort on the island to keep his distance, but every day he grew more enamored of her. The night with her before he'd received orders to return to Greece should never have happened.

He loathed himself for allowing things to get that far, but she'd been like a fever in his blood. Intoxicated by her beauty, by everything about her, he'd given in to his desires, and she'd been right there with him. Her loving response had overwhelmed him, setting him on fire.

There'd been other women in his life, but never again would he know a night of passion like that. What he and Stephanie had shared for those ten precious days had been unbelievable. His longing for her was still so real he could taste it.

When he'd awakened on their last morning together, they'd been tangled up in each other's arms. She'd looked at him with those sapphire eyes, willing him to love her, and he'd wanted to stay in that bed with her forever. After their dive that afternoon, it had shredded him to walk away from her and board the jet for the flight to Athens, but he'd had his orders. He couldn't imagine a world that didn't include her.

After meeting up with Kon for their next covert operation, Nikos had confided his deepest feelings, telling him that after this last mission was completed, he planned to resign his commission and marry her. But just three days after that, the enemy had struck, and his best friend was dead. Nikos was no longer a whole man. Stephanie could be only a memory to him now.

En route to the Caribbean he'd never dreamed he would meet the woman who would leave her mark on him. His mind went over the conversation he'd just had with his father.

You don't know what you're saying!

But I do. Natasa is a lovely person, but there's something wrong with a woman who waits around for a man who's never been interested in her romantically. I'm afraid a marriage between the two of us is out of the question.

Nikos had met the ideal woman meant for him, but she would have to remain in his dreams. If Kon were still alive he'd say, "Get in touch with her and tell her the truth about your condition. You trusted her enough to spend every living moment with her. It might ease the pain for both of you if she knew who you really were, and what happened to you."

A groan escaped Nikos's throat. With his spinal injury, he wasn't the same man she'd met. Part of the collateral damage had rendered him sterile. He'd never be able to give a woman a child from his own body. Nikos lived in a dark world now. He looked and felt like hell. No woman would want a man whose flashbacks could make him dangerous to himself and others. Stephanie would only hate him for lying to her. For using her for pleasure, then dumping her without explanation.

"Nikos?"

His eyes flew open. "Jeno?"

The steward looked at him with compassion. "Are you feeling ill? Can I get you anything?"

He shook his head. He'd come to a dead end. The woman he loved and desired was permanently beyond his reach now.

"We're getting ready to descend."

"Thank you."

He fastened his seat belt. Jeno was right about one thing: Nikos did feel ill. The meeting with the vice admiral was like the first handful of dirt thrown on top of the coffin. He saw the life he'd once known vanish into the void, leaving him to travel through a tunnel of blackness that had no end....

July 26

Stephanie was going to be a mother.

She ran a hand over her stomach, which had grown fuller, making it harder to fasten the top two buttons of her jeans. It still seemed unbelievable that she was carrying Dev's child. When she'd missed her period last month it hadn't alarmed her, because she'd always been irregular. In college she'd gone six months without a period.

But over the last three weeks she'd felt weak and

nauseated. In her depressed state she'd lost her appetite
and thought she had a flu bug. But it didn't go away
and then she started noticing other changes to her body.
It all added up to one thing, and the home pregnancy
test yesterday had turned out positive, shocking the
daylights out of her.

The trip to Dr. Sanders today had confirmed that
she was three months along with Dev's baby. *Incredible.* Her OB had ordered pills for her nausea, plus iron
and prenatal vitamins to build her up.

If she caught up to Dev, would he want to know he
was going to be a father?

Deep down, she'd been waiting for him to contact her. He knew she worked for Crystal River Water
Tours. It would have been easy enough for him to call
and leave a message. But that hadn't happened. He
hadn't planned on ever seeing or talking to her again.

Yet she felt certain the man she'd fallen in love with
would have wanted to hear the truth about his own
baby. But it seemed that man didn't exist. If she were
able to find him, would he still tell her he wanted nothing to do with her or the baby, once he found out?

For the next twelve hours she agonized about what
to do, vacillating over the decision she needed to make.
By morning, one thing overshadowed every consideration. She knew her child would want to know its
father. It would be the most important thing in her
baby's life.

Stephanie knew all about that, having always longed
to meet her birth father and know his name. It took two
to make a child, and it was up to her to inform Dev if
it was at all possible. What he did with the information was up to him.

But her hand hesitated before she reached for the phone to begin her inquiries at the resort. The two people she knew there might wonder why she needed information. They'd probably deduce she was some obsessed girlfriend.

How humiliating would it be to confide the truth about the baby to them? She just couldn't. But maybe it would work if she explained she'd been worrying about him ever since he'd disappeared, the very night they were going to have dinner together. She felt certain he'd been ill, thus the reason for his swift departure. Did they know any way she might get in touch with him, just to see if he was all right?

With her hand shaking, she called the number on the brochure she'd kept, and waited.

"Dive shop. This is Angelo."

She gripped the cell phone tighter. "Hello, Angelo. I'm glad it's you. I tried to reach you earlier, but you were out. This is Stephanie Walsh. You probably don't remember me. I was there almost three months ago."

"Stephanie? I always remember the pretty girls, you especially."

Her heart beat too fast. "You just made my day."

He laughed. "You had a good time on vacation?"

"Wonderful, thanks to you." *The best of my whole life until the box of gardenias was brought to the table.*

"That's good. How can I help you?"

"I'm trying to reach Dev Harris, the scuba diver from New York I partnered with that first week. Do you have a phone number or an email for him? Anything at all to help me? He left so suddenly, I've worried over the last few months that he might have been taken ill. I have pictures I'd like to send him via email."

"Let me check. Don't hang up."

"No. I won't."

She paced the bedroom of her condo while she waited. There were a lot of Devlin, Devlon or Devlan Harrises listed in New York City, but none she could reach was the man she was trying to find.

When she'd first gotten back to Florida, anger had driven her to phone New York information, but there was no such name listed for him. She'd spent several days phoning exporting companies where he might be working, but she'd turned up nothing.

After exhausting that avenue, she'd called various airlines that had landed planes on the island April 18, but got no help. The resort could tell her only what she already knew, that he was from New York. That was when she'd given up. But her pregnancy had changed everything.

"Stephanie? I'm back. Sorry, but there is no address or phone number. Perhaps one of the shops you visited would know something."

She bit her lip in disappointment. "We didn't do any shopping, but he did have some flowers delivered to me. Would they have come from the resort?"

"No, no. The Plant Shop in town. Just a minute and I'll give you the number." She held her breath while she waited. "Yes. Here it is."

Stephanie wrote it down. "You live up to your name, Angelo. Thank you so much."

"You're welcome. Good luck finding him."

After hanging up, she placed the call. Stephanie had once told him she loved gardenias. Tears stung her eyes. She had to admit his parting gift had been done with a certain style, while at the same time destroying her dreams. If there were no results, then the baby she was carrying would never know its father.

"The Plant Shop."

"Hello. My name is Stephanie Walsh. I'm calling from Florida. On April 27 a box of gardenias from your shop was delivered to me at the Palm Resort. I never did get to thank the gentleman who sent it to me. He left before I realized he'd gone. His name was Dev Harris. Could you give me an address or a phone number, please? He's from New York City. That's all I know."

It was a long shot, but she was desperate.

"I'm sorry, but we can't give out that information."

"Can you at least tell me what time he left the order?"

"Just a moment and I'll check." After a minute, the salesclerk returned. "It was phoned in at 5:00 p.m."

"Thank you for your help."

After she hung up, one more idea flitted through her mind. She called the resort again and asked if she could speak to Delia, the darling girl who'd been the maid for their rooms. Could Delia call Stephanie back collect, please? It was very important.

The front desk said they'd give her the message. Within a half hour, Stephanie's phone rang and it was the resort calling. Delia was on the other end.

"Hello, Stephanie."

"Oh, Delia. Thanks so much for calling me back."

"Of course. How is the handsome Dev?"

I wish I knew. "Actually, I'm not sure. I'm really worried about him. That's why I've phoned you. I'm thinking he must have left the island early because he was ill and didn't want me to know or worry. I thought

I would have heard from him by now, and need your help to find him if it's at all possible."

"Tell you what. My boyfriend works at the airport servicing the planes before takeoff. I'll ask him to find out what planes took off on April 27 after five in the evening. Perhaps he'll learn something that can help you."

"I'll make this worth your while, Delia."

"I would like to do this for you. I never saw two people more in love."

Tears scalded Stephanie's eyes. "Thank you," she whispered. "I just hope he isn't fatally ill."

"I don't blame you for being upset."

Whether Delia believed her excuse for calling or not, Stephanie couldn't worry about that now.

Two hours later her phone rang again. "Stephanie? He couldn't get you names, but there were three flights out that evening, if this helps. One was a nonstop flight to Los Angeles, California, another nonstop to Vancouver, British Columbia. The last was a private jet owned by the Vassalos Corporation, headed for Athens, Greece."

She blinked.

None of the planes had headed due north to New York. Her spirits plunged. If he'd been called back to his work on an emergency, surely he would have taken a direct flight to New York. There were dozens of them leaving the Caribbean for that destination.

"You're an angel for being willing to help me, Delia. Expect a thank-you in the mail for you and your boyfriend from me."

Stephanie rang off, shaking with the knowledge that Dev had lied to her without compunction. *Who are you, mystery man?* Had he pulled a fictitious name out of a hat on the spur of the moment? Was Dev a nickname?

One thing she was convinced of at this point: he was no New Yorker. And he'd been in an enormous hurry when he'd left Providenciales. Thousands of business-men traveled by private jet. Certainly if he'd needed to leave before they'd even had dinner, it would make sense he had his own special mode of transportation waiting. No long lines…

Before she did anything else, she went to her com-puter in the den of the condo she'd inherited from her mother, to make a global search of the name Vassalos in Greece. One source came up more prominent than all the rest and drew her attention. *Vassalos Maritime Shipping, Egnoussa, Greece.*

Shipping…

After more searches she discovered the Oinousses, a group of small islands in the eastern Aegean Sea near Turkey. Egnoussa, the largest inhabited one, was fourteen kilometers long. One of Greece's most im-portant naval academies was based there, due to the rich seafaring history of the islands. A smaller island, Oinoussa, was also inhabited.

Reading further, she learned Egnoussa was home to some of the richest shipping magnate families in the world. There were only four hundred or so inhab-itants, with some fabulous mansions. A naval com-mercial academy and museum were located on one part of the island.

She replayed the memories of Dev in her mind. His urbane sophistication and knowledge set him apart from other men she'd known. He'd possessed a natu-ral authority and spoke impeccable English. But when she thought about it, she realized he hadn't sounded like a New Yorker.

Had he come from a Greek island? If so, he would naturally be at home in the water.

He'd told her he worked for an international exporting company in New York. Did that company have an outlet in Greece? Did Dev work for it? Exporting could translate to mean shipping, couldn't it? In her mind it wasn't a far stretch to see where he might have come up with his lie.

What if Egnoussa was his home? Was he from *that* Vassalos family, with the kind of wealth that had opened every door for him? Maybe this was a stab in the dark, but the more she thought about him, the more the shoe seemed to fit. The cliché about looking like a Greek god fit him like a second skin.

She could phone the shipping company and ask questions. But since he obviously didn't want to be found, if he was there or got wind that she was trying to reach him, she might never get answers. Scrolling down farther, she found more information.

After a short flight from Athens to the island of Chios, an hour's boat ride takes you to Egnoussa Island. There's one hotel with only twelve rooms, one taxi. You can walk Egnoussa in a day.

Her mind reeled with ideas. She could take some pictures of him with her and show them to someone at the shipping office. Stephanie would know immediately if that person recognized him. Maybe she was a fool, but for her baby's sake she had to try to find him, and would use some of her savings to get there.

Stephanie called the doctor to make certain it was okay to fly. He told her she'd be all right for twenty-eight weeks. After that, she'd need to check with him about it. Since Greece didn't require immunizations for visitors from the United States, she'd be all right.

Luckily, she already had a passport. When she and her friends had decided to vacation together, they'd applied for passports in case they decided on a vacation along the French or Italian Riviera. But in the end, the Caribbean had won out.

If she traveled to Greece and it turned out to be a fruitless mission, then so be it. Whatever happened, the sooner she went, the better for her state of mind. Unlike her mother, who didn't attempt to tell her lover he was a father, at least Stephanie could explain to her child that she'd done everything humanly possible to locate the man who'd called himself Dev Harris.

Life was going to be difficult enough from here on out. She would have to discuss her condition with her boss. If he could give her a front desk job until after the baby was born, she'd be thankful and grateful. But if not, she'd need to start looking for another kind of job after she got back from Greece. Besides finishing paying off the mortgage, she needed to earn enough money to provide for herself and the baby.

CHAPTER TWO

July 28

Nikos had been out on the *Diomedes* for two weeks, but this afternoon he'd docked at the marina in Egnoussa. As soon as he replenished his food supply, he'd be leaving again. To his chagrin, he still needed support to move around, but had traded in his crutches for a cane. He used it only when he was exceptionally tired.

His right-hand man, Yannis, a seaman who'd worked for the family for over forty years, had just finished tying the ropes when Nikos's silver-haired father approached them.

"Where have you been, Nikos?"

"Where I've been every day and night since I was released from the hospital, exercising and swimming off shore." Battling his PTSD.

Despite taking medication, he'd had two violent episodes flashing back to the explosion. According to his doctor, with the passage of time they'd start to slow down, but it might take months or even years. For the time being Nikos had made the small custom-built yacht his home, where no one except Yannis could be witness.

What his family didn't know was that some of his time had been spent with Kon's grieving parents. He'd also had long talks with Kon's married brother, Tassos, about many things. He was only a year older than Nikos and lived on Oinoussa, an island close to Egnoussa. Before Kon's death the three of them had been close.

Tassos had gone into oil engineering and had recently returned after working on an oil rig in the southern Aegean. He had a brilliant head on his shoulders. He and Nikos had been talking a lot about Greece's financial crisis and the direction of the country. For the time being Nikos mostly listened to Tassos, but he could scarcely concentrate while he felt half-alive.

"I've been phoning you for the last hour! Why didn't you answer?" His father had to be upset to have come down to the dock.

"I was doing some shopping with Yannis, who's bringing things on board from the car. What's wrong?" His father looked flustered.

"You have a visitor."

"If you mean Natasa, you're wasting your time."

"No. Someone else."

"I can't imagine who could be so important it would send you here." Since returning home from the hospital, Nikos had stayed in touch with his family by phone, but he'd seen no one except Kon's family and Yannis.

His father's eyes, dark like his own, studied him speculatively. "Does this woman look familiar to you?"

He reached in his pocket and pulled out two snapshots. One showed Nikos and Stephanie in the dive boat. They'd just removed their gear and were smiling at each other. His breath caught at how beautiful she was. Angelo had taken the picture.

The other photo showed them on the beach with their arms around each other, right after the sun had set. In that sundress she'd looked like a piece of golden fruit. In fact that's what he'd told her, among other things. The girl Delia, in housekeeping, had taken their picture.

"I take it she's the woman who has erased thoughts of Natasa from your mind."

Nikos could hear his father talking, but at the sight of Stephanie in those photos, he reeled so violently he almost fell off the pier into the water. She was here on the island? But that was impossible! There was no way on earth she could have found him.

"You were careless to allow yourself to be photographed in the Caribbean while you were still in active service. What is she to you, Nikos? Answer me."

He couldn't. He was still trying to grasp the fact that she'd flown to Greece and known exactly where to come.

"After looking at these pictures," his father continued, "I've decided you're in much deeper than I thought. Her beauty goes without saying, and she has a breathless innocence that could fool any man. Even *you*, my son."

Nikos closed his eyes tightly.

"You've never looked at Natasa or any woman the way you're looking at this female viper. I admit she's devilishly ravishing in that American way, but she's a mercenary viper nonetheless, one who knows your monetary worth and has come to trap you.

"Surely after what happened to Kon years ago, you realize that getting involved with a foreign woman on vacation in those surroundings can only mean one thing. Don't let her get you any more ensnared. I know you well enough that if she's pregnant, it's someone else's."

His father's words twisted the knife deeper. The mention of Kon's tragedy brought back remembered pain. Was history repeating itself with Nikos? This just wasn't possible! No one in the Caribbean knew Nikos or anything about him. *No one.*

He rubbed the back of his neck. "Do you mean she simply walked into the building?"

"Like she knew the place, according to Ari," his father explained. "After arriving in the taxi, she approached him at the front desk and asked to speak to Mr. Vassalos. When she showed Ari the pictures, he phoned me at home. I told him to have her taken into my office, where she's waiting for word of you."

Nikos still couldn't believe it. For a number of reasons this seemed completely out of character for Stephanie. He could have sworn she was the one woman in his life who gave everything without wanting anything back. While he'd been diving with her, he'd trusted her with his life, and she him. Or so he'd thought. To have been so wrong about her gutted him in an agonizing way.

"Have you made a commitment to her?"

They'd made love all night, transforming his world.

"Though it's none of your business, the answer is no," he muttered in a gravelly voice, poleaxed by this revelation. Not then, and since the explosion that had blown his dreams to hell, *most definitely not now...*

After receiving the gardenias, the Stephanie he thought he'd known would never have come searching for him. She would have understood the gesture meant goodbye, but apparently that hadn't deterred her from what she wanted.

How had she found him? Was it his money she was after? He'd taken precautions, ruling out pregnancy as a factor. But as his father had said, she could be pregnant by someone else. The very accusation he'd turned on Nikos's mother, ruining their lives. The notion that Stephanie had been after Nikos for his money made him feel ill.

"It's little wonder you've displayed such indifference to Natasa. What do you intend to do?"

Just when Nikos thought life couldn't get worse, *it had.*

He stared at his father. "Nothing." He handed him back the photos. "Give Ari instructions to tell her I'm out of the country and won't be back."

"No personal message?"

"None." He bit out the word.

A gleam of satisfaction entered his father's eyes. His parent still had this sick fantasy about Nikos and Natasa. "I'll take care of it."

Stephanie sat in the chair, actually stunned that her intuition had paid off. The second she'd shown the photographs to the man in reception, she'd seen the way his eyes had flared in surprise.

The next thing she knew, he'd made a phone call and said something in Greek she couldn't understand. Before long he'd escorted her to an office down the hall filled with pictures of ships of all kinds, almost like a museum of navigational history. The man told her they were trying to locate Kyrie Vassalos.

Until that moment she'd believed this trip had been

in vain, and that something might be wrong with her mentally to have gone this far to trace a man who didn't want to be found. But a voice inside said he still had the God-given right to know a child of his was on the way.

She'd been waiting close to an hour already. But the longer she waited, the more she expected to be told he wasn't available. If so, she would leave Egnoussa and not look back. He was a member of the Vassalos family. That was all her child needed to know.

One day years from now, it was possible Dev—or whatever he called himself—would be confronted by his son or daughter. That would all depend on whether or not her child was like Stephanie, and wanted to meet the man who'd given him or her life. Some children didn't want to know.

No matter; Stephanie planned to be the best mother in the world. She loved this baby growing inside her with all her heart and soul, and would do everything possible to give it the full, wonderful life it deserved.

After another ten minutes had passed, she couldn't sit there any longer, and decided to tell the man in reception that she would come back. The weather was beautiful, with a temperature in the mid-eighties. The island was so tiny she could walk around the port and then return. The doctor had told her mild exercise like walking would do her good and help bring her out of her depression.

As she got up to leave, the man who'd been at the desk walked into the room. "Ms. Walsh? I'm sorry I took so long. It seems Kyrie Vassalos is out of the country and won't be back in the foreseeable future. I'm sorry." He gave her back the snapshots.

So, it was just as Stephanie had thought. She would

have handed him one of her business cards from Crystal River Water Tours, where she took tourists and groups on swimming tours. But at the last second she thought better of it. For their unborn child's sake, she hoped Dev would be curious enough to find her on his own.

"Thank you for your time."

"You're welcome," he said with a smile.

After putting the pictures in her purse, she left the office and walked down the hallway to the entrance of the building. If she hurried, she'd be in time to make the next boat going back to Chios. Her trip hadn't been wasted. She'd done her duty for her child. That was all that really mattered.

She made her way through picturesque winding streets paved with slabs. En route she passed mansions and villas with tiled roofs built in the Aegean island architectural style. Dev lived in one of those mansions, but she feared she'd never see the home where he'd grown up, and they'd never share anything again.

Stephanie kept going until she arrived at the landing area, where she sat on a bench and raised her face to the sun. This island was its own paradise. Evidently the lure of scuba diving had caused Dev to leave it. Being born here, he would have been a water baby, which explained his natural prowess above and below the surface.

Was he a true playboy? Or maybe a hardworking shipping tycoon who took his pleasure on occasion where he could find it around the world, as in the Caribbean? She knew nothing about him. He might even have a wife and children.

Stephanie shuddered to think she could have been

with a married man. If that were the case, she would never forgive herself for sleeping with someone else's husband. If he had a wife, it could only hurt her to see Stephanie's business card. She was glad she hadn't left it.

Face it. You took a huge risk being with him at all.

Disturbed by her thoughts, she reached in her purse for some food to help abate her nausea. She ate a sandwich and drank some bottled water she'd brought with her. The doctor told her she needed to eat regularly, to maintain her health. For once she *was* hungry, probably because she finally knew Dev Harris was a Vassalos and could be reached here.

After finishing her sandwich, she pulled out a small bag of grapes she'd purchased in a fruit market. On impulse she offered to share them with an older woman who'd just sat down by her.

The woman smiled and took a few. "Thank you," she said in heavily accented English.

"Please take more if you like."

She nodded. "You are a tourist?"

"No. I came to visit someone, but he wasn't here."

"Ah. I wait for a friend."

"Do you live here?"

"Yes."

Stephanie's pulse raced. "Do you know the Vassalos family?"

"Who doesn't! That's one of their boats." She pointed to a beautiful white boat, probably forty-five to fifty feet long, docked in the marina. "Why do you ask?"

"It's their son I came to see."

"They have two sons. One works here. The other I never see. He's always away."

Did that mean he was always doing family business elsewhere?

Unable to sit there after that news, Stephanie got to her feet. Maybe all wasn't lost yet. "It's been very nice talking to you. Keep the grapes. I think I'll take a walk until the boat gets here."

Without wasting another second, she headed in the direction of the moored craft. Maybe one of the crew would tell her where she could reach Dev. She'd come this far....

Closer now, she realized it was a small state-of-the-art recreational yacht, the luxurious kind she occasionally spotted in Florida waters, but she saw no one around. After walking alongside, she called out, "Hello? Is anyone here?" But there was no answer.

Upon further inspection she took in the outdoor lounge with recliners and a sun bed. Beyond it was the transom, with water skis, a rope and scuba gear. The sight of the equipment brought back piercingly sweet pain.

She stepped closer and called out again. Still no answer. Since the boat that would take her back to Chios wasn't in sight yet, she decided to wait a few more minutes for someone to come.

Praying she wouldn't get caught, she sat down facing the open sea and hooked her arms around her upraised knees. Before long she spotted the boat in the distance, headed toward the harbor.

Time to go.

Her spirits reached rock bottom because she'd come to the end of her journey. With her head down, she retraced her steps along the pier. "Oh—" Stephanie cried out in surprise as a hard male body collided with hers. She felt a strong pair of hands catch her by the upper arms to prevent her from falling.

Through the wispy cotton of her white blouson top the grip felt familiar. But when she lifted her head, nothing was familiar about the narrowed pair of glittering black eyes staring into hers as if she were an alien being.

"Dev—"

It *was* him, but he was so changed and forbidding, she couldn't comprehend it. He released her as if she'd scorched him, and kept walking.

"Dev!" she called in utter bewilderment. "Why won't you even say hello? What's happened to you?"

He continued walking, not fast or slow, never turning around.

She thought she'd been in pain when she'd opened the box of gardenias to discover he'd gone, but this pain reached the marrow of her bones.

Let him go, Stephanie. Let it all go.

Turning away from him, she kept walking, and had almost reached the beach area when he called to her in his deep voice. "Stephanie? Come back."

She looked over her shoulder at him. "When you left the Caribbean so fast, I worried you were ill or even dying, but obviously you're fine. Don't worry. I'm leaving and won't venture near again."

"Come back, or I'll be forced to come after you."

She heard the authority in his voice that left her in no doubt he'd do exactly that. With her heart thudding, she started toward him. By the time she reached him, her khaki-clad legs would have buckled if he hadn't helped her onto the nearest padded bench aboard the yacht.

The last time she'd seen him he'd been in his bathing suit after their dive. His eyes had smoldered with desire as he'd kissed her passionately, before they'd parted to get ready for dinner. He'd told her to hurry, then had pressed another long, hot kiss to her mouth. Neither of them could bear to be separated.

Or so she'd thought.

This brooding version of Dev looked formidably gorgeous. He was wearing white cargo pants and a gray crew-necked T-shirt. His black wavy hair had grown longer, setting off the deep bronze of his complexion. With his height and fit physique, he bore the aura of a man in command, just as she and the girls had supposed. But he'd lost weight.

He lounged against the side of the boat, his hands curled around the edge, his long legs extended. *Legs he'd wrapped possessively around hers, whether under the water or in bed.* But there was a gauntness to his handsome, chiseled features that suggested great sorrow or illness. She'd been right about two things: he'd left the Caribbean on some kind of emergency, and was a native Greek down to every black hair on his head.

"I heard you showed up at the shipping office, but I never dreamed I'd find you outside the *Diomedes*. What are you doing here?"

Stephanie could hardly fathom the frigidity of his words. "I told you. After what we shared, you left so fast without an explanation I could live with, I feared something terrible must have happened to you. I—I needed to see for myself," she stammered.

"I thought the card I left with the flowers summed things up."

"It did, but I guess I'm a hard case."

She heard his sharp intake of breath. "I'll ask again. What are you doing here?"

"I came to Greece to find you, and was told you were away on business indefinitely. The man at the desk didn't give me any additional information, so I was trying to find someone on this yacht who might tell me where you were. But no one was about."

"Evidently that didn't stop you from waiting around." He spoke in a low wintry tone so unlike him she shivered in fresh pain. "In your desperation, I'm surprised you didn't come to Egnoussa much sooner."

Her desperation? What on earth was wrong? How could he have changed into a completely different person? He might not like seeing her again, but his demeanor bordered on loathing.

Though terrified at the thought he might be seriously ill, and stung by his hostile behavior, Stephanie still held her ground. "I would have been here the next day if I'd known where you lived. But the note you put with the gardenias didn't tell me where I could find you."

"How remiss of me." Coupled with his sarcasm was an icy smile, devastating her further. "Still, with the help you were given, you managed to track me down easily enough."

"If you're talking about God's help, you're right."

Evidently he didn't like her response, because he straightened to his full height. "Even knowing you as I thought I did, I have to admit I'm surprised you'd use that excuse to cover who you really are."

"Who *I* really am?" Despite being stymied, she lifted her chin proudly. "Then we're on even footing, because I don't know who you are either. The man I met in the Caribbean was named Dev Harris, an international exporter from New York on a scuba diving holiday. A man who made our dive master, Angelo, look like a beginner."

Below black brows, Dev's dark eyes pierced her to the core of her being. This frontal view of his face exposed shadows beneath them, and carved lines around his mouth that hadn't been there before. Despite her anger it grieved her that he could have been suffering all this time.

"And you made quite the seductress."

A gasp escaped her throat over the unexpected remark thrown out at her like that. Incredulous, she shook her head. "Seductress? I don't know what you're talking about."

"Come on, Stephanie. The game is over. Working for Crystal River Water Tours, you don't make the kind of money to send you all over the world, on two occasions in the last three months, without a definite agenda."

For a moment she was so shocked, she couldn't make a sound.

"However, I have to admit you played your hand with such finesse, you almost took me to the cleaners, as you Americans say. I barely got out of there in time."

"In time? For what?" She couldn't begin to understand him. In a slow rage over his indictment of her, she moved closer. "Curious you'd say that, because it seems I flew out of Providenciales too late."

He folded his powerful arms. "And now you're in

trouble up to the last silvery-gold strand of hair on your beautiful head."

"Yes," she answered in a quiet voice, without blinking. Trouble that came wrapped in a baby quilt, with a bottle of formula, among other things.

A white ring encircling his mouth gave evidence of the negative emotion fueling him. "So you're here to continue where you left off."

She swallowed hard. Two could play at this game he'd accused her of. If she could keep him talking, maybe she'd find out what was going on. He wasn't the same Dev. "Only if you still want me."

"That's an interesting proposition. Why don't you make me…*want* you." His voice grated the words. "If you can accomplish that feat, I'll let you name your price."

"What price are you talking about?" she cried in absolute shock.

His eyes narrowed to black slits. "One way or another, money is the reason *you're* here."

"You think?"

In spite of his cruelty to her, his dare emboldened Stephanie to take him up on it. Much as she wished she could turn off her desire for this man whose child she was carrying, it didn't work that way. With her only thought being to get to the bottom of this nightmare, she reached for him and slid her arms around his neck.

"I've missed you," she whispered, before pressing her mouth to his, needing to be convincing so he'd listen to her. "You have no idea how much." After three months deprivation, her longing for him was at full strength, despite her pain at being abandoned. She needed to feel his arms around her and be kissed the way he'd done before, as if he was dying for her.

At first she could wring no response from him, and couldn't bear it. Then, suddenly, she felt his groan before he pulled her closer, as if he couldn't help himself. Every remembered memory came flooding back…the rapture, the ecstasy of his mouth and hands doing incredible things to her.

If anything, the flame of heat licked at both of them even more strongly than before. She rejoiced that she'd found him and that he still wanted her. His response couldn't be feigned. He was definitely covering up something. But right this minute intense desire was the one truth between them, and she'd cling to it with every breath she possessed until she knew what had happened to him.

Their bodies swayed due to the intensity of their passion. He clung to her with surprising strength. Voluptuous warmth enveloped them, bringing her inestimable pleasure that was spiraling, taking her over the edge of coherent thought. "Could we go someplace private?" she begged against his lips. "I've needed to feel you like this for so long, but I'm afraid someone will see us."

After a slight hesitation, he tore his lips from hers and released her. Before he pulled away she thought she saw torment in his eyes. "Come with me." He sounded out of breath.

"Wait. I dropped my purse." She retrieved it from the deck floor.

"No luggage?" he asked, falling back into that accusatory tone she hated.

"I only planned to come here for a few hours, so I left it in my hotel room on Chios."

He studied her through veiled eyes, no doubt assessing the validity of her statement before grasping her hand. "We'll go below." Nikos pulled her to the top of the stairs and they descended. He led her down the hallway past the lounge. Beyond it was the galley and a laundry room. The master bedroom was on the end, with its en suite bathroom.

The bed was unmade. Had he slept on board last night? While she stood there, bombarded with questions she needed answers to, he shrugged out of his T-shirt. After throwing it on a chair, he sat on the end of the bed to remove his sandals. She took a quick breath when he stood up to get out of his cargo pants. Despite his weight loss, he was such a striking man her mouth went dry looking at his hard-muscled frame.

"What are you doing?"

He shot her a penetrating glance. "I thought this was what you wanted. I'll pay your price after we're finished. Let me help you." In a lightning move he reached for her purse and tossed it on the chair on top of his shirt, panicking her.

"Wait, Dev—"

But he was beyond listening to her. "Delightful as that blouse is, I'm aching to see you again without any artifice. It's been a long time since our all-nighter. Kissing you has caused me to remember how delightful you are. Do you want to remove it, or shall I?"

Suddenly apprehensive, she stepped away from him. The challenge she'd initiated, to break him down, had backfired and she started to be afraid. "Please don't be like this, Dev. We need to talk." She refused to tell him why she'd come all this way, until she understood the reason he'd changed into someone else. If he made love to her, he'd know what she was hiding.

His smile had a wicked curl. "I don't remember you being this coy with me before. Come here." He inched closer and caressed her cheek. "We were lovers. Why pretend to be shy now when you were—shall we say—so accommodating before?"

Heat flooded her face. He was the most irresistible male alive. She couldn't bear it that there was this awful anger emanating from him. "For one night I slept in your bed, but I wouldn't call us lovers, not when you took off the next day, never to be seen again."

She felt his hands circle her neck, where he rubbed his thumbs over the pulse throbbing in the hollow of her throat. "That must have been a shock, eh?" he taunted. "Didn't you like the flowers I left behind?" he whispered silkily. "You told me gardenias were your favorites."

Stephanie had promised herself she wouldn't break down in front of him, but she had to fight the sting of salt against her eyelids. "I loved them, and would have thanked you if you'd left me a forwarding address or phone number."

His hands slid to her hair, where his fingers curled around the strands of her ponytail. "Since you've found me anyway, come to bed and show me just how much you loved them. Don't worry. You'll get what you came for."

She shook her head. "Don't do this, Dev. Whatever terrible thing you think I've done, those ten days we spent together have to account for something to cherish."

"Cherish?" he mocked, wounding her all over again, before freeing her. His hands went to his hips in a stance of male beauty all its own. "That word connotes fidelity, loyalty. I wonder if an ounce of either quality exists inside that delectable body of yours." His response dripped like acid from his lips.

Dev would be shocked if he knew what existed inside her and was growing with every passing minute. She pressed her arms to her waist, unable to forget for one second that she was carrying his son or daughter.

"It's clear you believe I betrayed you in some way. How could I have done that? We were together constantly at the resort. On that first day you asked *me* to be your diving partner, not the other way around. I spent every waking moment with you instead of the girls who came with me. I never even left the resort to go shopping with them, because you wanted to be with me every second.

"When I read the note left in the flowers, you have no idea what it did to me. I realized I was only a spring fling to you. I—I thought it was more." Her voice caught. Feeling unexpectedly nauseous, she moved over to the bed and sank down to recover.

He pinned her with those jet-black eyes. "Yet even though you got the message that our interlude was over, you came here, anyway."

After what they'd shared, for him to say that it had been over since they'd left the Caribbean caused her spirits to plummet to a new low.

"Yes. It was important for me to see you again, to find out why you had to go back to your work so abruptly. What if you needed help? Possible reasons for your sudden disappearance plagued me, until I couldn't sleep. I feared it might have even been a medical emergency that prompted you to write me that note, and you didn't want me to worry about you.

"All this time I've wondered if something terrible had happened to you or your family, and you couldn't confide in anyone who knew you. I simply didn't know." She bit her lip. "A few days ago I couldn't stand it any longer and decided to search for you."

"How did you manage that? Who told you my name?" He sounded beyond livid.

"No one!" she cried. "At least not in the way you mean."

"Explain that to me."

She stood up again, kneading her hands together. "When I couldn't find a number or address for you in New York, I turned to the employees at the resort to try to get answers." By the time she'd explained everything she'd done, his expression looked thunderous.

His dark head flew back. "Are you telling me you figured out what plane flew me out of the Caribbean?"

"Not at first. Taking you at your word that you had an emergency at work, I thought about the flights. One to Los Angeles and one to Vancouver. Why would you go to either place when you were working in New York? The private jet to Greece made no sense, either, at least not at first.

"I spent all night wondering. By morning I looked the name up on the computer and discovered Vassalos Maritime Shipping located on the island of Egnassou. I didn't know if you were a Vassalos from Vassalos Maritime Shipping or an employee. But since you'd told me you worked for an international export company, I thought it was a close enough connection to find out.

That's why I brought the photographs, in case someone recognized you.

"I thought there might be a chance I could find you here. When the man at the shipping office desk recognized your picture, I knew I'd come to the end of my search. That's when I realized you'd been lying to me the whole time. Undoubtedly, you do that whenever you meet a woman to enjoy for a time before you disappear."

For a full minute he studied every square inch of her, his expression lethal. "Since you've accomplished your objective, let's go to bed for old time's sake, one more time, shall we? Then I'll send you on your way with enough money to have made your trip worthwhile."

Her body stiffened. "I don't want your money and have already gotten what I came for, Dev."

"The name is Nikos, as you damn well know!"

Nikos...

Somehow she'd thought Dev would soften while they were alone, and tell her why he'd lied to her. But the inscrutable man facing her bore little resemblance to her secret Adonis who'd brought her joy every second they'd been together. It hadn't mattered whether they'd been walking on the beach or finding glorious sights in the aqua depths of the sea.

She decided this man didn't deserve to know about the baby until it was born. He wouldn't believe her if she told him now, anyway. In fact, she was beginning to think he'd drummed up this betrayal business on purpose, to get rid of her. He'd probably pulled the same excuse on his other lovers when he was through with them. If that was true, he'd done a stellar job.

Now that she had the main phone number of Vassalos

Shipping, she could always leave a message for him next January. If he cared to answer, he'd learn then that he was a new father, not before.

His smile was beautifully cruel. "You've been playing me for a reason. Now I want to know what it is."

Stephanie drew in a fortifying breath. "I'd hoped to get an honest answer out of you, but you're not Dev Harris. Let's just say I don't want to ruin my memory of him. You, sir, are someone I don't care to know. For all I know you have a wife and children. The thought of committing adultery with you makes me sick."

She would have reached for her purse to leave, but that's when she saw a cane resting against the wall at the side of the closet. Stephanie looked up at Dev, noticing he'd lost a little color and was braced against the door to prevent her escape.

When he'd grabbed her earlier on deck, they'd both weaved a little. She'd thought it was because the impact had caught him totally off guard, but now she knew that wasn't true. He *was* unsteady. Something serious must have happened for a man as fit as he was to need a cane. Why was he being so brutal to her? She couldn't comprehend it.

"What is it you want, if not money?"

"A little honesty. I—I feel like I'm in the middle of a nightmare." Her voice faltered.

"You're part of mine, didn't you know?" he growled. "Can you still stand there and tell me you found me through Delia's boyfriend?"

"It's the truth!"

"Surely you can do better than that." His tone stung like a whiplash.

"Dev… Nikos… Tell me what I've done?" Her cry

rang in the cabin's interior. "Are you truly so devoid of feeling that you can leave me hanging like this without one word of explanation?"

"Isn't this a case of the pot calling the kettle black?"

Stephanie had taken enough of his abuse. "Let me pass." She feared she was going to be sick.

His black brows furrowed. "You're not wanted here, but since you've shown up anyway, you're not going anywhere until I get an honest explanation."

She shook her head. "Why do you continue to accuse me of something I don't understand?"

Anger marred his arresting features. "Who told you about me? How did you know I'd be staying at that particular resort? Where did you get your information?"

"I don't know what you're talking about."

"You were obviously lying in wait for me at the resort."

"You mean like some femme fatale, so I could get you to sleep with me?"

"Were you hoping to get pregnant by a rich man? Is that it? Your latest boyfriend didn't quite live up to your dreams?"

By this time she was fuming. "Let's presume for a minute you guessed it and that was my sin. What about *your* sin? You slept with me, too."

He hunched of his broad shoulders slightly. "So I did."

"Only it seems just one night was all you wanted before you moved on. Now that I've come here, you're disgusted to see me and obviously regret our interlude." With her hair caught back in a short ponytail, and her probable lack of color, she realized she must look dreadful to him.

"But not you." His eyes had become mere slits. "Who told you about me and my family? How did you know about me?"

She couldn't believe her ears. "No one!" *Only an innocent child who doesn't have a voice yet.* "I was foolish enough to come looking for you here b-because I couldn't believe it was over between us," she stammered. That was the truth, just not all of it.

His expression remained implacable.

Stephanie averted her eyes. "It was wrong of me to sleep with you. I was raised to be wiser than that, a lesson I learned too late. But no, Dev. No matter how much you despise me for coming here uninvited, I could never regret anything so beautiful. Now I'm leaving, but I need to use your bathroom first." She was going to be sick.

CHAPTER THREE

STEPHANIE SWEPT PAST him, causing Nikos to bite down hard so hard he almost cracked a tooth. That week in the Caribbean with her had been beautiful. The most beautiful experience of his life. To think it had been a deliberate setup!

Enflamed to realize she'd used him, Nikos snatched her purse from the chair and dumped the contents on the bed, hoping to learn something. Anything!

Among the contents were three vials of pills, a wallet, a phone, a key card for the Persephone Hotel along the waterfront in Chios, an airline ticket and her passport. He examined it but saw no red flag. Her wallet gave no clues except some pictures. Two of them were of her and Nikos. Another was of her friends and still another of a woman who looked to be her mother. He also found her business card from Crystal River Water Tours.

With a grimace he reached for one of the bottles, which contained vitamins. Nikos opened it and could smell them before emptying the pills on the bed. He examined the second vial, of iron pills. The third held a prescription drug issued from the same pharmacy in Florida. Dr. Verl Sanders. Three a day as necessary for nausea and/or vomiting. The date on all three bottles indicated they'd been issued two days ago.

She was pregnant. Just as his father had intimated…

He swung his head in her direction. By now she'd come back out and was sitting on the chair. "Please, Dev." Her blue eyes begged him, out of a face with a slight pallor he hadn't noticed before. Come to think of it, with that wan complexion, she didn't look the same. The glow of health that had radiated off her in the Caribbean was missing. "If I could have one of those small greenish pills with some water?"

She still insisted on using his fictitious name. Nikos picked up one of the pills, then grasped her upper arm and led her back into his bathroom. Her firm flesh, warm from walking on the island in the sun, was a potent reminder of what he'd been torn from at the resort, but that golden quality about her had disappeared.

"Use the cup from the dispenser."

Stephanie took one and put it under the faucet. When he handed her the pill, she swallowed it with half a cup of water. He'd expected resistance, but the eager way she drank and the slight tremor of the hand holding the cup revealed a vulnerability that brought out his protective instincts and caused his mind to reel.

"How far along are you?"

The empty cup fell into the sink. This was no act. She weaved in place, causing him to tighten his grip on her arm so she wouldn't fall. Her eyes stared at him in the mirror. "You do the math."

That comment—just when he'd felt himself softening toward her—caught him on the raw. He gripped her other arm to bring her close to him, and gave her a little shake. "Whose baby is it? Rob's?"

"You can ask me that?" she cried, sounding so wounded it almost got to him.

"Very easily."

Her head fell back on the slender column of her neck. "Rob? The guy I only had one dinner date with? I was never intimate with him or anyone else! I can't believe you brought his name up."

"I used protection, Stephanie."

"That's what I told Dr. Sanders. He said no protection was perfect, and informed me I was going to have a baby. I'm three months along."

She'd already gone through her first trimester? He'd been in absolute hell during that same time period.

"Call him and he'll confirm it. If you can conceive of my being with another man after what we shared on vacation, then your imagination is greater than mine could ever be. After it's born and you're still in doubt, then a simple DNA test will tell you the truth."

The blood hammered in his ears. He searched her eyes, trying to find any trace of duplicity in her, but could see none. His lips twisted. "So your carefully laid plan had the consequence you'd hoped for, and now you're ready to turn this to your advantage?"

"What advantage?" she blurted angrily. "When you were through with me, you sent me flowers and couldn't have made it clearer our interlude was over. But I happen to believe that a man who's a womanizer still deserves to know he's going to be a father. That's the real reason I'm here!"

The *real* reason. *Which truth was the truth?*

"I could have sent you a bouquet with a note congratulating you on your new status. But I had no idea where to send it, so I decided to do the decent thing and come in person, hoping to find Dev Harris. Instead I found *you*."

With her wintry indictment, she jerked herself out of his arms and hurried back to the bedroom. "Now that you've been given the news, I need to catch the boat back to Chios." She started to put the contents of her purse back, but his hand was faster, preventing her.

"I'm afraid not. There won't be another one until tomorrow." He slid her cell phone and passport in a pocket of his pants.

Her head swerved to meet his piercing gaze. "I never wanted or expected anything from you, and that's a good thing, because I don't know who you are."

"Nor I you." His voice grated. "Except in the biblical sense." He saw a glint of pain in her eyes before she started for the doorway. "Go ahead, but without a passport, you won't be allowed to board the plane back to the States."

"You can't keep me here! I have a job to get back to, a condo to take care of. My flight leaves for Florida in the morning."

"You should have thought of that before you ever targeted me."

Her naturally arched brows frowned in puzzlement. "You certainly have an inflated opinion of yourself. I've met men in Florida with a lot of money. Maybe not as much as the Vassalos family, but enough to keep a grasping woman in style for the rest of her life. Since you can't wait for me to be gone, how long do you intend to keep me here?"

"For as long as it takes to get the truth from you."

She sat down on the edge of the bed as if she was too weak to stand. Her pallor convinced him that part of her story was the truth. She was nauseous, but maybe it covered something other than pregnancy. Kon's wife had done a spectacular job of convincing him she was pregnant.

"Dev… We met purely by accident, when I was scuba diving at the resort with my friends from Crystal River."

"Yet you managed to locate me here without any difficulty whatsoever. Now you're telling me you're pregnant with my child. We both know you were already pregnant when you slept with me on vacation. If you're hoping to inveigle your way into my life with this announcement, it won't work."

By now her hands had formed into fists, and she jumped up from the bed. "I don't want to stay here!" she cried, sounding on the verge of hysteria. "I can't! I'm expected back at work. My friends will wonder where I am."

He would never have credited her with being an hysterical woman. It didn't fit with what he knew about her. Yet what did he really know, except what she'd allowed him to see while they were both on vacation? "No problem. You can call them and tell them you've been detained."

"Dev—"

"It's Nikos, remember?"

"All right then. Nikos. Please don't do this. I need to get back to the hotel in Chios for my personal belongings."

"We'll sail there and Yannis will collect them for you."

"Yannis?"

"He's a seaman who worked for my family when I was boy. Now he works for me."

"What do you mean, collect?" she asked in fresh alarm.

"After we leave Chios, we won't be touching land again for at least two weeks."

After letting out a moan, she started pacing, then stopped. "Call my obstetrician in Florida. He'll verify the dates so you'll have your proof."

"That won't prove anything. You could have been with a man the night before we met. Maybe several."

A gasp escaped. "Surely you don't believe that! There was only you. Phone Delia. She'll verify everything."

"How much did you pay her and her boyfriend to tell me a lie if I called her?"

Stephanie paled more. "Nikos…who are you?"

He raked a hand through his hair, wondering the same thing. After living through a hellish childhood with his father, plus the memory of Kon's disastrous marriage and divorce, Nikos had developed a much more cynical outlook on life.

Part of him couldn't help but wonder why Natasa had been waiting around for him all these years, if not to marry money. She'd lived with wealth all her life and needed a rich husband to be kept in that same lifestyle. The thought sickened him.

What if Stephanie was telling him the truth? His black brows furrowed. "Someone who doesn't like being taken advantage of. You were very clever to try and convince me you found me by sheer perseverance. For the time being you'll remain with me on the *Diomedes."* It was an impulsive decision, one he hadn't had time to examine yet.

She looked frantic. "Please don't do this."

For a moment he was carried back three months in time. She'd begged him not to tease her when he kept kissing her face, but not her mouth. He'd been on the verge of devouring her and couldn't hold back much longer. Just now that same appeal was in her voice, confusing him, when he needed to keep his wits.

"You don't have to worry. I'll let you contact your boss and make it right with him. Tell him your medical condition has made it necessary for you to stay in Greece for an indefinite period. Your boss will have to understand."

"But Nikos—"

"No doubt your friend Melinda will run by your condo for you and check your mail." He put his T-shirt back on and slid into his sandals. "As for you, I'll make sure you're taken care of in your fragile state. Just be grateful I'm not turning you over to the authorities for trespassing on private property. You wouldn't last long in one of our jails."

Her appealing body shuddered.

"It would be interesting to know who told you I was on the yacht. No one knows except my parents."

"I—I met an older woman waiting for the boat that would take me back to Chios," Stephanie stammered. "She pointed to this yacht and said it belonged to the Vassalos family."

"Why would she do that?"

"Because I asked her if she lived here and knew your family."

"What did she say?"

"That everyone knew your family."

"Did you exchange names?"

"No! I simply offered her some of my grapes while we were waiting for the boat."

"So at that point you just decided to walk over to the yacht and see if it met your high expectations, did you?"

"No. My intention was to find out if anyone on board knew where you really were."

"I guess I'm not surprised you decided to use your beauty to sweet-talk the crew into revealing my whereabouts."

She stiffened. "There *was* no crew."

"Yet having been told I was out of the country indefinitely, you still waited for someone to come to the yacht."

She moistened her lips. "I was afraid that if you were at work and knew I was looking for you, you'd pretend to be away. It was my last resort to try and reach you."

"Therefore once again it was pure luck that you didn't take no for an answer and sought me out at the yacht."

"It appears that way," she whispered.

"I'm afraid your luck has run out." Before he walked out of the bedroom, he said, "Go ahead and fix your own meal. There's food and drink in the galley. We just restocked everything. You're paler and weaker than I remember. That couldn't be good for you in your condition."

"I notice you've lost weight and don't look as well, either!"

Touché.

"In fact, you—" Suddenly, she stopped talking.

"I what?" he demanded.

Stephanie averted her eyes. "Nothing."

He'd seen her glance at the cane, and had an idea what she'd intended to say. It angered him further. "Don't try to go up on deck while we're leaving port."

Adrenaline drove him out of the room and down the hall to the stairs. But he paid the price for not taking care because when he reached the top deck, he felt pain at the base of his spine and realized he'd exerted himself too much without support. *Damn it all.*

CHAPTER FOUR

AFTER A FEW minutes of enforced solitude, Stephanie could feel the yacht moving. Good heavens! Nikos had really meant it. They were leaving the port and she was his prisoner! It certainly wasn't because he was enamored of her. She'd changed physically since they'd been together, making her less attractive.

His looks had altered, too, but in his case the weight loss and dark brooding behavior didn't detract from his virulent male charisma. If anything, those changes made him even more appealing, if that was at all possible.

By now she'd passed the stage where she still believed she was having a nightmare. Rage and bewilderment had been warring inside her, but her greatest need at the moment was for food, so she wouldn't throw up again. No matter what was going to happen, she needed to take care of herself and her baby.

Taking him at his word, she walked to the galley. He'd stocked his fridge well in a kitchen that rivaled that of even the most rich and famous yacht owners. Anything she could want was here. But after she'd eaten, she started going crazy with nothing to do, and decided to go up to the top of the stairs for some fresh air.

To her dismay the tough-looking seaman, Yannis, probably in his sixties, barred her way. "Go back down, Ms. Walsh," he told her in a heavily accented voice.

"Just let me stand here for a little while and breathe some fresh air." There was no sign of her baby's father. The sun had fallen below the horizon.

"Nikos doesn't want you up here until we're out on open water. It's for your safety. I promised him that I would take care of you."

There'd be no point in begging his guard dog to let her walk around on deck. "All right." She turned around and went back to the dimly lit passage below, and finally Nikos's bedroom. Stephanie couldn't believe this was the same man she'd fallen madly in love with.

Since he wasn't working at Vassalos Shipping right now, what was he doing on this yacht? Needing to figure out why he was being so cruel and secretive, she opened his closet, but all she found were casual clothes. Nothing that told her anything. The clothes in the dresser didn't reveal anything, either.

Needing answers, she left the bedroom and went along the passageway to the next door, on the left. It was another bedroom, with a queen-size bed and its own bathroom.

She tried the next door, but it was locked. Maybe it was the bedroom of the man who was crewing for Nikos. Stephanie's gaze darted to the lounge across from it. One end contained a couch, table and chairs, and an entertainment center. The other end had been made into a den, equipped with a computer and everything that went with it.

After checking out his desk, she came across sets of

maps and charts with Greek words she couldn't read. Stephanie was afraid she'd be caught snooping and it would intensify his anger. Quickly, she put them back in the drawers and hurried down the corridor to his bedroom.

Once she'd shut the door, she leaned against it with a pounding heart while her mind tried to make sense of what he was doing on the yacht. When she'd calmed down, she was so exhausted she stretched out on the bed. In case he came to check up on her, he would think she'd been sleeping instead of exploring the yacht without his permission.

Emotionally spent, she closed her eyes for a minute, trying desperately to put all the disjointed pieces together. The man at the reception desk had told her Kyrie Vassalos was out of the country and wouldn't be back in the foreseeable future. It was a blatant lie, since Nikos had obviously been living on this yacht for some time. Why?

Stephanie racked her brain for answers until she knew nothing else. When she next became aware of her surroundings, the yacht was still moving. To her surprise Nikos had thrown a blanket over her. How long had she slept? Her watch said it was 11:00 p.m., Greek time.

When she rolled over to get up, she realized he'd removed her sandals. At the end of the bed she saw her suitcase. That meant he'd already sailed to Chios, and had no doubt taken care of her hotel bill.

She started to tremble. No one in the world knew where she was right now. No one would be looking for her yet. Stephanie was being held against her will in the middle of the Aegean Sea by a man she didn't begin to know.

After slipping on her sandals, she left the bedroom and walked down the hall to the stairs. No one met her at the top. She walked to the railing and looked all around. Night had descended. In the distance she could see lights twinkling from land far away. Though the sight was beautiful, she shivered to think she'd been so foolish as to climb aboard the boat of a perfect stranger. In Greek waters, no less...

Didn't Greek mythology tell of Pandora, the first woman on earth? Zeus had given her a beautiful container with instructions not to open it under any circumstances. But her curiosity had prevailed and she did open it, letting out all the evil held inside. For what she'd done, she'd feared Zeus's wrath.

Another shudder rocked Stephanie's body. Today she'd opened that container, knowing she shouldn't have. The action had seemed so small at the time. But what she'd done, in order to find the father of her baby, had turned out to have severe and far-reaching consequences for her, inciting Nikos's wrath.

"You're not supposed to be up here."

At the sound of Nikos's deep voice, a cry escaped her lips and she spun around. The warm night breeze flattened the T-shirt against his well-defined chest, ruffling his black wavy hair. Despite his hostility, his male beauty captivated her.

"I was looking for you."

"It's dangerous to walk around at this time of night. You're lucky I didn't set the wireless security system yet, or you would have received the fright of your life by the noise."

Her hand clutched the railing. "I'm used to being on boats," she said defensively.

His lips tightened into a thin line. "Go back down. *Now.*"

Nikos's mood was too dark and ominous for her to dare defy him. Taking a deep breath, she turned around and walked back to the stairs, which she descended. She felt him following her, all the way to the bedroom.

After he came inside, she looked at him. "Was the alarm set this afternoon while I was waiting to talk to a crew member?"

"Yes, even if that part of the marina is Vassalos private property. There are some people who will trespass no matter what."

She lifted a hand to her throat. She'd considered going on board, but had held back, thank goodness. "You mean all those other boats belong to your company?"

"That's right." His chiseled features stood out in stark relief. "I must admit I'm surprised you didn't step on the *Diomedes* without permission. When we were together on Providenciales, I noticed what an adventurous person you were, unafraid to explore the depths where the others held back. I guess it doesn't really surprise me you would show such tenacity in trying to find me, regardless of the consequences."

Her softly rounded chin lifted. "That's because I was on a sacred mission."

"*Sacred?*" he queried silkily. "What an interesting choice of words."

Salty tears stung her eyelids. "You wouldn't understand."

"Try me."

Stephanie shook her head. "You'll only mock me, so there's no point."

"You're trying my patience, what little I have left," he said, his voice grating. He lounged against the closed door. The stance looked familiar, but she had an idea he needed the support. Stephanie wished she didn't care about his condition, but the signs of his suffering, both physical and emotional, had gotten to her. "I'm waiting."

"When we were in the Caribbean, you asked me about my father. I told you he and my mother never married and she raised me alone. But I never went into the details."

"Why was that?"

She sank down on the side of the bed. "Because it's such a painful subject for me to talk about, and because I barely knew you. Eventually I would have told you everything, but we ran out of time." Her voice shook.

His jaw hardened. "That must have been a shock to your carefully laid plans."

"I didn't have any plans, Nikos. I don't know why you won't believe me. You say you want answers, so I'm trying to give them to you. Mom met my father on a winter skiing holiday in Colorado. They spent a glorious week together before he said he had to leave, but would fly to Crystal River to see her.

"She worked in hospital administration. He could have found her at any time, but he never called or looked her up. Mom had her pride and waited in vain for him to get in touch with her."

Nikos eyed Stephanie skeptically. "If she knew where he lived, why didn't she seek him out?"

"By the time I was born, she was so ashamed of

what she'd done, she made up her mind that I would never know his name or where I could find him. She felt he didn't deserve to know he was a father. I was put in day care and she raised me with the help of my grandparents until they passed on."

Struggling with the rest, Stephanie sprang to her feet. "Since you left me at the resort, I have a crystal-clear understanding of what my mother went through and why she was so shattered. But she forgot one thing. She didn't realize how important it was for me to know who my father was, if only to see him once and understand my own genes, to gain more of an identity."

Stephanie heard Nikos take an extra breath in reaction.

"Mother robbed me of that. It's the only thing in our lives that caused pain between us. I loved her. Though she was the best mom in the world, I had a hard time forgiving her for that. However, I finally have. Still, her omission has left scars, because I'm my father's flesh and blood, too. When she died, her secret died with her, leaving me in agony and always wondering about him.

"Do I have grandparents who are still alive? A half brother or sister? Does my father like doing the things I like? Do I look like him? Those are questions for which I have no answers. Unfortunately, I'll never be given them."

She clutched her arms to her waist. "Such is the story of the Walsh mother and daughter. We were both open to a good time, until it was over. I can't believe I've repeated my mother's history, but they say experience is the best teacher."

Stephanie threw her head back. "How I've learned! I had to believe it when the doctor told me I was pregnant. He said a good condom hardly ever fails, but it can slip. That's probably what happened with us."

By now Niko's countenance had grown dark and lined.

"Believe it or not, my very first thought when I learned of my pregnancy wasn't about you or money, but about the life we'd created. I felt all the joy of being told I was going to be a mother, and I loved my baby instantly.

"But I have to tell you, I damned myself and you for the weakness that caused us to reach out for pleasure without marriage or commitment of any kind, without really knowing the most basic things about each other. We were both incredibly selfish, Nikos."

"You're right," he admitted, with what sounded like self-loathing.

"In hindsight I realize I don't hate you for what you did, leaving without a personal goodbye. I took a risk with you. We were equal partners in doing what we did. That's why I did everything I could to find you and let you know you're going to be a father. To *not* tell you would be an even more selfish act.

"I wouldn't be honest if I didn't admit that I wanted to be with you the moment we met in the Caribbean, and I made no secret about it. That time was beautiful beyond belief and something I will always treasure. It's the reason I don't want to make something ugly out of something that was sacred to me at the time, even if it was illicit. I still don't know if you have a wife or other children."

"I don't," he whispered in a bleak tone.

"If that's the truth, then I'm glad I don't have to carry that burden, too. You've accused me of coming after you because of the great Vassalos fortune. Let me say now that I wouldn't ask for money or take it under any circumstances. What we had together wasn't love. It couldn't have been, since it was based on a lie."

At her comment his features hardened.

"You owe me nothing, Nikos, but you have the right to know we're going to have a child. When the baby's born, I plan to give it the last name of Walsh. But I did want to be able to tell our daughter or son your true name—that it wasn't Dev Harris, and that you come from a fine established family from Egnoussa, Greece, and not New York.

"That's why I did everything possible to find you and learn your true identity. I realize I've gone where angels fear to tread, even to trying to find out about you from someone working on your yacht. But I've done it for our child, who doesn't deserve such selfish parents."

"It's very noble of you to take on partial blame." But his mocking tone robbed the sentiment of any meaning.

"Once you let me off this luxury vessel, I'm going back to Crystal River, knowing I've done my best for my baby. One day, when our child asks about you, I'll tell him or her all I know and learned about you during those ten days we spent together. They were the happiest days of my whole life.

"It will help satisfy our child's great need to know about his or her beginnings. Every human born wants to know who they are and where they come from. Were they wanted? I want our child to know he or she was wanted from the second I found out that I was pregnant. Once grown, it will be up to him or her if you meet. I'll play no part in it.

"Now if you'll excuse me, I need to use the bathroom again. After I've gotten ready for bed, where do you want me to sleep?"

"Your bedroom is the next one down the hallway, on the left. I'll show you. You can freshen up in your own bathroom."

He picked up her suitcase and took it to the guest bedroom she'd looked in before. "Get a good night's sleep. It appears you need it," he muttered. The unflattering observation shook her to the foundations.

Nikos had told Yannis to drop anchor off Oinoussa Island for the night. Afraid to go below and fall asleep, where he might have one of his flashbacks and Stephanie would hear him, he opted for a lounger beneath the stars, and covered himself with a light blanket.

All was quiet except for the frantic pounding of his heart at every pulse point of his body.

For the rest of the hours before dawn he lay there in torment, going over their conversation in his mind.

Even if he'd used her while on vacation, Stephanie had claimed she wanted him to know in person that he was going to be a father. At the heartbreaking story of having all knowledge of her own father kept from her, Nikos had been moved beyond words.

To go to so much trouble and expense to find Dev Harris—to risk her health in the process—led him to believe she must be telling him the truth. Otherwise she would have sought out the other man she'd been with, *if* there was another man.

But if she'd been with another man before Nikos, no one had proof of paternity. Only a blood test after the baby was born would prove it. Any earlier attempt would be a risk to the unborn baby and possibly cause a miscarriage. He didn't dare insist on it. Much as he wanted to believe he was the father, and that her true reason for coming to Greece was to inform him of the fact, he was still riddled with doubts.

Nikos closed his eyes tightly. When Kon had been confronted with a similar situation, before they'd gone into the military, he'd believed the nineteen-year-old girl who'd told him she was pregnant. Kon had gotten in over his head with an attractive French girl he'd met on vacation in Corsica, but before returning home, he realized he wasn't in love, and had ended it with her while they were still together.

To his chagrin, she'd showed up a month later with a positive result on a home pregnancy test, claiming he was the father. She was terrified of having her parents find out. What should she do?

Kon was an honorable man and had been willing to take responsibility, so they got married privately at the local church, where Nikos stood as one of the witnesses. His parents accepted her into the family and they'd lived with them until Kon could afford to find a place for them to live on their own.

But two months later his friend realized she'd lied to him and there was no baby. He got medical proof from the doctor at the hospital. She was forced to admit she'd made up the fabrication because she loved him and didn't want to lose him. If he thought they were going to have a baby, then they could get married. As it turned out her plan had worked...for a while.

Betrayed to the point he couldn't look at her anymore, he divorced her and put the whole ghastly affair behind him. But there'd been a heavy emotional price to pay, and the divorce had cost him a great deal of money, which Nikos insisted on funding from his own savings account. It was the least he could do for his friend.

After the agony Nikos had seen Kon go through when he'd realized he'd been deceived, the possibility that Stephanie was lying, too, gutted him. He didn't honestly know what to believe.

Short of making love to Stephanie to learn if she was truly pregnant, which wasn't a viable option for too many reasons to consider right now, he could phone her doctor. Yet somehow that idea was repugnant to him.

The only sure thing to do was wait for physical signs of her pregnancy. In order to do that, he would have to keep her close for the time being.

When Nikos thought back to their first meeting, he recalled he'd been the aggressor. Unlike her friends, who worked at a local hotel in Crystal River, Stephanie had done nothing to come on to him. While they'd flirted with him, she'd kept her distance and been totally serious about diving.

It turned out they didn't have her skills and snorkeled only part of each day. Oftentimes they preferred to laze on the beach and go shopping in town. Not Stephanie. Quite the opposite, in fact, which was why he'd asked her if she'd be willing to be his diving partner for the duration. He'd felt her reluctance when she'd said yes, but it was obvious she loved the sport and couldn't go diving without a partner.

Scuba diving wasn't for everyone, but she was a natural. Together they'd experienced the euphoria of discovering the underwater world. Besides her beauty, there was an instant connection between them as they'd signaled each other to look at the wonders exploding with color and life around each gully and crevice.

When they'd had to surface, he hadn't wanted it to end, and had asked her to eat dinner with him. She'd turned down his first invitation, but the second time she'd agreed. That's when he'd learned she'd grown up along Florida's Nature Coast. She'd learned to scuba dive early with her mother. After college she'd gone to work for a water tour company that took tourists scalloping and swimming with the manatees. It explained her prowess beneath the waves.

If he was truly the only man she'd been with, then her news represented a miracle. Nikos was sterile now, the hope of ever having a child from his own body having gone up in flames during the explosion.

Yet he could feel no joy if she'd set him up—no elation that a deceitful woman would be the mother of his child. If indeed he was the father...

But what if you are, Vassalos?

Think about it.

Your own flesh and blood could be growing inside Stephanie. The only son or daughter you'll ever have.

More thoughts bombarded him.

After his last mission he'd hoped to resign his commission and go after her, marry her. What if she truly was innocent of every charge, and he'd totally misread the situation? If that was the case, then one misstep on his part could hurt her emotionally and damage any chance at real happiness, with their baby on the way.

He got up from the lounger and walked over to the railing, watching the moonlight on the water. His training as a SEAL had taught him that you had to set up your perimeter and have everything in place before you mounted an assault. This time Stephanie was the target. Unfortunately, after leaving her behind, he'd unwittingly planted an almost impenetrable field of land mines and booby traps that would destroy him if he wasn't careful.

If his suspicions about her were correct—that she'd calculated every move since meeting him at the resort, in order to trap him—it meant maneuvering through them with surgical precision while he waited to see if she was pregnant, then awaited the DNA results.

How would he begin making it up to her if he was wrong?

In retrospect, Nikos realized he'd accused her of duplicity, when he'd been the one who'd committed a multiple number of sins. Not only had he forsaken her on the island without giving her an honest explanation, he hadn't tried to reach her during his stay in the hospital.

The moment his father had handed him those snapshots, Nikos had been carried away by his own suspicions that she was after his money and the lifestyle he could provide her. His anger had quickly turned to white-hot pain at the thought she'd been only using him during that time on vacation. In retaliation, he'd treated her abominably.

Nikos let out a groan. Was he turning into his father? A man who'd believed the worst about the wife who loved him, because of a rumor? Whose doubts and suspicions had turned him into an impossible man to live with, catching Nikos in the crossfire?

Stephanie's words still rang in his ears. *What we had together wasn't love.*

But what if it *had* been love on her part, and it was

only her anger talking now? Otherwise why would she have gone through all she'd done to find him?

He owed it to both of them to discover the truth. Otherwise he might be dooming himself to repeat his father's history. Until Nikos had proof, he decided he would believe her story, because his entire happiness could depend on it.

By the time the sun had risen above the horizon, he'd made his plans. The first thing he'd do was shower, then fix breakfast for the two of them. *Or the three...*

A knock on her bedroom door brought Stephanie awake. It was ten after eight. She'd slept soundly, likely because of the gentle rocking of the yacht. But it didn't feel as if they were moving now.

"Yes?"

"Your breakfast is waiting for you in the lounge down the hall, whenever you're ready."

She blinked. "Nikos?"

"Of course."

There was no "of course" about it. Last night he'd told her to fix her own food. This morning it seemed he'd decided to be more civil. That was a good sign, since she needed to go home today, and couldn't without his cooperation.

"Thank you. I'll be right there."

She took all her pills with a cup of water she'd put by the bed, and then got out from under the covers. Once in the bathroom she showered quickly, then brushed her hair and left it loose. A little blusher and lipstick and she felt ready to face Nikos.

Stephanie hadn't packed a lot. She'd brought extra undergarments and a smoky-blue knit top she wore loose over her khaki pants, which were uncomfortable now. She needed to buy some maternity clothes the moment she got back to Florida.

In spite of the fact that she would have to go through the entire pregnancy alone, she was looking forward to it. Having found the baby's father, and knowing his real identity, she felt a bit more lighthearted. Soon she'd start getting a nursery ready, and couldn't wait.

After putting on her sandals, she left the bedroom and moved across the hall to the lounge, where she found Nikos at the table, waiting for her. He stood up when she walked in. She detected the scent of the soap he'd used in the shower. Her senses responded to it, though she tried to ignore them.

"It looks like you've made a fabulous breakfast." He'd fixed coffee, too, but so far she hadn't been able to tolerate it. "We could have eaten in the galley and saved you the extra trouble."

"True, but you're a guest, so I thought this might be more enjoyable."

"For a prisoner who has to stay below deck, you mean," she muttered.

He ignored her comment. "Let's hope there's something here that you can keep down." He helped her into a chair before he sat opposite her at the rectangular table.

"Those rolls and fruit look good." So did he.... This morning he was freshly shaved and wearing a white crew neck shirt with jeans. It was sinful how handsome he was!

While he ate eggs and a roll, his jet-black eyes played over her several times. "Your hair is a little longer."

"So's yours." But she refused to tell him how much she liked it.

He appeared to drink his coffee with pleasure. "What did your doctor tell you about swimming and scuba diving in your condition?"

The question was totally unexpected. "I can do some limited swimming, but diving during pregnancy increases the risk to the fetus, so I'm not taking any chances. Why do you ask?"

One black brow lifted. "Your job. Now that you're pregnant, the kind of work you do swimming with the manatees will have to be curtailed."

She munched on a banana. "I realize that and plan to discuss it with my boss when I get back. Which raises the question of when you're going to take me to Chios so I can get a flight home."

"That all depends." He bit into a juicy plum.

Stephanie fought to remain cool-headed. "On what?"

He finished it, then lounged back in the chair, eyeing her for a long moment. "I have a proposition for you."

"I'm not interested."

"Surely after all the trouble you took to find me, can't you admit you're a little curious?"

"That curiosity died when I didn't find Dev. You're the dark side of him, a complete stranger to me with your lies and secrets. I have no desire to listen to anything you have to say, except to hear that you'll let me go."

"Be that as it may, you've convinced me you were an innocent tourist on vacation in the Caribbean. I take full responsibility for finding you attractive and pursuing you. Since you're pregnant, it's only right that I take care of you and the baby you're carrying."

For him to say that to her now… Pain ripped her apart. "For the last time, I don't want your money, just my freedom."

His eyes narrowed on her features. "You can have it in time *if* it's what you want. That's what divorces are for."

Shaken by his words, she sprang from the chair. "What are you talking about?"

"Our marriage, of course. You came all the way from Florida to let me know I'm going to be a father. But that's not all I want. I want my name on the birth certificate along with yours. To a Greek male, it means everything."

"Since when?" she blurted.

"Since learning that you've known nothing about your own father—not even his name. I can see how devastating that has been for you, which makes it more vital than ever that the baby growing inside you has my name so it can take its rightful place in the world."

Stephanie reeled in place, clinging to the back of the chair. "You don't want to marry me." Her tremulous words reverberated in the lounge.

Now Nikos was on his feet. "On the contrary. It's all I thought about during the night."

"Why?" she cried in torment.

"Because this baby is already precious to me."

Her anger flared. "Last night you questioned if it was even yours."

"Last night I was in denial that a miracle had happened."

She shook her head. "What do you mean?"

"A lot has occurred since we last saw each other."
He didn't need to tell her that. Her whole world had
been turned upside down. "I was in a boating accident
that landed me in the hospital with a spinal injury."

Stephanie bit her lip, pained by the news. "I knew
something was wrong," she whispered. "Sometimes
you're a little unsteady. I noticed it wh-when you were
holding me."

"Nothing gets past you, does it? Your unexpected
presence on the *Diomedes* gave me away. Fortunately,
I'm getting stronger every day and use the cane only
when I'm tired. But I'm not the man I once was and
never will be. Furthermore, the accident had certain
repercussions I can't do anything about."

Her mouth went dry. She was almost afraid to hear.
"What are they?"

"For one thing, my injury left me sterile."

Sterile?

A slight gasp escaped her lips, for she knew that
kind of news had to be soul wrenching to a man.
"Surely it's only a temporary setback?"

"No." His eyes again narrowed to slits. "It's permanent." The throb in his voice carried its own haunting tale.

Stephanie pressed her hand to her mouth to stifle her
cry. "I'm so sorry, Nikos. I hardly know what to say."

"Perhaps now you understand why your coming
here to tell me you're pregnant, at the very moment
I've been dealing with my news, made me go out of
my head for a little while. After having to give up all
hope of having my own child, I suppose I was afraid
to believe you were telling me the truth."

Stephanie's lungs tightened while she tried to absorb

the revelation. "What was the other repercussion?" She feared it was going to be horrible, too.

"My best friend died in the accident."

"Kon Gregerov?"

Nikos nodded gravely.

"Oh, no…" She couldn't hold back the tears. They rolled down her cheeks. He'd mentioned his friend several times while they'd been diving. He'd told her they were closer than he was to his own brother. They'd grown up together and would have done anything for each other.

After such trauma, was it any wonder he'd changed so completely in every way? Other than anger over what life had dealt him, Nikos had to feel dead inside. If their positions were reversed, Stephanie knew her life would look black to her.

"Now that you've heard the truth from me, here's my proposition. I want to marry you as soon as possible, and we'll live here. It will mean having to give up your job. You can either sell or rent your condo, and put your car and furnishings in storage for the time being.

"It's the only way I can protect you and the baby. But it wouldn't have been fair to you if I hadn't told you I can't give you more children. Millions of other men can. You need to think about that very carefully before you commit yourself legally to me."

Stephanie *was* thinking. It was a shock that she was going to have a baby at all. Right now she couldn't contemplate having more children. Though she knew Nikos wasn't in love with her, she had proof he'd been deadly honest with her just now. Knowing the only child he would ever have was on the way might give him a reason to go on living.

But there was a part of him that didn't know if he was the father or not. And she had concerns, too, if a marriage between them was going to take place. She knew so little about him.

"Nikos?" She wiped the moisture off her face. "What is it you do for a living?"

He put his hands in his back pockets. "I used to work for the family shipping business. Now I'm in the process of starting up something new with Kon's elder brother. It's a project we used to talk about a lot."

"What's his name?"

"Tassos. He's a good friend, too, and married, with a child."

"Does it have to do with shipping?"

"No. We're planning to drill for natural gas in this part of the Aegean."

She knew Nikos was extraordinary, but to consider such an undertaking meant he was a man with vision. It took away her fear that he may have lost interest in everything, including life. To know he was working on something so vital for his own well-being, not to mention his country, thrilled her. Suddenly all those maps and charts she'd seen in the desk made sense.

"You don't need to worry that I can't take care of you," he said mockingly.

"Don't be absurd. The thought never crossed my mind. Nikos? Have you ever been married?"

A caustic laugh escaped. "No, although my family has had a girl picked out for me for years now."

Someone he loved? "You mean a beautiful, well-heeled Greek woman of a good family from your social class. Until I showed up yesterday, were you planning to marry her?"

"No. Natasa wants children. That's the one thing I can't give her."

But he's given one to me, his only one. Stephanie's heart rejoiced, despite the fact she knew he wasn't in love with her.

"When the news gets out that you and I are married, she'll have to move on," he muttered.

Nikos hadn't answered her question, but it didn't matter. Having another woman waiting at home, approved of by his family, explained why he'd never made a commitment to Stephanie on the island. She had enough charity in her heart to feel sorry for Natasa. Nikos was a prize who stood out from every male she'd ever met.

"If I were to agree to marry you, I wouldn't want a big wedding, Nikos."

"That's one area we fully agree on. We'll have it take place in private, with only Yannis and the Gregorov family as witnesses."

Alarmed, she turned to him. "Not even your parents?"

"Especially not them." Stephanie cringed, there was so much heat behind his declaration. "My father and I have been at odds for a long time."

"Your mother, too?"

"Let's just say she's loyal to my father and takes his part in most everything, to keep things civil."

That's why Nikos had never spoken of them on vacation. What could have happened to cause such a breach? "I'm sorry."

He eyed her soulfully. "No more sorry than I am for you to have lived with the hurt your mother inflicted, even if she did it for what she believed were the right reasons. My father justifies his decisions in the same way, without considering the damage. You and I share a common bond in that regard."

A world of hurt laced his words.

"After we're married, we'll drop by the house for a visit and tell them. They'll come around after the baby's born. My parents want grandchildren."

Stephanie eyed him carefully. "Do they know that the accident made you s-sterile?" she stammered.

Frown lines marred his face. "No. To them, children are everything. I don't ever want them to know."

She could understand that. If his family pitied him, he'd never be able to handle it. Stephanie was coming to find out what a private person he was. "Have you considered how they'll feel about me when we're introduced? I'm afraid they'll never see a pregnant American woman from a single family, with no father in the picture, as worthy to be your wife."

His features hardened. "You're carrying a Vassalos inside your body. That makes you the worthiest of all."

Her baby was a Walsh, too, but Nikos had his pride, and right now she knew he was clinging to that one bright hope. More than ever Stephanie realized he was planning on the baby being his. Otherwise there'd be no visit to his family, and her marriage to Nikos would be dissolved.

In order to put him out of his pain, she could swear on the Bible that he was the father, so he'd be reassured, but it would do no good. He needed proof.

Last night he'd told her to go below. She'd thought he was just being mean-spirited, because he was angry. But hearing about the boating accident that had cost his friend his life made her realize Nikos was being protective.

He'd been that way with her scuba diving, always watching out for her. It was his nature. She'd found that trait in him particularly reassuring and remarkable, but she still had reservations about marrying him.

"Earlier you mentioned divorce."

"That's because we don't know what the future will bring after the baby is born."

"You mean you might not want to live with me anymore, under the same roof."

He cocked his head. "As I recall, you were the one who said that what we had on vacation wasn't love. I'm just trying to cover every contingency so there won't be any more surprises. I'd say we've both had enough of them since we met in the Caribbean, and need to lay the groundwork if this is going to work."

Pragmatic was the operative word. She could hardly breathe. "Where would we live?"

"Because of my work with Tassos, I prefer the yacht for the time being. We'll dock at various ports so you can go ashore and explore. A little later on I'll buy us a villa on Oinoussa Island, near the Gregerov's, where you can set up a nursery. Tassos's wife, Elianna, and his younger sister, Ariadne, both had babies recently and speak excellent English. They're warm and friendly. You'll like them."

"I'm sure they're very nice."

The problem was, Stephanie didn't speak any Greek. Yesterday she hadn't known if Dev was even in Egnoussa. Last evening he'd turned into Nikos Vassalos; today he was talking marriage to her. But he wasn't the man she'd fallen headlong in love with on vacation.

That time with Dev could never be recaptured, and she found herself grieving all over again.

Unfortunately, she didn't have the luxury of shedding more tears. For the sake of their child, it was Nikos, not Dev, who'd proposed to her, in order to give their baby a legitimate name and legacy.

"Any more questions?"

"I'm sure more will come up, but right now I can't think of any." She clutched the chair railing. "Is there anything else important you haven't confided to me?"

He rubbed the side of his jaw. "Yes. If you agree to marry me, then I'll tell you the rest. But if you would prefer that I set you up on Oinoussa as my pillow friend and a kept woman, so I have access to you when the baby comes, then there's nothing more you need to know."

She'd heard the Greek phrase "pillow friend" before. A woman with no claim to the man who provided for her until he tired of her and sent her away. Stephanie couldn't imagine anything so awful.

"It's either one or the other, Stephanie, because under no circumstances will I let you leave Greece now."

Nikos meant it with every breath of his body. As he'd told her earlier, this baby was doubly precious to him now.

How bizarre that she was hesitating, when she'd come to Greece to find her baby's father and do the right thing for her child. But nothing had gone the way she'd envisioned it. Theirs would be a marriage without love.

"When do you plan for us to be married?"

"Tomorrow."

So soon! "Isn't there a waiting period?"

"Not with my contacts."

Naturally, Nikos knew someone in high places who could move mountains. Of course he did! Stephanie didn't doubt he could make anything happen, if he wanted it enough. "Where will ours take place?"

"At the small church on Oinoussa, with Father Kerykes, the village priest. He performed Kon's marriage. The man can keep a confidence and be trusted to honor my wishes."

Stephanie moistened her lips nervously. At least they would exchange vows in a holy place.

"What's it going to be, Stephanie?"

As a marriage proposal, it lacked all the passion and romance of her dreams. Without looking at him, she said, "For our child's sake, I want to marry you to give it your name."

"In that case, follow me. I have something to show you."

He left the lounge and walked across the corridor to the locked door, which he opened with a key. It was another bedroom, with two twin beds. "You're welcome to look in the closet."

What on earth?

Stephanie stepped past him and opened the double doors. On one side she discovered two military dress uniforms hanging, one was white, the other navy blue with gold buttons and braid. Next to them was a pair of crutches.

When she glanced on the other side, she was startled to discover half a dozen rifles and a special black scuba diving suit, along with a ton of very official looking gear that would be used by someone in the military.

She turned slowly and sought his gaze. "This equipment belongs to you. What does it mean? I thought you worked for your family's company."

"I did until I was twenty-two. By then Kon was divorced and we decided to join the Greek navy, much to my father's chagrin. We were in for ten years, but for the last five we've been Navy SEALs doing covert operations for our government."

That's why he was such an expert scuba diver.... All those years, Nikos had been fighting for his country. So far every minute she'd spent with him since she'd flown here provided one revelation after another.

"While I was on vacation with you, our unit got called up to do another highly classified mission. Since I can never use my own identity when I travel, and had to leave immediately, the note I left you was the best I could do."

The memory of that note flashed through her mind. *Unfortunately, I've had to leave the island because of an emergency at my work that couldn't be handled by anyone else.* Stephanie was so stunned, she sank down on one of the beds for support.

"Two days later the enemy ambushed our underwater demolition team. They bombed out of the water the fishing vessel we were using for surveillance. After it was detonated, I saw one of them swim away, before I could warn everyone. Kon died in the explosion. I was knocked unconscious and would have died if I hadn't been picked up and flown to the hospital."

"Nikos—"

"At first I was told the injury to my spine meant I'd be paralyzed from the waist down, but slowly feeling came back to my limbs."

"Thank heaven," she whispered in a trembling voice.

"The explosion should have taken me out, too!" His own voice shook with despair.

"But it didn't, and you have to believe there was a reason you survived."

His grim expression devastated her. "If you can make me believe that, then you're a saint."

Anger swept through her. "Kon didn't leave a child behind, but you did! Think about the fact that you're not paralyzed. Otherwise your child would grow up knowing you only in a wheelchair."

He bit out a Greek epithet before he murmured, "It turned out I'd been deeply bruised, but I could walk."

"You're one of the lucky vets, Nikos, and it's going to mean the world to your child that you continue to get better and stronger. Are you seeing a doctor regularly?"

"Yes," he whispered.

"What about exercise?"

"Among his many jobs, Yannis helps me do mine up on deck."

"I can help you with them, too."

"That won't be necessary, but since you're going to be my wife, I wanted you to know about my past. Now we don't ever have to speak of it again."

Nikos closed the closet doors and pulled her cell phone from his pocket. "Before we make any plans, you need to talk to your boss and tell him you can't work for him anymore." He handed it to her. "While you do that, I'll be in the galley. Come and find me after you've talked to him. If I'm not there, I'll be in the lounge."

With her heart thudding, she got to her feet. "Nikos?"

He paused in the doorway, darting her a piercing glance. "What is it?"

With that intimidating look, the question she would have asked him never made it past her lips. In fact, she already did have the answer to what would have happened to them if he hadn't had to leave the island to go on a covert operation.

Nothing would have been different. Like her father, when he'd left her mother, Nikos would have said goodbye to Stephanie, telling her the lie that he'd see her again, and that would have been the end of it.

Until his accident, Nikos's future had been tied up with another woman. As he'd told Stephanie a little while ago, Natasa wanted children....

CHAPTER FIVE

WHEN NIKOS BROUGHT the dishes from the lounge into the galley, he found Yannis enjoying breakfast. The balding seaman needed a lot of food to keep going. He looked up. "What are your plans for today, Nikos?"

"After you finish eating, we'll pull up anchor and head for Oinoussas . Once we've docked I won't need you until tomorrow. That ought to give you some time to do what you want with Maria." The widow who ran a small shop had become his love interest.

"She'll like that."

"But not you?" he teased.

Yannis stared at him. "What's going on? You no longer act like you're on the way to your own funeral."

"I'm getting married tomorrow to Kyria Walsh at the church of Agios Dionysios. *That's* what's going on. I need to make preparations."

His longtime widower friend looked shocked. "Married? To her? But what about Kyria Lander?"

Nikos started doing the dishes. He and Yannis took turns cooking and cleaning up. "She's not pregnant with my child, Yannis. Stephanie is."

"Ah…" The older man crossed himself. "This happened while you were on vacation in the Caribbean?"

"Yes."

A huge smile broke out on his weathered face. "Now I understand. I told you the scuba diving there was the finest in the world. I'm glad you listened to me. She's a real beauty, Nikos. It's about time you had some happiness in your life. Does your father know?"

"Not yet." Nikos was functioning on faith that she was pregnant and carrying his baby.

"There will be an explosion when your family finds out."

"It won't matter, because by the time they hear the news, she'll be my wife. You're going to be a witness, like you were for Kon."

"I'll be honored. Are you having a boy?"

"It's too soon to know. Maybe in another month. For the present we'll live on the yacht. Stephanie needs pampering and must eat for two. Since the last time I saw her, she's lost her glow, and needs to take care of herself." He refused to entertain the thought that she wasn't pregnant.

The older man nodded.

"Just so you know, I've told her how I got injured." He turned his head away from Yannis. "We have no secrets."

His friend got up and added his plate and mug to the dishwasher. "That's good. Otherwise, she'll find out soon enough," he said before leaving the galley. Since Nikos knew that, he would take steps to make certain Stephanie remained clueless about his PTSD.

After reaching for another roll, he headed for the lounge to phone Father Kerykes. They talked for a few minutes to settle on a time for the wedding, which was finally arranged to take place at four in the afternoon.

Next Nikos called Tassos, who seemed overjoyed to learn about the imminent marriage. He insisted that his wife and the Gregerov family would all be there to join in the festivities and take pictures. Later they would treat the bridal couple to dinner at their favorite local taverna.

Just as Nikos hung up, Stephanie walked into the lounge. Her closed expression told him little. "Did you reach your boss?"

She nodded.

"How did he take the news?"

"He wasn't happy about it and complained it would be hard to find someone to replace me."

"I don't doubt it. You're an expert diver and swimmer."

"There are enough qualified applicants in the file drawer that he'll have no problem. It's my reason for resigning he doesn't like."

"How so?"

"Grant is the fatherly type and feels I haven't known you long enough to consider getting married."

"Did you tell him you're pregnant?"

"I had to, otherwise he wouldn't let it go. In the end he grudgingly wished me well and told me he was glad I wasn't going to make another flight back to Florida, considering my condition. He's really a wonderful man. I promised him that after the baby was born, I'd send him a picture of the three of us."

Nikos liked the sound of that. But what if none of it turned out to be true? He rubbed the back of his neck. *You can't afford to think like that, Vassalos.*

"He'll send me my final paycheck when I give him an address."

"Good. What about your friends?"

She lowered her head. "I'll phone them after we're married." She'd called Melinda from Chios to let her know she'd arrived safely. "Otherwise they'll tell me to wait. I can't deal with that kind of pressure right now."

Nikos knew all too well about pressure, especially the parental kind. "In that case let's go up on deck, where you can sunbathe on one of the loungers until we dock at Oinoussa. After that we'll enjoy lunch in town. Among other things we'll do some shopping for clothes, since you only packed enough for a day or two."

Her jewel-like blue eyes fastened on him in apprehension. "What other things?"

"When did your doctor want to see you again?"

"In a month."

"Was everything fine?"

"Yes, except that I need to take iron."

"I saw the pills. To be on the safe side I want to stop in at the clinic, so we can meet the doctor who'll be taking care of you from here on out. Dr. Panos looks after Elianna and Ariadne, who both live on Oinoussa and have great faith in him. You'll need to set up your next appointment."

To his surprise she looked relieved. "I'm glad you thought of a good doctor for me. I really like my OB. He was my mother's doctor and has cared for me since my teens. It's hard to gain trust with someone else."

It was hard to gain trust, period, but since she hadn't fought him on this, Nikos was in a better mood than he'd been since leaving the hospital more dead than alive.

They were coming in to dock at Oinoussa. To Stephanie it looked surprisingly large and beautiful. Tranquil.

The town appeared to be draped over green hillsides, with several churches and charming houses displaying more of the local neoclassical style. Nikos told her there were no springs, so the water came from wells and a reservoir.

She looked over the yacht railing to the brilliant blue water beneath them. Everything was so clean and calm, it almost didn't seem real. This heavenly island was going to be her new home. While Nikos talked of the many beaches she could explore, her mind was on her baby who would be born here, a baby whose father wasn't a New Yorker named Dev Harris.

It started to hit her that she'd done something miraculous for her child, something her own mother couldn't bring herself to do for Stephanie. Because she'd found Nikos, this baby would have a full identity from the very moment of its birth.

Experiencing a sensation of euphoria, she turned to Nikos, who'd come to stand next to her. His hard jawline and arresting Greek profile stood out against the white houses and tiled roofs in the distance.

Suddenly, his black-fringed eyes fused with hers. For a moment, the dullness that had robbed them of their vitality since she'd come here vanished, and they shone with that same energy she'd glimpsed on vacation. "What were you going to ask me?" he murmured in a voice an octave lower than normal.

Her heart raced, because there were times when they seemed to be so in sync, they could read each other's minds. "What's your full name?"

She watched his chest slowly rise and fall. "Theodoros Nikolaos Vassalos."

Stephanie blinked. "Is Theodoros your nickname?"

"No. I don't have a nickname. It's my father's name."

"So when our baby is born, it will take your name first?"

"Yes, because it will be our first and only child."

"Are there rules about naming it?"

"You can name our baby whatever you like."

"But what if we follow the rules?"

"Then if it's a boy, we'd name it Alexandros, after my father's father."

She experimented outloud. "Nikolaos Alexandros Vassalos."

"That's right."

"And if it's a girl?"

"After my mother's mother, Melitta."

"I like both names. Are they still alive?"

"Yes."

She smiled up at him. "Our child will have great-grandparents, too. What a blessing," she said as he studied her hair and features.

"Nikos?" Yannis called out.

"I'm coming," he said, still staring at her with an enigmatic expression she couldn't read. "Get what you need to take with you. We're going ashore."

On legs that felt like mush, she hurried downstairs to freshen up and gather her purse. In a few minutes the men had secured the ropes, and Nikos walked her along the dock to a parking area, where he helped her into a dark blue car.

"Feel free to use this whenever you want to come into town. I'll give you a key when we're back on the yacht."

"Thank you."

She noticed he moved a little slower, but considering his horrendous accident, it was miraculous he could walk without most people noticing anything was wrong.

"Are you hungry?" he asked.

"I'm getting there."

"Did you take your pill for nausea?"

"Just a few minutes ago."

"Good. There's a taverna where you eat in the garden at the back. I'll introduce you to some authentic food I love."

Stephanie couldn't wait to see what he chose for them, especially since these islands were home to him and he knew the streets and shops like the back of his hand.

The proprietor of the small restaurant beamed when Nikos escorted her inside. They spoke in rapid Greek before the older man led them through some doors to a charming garden in bloom with fabulous wild hyacinths and orchids.

There were a dozen or so tables filled with tourists and locals. After settling at a table for two, they were brought fruit drinks and appetizers. One dish, something yellow, was prepared with olive oil, onions and fava beans, Nikos told her. Another, called *caciki,* tasted like cream cheese with cucumber and was served with slices of freshly baked, crusty *psomi* bread. It was followed by shrimp risotto and the grilled calamari.

Stephanie made inroads on everything but the octopus. "Maybe another time," she said to him. After his morose, brooding demeanor yesterday, the white smile he suddenly flashed her, the first she'd seen since her arrival, was so unexpected and startling that her breath caught. She found herself praying this side of him wouldn't disappear.

"Dessert?"

He had to be teasing her. She shook her head. "Thank you. The meal was delicious, but I couldn't possibly eat another bite or it might turn on me."

"Since we can't have that, let's go buy you some clothes."

They went back to the car and he drove to the other side of the village, where he stopped in front of a boutique. "Ariadne likes this store. She says it's trendy. I think you'll find something to your taste."

Inside, Stephanie discovered some great short-sleeved tops, pants, skirts, a couple sundresses and several dressy, long-sleeved blouses in filmy material for evening. Along with those she bought more lingerie, sleepwear and a bikini.

An older woman waiting on her spoke excellent English and was very helpful. As she was putting a white sundress and jacket with small purple violets around the hem in a box for Stephanie, she said, "You will look beautiful in this."

"Thank you."

Nikos stood at the counter with her. "It will make a lovely wedding dress, don't you think?"

Stephanie's heart plummeted. She knew Nikos wanted their wedding to be simple, but she'd still hoped to wear something more bridal to her own nuptials. The saleswoman must have seen her reaction, because to Stephanie's surprise she frowned at Nikos.

"A wedding dress? Oh, no. For that you need to go across the street."

"It's all right," she quickly told the woman.

In order not to upset Nikos, Stephanie forced herself to recover from her disappointment in a big hurry. "I love this dress. It will be perfect. Here's my credit card." She'd come to Greece unprepared, and didn't expect him to pay for a new wardrobe.

Too late, she realized her mistake. In front of the other woman he took the card away and replaced it with one from his wallet. Stephanie gave him a covert glance and saw that his dark expression was back. She should have guessed Nikos had too much pride to allow a woman to pay.

There were so many things she needed to learn about him. On the island they hadn't gone anywhere except the resort, rarely interacting with anyone other than the staff. This was a totally different situation.

He collected her purchases and walked her out to the car, putting everything in the backseat. While he did that, she climbed in the front passenger seat, but he held on to her door so she couldn't close it.

Stephanie looked up at him. "Aren't we going to leave?"

His jaw had hardened. "I saw the look on your face in there. You want a traditional wedding dress? We'll get you one. The most elaborate we can find."

She was crushed. "No, Nikos. Please get in the car so we can talk without everyone hearing us."

"There's nothing to discuss. Come."

After she got out, because he'd left her no choice, he locked the car and ushered her across the street to the bridal shop. An elegant, striking young woman, probably in her mid-twenties, caught sight of Nikos and couldn't look anywhere else. When she spoke in Greek, he responded in English.

"We'd like to see your designer bridal gowns for my fiancée."

Fiancée. What a joke.

"Right over here." She led them to a rack of sumptuous-looking dresses with price tags that meant this was a high end shop. "Go ahead and start looking."

Stephanie hated being in this position. The whole time she examined each dress, she could hear the ringless clerk talking to Nikos in Greek instead of waiting on her. The younger woman was deliberately flirting with him. Stephanie had to get a grip. In the mood he was in, she knew he wouldn't leave this shop until she'd found something for their wedding.

Last night, when she'd opened the closet containing his uniforms, she'd imagined him as a groom wearing the navy one with the gold buttons. With his black hair and olive skin, he'd look magnificent in it. Such an outfit required a wedding dress that lived up to it. If he was now intent on her wearing a designer gown, then she expected him to dress accordingly, too.

After some deliberation, she chose the most expensive dress on the rack. It was a simple princess style, but the floor-length veil of Alençon lace gave it elegance. It cost a fortune, but she didn't care. He'd accused her of using him for his money. *So be it.*

She turned to the clerk. "If you have this one in stock, I'll take it. In America I'm a size 4." Of course, Stephanie wouldn't be that size much longer, but she figured she could squeeze into it once she'd worn off her meal.

The clerk looked taken back. "I believe we do."

"Then please ring it up for me. My *fiancé* will carry it out to our car. Thank you."

Once the clerk went into the back room, Stephanie glanced at Nikos, who was leaning against the counter, his face implacable. No doubt he was feeling some pain, but he'd hate it if she drew attention to it. Maybe she could give him an out.

"Do you still want to stop by the clinic before we go back to the yacht? We could go there tomorrow instead."

His black eyes had taken on that glittery cast. "There's still time this afternoon, unless you're not feeling well."

She wasn't. Not exactly. But for once it had nothing to do with nausea. She sensed he still didn't trust her, and could cry her eyes out after the lovely meal at the restaurant, where he'd been more like...like Dev. "I'm fine."

Stephanie turned her back while he dealt with the saleswoman, then they left the shop.

He laid the dress and veil on top of the other packages before they left for the clinic, which appeared to be closer to the port.

When they went inside to Reception, they learned that Dr. Panos was operating and wouldn't be available. Not to be thwarted, Nikos made an appointment for her for September 1, a full workup.

With that accomplished, they drove to the parking area at the dock. He let her take a few bags, but he carried the rest, along with her wedding finery. Nikos should have brought his cane and let her do more to help, but that infernal pride of his got in the way.

Odd how she hadn't seen it manifest itself when they'd been on vacation. He'd been so mellow and easygoing then. She longed for that time to come back, but it never would.

Once he'd carried everything to her bedroom, he told her he'd be on the phone in the lounge if she needed him. For the next little while Stephanie removed the tags from her purchases and put them away in the closet and dresser.

She checked her watch. It was going on five o'clock. By this time tomorrow they would have been married an hour already.

She supposed she should try on her wedding dress, but for the moment she was too tired, and she'd need a shower first. Emotional fatigue had set in. Maybe later, after she got ready for bed, she'd take it out of the plastic cover and see how it looked on her.

With a sigh she removed her jeans, which were too tight, and lay down on the bed for a minute. She turned on her side, while her hand went automatically to the little bulge, which was definitely getting bigger. Tears trickled out of the corners of her eyes.

"All this is for you, my darling. Are you a little Alex who will be impossibly handsome like your father and turn the head of every girl? Or are you a beautiful little Melitta with flashing black eyes and hair like your daddy? Maybe by my next appointment, or the next, I'll know what to call you."

CHAPTER SIX

WHEN IT GOT to be seven, Nikos hung up the phone with the florist who would bring some flowers to the church tomorrow. All he had left to do was buy a ring. He'd do it in the morning, after Yannis came on board and Nikos had done his exercises.

Now that he'd taken care of everything he could, he got up and walked down the corridor to Stephanie's bedroom. He knocked, but couldn't hear any noise. Since he would have noticed if she'd gone up on deck, he knocked again.

Was she sick? She'd eaten more at lunch than he'd expected. Though he was relieved to see she had an appetite, he worried. Being very quiet, he turned the handle and opened the door a crack.

What he saw made his heart fail. Stephanie had removed her jeans and left them on the floor where she'd stepped out of them. Could he hope it was because they were too tight?

She was out for the count, with her long gorgeous legs uncovered. Jet lag had caught up to her. Her gilt-blond hair splayed out on the pillow. He'd seen this sight before, when she hadn't been wearing any clothes.

The memories came rushing back, increasing the

ache for her that had never gone away. Before he lost control, he closed the door and went to the galley to fix himself a cup of coffee and throw a salad together. Anything to keep busy. When she awakened, he assumed she'd want some dinner.

Nikos had just added the feta cheese when she appeared in the doorway. He shot her a glance. She was wearing a new pair of jeans and one of the flowered print blouses she'd picked out, this one in aqua and white. He noticed that she'd brushed her hair. Beneath the light it shone a silvery-gold, and given those dazzling blue eyes of hers, he'd never seen a woman with such fabulous coloring.

"At last."

"I didn't mean to sleep so long."

"You're still catching up. Are you hungry?"

"I am, if you can believe it. I just took another pill to make sure I stay feeling good."

"It seems to be working. Come all the way in and join me."

He'd already set the galley table with fresh fruit and rolls, plus apple juice and water for her. After serving the salad, he poured himself coffee and sat down opposite her. She reached for the water first and drank a full glass before eating a roll.

"The hot weather this time of year will get to you if you don't stay hydrated."

"So I've noticed. I'll start carrying a bottle around with me. Thank you for fixing dinner, but I hope you know I don't expect to be waited on."

"I enjoyed fixing our prenuptial meal."

She ate some of her salad, then rested her fork on the plate. "Speaking of our wedding, I'd like to explain about today. I didn't want to leave the impression that the white sundress wasn't good enough to wear at the church."

"You owe me no explanation."

"Yes, I do." She wiped the corner of her mouth with a napkin. "The clerk at the boutique mirrored my surprise, but she shouldn't have said anything."

"It's fortunate she did. As I understand it, the wedding day is for the bride."

Defeated by his attitude, she said, "You're right. Women are hopeless romantics in that department, but for me it's more than that. I know you wanted to keep the marriage simple, and I would have been perfectly happy with that if I wasn't pregnant, and our situation was different."

"What do you mean, different?" His question came out sounding like ripping silk, alarming her.

"We're not marrying for the normal reason and I've been thinking about the baby. When it's old enough, our child will want to see pictures of the wedding. Blame it on me for wanting to give it everything I was denied.

"I'm sure there are wedding pictures at your parents' home, of them in their finery. A child wants to see what its mother and father looked like on that special day, the way they wore their hair, what they were wearing. The moment I opened the closet in the extra bedroom, I could envision you in the navy blue uniform."

She leaned toward him excitedly. "Think what it would mean to our child to see you in it on your wedding day. He or she will know about your injury and why you had to leave the service earlier than you'd planned. It'll be preserving a piece of history.

"I have no history from my father, but you can leave some for our child. That's why I chose the dress in the bridal shop with the long lace veil. I know it was expensive, but the sundress wouldn't do justice to your uniform. There's nothing like a handsome man in his dress blues. Any woman would tell you the same thing."

"Stephanie—"

She took a quick breath. "Don't deny it. You *are* exceptional, Nikos. My friends on the island never did get over you. The girl in the bridal shop couldn't take her eyes off you, either. Our son or daughter will be so proud of you and the honorable way you served your country."

Nikos jumped up from the table, too full of conflicting emotions to sit there any longer. He'd leaped to the wrong conclusion after she'd chosen the most expensive gown in the shop. How easily his trust had worn thin. But he'd been remembering the conversation with his father.

You've never looked at Natasa or any woman the way you're looking at this female viper. I admit she's devilishly ravishing in that American way, but she's a mercenary viper nonetheless, one who knows your monetary worth and has come to trap you.

"Don't make me out to be a hero, Stephanie."

"Any man or woman who serves in the military is a hero, Nikos. I'll make two albums to preserve our wedding day. One for our child and one for your parents. Maybe Yannis will take pictures for us." After a pause, she added, "And perhaps the day will come when you'll tell me what they did to you that was so terrible you don't want them at the wedding."

Without looking at her he said, "My reasons run

fathoms deep, but they have nothing to do with you."
He doubted he could ever talk about it.

"Still, they *are* your parents and our baby's grandparents. I know an album of our wedding day will
mean everything to them, too. Please tell me you'll
wear the uniform."

"I'll think about it," he muttered. "I have to go
ashore again. When I leave, I'll set the security system. If it goes off, the harbor police will be alerted and
a signal will be sent to my cell phone. You'll be perfectly safe while I'm gone."

"Where are you going?"

"If you must know, to visit a friend."

"Tassos? Have you told him about the baby?"

"No one knows except Yannis. I'll see you in the
morning."

He left the boat and took off for the cemetery. It
would be his first visit to Kon's grave. Nikos had been
in the hospital when his buddy had been buried in the
Gregerov family plot. They'd always talked over everything important....

At three-thirty the next afternoon, Nikos waited at the
car, ready to take pictures that he knew were so essen-
tial to Stephanie's happiness. After breakfast he'd gone
into town to purchase her ring. When he returned, he'd
discussed the details of the wedding ritual with her.
Now it was time to go.

In a moment she stepped off the yacht. With Yannis's help she started walking along the dock in her
wedding dress. He doubted there'd ever been a sight
like her before, and he started clicking frame after
frame.

The few people around the port watching her would think they were seeing a heavenly vision of femininity in flowing white silk. Angel hair glinted silver and gold through the lace in the late afternoon sun. His throat swelled with emotion to realize this bride was going to be his.

In his gut he wanted the child she was carrying to be his. If it wasn't…

After seeing those jeans lying on the floor at the side of her bed last evening, he was convinced she was pregnant. He couldn't let any more doubts ruin today, which would never come again.

Stephanie's urgent plea had gotten to him and he'd put on his dress blue uniform. With nothing more than a few clues, she'd come all the way from Florida to find him, so he would know he was going to be a father. The least he could do was accede to her desires on this issue. He'd told Kon as much.

Nikos had been thinking a lot about Stephanie's father. Maybe he could be found through the help of a good private investigator. It was worth looking into, but that would have to wait until another day.

Yannis, acting in the place of her father, who would probably have given her away if he'd known of her existence, had worn his best white suit for the occasion. Nikos suspected the older seaman was enjoying this. He and Stephanie seemed to be getting along well already. Yannis was an old softie beneath his gruff looking exterior. It was clear she had already charmed him.

Nikos kept taking pictures until they reached the car. Her eyes, so solemn, met his for an instant before Yannis took over, asking them to pose together before they got inside. After some careful maneuvering to protect her dress, they helped her into the backseat, and Nikos sat in front while Yannis drove.

"Oh, Nikos!" she cried softly when they'd traveled a distance up the hillside. The small domed gray-and-white church of Agios Dionysios stood overlooking the sea. "How beautiful! I can't believe we're going to be married here."

"My wife and I were married in that same church forty years ago," Yannis said over his shoulder.

"Were you childhood sweethearts?"

"How did you know?"

Her gentle chuckle found new areas inside Nikos's body to warm. "Do you have children?"

"Two married sons and six grandchildren. They're fishermen and live here."

"You're a very lucky man."

"It was a lucky day when Nikos met you."

Well, well. Stephanie's takeover of Yannis was now complete.

"Thank you, Yannis."

The next few minutes were a blur as they pulled up to the church's parking area, where the Gregerov family was waiting *en masse* to greet them. Nikos introduced her to Tassos's parents, Castor and Tiana Gregerov, and his pretty wife, Elianna, who had dark blond hair. The other women were various shades of brunette. More pictures were taken. Nikos had hired a professional photographer to film everything.

In the rush he noticed Tassos reach for Stephanie and press something in her hand. Nikos was curious to know what it was, but he would have to wait. He saw her eyes glisten with tears before she kissed him on the cheek.

After embracing Tassos's mother, Nikos reached for Stephanie and they proceeded inside the church. He cupped her elbow, taking care with her veil, and walked to the front, where a dozen sprays of flowers filled the nave with perfume. He'd made certain there were some gardenias among the arrangements.

He had the distinct impression Stephanie was pacing herself carefully in deference to him not being able to move quite so fast. Small courtesies seemed to come naturally to her, another trait he couldn't help but admire.

Father Kerykes chatted with them before asking Tassos and Yannis to take their places on either side of the couple. The others sat in a group. For Stephanie's sake he presided in English, promising to keep it as short as possible. But as Nikos had explained to Stephanie earlier, there was no such thing as a short Greek wedding.

First came the service of the betrothal with the rings. Nikos had bought her a diamond ring, and a gold band for her to give to him, but she produced a ring he immediately recognized as Kon's. Nikos was so moved by Tassos's gesture, he choked up during the marriage sacrament.

It was followed by the crowning and ceremonial walk. Three times around the priest, who at the end removed their flowers. After they kissed the Bible, he pronounced his blessing on them.

"For better or worse, you're Mrs. Vassalos now," Nikos whispered as they walked down the aisle holding hands. "Are you feeling all right?"

"I—I'm fine." Her voice faltered. "Just thirsty."

"There's water in the vestibule, where we'll sign the documents. Then we'll go outside for more pictures."

By the time she emerged from the church with her bouquet, her cheeks looked flushed. Nikos urged everyone to hurry with the well-wishing and the pictures, but all of them were pressing for the bridal kiss. He did it swiftly, noticing Stephanie was fading fast. No wonder there was little response.

"Are you going to be sick?" he asked as he helped her into the car.

"No," she replied, but her voice trembled. "I'm just feeling weak and overheated. I'll be all right in a minute."

"In this weather a wedding like ours is brutal, but it's over now. The taverna will be cool. It's only a mile away. Drive fast, Yannis."

"I feel a fraud, Nikos. I'm a hot weather girl and don't know what happened to me in there."

"You're pregnant and have been through an arduous marriage ritual."

She lay back in the corner with her eyes closed. "Once was enough. I fought so hard not to faint in front of you."

"You made it. I'm very proud of you."

Stephanie started laughing. "I had no idea it would be an endurance test."

"Why do you think I put it off all these years?" he teased.

"Sorry. You must be stifling in your uniform. In hindsight I can see why you wanted me to wear the sundress." She let out a little moan. "I shouldn't have tried to find you in the first place. It forced you to have to go through all this."

With those words he felt as if he'd been rammed in the chest. She had no idea what was going through his mind. *"Don't ever say that again."*

Stephanie groaned. She'd said the wrong thing and had upset him, but it was the truth.

She might not have forced him with a sniper's rifle, like the ones in his closet. But the chance that this baby *could* be his had served as the ultimate weapon. Stephanie wasn't a fool. She knew he had doubts about its true paternity and wouldn't be satisfied until a DNA test was done, thus the reason for bringing up the possibility of divorce.

Over the last three months her heart had been hardened against him for his desertion of her, only to be softened after he'd insisted on either keeping her as his mistress or marrying her for the sake of their unborn child.

The *only* child he would ever have...

Their child, who would know its father and love him.

That's what this whole day had been about. She couldn't lose sight of that pertinent reality. After letting out an anxious sigh, she sat up straighter in the seat. "Forgive me for my show of temper. I can be a crosspatch sometimes. This has been a beautiful day and a wedding every bride dreams of. The flowers were beautiful and I love my ring. Thank you for making it all possible, Nikos."

"As long as you're feeling better and there's no harm to the baby, it's all that matters."

His need to protect had come out. No wonder he'd

snapped. She had to remember that and watch what she said from now on.

"We're headed for the most traditional taverna on the island, where there are few tourists. The owner's family makes their pasta and *dolmadakia* by hand. Besides oven-baked lamb and spit roast with lemon potatoes and garlic, you'll enjoy stuffed zucchini and meatballs, called *keftedes,* that melt in your mouth."

"I love meatballs."

"They're made in a tomato sauce that's out of this world."

Nikos sounded hungry.

Within fifteen minutes they were all assembled inside the authentic Greek restaurant, where everyone laughed and ate with great relish to the accompaniment of music. Stephanie found Kon's family members charming and felt the women's acceptance.

More pictures were taken, and toasts rendered, along with speeches from everyone including Yannis. It was clear they all loved Nikos. At one point he reached for her and kissed her warmly several times on the mouth, to the delight of their wedding party.

She couldn't drink alcohol and instead opted for a spoon sweet, which was a fruit embedded in syrup. "You taste delicious," he murmured as she kissed him back, always telling herself it was for the pictures that would go in the family album.

The evening wore on in a celebration she would always cherish, but when she looked around, she felt an ache in her heart that Nikos's family wasn't a part of it. As for herself, she wished her mother were still alive and could have been here.

If there'd been time, Stephanie would have invited

her friends who'd met Nikos on vacation. But it wasn't meant to be, because this had been pulled together on an emergency basis. Every flash of light from the diamond solitaire on her finger seemed to be sending a warning. *You may have had a wedding with all the trappings, but remember, it's the baby he wants, if it's his....*

She felt Nikos's gaze on her. "It's still too warm in here for you. I can see your eyelids are drooping. It's time to get you back home to bed, where you'll be cooler."

He stood up and announced they were leaving. "Stephanie and I thank you for making this day the most memorable of our lives." On that note he ushered her out of the taverna. Twilight had stolen over the island, giving it a magical feel. Nikos helped her into the car. Once more Yannis drove them down the hillside.

In the distance she saw the yacht. Nikos had called it home. Until he bought them a place here on the island to live, it would be hers, too.

Tassos and Elianna had followed them and brought half a dozen of the flower sprays from the church to decorate the lower lounge. His kindness today had touched her deeply and she gave him a hug before Nikos went up on deck with him. Besides being a good friend, he and her brand-new husband were in business together and had a lot to talk about.

Elianna started to leave, but Stephanie touched her arm. "Before you go, would you mind unbuttoning the back of my dress?" She put her veil on the couch to make it easier.

An odd smile broke out on the other woman's face. "You don't want Nikos to do it?"

Stephanie averted her eyes. "He wants to talk to Tassos right now."

"If you're sure."

"I am."

Elianna got busy. "It's the most beautiful dress I ever saw. How did you get it fastened?"

"Yannis helped me."

She let out a quiet laugh. "With all these buttons, it must have taken quite a while. Nikos didn't mind?"

"Yannis told Nikos to go away so he wouldn't see me until we left for the church."

"You are the envy of every woman in the Oinousses. People here thought he would marry Natasa Lander."

"I understand she's very lovely."

"Yes, and very rich. Her family is in shipping, too. They have the largest mansion on Chios Island. Nikos has surprised everyone."

"Our marriage surprised me, too," Stephanie said in a tremulous voice.

"Tassos tells me you two met on vacation in the Caribbean before the explosion happened."

"Yes. We were both scuba diving and paired up to explore." She was tempted to tell Elianna she was pregnant, but then thought the better of it, since Nikos hadn't chosen to tell Tassos yet.

"Ah. Nikos and Kon tried to teach me, but I got too frightened and couldn't control my breathing. I panicked."

"With more practice, you can overcome your fear of it, Elianna. I'd be happy to work with you if you'd like."

"Tassos wants me to dive with him."

"It's a beautiful world under the sea. If you can shake your fear, you'll learn to love it."

Stephanie felt the last button release and turned around. "What do you say?"

"Maybe I'll try again with your help."

"That's wonderful! I'll call you in a few days. We'll have lunch and make plans. Bring your baby. How old is he?"

"Theo is ten months and trying to walk."

"I can't wait to see him."

Elianna's dark brown eyes widened in surprise. "You won't be on your honeymoon?"

"We already had ours in the Caribbean. Right now Nikos is anxious to get started on the drilling with your husband. Since the accident that killed Kon, Yannis tells me he's been morose and unhappy. Now that he can't be in the navy, he needs to plunge into something else."

The other woman nodded. "Everyone took Kon's death hard, especially Tassos. He's thrilled that Nikos is interested in his ideas to start their own company."

"Then we need to help them. Right?"

They stared at each other for a moment before she nodded. "Yes. I'm glad he married you."

"I'm glad, too." If Elianna only knew the half of it. "Thank you for helping me." She gave her a hug before they parted.

While Tassos's wife disappeared up the stairs, Stephanie reached for the veil and walked down the hall to her bedroom to remove her wedding finery. First she stepped out of her dress and underskirt, which she hung in the closet. What a relief, so her stomach could expand! Another week and she wouldn't have been able to wear a size 4. The shop probably wouldn't have sold that gown any larger.

After a quick shower, she wrapped herself in her plaid flannel robe, then folded the veil with care and put it on the shelf above. Since she had no idea how long Nikos would be, she decided now would be the perfect time to phone Melinda.

With the room pleasantly cool, she lay down on top of the bed to make the call. So much had happened since her arrival in Greece, it felt like a century instead of a few days since she'd talked to her friend, let alone seen her.

After three rings Melinda picked up. "I'm so glad it's you, Steph. I've been worried."

"Don't be. Everything's fine. I have a lot to tell you, but if this is a bad time—"

"No, no. I'm taking a late lunch. Tell me what's going on. I'm dying to know how your hunch is panning out. Are you onto anything?"

Stephanie sat up, almost crushing the phone in her hand. "I found him, Melinda."

"You're kidding…"

"No. His real name is Nikos Vassalos. I don't know how much time I have before he comes to find me, so I'll make this quick."

For the next few minutes she told her what she could, ending with, "We were married a little while ago and now we're back on the yacht."

"Wait, wait, wait. You're *married?*"

"Yes, and I won't be coming back to Florida until after the baby is born and it's safe to fly." A noise in the hall attracted her attention, followed by a tap on the door. "Listen, Melinda— I'm not alone. I'll have to call you tomorrow. *Ciao.*"

She hung up and tightened the belt on her robe before opening the door. Nikos was still dressed in his uniform. His dark gorgeous looks affected her the same way they'd done on the island when she'd first laid eyes on him. She couldn't breathe then, either.

"I take it Tassos and Elianna have gone?"

He nodded. "I could hear your voice just now."

"Yes. I was talking to Melinda."

His black eyes searched the depths of hers. "Elianna told me you've invited her over in a few days."

Nervous, Stephanie clasped the lapels of her robe. "Yes, if that's all right. But if you have other plans for us, I'll phone her and we'll decide on a later time for a visit. I just assumed you would want to get back to work." When he didn't respond, she added, "Ours isn't a conventional marriage, and my coming to Greece interrupted everything. I don't want you to think you have to entertain me."

"Elianna told me you were going to try and help her get over her fear of scuba diving. How did she know you're an expert?"

At the way his brows furrowed, alarm shot through Stephanie's body. "While she was helping me out of my dress, I mentioned that we met scuba diving in the Caribbean. Did I say something wrong?"

He undid his tie and removed it in a way that made her pulse pick up speed. "Have you forgotten you're having a baby? You told me you were giving up diving."

"Nikos…that doesn't mean I can't swim at all. A little exercise for pleasure will be good for me. As for helping her, I won't be descending with her. I'll only work with her on the surface and encourage her until she overcomes her fear. Tassos wants her to do it, but she would probably feel better around someone like me who doesn't intimidate her."

"You mean Tassos *does,*" Nikos drawled in a tone with an edge.

"He's her husband. She wants him to be proud of her, not watch her struggle."

In a quick move Nikos unbuttoned the jacket of his uniform. "Anytime you go in the water, I intend to be close by." With that parting remark, he started walking down the corridor.

"Wait…"

He paused midstride and looked back.

"Is Yannis still on board?"

"No. He won't be coming until morning. Why?"

That meant they weren't going out to sea. "I just wanted to thank him for everything he did for me today."

Nikos turned to face her. "It was no penance for him to button you up. He asked my permission, by the way. Yannis was worried you had no one to attend you."

Silly as it was, she felt heat swarm her cheeks. "He was very sweet."

"You can tell him that tomorrow."

She shoved her hands in her robe pockets. "Let me thank you now for making this day perfect. The Gregerov family couldn't have been kinder. I can see why you feel so close to them. I—I wish I'd been able to meet Kon." She stuttered over the words. "Your heart must have been touched to receive his ring."

"You can't imagine. It belonged to his grandfather, who gave it to him before he died. Kon wore it until he entered the military, then put it away to make sure nothing would happen to it until he retired. He planned to give it to a son if he ever had one."

Stephanie heard tears in Nikos's voice. She wasn't at all surprised at the depth of his grief and understood more than ever why she'd found him so broken when she'd first collided with him on board. "I'm sure Kon would have wanted you to have it."

She bit her lip, not knowing what else to say to comfort him. In fact, she feared her talking was irritating him. "Do you mind if I go up on deck for a while?"

He gave an elegant shrug of his shoulders. "This is your home. You can do whatever you like. When I was in town this morning, I bought some English speaking films on disk, which you can watch in the lounge. I won't set the security alarm until we're ready for bed."

"Thank you," she said to his retreating back.

After drinking some water from the galley, Stephanie went up on deck to take in the wonder of the night. She'd always lived by the water, but no place in her experience lived up to the beauty of these isolated islands set like glittering jewels on dark velvet.

Time passed, but Nikos still didn't join her. She had assumed that, in marrying her, he intended to sleep with her. She didn't know and he hadn't spelled out a detail like that, but without love on his part, she wouldn't be able to respond.

The problem was this was their wedding night. The kisses he'd given her at the restaurant had felt like a prelude to making love, but maybe they'd been for show. *For the photographs.*

Deciding not to wait for him any longer, she went below. There was no sign of him in the lounge. She could go down the hall and knock on his door. Was he waiting for her to come to him? Stephanie had no idea what to do. When they'd been together on the island, he'd never left her alone.

But they weren't married then, and he'd never intended to propose to her. They'd found intense pleasure together, but in his mind it had been temporary until he returned to his unit and ultimately to Natasa Lander.

Even leaving the other woman out of it, the more Stephanie thought about the situation, the more she understood that if he still didn't believe she was carrying his child, he wouldn't want to sleep with her. Maybe the thought was distasteful, even repugnant to him. Shivering at the possibility, she made up her mind never to expect a physical relationship with him.

After brushing her teeth, she took a pill and turned out the light. But once she was under the covers another thought came to her, with such force she let out a small cry and sat up. She didn't know why she hadn't considered it before. Since he was sterile, it was more than possible he was impotent, too.

Nikos...

If that was the case, then her heart grieved for him. He was such a proud man, it was only natural that since the explosion he wouldn't want to marry Natasa or *any* woman.

But he'd trusted Stephanie enough to marry her in order to give their child a father. In the process he'd become her husband in name only, to make it legitimate while he waited to find out the results of the DNA test. The dots were lining up.

No wonder he hadn't wanted his family to be a part

of today's nuptials. Everything was based on whether or not he was the father. She fell back and buried her face in the pillow to stifle her tears until oblivion took over.

CHAPTER SEVEN

THERE WAS AN animal suffering in the darkness. Stephanie kept looking for it, but couldn't find it. The whimpering turned into moans, torturing her. If only she could do something to help it. When it let out a piercing cry, the sound brought her awake.

All this time she'd been dreaming!

Trembling, she shot out of bed, incredulous that her mind had conjured anything so terrible. Something she'd eaten at the restaurant must not have agreed with her. Maybe a drink of water would help. She hurried to the bathroom. When she reached for a cup, her watch said 3:30.

After draining it, she went back to bed, but before she could fall asleep again she heard another blood-curdling cry. This time she wasn't dreaming. Without hesitation she threw on her robe and ran down the hall to Nikos's room. Though she knocked several times, he didn't respond. That was odd.

She knocked again before turning the door handle, hoping he wouldn't mind the intrusion. One glance inside the room told her he hadn't been to bed. It was still made. Had he gone to town?

Again she heard a moan, louder this time. It was

coming from the deck. An animal had to be trapped there. Maybe a cat or a dog, but she hadn't heard the security alarm go off. Needing something to protect her, she grabbed a fluffy bath towel from the bathroom and gingerly went up the stairs.

Once she was on deck the cry sounded like human sobbing. It was coming from the area of the transom. She walked toward it, then stopped dead in her tracks. There, crouching on the floor, was a man in a pair of sweats and nothing else. A crumpled blanket and sun bed lay nearby. He was on his knees with his head in his hands. As she got closer, she put a palm over her mouth.

Nikos!

Except it wasn't the man she knew. This version of him wasn't cognizant of the world right now. In a deep sleep, he was heaving great sobs, and fell over on his side. In the moonlight his tortured features glistened with moisture. Greek words broke from his lips. She couldn't make out anything except Kon's name, which he cried over and over again.

He'd been reliving the explosion. She knew about PTSD, but she'd never been with someone who was in the middle of a flashback. Without conscious thought she sank down on the sunbed next to him and put her arms around him.

"Nikos, wake up! This is just a bad dream." She rocked him for a few minutes, but he was too immersed. At one point he grasped her arm and let out a scream that raised the hairs on the back of her neck.

"It's all right, Nikos. It's over. Go back to sleep."

He twisted and turned, but held on while he sobbed on and off for another half hour. His fingers bit into her skin through the thin material of her robe, with such force she knew she'd have bruises. As terrifying as it was to see him like this, she felt a new closeness to him. His cries let her into his psyche, where he suffered. He'd seen the horrors of war, but the explosion that blew up his friend had traumatized him dramatically, and she was a vicarious witness.

Her gaze flew to Kon's ring. The reminder of their friendship must have set him off during his sleep. While she kissed Nikos's face, she put her leg over his to help quiet him, and murmured endearments.

Nothing seemed to help. Not at first. Then slowly, his fingers slid away and he fell quiet. Yannis would know all about this. Tomorrow Stephanie would get him alone and find out the name of Nikos's doctor. He needed help getting through his nightmares.

She held on to him. He'd said this yacht was home to him now. Had he decided to sleep up here? If so, how often did he do that? A few days ago, when she'd explored the lower deck, she'd noticed his unmade bed. The poor darling had probably suffered these incidents since being hospitalized.

Did he have more than one episode a night? She'd read that a flashback could be triggered by something and come on at any time. While he stayed on this yacht, he could be away from people.

It made perfect sense that he didn't want to be with family. But what if he hurt himself while up here on deck? What if he walked in his sleep and fell overboard? She'd heard the military wouldn't take sleepwalkers because they could be a danger to themselves and others.

After a few more minutes she eased away from him

and got to her feet. In his trauma, he'd flung his arm around and his elbow had caught the corner of her jaw. Both it and her arm felt sore, but it didn't matter. She covered him with the blanket, then reached for the towel and sat down in the lounger to watch over him. It was quarter to six. Who knew how long he'd sleep?

Since her arrival, he'd been watching her like a hawk because of the baby. What an irony, since it was *his* welfare she would be worrying about, along with her own, from here on out! He could injure himself without realizing it. She couldn't bear it if anything happened to him.

Before this new day was over, she planned to talk to his doctor. Nikos needed watching. One thing was certain: Stephanie wouldn't let him go to bed without her. Wherever he chose to sleep, that's where she'd be.

She'd sat there for another half hour when she saw Yannis come on board. The second their gazes met, she got up without making a sound and padded across the deck toward him.

"So you know," he whispered with a grave expression.

"Yes. I heard him during the night and came up to investigate. He's resting now, but I need to talk to his doctor."

He nodded. "The one he sees now is at the main clinic here on the island." The same place her new OB practiced. "His name is Dr. Ganis."

"Thank you. I'm glad you're back. I don't want him to know I heard anything until I've talked to the doctor."

"I think that would be best."

"Does he have flashbacks often?"

"Since he got out of the hospital, he had one the first night on the yacht, and last night."

"The wedding must have triggered thoughts of Kon. I'd better go below so he doesn't know I was up here."

"That's a good idea. He'll notice the red mark along your jaw."

Yannis didn't miss much. "I'll cover it with makeup." She patted his arm before hurrying toward the stairs.

The first thing she did on entering her room was get the card for her appointment out of her purse. Once she found it, she phoned the off-hours service at the clinic and left word for Dr. Ganis to call her back ASAP. As soon as she mentioned it was Mrs. Nikos Vassalos calling about her husband, the receptionist said she'd get in touch with the doctor right away.

For the next hour Stephanie got ready for the day. First her pills, then she took a shower and washed her hair. By the time she'd finished blow drying it, marks had come out on her left arm. She'd been afraid of that.

An application of makeup to the small blotch near her chin helped, plus a coating of mango frost lipstick. Then she headed for the closet. Stephanie thanked providence she'd had the foresight to buy a long-sleeved blouse. It was an all-over print in a gauzy fabric that hung just below the waist. She put it on and matched it with a pair of white pleated pants that accommodated her thickening figure.

Stephanie had just put on some lotion when the phone rang. She grabbed for it and clicked on immediately. It was Dr. Ganis's nurse, who indicated he had an opening at 11:00 a.m. if she could make it. Stephanie said she'd be there and hung up.

Things couldn't be working out better. She'd

planned to go into town, anyway, and buy some picture albums. While she was at it, she'd look for a handicraft store in order to start making a quilt for the baby. While Nikos did business, she intended to stay busy and not bother him.

Nikos had told her she could use the car. While she left him alone to work, she would carry on with her new life. Besides loving to explore new places, Stephanie liked to cook. She could shop for food and fix their meals from now on. This evening she planned to prepare a totally American meal and surprise him. She wanted to help him. There was no use kidding herself any longer. She loved him desperately.

Once Nikos had showered and shaved, he got dressed and walked down the hall. Just as he knocked on Stephanie's door, she stepped out of the bedroom and then collided, wringing a small cry from her. He grabbed her arms to steady her. To his surprise he saw her wince. Not only that, he noticed a slight bruise along her jaw that hadn't been there when she'd gone to bed last night.

"You've hurt yourself!"

She averted her eyes. "It's nothing." She tried to ease away, but he prevented her from walking out the door.

"What's wrong with your arms?"

"Not a thing."

"Since you're wearing long sleeves, I'll be the judge of that. Let me see." With care he pushed the sleeve of her blouse up her right arm, but found nothing. When he did the same thing to the left, it was a tug-of-war, but he prevailed and saw bruising both above and below the elbow. "Who did this to you, Stephanie?"

"No one. When I was in the galley, I was clumsy getting something down from the cupboard. It hit my jaw and jammed my arm against the counter by accident."

"I don't believe you. Look at me." When she refused, he said, "These marks were made by someone's hand. You're trembling. Tell me the truth."

Finally, she lifted her eyes to him. Those dark blue pools stared at him in pain. "About three-thirty this morning I heard moaning sounds coming from the deck and thought it was an animal. When I went up to see…"

Nikos drew in a burning breath. "You found *me*."

"Yes. I knelt down to try and comfort you."

He raked a hand through his hair, gutted to think she'd seen him like that and he didn't even remember it. "I could have done real damage to you and the baby. I could have given you a permanent injury, or worse!"

"But you didn't, Nikos. You were jerking, but you weren't violent and didn't walk around. Mostly you were crying Kon's name. I wouldn't have let myself get close to you otherwise."

"I should have told you about my PTSD. The doctor gave me medicine, but sometimes the nightmares come on, anyway. By not saying a word to you, I put you at risk and have done the unforgivable."

"That's not true!" She cupped his face between her hands. "I'm glad I saw you like that. It helped to understand what you've been going through since the explosion. You've suffered so terribly. All I wanted to do was calm you down." She kissed his lips. "After a little while you started to sleep peacefully again. I sat there until Yannis came on board."

Nikos backed away from her. "Forgive me."

"For deserting me on our wedding night?" she teased.

"You know what I mean." He rapped out the words angrily.

"Nikos, there's nothing to forgive. Now that I know, I have a suggestion, because I'm worried about you sleeping up on deck when one of those flashbacks hits. As you told me on the way out of the church, I'm your wife now, for better or worse, so why don't we sleep in the room with the twin beds? That way we can keep an eye on each other. When you have a bad night, you'll be safe and so will I."

"I'm not safe to be around anyone, especially not you when you're pregnant."

"Where did you get an idea like that? Thousands of soldiers come home from war with battle fatigue. They resume their lives with their wives, who are pregnant or not, and they work things out. To be honest, I asked Yannis for the name of your doctor this morning. I have an appointment at eleven. I'd like to hear what he has to say, and want you to come with me. But if you won't, I'm going anyway, because I need to know the best way to help you."

She headed for the galley. Nikos followed her and watched her reach for a roll. She darted him a glance. "Have you had breakfast?"

"I couldn't." He wasn't able to tolerate the thought of food after what he'd done to her. "Stop being so damn brave."

"That's what I've wanted to say to you since I saw that cane you've refused to use in front of me. Why don't we agree that *you've* tried to be brave long enough? Now it's time for us to be totally honest with each other. Otherwise how are we ever going to get through the rest of this pregnancy without losing our minds?"

Totally honest?

Since Stephanie had shown up on board the *Diomedes,* he wasn't sure he was in control of his mind or his fears. Deep down he wanted the baby to be his more than anything in this world.

She poured herself a glass of orange juice and drank it. "I'm planning to do some grocery shopping while we're in town."

"We just stocked up a few days ago."

"Have you forgotten you've picked up an American wife since then? She'd like to make you some of her favorite foods." He blinked. "Oh, and will you bring the camera? We can take it to a print shop and have the pictures downloaded so we can mount them."

He cocked his head, amazed by this unexpected domestic side of her. Being with Stephanie on vacation hadn't prepared him for this aspect of her. "Anything else?"

She flashed him a full, unguarded smile that knocked him sideways, though the sight of the bruise on her jaw tortured him. "Since we don't know the gender of the baby yet, I think I'll work up a white puffy quilt and stencil it with the outline of a lamb. I'd love your input on the materials."

She washed out her glass in the sink. "I'll get my purse and see you at the car. If not, would you give me the keys?"

He ground his teeth. "I'm coming with you." As they left for town it occurred to him he needed to buy them a house, preferably today. The yacht was a great place for him to do business with Tassos, but it was no place for a woman whose nesting instincts had already kicked in.

While Nikos waited for her outside the local photo shop, he called Tassos, who knew of a villa he'd had in mind for Nikos for a while. It was in a more exclusive area of town that would be perfect for them.

With a phone call to a friend who was a Realtor, he made the arrangements and gave Nikos the address. The man agreed to meet Nikos and Stephanie there at one o'clock. That would give them enough time to see the doctor first.

It seemed to make Dr. Ganis's day to find out Nikos was married to a wife who intended to be proactive over his PTSD. He gave them a card they should both read regularly, but all the time he spoke, he couldn't take his eyes off her.

Nikos had already come to learn that with Stephanie's blond beauty and lithe figure, taking her out in public was proving to be a hazard. He could already count one traffic accident because the male driver had taken one look at her and driven right into the back of another car. It served the poor devil right.

Nikos read what was on the card.

Always be truthful with your vet, always keep safety in mind. Don't walk on eggshells. Grieve for what is lost and move on. Stay on top of medications. Short periods of withdrawal to help control anger make sense, but withdrawing from life into a "bunker" is not helpful. Conflict is normal. Focus on the issue at hand and resist bringing up

issues from the past. Exercise, get regular meals,
good nutrition, plenty of rest and time for play.
Enjoy the good times. When bad times come, hang
on. Good times will come again.

As they got up to leave his office, Stephanie won
the doctor over with her final comment. "I consider
these bruises *my* mark of bravery." His laughter followed them out the door.

Unable to help himself, Nikos gave her waist a
squeeze as they left the clinic for the car. "Do you mind
if we put off all the shopping until tomorrow? I have
a surprise for you that could take up most of our day.
Let's grab a bite to eat before we meet Mr. Doukakis."

Stephanie couldn't imagine what it was. However, she
was so happy to see that Nikos had forgiven himself
for the bruises, and seemed to be in a mellower mood,
that she didn't care what they did as long as it was together. When he'd interrogated her in the doorway of
her bedroom earlier that morning, she'd been frightened that irreparable damage had been done to their
relationship.

At one of the sidewalk cafés she ordered a lime
crush drink and discovered she adored the bruschetta
made with apple and goat cheese. Nikos downed a
whole loaf of lamb rolled slices. Taking the doctor's
advice, he passed on caffeine-laden coffee and ordered
decaf. Stephanie made a mental note to buy the same,
so he would sleep better.

When she couldn't eat another bite, he drove them
up a hillside covered with flowering vegetation. They
came to a charming, two-story villa, where he stopped

behind the car parked in front. The man at the wheel had to be this Mr. Doukakis he'd mentioned.

She flicked a glance at Nikos's striking profile. "What are we doing?"

He shut off the engine and turned to her. "Hoping to buy us a house."

What? "But I thought—"

"Let's not go there." He cut her off. "I'll use the yacht for business, but decorating one of the rooms below deck for a nursery is absurd."

"I agree, and have no intention of doing any such thing. As for the quilt, it'll be a gift for our baby. I'm looking forward to making it, that's all."

"You're avoiding the issue, Stephanie, and I know why. If you don't like the looks of this house, we'll find something better."

Just when she'd been on a real high, he'd sprung this on her. Already she could see the writing on the wall. While she was at the house, he'd work late, then call to tell her he was staying on the yacht overnight. No way!

"I don't want a house, not with you coming and going when the mood takes you."

"You mean you don't like *this* one," he thundered. "If you want a mansion, just say so and I'll accommodate you."

Now *she* was angry. "I thought we left that issue in the past, but I can see you won't let it go, about me wanting to marry you for your money. For your information, I *love* living on the water."

She watched his hands grip the wheel tighter. "It's no place for a baby."

"The baby won't be here for months! Why did you bother to marry me, Nikos? Sticking me in a house will make me feel like a kept woman. I thought you'd been honest with me, but you weren't."

His features had turned into a dark mask of anger. Good!

"Since it obviously irritates you to have a woman around, I'll settle for living on my own boat, to stay out of your way. Instead of a house, buy me one of those little one-person sailboats bobbing at the marina on Egnoussa. I'll pay you as much as I can when the condo sells."

"Don't say another word, Stephanie."

"You started this, so I'll say what I like. It would cost only a fraction of what it would take to buy me a mansion I don't want to live in by myself. Or better yet, let me *rent* a sailboat. That would be fair. Yannis could take me to pick one out, and bring it across to moor by the yacht. 'His and hers.' We'll be the talk of the island."

While she was still shaking from their angry clash, he got out of the car and walked to the other one. The two men spoke for a few minutes before Nikos came back and levered himself into the front seat once more.

She sensed he'd love to wheel away on screeching tires, but he controlled himself on the drive back to the dock. By the time they reached the parking area, she'd repented of the way she'd blown up at him.

The doctor's advice came to mind. Conflict was normal. Focus on the issue at hand, not past issues.

"Wait, Nikos," she said as he opened the door. "I apologize for my behavior. Instead of welcoming your gift, I threw it back in your face. I'm so sorry. Please forgive me."

He shifted his gaze to her. "I should have prepared you for what I had in mind."

She shook her head. "I'm afraid my reaction would have been the same. Look, I realize you were happy living by yourself on the yacht with Yannis. Then I came along and disturbed your world. If I promise not to be a nuisance or get in your way, can we start over? But I can't just be a lump around here. Give me a job and I'll do it, besides my share of the cleaning."

One dark brow lifted. "You really want to cook?"

"Yes. As many meals as you'll let me."

"Then so be it. That'll free up me and Yannis to do other work." Nikos closed the door. "Let's drive to the market. Ever since you mentioned American food, I've been relishing the thought of it."

Stephanie sighed in relief that they'd survived another skirmish. "Thank you. I promise you won't regret this."

Following her fried chicken for dinner that evening, both men finished off the apple pie. The fact that there were no leftovers told her she'd hit a home run on her first try.

Yannis got up from the table and winked at her. "If all your meals are this good, I'm going to put on weight."

"I'm glad you liked it."

After he disappeared, Nikos sat back in his chair with the hint of a smile. "I guess you know you're permanently hired. I'd help you with the dishes, but we're headed for Engoussa right now. I need to assist Yannis."

"Do you have business there?"

"Yes. I want my parents to meet you tonight."

Her heart started racing. "Do they know about us?"

"Not yet. I phoned and told them I'd be coming by. They'll send a car. It's time they met their daughter-in-law, before the news of our wedding reaches them."

The surprising revelation filled Stephanie with ambiguous feelings, of relief that their secret would be out, and anxiety because she wanted to make a good impression for Nikos's sake. "I'll wear the long-sleeved blouse with one of my new skirts."

He nodded his dark head. "Stephanie…" The way he said her name made her think he was dead serious. "Follow my lead and don't let my father intimidate you."

After Nikos left the galley, she put their plates in the dishwasher, already feeling intimidated. She wished she knew what kind of deep-seated trouble lay between Nikos and his father. If he'd just given her a hint…

She dressed for the evening, then waited up on deck as the yacht pulled up alongside the dock on Egnoussa. Fairyland at night. Few people were out.

Nikos joined her, looking fabulous in a silky black shirt toned with dark gray trousers. To her surprise he'd brought his cane. This was a first. Using it for support, he reached out with his free hand and grasped hers. They left the yacht and started walking along the pier, toward a black car she could see waiting in the distance.

It appeared the ordeal he was about to face had drained him physically. Stephanie would do everything in her power to help him. As they reached the car, she gave his hand a squeeze. But whatever his reaction might have been was lost when a stunning dark blond woman with appealing brown eyes opened the door and stepped out of the driver's seat.

"Nikolaos. It's been such a long time."

"Natasa." He let go of Stephanie's hand long enough to kiss the woman on both cheeks. "I didn't know you were on the island."

Stephanie felt de trop. This was the woman he would probably have married if Fate hadn't stepped in to change his life.

"When I heard you were coming, I arrived early and asked your parents if I could meet you at the dock so we could talk in private. They assumed you'd be alone. Who's your friend?"

Nikos turned to Stephanie. "This is Stephanie Walsh from Florida, in the States. She arrived a few days ago. Stephanie? This is Natasa Lander, an old friend."

"How do you do, Ms. Lander."

In the semidark, Natasa's face lost color. "Ms. Walsh," she acknowledged. "How is it you know Nikos?"

Stephanie groaned inwardly for this poor woman, who'd carried a torch for him all these years. It was no wonder. How could any other man compare?

"I was on a scuba diving vacation in the Caribbean months ago and we met."

"Why don't I drive?" Nikos offered. "When we reach the house, we can all catch up on each other's news at once."

Nikos... This was a terrible idea, but what could she do? While he helped Natasa into the backseat, Stephanie grabbed his cane and hurried around to the front to get in. As far as she was concerned, this was worse than any nightmare.

En route, Nikos chatted with Natasa the way you'd do with an old friend, drawing her out, until they reached the impressive Vassalos mansion with its cream-and-beige exterior. His ancestral home stood near the top of the hill next to equally imposing ones Stephanie had seen on her first day here. The burnt-orange-tiled roofs added a certain symmetry that gave the town its charm.

He pulled the car around to the rear and parked. Both Stephanie and Natasa moved quickly, not waiting for his help. Natasa went in the rear entrance first. Stephanie handed Nikos his cane, but he put it back in the car, then reached for her hand.

"Ready?" he asked under his breath. That forbidding black glitter in his eyes had returned. It was clear he hadn't been expecting Natasa. Stephanie suspected the other woman's appearance had been orchestrated by Nikos's father. Yet unseen, the older man made an adversary that caused the hairs on the back of her neck to stand up.

When she nodded with reluctance, she heard his sharp intake of breath. "Maybe this will help." He pulled her into his arms and found her mouth, kissing her with a fierceness she wasn't prepared for, almost as if he was expecting her to fight him.

Stephanie clung to him, helpless to do anything else, and met the hunger of his kiss with an eagerness she would find embarrassing later. At last he was giving her a husband's kiss, hot with desire, the one she'd been denied last night. Whether he was doing this to convince himself he was glad he hadn't married Natasa, she didn't know. But right now she didn't care.

The way he was kissing her took her back to that unforgettable night on the island, when they'd given each other everything with a matchless joy she couldn't put into words. He pressed her against the doorjamb to get closer. One kiss after another made her crazy with desire. Stephanie was so in love with Nikos that nothing existed for her but to love him and be loved.

All of a sudden she heard a man's voice delivering a volley of bitter words in Greek. It broke the spell. Gasping for breath, she put her hands against Nikos's chest. He was much slower to react. Eventually, he let her go, with seeming reluctance.

Still staring at her, he said, "Good evening, Papa. Stephanie and I will be right in. Give us a minute more, will you?"

Another blast of angry words greeted her ears.

"She doesn't speak Greek, Papa."

"How dare you bring this gold digging American into our home!"

That was clear enough English for Stephanie, who was thankful Nikos was still holding her. She eyed his father covertly. Except for their height, the formidable older man with gray hair didn't look like Nikos.

"I dare because she's my wife. We were married in a private church service yesterday. I wanted you to be the first to know."

"Then we'll get it annulled," he answered, without taking a breath.

"Not possible, Papa. Father Kerykes officiated. Naturally, I expect you and Mother to welcome Stephanie into the family. If you don't, then you'll never be allowed to see your grandchild."

Stephanie could hardly breathe. Nikos was claiming their child as his own even though he didn't have proof?

"So you *are* pregnant!" his father virtually snarled

at her. "I told Nikos I suspected as much when I heard you'd come to Egnoussa to track him down. Trying to pass off your baby as my son's? There's a word for a woman like you."

The man had just provided part of the source for Nikos's basic distrust of her. She eased away from him and stared at his dad without flinching. "I'm sorry you feel that way, Mr. Vassalos. I've been anxious to meet the father of such a wonderful, honorable man. You're both very lucky. I never knew my father.

"But I have to say I'm sad you're on such bad terms. Our baby is going to want to know its grandparents. I can only hope that one day you'll change your mind about me enough to allow us into your life. Now if you'll excuse me, I'm going to wait in the car while Nikos spends some time with you and your wife. *Kalinihta.*"

Good night was one of the few words in Greek she'd picked up, from listening to Nikos and Yannis.

No sooner had she climbed in the front seat and shut the door than Nikos joined her behind the wheel. He didn't speak the whole time they drove to the port. Stephanie knew better than to talk, but her heart was heavy for him and the tragic situation with his father.

After he pulled around to the parking area of Vassalos Shipping, Nikos left the keys on the floor of the car and they walked back to the yacht. "I want to get to know your family, Nikos, but I couldn't possibly stay in their house, since it would cause too much stress for everyone.

"Much as I want to make things right, I can't tolerate your father's attitude or the way he spoke about me.

Maybe in time things will get better. I could hope for that, but not right now. I trust you understand."

Silence followed her remarks, until he helped her step on the deck. "I owe you an explanation."

She threw her head back, catching sight of his tormented expression. "If you mean that kiss you gave me at the back door was supposed to be an in-your-face gesture for your father's digestion, I already got the message."

"If you think that, you couldn't be more wrong," Nikos grated. "Just when I thought my father had run out of tricks, there he was once again, trying to set me up with Natasa. But this time you were there. No amount of makeup could conceal the bruise on your jaw. It stood out in the moonlight, reminding me that you'd unwisely faced my demons and held me during the night, despite the consequences to you and the baby.

"Tonight I realized how very beautiful you are and how courageous to have forgotten yourself to help me. No one has ever been that self-sacrificing for me. In a rush of emotion I felt the need to show you how I felt. Since my father chose that moment to appear, then he has to live with that picture, because I refuse to apologize for something that had nothing to do with him."

Stephanie swallowed hard. Nikos's sincerity defeated her. "Do you think Natasa saw us?"

He gave an elegant shrug of his shoulders. "If she did, let's hope it was cathartic."

For the other woman's sake, Stephanie hoped so, too, and looked away. "I would have liked to have met your mother."

"One day I'll introduce you to her and the whole family. They're very nice people."

One day. That sounded so lonely.

"Nikos…about the baby—"

The mere mention of it brought a look of anxiety to his dark eyes. "Are you all right?"

"I'm fine!" she assured him, not wanting to add to his worries. "I was just surprised you told your father."

Nikos's hard body tautened. "Hearing the truth from my lips has put an end to his dream of my marrying Natasa in order to consolidate our families. He's been stuck in that groove for a decade. Since I've refused to work in the company, he has lost his hold on me."

Stephanie drew closer to him. "What's he afraid of?"

Nikos studied her for a long moment. "At one time he thought I was Costor Gregerov's son."

It took a second for Stephanie's brain to compute. When it did, she let out a gasp. "Your mother and Kon's father?" Surely she'd misunderstood.

"It's complicated. My mother and Kon's mother were best friends growing up on Oinoussa. My parents married first and had two children before I came along. But Tiana's eventual marriage to Costor brought a lot of grief to her family, because he's part Turkish.

"In some corners of society, the Greeks and Turks refuse to mix. The built-in prejudice against him caused a painful division. For Tiana, it was she against the world once she'd married Costor. They had four children before Kon came along."

As Nikos peeled back the layers, Stephanie's anguish for his pain grew.

"My mother defended Tiana's decision and was always sympathetic to Costor. At one point someone started a rumor that she got too close to him. It wasn't true, and both my mother and Costor always denied it, but my father was a bigoted man. He believed it and there was an ugly falling out that never healed."

Stephanie bit her lip. "DNA testing wasn't available when you were born."

"No, but it wasn't needed. As Tiana once told me, the stamp of a Vassalos was unmistakable. Unfortunately, my parents' marriage suffered. It's a miracle my mother didn't leave him, but she loves him. She remained close friends with Tiana, which threw me and Kon together, but the damage done to both families during those early years was incalculable."

Stephanie clutched the railing. "What a tragedy."

Nikos nodded. "My father became controlling and possessive. He tried to rule my life and choose my associates, making sure I didn't mix with people like Kon's family. By my teens he'd cultivated a friendship with the Lander family, laying the groundwork for the future he envisioned for me. But he went too far when I was forbidden to spend any more time with Kon, who'd become like a brother to me. Naturally, I defied my father, because Kon had done nothing wrong."

Stephanie darted him a glance. "Except to be a constant reminder of the past."

Nikos breathed deeply. "Everything reached a boiling point when Kon needed money for his divorce. I gave him what I'd saved from working. My father found out and threatened to disown me. I told him it wouldn't be necessary, because Kon and I had already joined the navy and would be shipping out."

The night breeze had sprung up, lifting the hair off Stephanie's cheek. "You and Kon shouldn't have had to suffer for your father's paranoia. How long did it take him to beg your forgiveness?"

"His pride won't allow him to beg. For my mother's sake I visited them on leave, but things have never been the same. Underneath he's still a bigot and distrustful."

"Evidently he doesn't like Americans, either," she whispered.

"He's predisposed to dislike anyone whom he imagines might have control over me. I invested my military pay and bought the *Diomedes* so I would never have to be beholden to him."

Heartsick for Nikos, Stephanie looked at her husband through new eyes. Here she'd suffered all her life, wishing she knew anything about her father, while Nikos... Her ache for him grew worse. "I can't tell you how sorry I am."

"You've married into a complicated family. Don't try to sort it all out tonight. You look tired, which comes as no surprise after your wrestling match with me last night."

Stephanie would do it again and again if he'd let her, but after this incident with his father, she sensed he was unreachable. True enough, his next words left her in no doubt.

"You go below. I'll stay up here and wait for Yannis. As soon as he comes, we'll leave port and head back to Oinoussa."

CHAPTER EIGHT

September 1

NIKOS HAD SEEN his wife in a bikini when they swam on one of the isolated beaches. Oftentimes Elianna came with them. With the growing evidence of her pregnancy, there'd been a decided change in her since April, when they'd met. But he broke out in a cold sweat as he watched the doctor spread the gel on Stephanie's tummy to do a Doppler ultrasound.

"Ooh, that's cold."

"All my patients say that."

"Are you all right?"

"Of course she is." Dr. Panos smiled at Nikos. "Sit down, Kyrie Vassalos, and watch the screen. We'll take a peek inside to see how your baby is progressing. This will take about ten minutes."

Nikos couldn't sit. More than his concern about the gender of the baby was the fear that something might show up to indicate a problem. The doctor moved the probe over her belly. Pretty soon the sound of a heartbeat filled the examination room.

"Can you hear that?" Stephanie cried in excitement.

"Your baby has a good, strong heartbeat. Keep watching the screen."

Whether it was his baby or not, Nikos stood there mesmerized by the sight of pictures that gave evidence of the living miracle growing inside her.

The doctor nodded. "I like what I see."

"Then it's healthy?" Stephanie's anxious question echoed that of Nikos.

"At this stage everything looks fine and normal. The baby could fit in the palm of your hand."

Yet you could see it was a perfect baby. Nikos could only shake his head in awe.

"But it needs to turn for me if we're going to find out its gender." Dr. Panos pressed in various spots. "I know you're uncomfortable after drinking all that water, Stephanie. Just a few more minutes, then you can use the bathroom."

She let out a big sigh. "As long as there's nothing wrong, I don't care if it's a boy or a girl."

Since the night she'd held him during a flashback, Nikos had secretly worried he might have damaged the baby in some way. At the good news, exquisite relief swamped him.

Though she'd promised not to come near him at night, that fear had caused him to lock his bedroom door when he went to bed so she wouldn't try to help him during an episode. Much as he desired sleeping with her, even if it would only be in the cabin with twin beds, he didn't dare.

"From the positioning, I don't know if we're going to be successful. I need a better angle. Otherwise we could try another one in eight more weeks, at the end of your second trimester." He continued to move the probe. "This one is active and kicking."

"That sounds good to me," Stephanie told the doctor. "I want to teach it to scuba dive."

"So you're a diver."

"We both are," Nikos volunteered.

After a surprisingly long period of silence, Dr. Panos said, "Then let's hope he shares your interest."

"He?" they exclaimed in unison.

"See that?" He pointed to the baby's anatomy. "There's your boy. Got a name for him yet?"

Her eyes filled with tears as she looked at Nikos. "Nikolaos Alexandros Vassalos!"

Stephanie...

Dr. Panos chuckled. "Well, that sounded definite." He turned off the machine and handed each of them a photo. "You can get up and use the restroom now. Keep taking your iron and vitamin pills, get plenty of rest, and I'll see you in a month. Make your appointment with my receptionist on your way out."

"Thank you!" Stephanie murmured emotionally.

"You're entirely welcome. Congratulations."

Nikos shook his hand, then studied the pictures while he waited for her. He couldn't help remembering the time in the hospital when he'd been told he would never father a child, would never know the joy of hearing those words from a doctor, let alone be given pictures.

Stephanie's glowing face was the first thing he saw when she met him out in reception. With excitement she scheduled her next visit, for early October.

Don't let your doubts drag you down now, Vassalos.

He ushered her outside to the parking lot. "This calls for a celebration. What would you like to do?"

"Go to a furniture store and buy a crib. I've almost finished the lace edge on the quilt and can't wait to see it set up in my room."

"Be honest with me, Stephanie. Wouldn't you rather we went looking for a house first?"

His question brought shadows to her eyes. "I thought we went through this a month ago."

"I was afraid you were humoring me. I thought to give you a little more time."

She put her hands on her hips. "I think it's time you were honest with me. Are you dying to live in a house? Or have you decided you want to deposit me in one before you go crazy? I'm getting the message you need space away from me, while you conduct your business meetings on board. If that's the case, please say so now."

"Space is not the issue."

Color tinted her cheeks. "Then what is?"

"I was only thinking of your happiness while you make preparations for the baby that's coming."

"I'm perfectly happy, but apparently you're not. So I have an idea. While I go back to the yacht, you can look at furnished homes to your heart's content with Mr. Doukakis. Let me know when you find the one you think will suit me best, and I'll move into it."

Damn. On this red letter day he'd mentioned a house only to please her, not to undo all the joy she'd been feeling since her visit to the doctor.

"Not every woman with a baby coming wants to live on the water."

"But I'm not every woman," she retorted. "The yacht

is home to me. From my condo I used to watch ocean-going vessels out on the water and dream about sailing around the world on one. That idea has always intrigued me."

He nodded. "Then I won't mention buying a home again. After we find the right crib, let's have lunch on the island before we return to the *Diomedes*."

Now that she had run out of steam, she seemed to droop a little. "Nikos? Forgive me for snapping at you. I can't believe I talked to you like that when you're always so wonderful to me. The truth is I've been so happy, I haven't wanted anything to change. But that's the selfish part of me talking. I'll go with you to look at a house, and never complain again. The last thing I want to be is a carping wife." Her voice caught.

"Carping?"

"Yes, as in a petty woman who looks for trouble and finds fault at every turn, appreciating nothing. With your command of English, I'm surprised you haven't heard that word."

He cradled her lovely face in his hands, forcing her look at him. She'd picked up a golden glow since living on the yacht. Her eyes shimmered an intense blue. Nikos could easily get lost in them. "You're none of those things and you know it."

"I'm the ball on your chain, holding you back." She was serious.

Laughter rose out of his throat. "From what?"

She averted her eyes. "From whatever you planned to do before I ventured into Vassalos territory without permission. I look back on it now and can't believe I was so audacious."

Right now he couldn't relate to the man who'd

collided with her along the pier. That man had been drowning in despair, without a glimmer of hope. For a moment he'd thought he was hallucinating. But the minute he'd touched her, he'd realized she was no figment of his imagination. Stephanie Walsh had materialized in the flesh.

Nikos slid his hands to her shoulders, covered by her leaf-green top. His fingers played with the ends of her silvery-gold hair. Desire for his pregnant wife was eating him alive. Oh yes, she was pregnant. He had the proof resting in his pocket.

With their mouths so close, it was all he could do not to devour her in front of the people coming and going from the clinic. But he did kiss her very thoroughly, and was shaken by her powerful response.

"I dare you to kiss me like that when we're back on the yacht and no one is watching," she teased.

That's what drew him to Stephanie. Though she could be fiery, she didn't take herself too seriously, and retained a sense of humor lacking in the women he'd known. They'd had a month of togetherness and he still wasn't tired of her. If anything, he couldn't wait to get her back to the yacht. He'd taken the day off work and no one else would be around.

"I'm so glad you know how to put this crib together. I wouldn't have a clue." Stephanie sat propped on her bed, finishing the lace edge of the baby quilt while she watched her husband work. As she studied his dark, handsome features, a feeling of contentment stole through her.

She picked up the ultrasound picture and studied it for the hundredth time. Knowing she was carrying his son made this day unforgettable. How could Nikos possibly not know and feel that this was *his* baby?

But every time she put herself in his shoes, she remembered the horror story about his parents. And not just his parents, but the tragic lie that had bound Kon to the Frenchwoman. Trust was one of the most vital essentials in a relationship, let alone a marriage. Nikos's view of life and women had been flawed because of circumstances, yet there was a part of him that was still giving her a chance. She loved him for that modicum of trust in her, loved him with every fiber of her being.

"It's your fault I feel stuffed after eating lunch." It had been a marvelous lunch of filet of sole with grapes and capers. "I've gained too much weight since my first doctor's appointment, in Florida. Do you realize there's no such a thing as a bad meal on Oinoussa?"

He darted her an all-encompassing glance that sent a shiver of excitement through her body. "Nor on the *Diomedes*. The acquisition of my new cook is putting back the pounds I lost in the hospital. When we were on the island, you never told me you're such a fabulous cook."

"You and Yannis are full of it, but it's nice to hear. Mom was always at work, so my grandmother taught me a lot of her recipes."

"Yannis says you put Maria's cooking to shame."

"It's the butter instead of the olive oil."

"I like both."

"So do I. The blending of two worlds." She let out a sigh. "Nikos? I've started picking up some Greek around you and Yannis, but it's a slow process. I want to be able to talk to the baby in both languages. How would you feel if I found someone on Oinoussa to tutor me for a few hours every day? You speak perfect English. I feel embarrassed that I can't converse in Greek."

"I think it's an excellent idea."

"You do?" She'd been holding her breath in case he told her the future was still uncertain and he didn't think it was necessary.

"I'll look into it." On that satisfying note he got to his feet. "The crib is finished. What do you think?" He'd placed it against the wall opposite the end of her bed.

"I love it! I'm glad we picked the walnut for Alex." She rolled off the bed. Together they added the mattress and padding. When she'd fastened the ties, she reached for the baby quilt and spread it along the railing.

Nikos examined the hand stitching. "You do perfect work. Anyone would think you'd bought this. I'm more impressed than I can say."

"It's full of mistakes, but thanks. I hope he has your black hair. Against the white material, he'll be gorgeous. I can't wait to wrap him in it."

In the next breath Nikos pulled it off the railing and wrapped it around her neck and shoulders. "If he has your blond hair, the effect with this quilt will be sensational." Still holding the material, Nikos drew her close. "All his friends will say he has the most beautiful mother in the Oinousses."

"*Nikos,* I—"

The rest of her words were smothered as he claimed her mouth and slowly savored her as if she were something fragile and precious. Heat began to course through her body, making her legs tremble. She slid her hands up his chest, where she could feel the solid pounding of his heart beneath his sport shirt. For so long Stephanie had been waiting for a sign that he still wanted her. Her great need caused her to respond with an ardor she didn't know herself capable of.

He picked her up and laid her on the bed before stretching out next to her. "Today when I saw the doctor spread the gel and use the probe, I wanted to be the one to feel the baby, Stephanie. Let me feel you now." His voice throbbed.

She responded with a moan as he lifted the hem of her blouse and pulled down the elasticized waist of her skirt. When his hand moved over her belly, sensation after physical sensation swept through her. "Our baby is right there."

As he lowered his mouth to the spot, the shock of his kiss traveled through her womb. Stephanie was filled with indescribable delight and the hope that everything was going to be all right. She let out a helpless cry and once again their mouths sought each other and clung.

There were so many things she'd been wanting to tell him. Now she could show him, without words getting in the way. She'd thought she'd loved him before, but after living together for a month her feelings for him had deepened in new ways and had taken root.

"Don't be afraid you're going to hurt me," she begged, wanting him to crush her in his arms. Though she sensed his growing desire, he held back, kissing her with tenderness rather than the kind of passion she'd once known with him. She wanted more.

He buried his face in her neck. "I don't want to do anything that could injure the baby."

Surely he knew that couldn't happen. Or was he covering for something else she'd secretly worried about from the moment he'd told her he was sterile? "There's no fear of that, unless it's your own injury stopping you."

Nikos lifted his head and looked down at her in confusion. "What do you mean?"

"I'm talking about the deep bruising to your spine from the explosion. When you push yourself too hard, I can tell when you're in pain, but I'm wondering if it's more than that."

To her chagrin he rolled off the bed and got to his feet. "Explain what you mean."

Stephanie sat up, furious with herself for ruining the moment. "I've wondered if your PTSD wasn't the only reason you didn't want to sleep with me in the cabin with the twin beds. If you can't make love, then please tell me. Don't you know it could never matter to me?"

He reared his head in obvious surprise. "There's nothing wrong with me in that department."

For a moment she couldn't breathe, she was so thrilled to hear that news, for his sake. "I—I'm sorry if I jumped to the wrong conclusion," she stammered. "Thank heaven you're all right."

But another part of her was humiliated to have given herself away. It meant he had another reason for not making love to her. Afraid she knew what it was, she got off the bed and put the fallen quilt back on the crib railing.

"Looking back on the explosion, I suppose you could say the collateral damage didn't take everything away," he murmured.

Needing to do something to deflect the pain after that grim assessment, she started cleaning up the mess they'd made. He took the plastic from her hands. "I'll take care of this."

Unable to meet his gaze, she reached for a book she'd been reading, and hurried up on deck to put distance between them. Now that she knew the whole truth of their situation from her husband's lips, she could envision what life had been like after Nikos's father accused his mother of being unfaithful, all of it based on a vicious rumor. The thought that the baby might not be his had changed the dynamics of their marriage.

Was Nikos following the same pattern? Unsure of her still, would he go only so far and no further while he waited for the result in January?

Stephanie had thought her husband was beginning to believe their baby was his. A few minutes ago she'd felt closer to him than she'd thought possible. Though she could shout it to the heavens that the stamp of a Vassalos would be on their little boy, she would never be able to convince Nikos of it until after the delivery.

"Stephanie?"

She wheeled around just as she'd arranged a lounger to sit in while she read. "Yannis! I didn't know you were here. We thought you wouldn't be back until tonight."

"I've got some repair work to do and decided to get at it before dark."

Put on a good face.

She could tell he was dying to know how her doctor's visit went, but he was never one to pry into her business. "We got back a while ago. Nikos set up a crib in my room. You'll be impressed what a good job he did. Our baby boy will be very happy in it."

A grin broke out on the man's bronzed face. "You're going to have a son?"

"That's what the doctor said. We plan to call him Alex."

"That's a fine family name."

"Yes. Ask Nikos to show you a picture."

The older seaman's eyes looked suspiciously bright. "I'm very happy for you."

"We're happy, too." She would keep up the pretense if it killed her. "Thank you for all your kindness to me, Yannis. You do so many things to help me, and I'm grateful."

"It's my pleasure."

"Nikos couldn't get along without you, even if you do put him through torture every day helping him do his exercises. But you already know that, don't you?"

For once she saw him blush.

"He's a slave driver, all right." Nikos had just joined them. "I guess my wife has told you the news."

Yannis clapped him on the shoulder. "She says you have a photo."

"Right here." Nikos pulled it out of his pocket.

The seaman's eyes squinted against the light to get a good look. "He's beautiful, like his mother."

"I was just telling her he'll have the most beautiful woman on the island for his *mana*."

But you can't take credit for being the father yet, her heart cried.

Stephanie would have to harden herself, because this was going to be the way of it for the next five months.

CHAPTER NINE

December 10

STEPHANIE LOVED HER Greek lessons. For the last four months Yannis had driven her faithfully to and from the school on Oinoussa every weekday after breakfast for her two-hour session with Borus. The forty-year-old was a part-time counselor who was glad for the extra money. He was also a lot of fun.

The closer she drew to her delivery date, the more taciturn and anxious Nikos had become. Whether or not he believed this child was his, she knew he worried. Even though Dr. Panos had assured him at every appointment that she was coming along normally, with no unexpected complications, he didn't seem to quite believe it, and hovered over her until there were times when she wanted to scream.

With the baby due in three weeks, he argued with her that she should stop the lessons. A month ago he'd told her no more swimming with Tassos's wife in order to give her scuba pointers.

While they were eating breakfast this morning, she asked Nikos if he was ordering her to stay home today. The question turned his features into a cool mask before he told her the lessons would end when her teacher left for the Christmas holidays on the seventeenth.

With that pronouncement Nikos got up from the table, taking his coffee with him to the lounge to work. These days the *Diomedes* stayed in port and he used a small cruiser to travel back and forth from the rig erected offshore.

To her joy his business with Tassos was growing, and he'd acquired rights to drill off some of the other uninhabited islands of the Oinousses cluster. His strong concern for the environment made certain there'd be no damage to the local habitat.

As usual when Stephanie came out of class, she tried out what she'd learned on Yannis, who was an excellent teacher himself. But today when he greeted her, she could tell he had something serious on his mind.

"What's wrong? Has something happened to Nikos?" she cried in alarm.

"No, no."

"Thank goodness." She had to wait for her heartbeat to slow down.

"You have a visitor on board. She's very anxious to talk to you."

Stephanie frowned. "Who?"

"Kyria Vassalos, Nikos's mother."

"Oh…" She couldn't believe it. "Is Nikos with her?"

"No. He's gone to the rig. She came when she knew he wouldn't be here."

"How did she know?"

"Because I worked for her when he was just a boy. We've always been friends."

"Which means you've always kept her informed." Stephanie got it.

"Yes. Today Nikos's father is away in Athens on business. It's been her first chance to come and visit. I sent my son to fetch her in his boat. But if you don't want to meet her, I'll tell her to go back to Egnoussa."

"No. Don't do that." More than anything in the world Stephanie had wanted to meet his mother. She just hadn't expected their first meeting to happen when she was in full bloom, with swollen feet and her face marked with chloasma, the pregnancy mask. If she could be thankful for one thing, it was that she could carry on a basic conversation in Greek.

Her nervousness increased as Yannis drove her to the port. Together they walked along the pier to the yacht. Stephanie could see his mother looking out from the rail. Her luxuriant black hair was pulled back in a stylish twist. She was trim, and shorter than Stephanie by several inches. With her white slacks and stunning blue blouse setting off her olive skin, she was a true Grecian beauty. This was where Nikos got his fantastic looks.

As Stephanie stepped on board, the older woman turned, focusing her soft brown eyes on her. "I hope you don't mind," she said in accented English. "I've wanted to meet the woman my son married. I'm sorry it didn't happen when you came to our home. You need to know I'm ashamed of my husband's behavior toward you. My name is—"

"Hestia." Stephanie supplied it for her. "I know your name and I'm so glad you're here now," she said in her best Greek. "You raised a wonderful son. I love him very much."

His mother made a quiet study of her. "For him to

have married you the day after you arrived in Greece, it's obvious how he feels about you."

Stephanie shook her head. "He married me for the sake of the baby." Taking a risk, she added, "He doesn't believe he's the father."

Hestia looked stunned. "I don't understand."

"Come downstairs with me and we'll talk." They went below. "Can I get you something to drink?"

"Nothing, thank you."

"Then come to my room."

A gasp escaped Hestia's lips when she saw the bedroom turned into a nursery. Between Stephanie's bed and everything a mother needed to take care of her new baby, there was barely room to move.

At this point Stephanie's speech was sprinkled with Greek and English. "Please sit down in the rocking chair. I have something to give you." She went over to the dresser and pulled out a photo album. "I wish you had been at the wedding. You should have been there. I made this for you and your husband to keep."

The older woman opened the cover. For the next five minutes she remained speechless as she looked at all the pictures. When she finally lifted her head, tears were rolling down her cheeks. Stephanie saw in those brown eyes all the sorrow a mother could at missing out on her child's wedding day.

"Nikos told me about your husband's distrust when you were pregnant with him. I'm afraid the same thing has happened to me. We had only ten days together on vacation last April. We don't know that much about each other, and so much happened after he had to return to active duty, it raised his doubts about life. About everything."

His mother nodded sadly. "Even though he could walk, he was on the verge of giving up when we took him home from the hospital."

Tears welled in Stephanie's eyes. "He's much better now, but he won't believe this is his baby until after Alexandros is born."

"You can forgive my son for this?"

She smiled. "Didn't you forgive his father?" Stephanie reached for the sonogram picture and showed it to her. "That was at four months. He was only four and half inches long. Now look at him." She placed her hands on top of her big stomach.

Hestia didn't give her a verbal answer, but got to her feet. After setting the album on the dresser, she put her arms around Stephanie and hugged her. "You must come for Christmas and stay the whole day. Everyone wants to meet you. I won't take no for an answer."

Stephanie's heart warmed. "We'll be there. Even if Nikos is still upset with his father, he won't dare refuse to accompany me if I go. He hovers around me constantly these days. Sometimes he follows me when I have to go to the bathroom!"

Laughter bubbled out of her mother-in-law. "That's how my husband was with all three of our children, doubts and all." She wiped her eyes. "I'm going to leave so Nikos won't find me here when he comes home."

"Yannis will see you out to the dock." Stephanie handed her the album to take with her.

"He's a treasure, but I'm sure you've learned that for yourself by now."

"Definitely."

"Take good care of yourself, Stephanie. Your time is close."

"Don't worry. Nikos does it for both of us."

They both laughed as they started up the stairs. Stephanie felt as if she was floating. Already she loved Nikos's mother.

December 17

Nikos lounged against the door of the car while he waited for Stephanie to come out of the school. After going to her doctor's appointment with her, he'd driven her straight here. He was glad this would be her last day of Greek lessons. Her due date was two weeks from tomorrow. Dr. Panos had told her to rest and keep her feet up. Nikos intended to see that she followed his instructions.

Just when his patience had worn thin and he was ready to go in and get her, the school doors opened and his wife emerged with her teacher. Borus Paulos had come highly recommended, but all Nikos could see was that he was enamored of her in the jacketed white sundress she'd bought that first day shopping.

The man gesticulated while he continued talking. Nikos doubted he'd noticed him waiting, but Stephanie saw him. She waved before saying goodbye to her teacher. Then she started walking toward him.

For a moment he was transported back to the Caribbean. He'd been walking along the beach with Angelo when he saw this woman in a wet suit with a fabulous body. Her hair looked gilded in the sun. She was coming to meet Angelo on those long, elegant legs.

When she drew closer, her gaze suddenly switched to Nikos. Her eyes were an impossible blue color, dazzling like rare gems. Her voluptuous mouth curved into a friendly smile. She looked happy and excited because they were going to dive. At that moment the most remarkable sensation had passed through Nikos's body and he was never the same again.

That same electrifying feeling was attacking him now as Stephanie approached the car and their gazes met. He lost his breath. This woman with child was his wife! Whether the baby was his or not, he realized it no longer mattered to him. Somehow over the months they'd become his family. If he'd seen this day while he lay recuperating in the hospital, he would have thought he'd lost his mental faculties along with the ability to walk.

"Sorry it took me so long to get away," she said a little breathlessly. "Borus is a talker when he gets going."

"It wasn't your fault." Her tutor couldn't help his hormones raging in her presence. In fact, the way Nikos himself was feeling at the moment, he didn't dare touch her while they were in front of other people. He opened the passenger door to help her in, seduced by the strawberry-scented shampoo she used in the shower. When her swollen belly brushed against him by accident, his heart gave an extra beat in wonder, while she let out a gentle laugh.

By some miracle she'd stayed incredibly healthy throughout her pregnancy. She'd never developed the serious problems he'd heard various married business associates talk about. Though she complained of swelling and the chloasma she insisted made her resemble a raccoon, he'd never seen her more beautifully feminine.

It had taken control almost beyond his endurance to stay away from her. Because of his injury she'd wrongly assumed he couldn't make love to her as he'd done on the island. But only one thing had held him back. Stark staring fear.

She didn't know what it was like to worry that he might cause harm to her and the baby during a flashback. It was the only force strong enough to keep him locked up in his room night after night. After living together this long without an incident that left bruises on her, he refused to allow anything to go wrong now.

After lunch they were going to do the last of their Christmas shopping. Just a few more presents, nothing taxing. While they were gone, he'd instructed Yannis to put up the little Christmas tree with lights he'd bought and smuggled on board. The lounge was the best place to surprise her. It wasn't a tradition Nikos followed, but he knew Americans were big on it, and such things were important to his wife.

He darted her a glance before he started the car. "Hungry?"

"You know, for once I'm not? But if you want to eat before we shop, that's fine with me."

"What I'd like to do is get the gift buying over with as fast as possible and go back home. I'll cook today and surprise you with something you haven't had before."

She smiled at him. "I'd love that."

"Good."

With the much cooler late autumn temperatures, she appeared to thrive. He could only marvel at her energy.

"Let's shop at the main department store," she suggested. "That way we can find everything we want under one roof."

"I was thinking the same thing." He headed in that direction. "Just so you know, Tassos phoned while I was waiting for you. He and Elianna have invited us to their house for their family's Christmas Day party."

He felt Stephanie stir restlessly in the seat. "That's very nice of them, but we can't go."

He frowned. "Why not?"

When she remained quiet, he slanted her a glance. "Stephanie? What's wrong?"

"Nikos," she began, but her hesitation was plain as day. He saw a guilty look enter her eyes. It surprised him no end.

"You don't want to go?"

"Under other circumstances I would, but that's not it." She shook her head. "I have a confession to make."

Just when he'd been thinking nothing had gone wrong with her pregnancy, he was terrified she was going to tell him something he didn't want to hear. On impulse he pulled over to the side of the street and shut off the engine. Turning in the seat, he slid his arm behind her and tugged on a few strands of her hair.

"Are you ill? Is there something you didn't tell the doctor this morning?"

"This isn't about me. I…it's about us."

In an instant his blood ran cold. "You mean after all this time, you've chosen today instead of Christmas to tell me who the father of your baby is?"

"No! Nikos." Her horrified cry reverberated in the car. "I'm going about this all wrong. Your mother came to see me last week while your father was away in Athens. We had a frank talk about everything. I showed her the sonogram picture. She's wonderful and I love her already. Before she left, I gave her the wedding album I made for them. She has invited us to spend Christmas Day with your family. I accepted for us."

After he'd imagined every horrific thing possible that could destroy life as he knew it, her explanation came as a complete shock. It took a minute for him to assimilate what she'd just said. He waited until he'd calmed down enough to talk. "That won't be a problem. I'll phone and tell her we've made other plans. She'll understand."

"No, I don't think she will. Nikos," Stephanie said in a tremulous whisper. "She adores you and needs to see her son. They've missed out on more than a decade of your life. You can't disappoint them. Life's too short."

He sucked in his breath. "My father's bias against Castor and his children for being who they are has been unconscionable, Stephanie. After what he did to my mother and the way he spoke to you, I can't be in the same room with him."

She put a hand to his cheek. "But she's forgiven him and so have I. As you told me, he's afraid and doesn't know how to make things right. If you don't show him the way, his fear of losing you will send him to the grave a desperately unhappy man. What joy could there be in that for any of us?"

Nikos felt sick to his stomach. "I can't do it. Don't ask that of me."

Stephanie pulled her hand away from him and stared out the window. "Then you go to Tassos's family for Christmas. I'll go to your parents and take your family their gifts."

Seeing black, Nikos started the car and drove straight to the dock.

As Stephanie passed the lounge on her way to the bedroom, she saw a five-foot Christmas tree studded with colored lights set up over by the entertainment center. Yannis had been busy while they'd been gone. She walked over to it and examined some of the ornaments.

After the devastating silence in the car while Nikos drove them back to the yacht, the sight of this brought her immeasurable delight. There was no one like Nikos. But the lights brought pain, too, making a mockery of the peace and joy Christmas was supposed to bring. They'd reached an impasse. His mother's invitation and Stephanie's acceptance had ruined this beautiful day.

Desperate to make things right between them, she hurried to his room before he could lock her out. That's what he'd been doing for months. The night before last she'd heard the gut-wrenching moaning and sobbing that came from his bedroom. So far she'd counted four episodes she knew about since their wedding.

When she discussed this with Yannis, the older man said it was a good sign that they weren't happening as often as they had in the beginning, which could only mean Nikos was slowly getting better. Stephanie wanted that for him more than anything.

He was such an outstanding man; she couldn't reconcile everything she knew about him with the side of his nature that had caused him to shut down just now. She couldn't leave it alone. This was too serious. Without knocking, she opened the door, determined they were going to talk everything out.

She couldn't prevent the cry that escaped when she discovered he'd removed his clothes and had just pulled on his black bathing trunks. With his back still to her, she saw the bruising at the lower part of his spine. Since he'd always worn his wet suit when they went swimming, she hadn't realized how deep and pervasive his injury had been. To think of his lying in that hospital bed broken and in despair... She couldn't bear it.

He wheeled around, a live, breathing, angry Adonis. That awful glittery look in his jet-black eyes impaled her, freezing the breath from her lungs. "I don't recall inviting you in here." The wintry tone he'd once used with her was back in full force.

Stephanie couldn't swallow. "I was afraid I might not get an invitation. I came in to tell you how sorry I am that I didn't let you know about your mother's visit until now. You've suffered years of pain over a situation I haven't fully comprehended until today. I'll call your mother and tell her we can't come."

It was as if he'd turned to stone. She couldn't reach him.

"I should never have attempted to tell you anything about your life or your thoughts," she went on. "I do have an audacious nature and realize it's a glaring flaw in my makeup. So I'll make you a promise now that I'll never keep anything from you again, or try to influence your thinking in any way. I swear it."

Desolate at this point because of his silence, she turned to leave, but paused in the doorway. "I love the Christmas tree. No woman in the world has a better husband than you. I'm sorry you can't say the same thing about your wife. To tell you I'm sorry I came to Greece would be a lie, but I'd give anything if I'd been honest with you after your mother left the other day. I've trespassed on your soul, Nikos. Forgive me. It will never happen again."

She rushed to her room and lay down on her back, pressing the pillow against her face to stifle her sobs. It wasn't long before she heard the familiar sound of the cruiser. Who knew when Nikos would be back? And when he did return, there was no guesstimating how soon he'd speak to her again.

Stephanie knew he couldn't tolerate the sight of her right now. She didn't blame him. That's why he'd taken off. Perhaps the best thing to do was give him some space. The more she thought about it, the more she liked the idea. While she put a plan into action, she ate a substantial lunch and made a phone call.

Once that was done she packed an overnight bag with several days' worth of clothes. On her way out she stopped in the lounge to put some presents under the tree for Nikos. Presents made it look ready for Christmas. After that she wrote him a note, leaving it on his desk where he would see it.

> *Dear Nikos. We've been together constantly since I barged into your life. What was it Kahlil Gibran once wrote? "There should be spaces in your togetherness." I agree with his philosophy, so I'm taking myself off until the day after Christmas. Don't worry. I won't be far. Please be assured I won't embarrass you by bothering anyone you know or care about. Our business stays our business. I think you know I would never do anything that put me or the baby in danger. I want Alex to know his father. S.*

Nikos could be gone for the rest of the day. As for Yannis, he'd said he'd be back at three. She had a half hour to leave without him seeing her.

The town had only two taxis. One of them was waiting for her at the dock. She got in and told the driver to drop her off on a corner where she'd seen used cars for sale. Her passport still showed she was single. The man who sold her the car had no idea she was Kyria Vassalos. That suited her fine. It didn't take long before she was in possession of a clunker that cost only five hundred dollars.

Free to do what she wanted, Stephanie drove to a wonderfully sited convent nestled among pines and ringed with a magnificent garden. The weary traveler was welcome to stay at their hospice, which was located on the west side of the island, about ten minutes from town. During one of their lessons Borus had told her she should visit to learn its history.

En route she passed several quiet coves, enchanted by the scenery and grateful she could use her bank card to draw money from her final paycheck. She still had enough to pay the fee for board and room for a week.

The convent suited her perfectly. For the time being she intended to get some reading done and keep her feet up. But when she got restless, she could take short drives around the island. It helped to know she'd be out of Nikos's hair for a while. He'd been hurtled into a world of pain after he'd left the Caribbean, and deserved a break.

As she'd told him, she was the ball on the end of his chain. By her staying here at the convent, out of sight, he didn't have to drag it around. For the time being he didn't know where to find her and that was good. He hovered too much.

On the plus side, she could give in to her emotions, which were out of control at this stage of her pregnancy. If she wanted to cry her heart out at night, no one would hear her through the thick walls.

Once in her simple room, she sank down on the bed. Right now she was so exhausted she couldn't move. For the last hour she'd had pain in her lower back. It was from all the walking she'd done today. Tomorrow she'd go out in the garden, but not now.

Evening had fallen before Nikos returned to the dock. Yannis was waiting to help him tie up the cruiser. But there was a worried look on the older man's face that raised the hair on the back of Nikos's neck.

"Is Stephanie all right?"

"That's the problem, Nikos. I don't know. When I came back at three she was gone, but she left a note on the desk in the lounge."

Forgetting the pain in his back, Nikos raced along the pier to the yacht and hurried down the stairs. As he read her message, his heart plunged like a boulder crashing down a mountain. "She had to have called for a taxi to take her to one of the tourist lodgings. I'll call and find out which one."

But when he finally reached the driver who'd picked her up, the man was no help. "I dropped her off on a corner by the Pappas Market. She was carrying an overnight bag."

Searing pain ripped Nikos open before he hung up. "I've got to find her tonight!"

Yannis looked grim. "You get dressed and we'll go to every place where she might be staying."

Nikos changed into jeans and a sweater before they took off for town in the car. They combed the whole area for an hour, without results. "I should never have closed up on her like I did earlier. She couldn't help it that Mother came to see her."

"That was my fault, Nikos."

He stared hard at his friend. "No. The fault is all mine for letting old wounds fester until the result caused Stephanie to run away from me. I can't lose her, Yannis." His voice shook. "Where in the hell has she gone?"

"How did she find you?"

The shrewd seaman's question gave Nikos pause. He struggled for breath. "Through sheer persistence and determination." His mind reeled with possibilities. "Since she's not at any local lodgings, she had to get a ride with someone to somewhere else." His turmoil grew worse.

Yannis patted his shoulder. "Perhaps she went to another part of the island."

"Maybe. But there's no place for her to stay, only ruins and churches."

"Could she have gone back to the dock, to take the boat to Chios?"

"Anything's worth looking into." Nikos got the port authority on the line. The captain in charge of the last crossing was emphatic that a blonde, pregnant American woman had not been on board.

Nikos shook his head. "She's here somewhere, Yannis. Maybe she crept on some fishing boat down at the harbor to spend the night."

Yannis scratched his head. "I don't think she'd do that, not in her condition. She's so excited about that baby, she'd never put herself in precarious circumstances. Besides, everyone knows you. I doubt she'd do anything that could embarrass you. She said as much in the note."

Nikos stared blindly at the water in the distance.

"She had to get help from someone, but in my gut I know she wouldn't turn to Tassos or my family. She hasn't made any friends yet."

"That's not exactly true."

His gaze swerved to Yannis. "What do you mean?"

"Bulos."

Though she'd spent ten hours a week for months with her language teacher, Nikos still ruled him out and shook his head. "Let's go home and see if she's back on board the *Diomedes*. If not, I'll think about bringing in the police."

Except that she expected him to trust her enough to take care of herself and come back when she was ready. The police would want to know why she was missing and would figure out she and Nikos were having a domestic quarrel. It would be the talk of the Oinousses.

By three in the morning it was clear she wasn't coming back. Nikos thought he'd been at the end of his rope in the hospital, but this was agony in a new dimension. If anything untoward happened to her or the baby because of him, life wouldn't be worth living.

Yannis made them coffee. Both of them were too wired from anxiety to do anything but pace. They were waiting for morning so they could begin their search all over again.

At five to four Niko's cell phone rang, causing him to almost jump out of his skin. He clicked on. "Stephanie?"

"No, sir. This is Sister Sofia at the Convent of the Holy Virgin on Oinoussa. Are you Kyrie Vassalos?"

Beads of perspiration broke out on his forehead. "Speaking." He couldn't imagine why she'd called.

"Your wife checked into our hospice this afternoon." *The hospice! Of course!* "But she's been in labor ever since and is now at the hospital."

Nikos weaved in place. "God bless you, Sister. You've just saved my life!" He hung up. "Yannis? Stephanie is at the hospital having the baby!"

With Yannis driving, they made it there in record time. Nikos burst inside the emergency entrance. "My wife!" he said to the surprised attendant. "Stephanie Vassalos—"

"She's in the delivery room."

"Has she had the baby?"

"Not yet. Dr. Panos says for you to come with me. I'll get you ready. We need to hurry."

The next few minutes were a blur as Nikos was instructed to sanitize his hands before being led into the delivery room. He was told to sit.

"Nikos!" He heard Stephanie call out to him.

"You're just in time," the doctor said without missing a beat. "Your baby fooled everyone and decided to come a few weeks early. Push, Stephanie. That's it. One more time."

Nikos's wet eyes flew to his brave, beautiful wife, propped on the bed. The strain in her body and the way she worked with the doctor was something he'd never forget.

"Ah, there's the head. This guy's got your husband's black hair."

He heard his wife's shouts of excitement.

"Keep pushing. Here comes Alexandros." Dr. Panos held the baby up in the air by the ankles and Nikos heard a gurgle, followed by a lusty cry.

Stephanie started sobbing for joy. "How does he look?" she begged the doctor.

"You can see for yourself after I've cut the cord." A minute later he laid the baby across her stomach and wiped off the fluid. "Come on over here, Papa. You can examine your son together."

As wonderful as that sounded, Nikos leaned over to kiss Stephanie's dry lips first. "Are you all right? I'm so sorry I wasn't there for you."

Her eyes were a blazing blue. "But you have been, all this time, and I've never been so happy in my life. Isn't he beautiful?"

His gaze flew to the baby, who'd stopped crying and gone quiet. His dark eyes looked at Nikos so seriously, reminding him of the way Stephanie sometimes did. He studied the rest of him. His perfect hands with their long fingers were curled into fists. It was like looking through a kaleidoscope, where all the bits and pieces formed a miraculous design. This one was made from the molds of a Walsh and a Vassalos.

Nikos saw Stephanie's mouth and chin, his brother's ears, his mother's black hair, his own fingers and toes, his father's body shape. *My son. My one and only.*

"He looks exactly like you, Nikos."

He turned his head toward her. "You're in there, too. But I want you to know that even if he didn't look like me, it wouldn't matter, because I fell in love with the two of you a long time ago. A miracle happened on the island."

"I know." Tears gushed from her eyes. "I love you, darling. So much I can't begin to tell you."

"No woman ever fought harder to show her love than you did when you came all the way to this remote island to find me. I'll never forget," he said against her mouth. "I've got to tell Yannis. Then I'm going to call the family and tell them they've become grand-parents again."

CHAPTER TEN

January 24

YANNIS WAS WAITING for her at the car outside the clinic.
The temperature had to be in the forties. Her sweater
felt good. There'd been some light rain that afternoon,
but now that the sun had dropped into the sea, it had
stopped.

Stephanie had decided to get her six weeks checkup
a few days ahead of schedule, without Nikos knowing.
The whole point was to surprise him.

"Dr. Panos says I'm 100 percent healthy, but I need
to lose weight."

"You look good for a new mother."

"Thank you."

"Now remember our plan."

"Are you sure you want to do this, Yannis?"

He grinned. "Nikos's parents have spent more time
on the *Diomedes* than they have at their house. It's my
turn."

"Alex is crazy about you."

"I love him. Maria and I have been waiting to tend
him. We have it all planned for tonight. Everything's
ready for you on the cruiser."

"Do you think Nikos suspects anything?"

"No. Tassos is with him and so are your parents. Between family, the demands of the business and the duties of a new father, he's too exhausted to be doing much thinking."

She took a shaky breath, so nervous and excited at the same time that she couldn't hold still. "Then I'll just keep walking past the yacht to the cruiser, and wait for him to come."

"When he asks where you are, I'll tell him that after you got back from shopping, you went in search of the camcorder, since you couldn't find it in the lounge. In the end he'll come looking for you."

This was the first night they would be away from the baby. "We'll be in that little cove around the point if there's a problem."

"Don't you worry about anything."

"Alex isn't too crazy about formula, but he'll drink it when he gets hungry."

"Of course he will. It's Nikos you should be worried about. He needs some attention."

She had news for him. *So do I.* "You're an angel, Yannis."

After he'd parked the car at the dock, she gave him a hug, then ran along the pier to the cruiser and hurried on board. There was just one bedroom below. She turned on the heat to warm things up. While she waited, she took a quick shower and changed into a new nightgown her mother-in-law had given her for Christmas.

Though she was already missing her little boy, she was dying to be with her big boy. They hadn't been intimate since her vacation on Providenciales. Right now she was horribly nervous. If he still wasn't prepared to make love to her because of his PTSD, she needed to know before she made herself sick with expectations.

For weeks now they'd shared tender, loving moments with the baby, but Nikos went to bed alone every night like clockwork.

Not tonight!

After leaving the light on in the hallway, she brushed out her hair and climbed under the covers with a novel. For fifteen minutes she kept reading the first page, until she heard him call to her.

"Stephanie? What are you doing? The camcorder was in your bedroom. Come on up. The family's waiting for you."

Her heart thudded too hard. "If you don't mind, I'd like to stay down here for a while."

In the silence she could almost hear him thinking. "Why?"

"Because I'd like to have my husband to myself for a little while."

She heard him come down the stairs. "Are you upset about something?" His voice had suddenly deepened. It did that when he suspected trouble.

"Actually, I am."

He burst into the bedroom. The worried look on his handsome face was priceless. "What are you doing in bed?"

She sat up, feasting her eyes on him. "I've been waiting ten months for you. This afternoon Dr. Panos gave me a clean bill of health, so—"

"You've been to see him already?" he interrupted. If she wasn't mistaken, the news seemed to have shaken him.

"Yes. I couldn't stand to wait until next week. Everything's been arranged. Yannis and Maria are taking care of Alex until tomorrow. I told him we'd motor around the point to the cove and stay for the night. I grabbed your medication earlier today. It's in my purse. So there's nothing you need to go back for. Your parents and Tassos will understand."

A haunted look crept over Nikos's features. "Stephanie—"

"If you have a nightmare, you won't have to worry you're hurting the baby. He's safe and sound on the *Diomedes*. I'm tough, Nikos. I can take whatever happens if you'll give me the chance. I want to be your wife. Won't you let me?"

She watched his throat working. It felt like an eternity before he said, "It's cold on deck. Stay right where you are."

"I promise."

In a few minutes she felt the cruiser reversing. After traveling at wake speed, Nikos opened it up and they were flying across the water. It didn't take long to round the point. He eventually slowed down, and she felt them glide onto the sand in the cove.

More waiting while she heard him take a shower.

Before the light went out, she saw his silhouette in the doorway. He'd hitched a towel around his hips. "I have a confession to make, Stephanie."

Not another one. She couldn't take it. "What is it?"

"When I got back to my unit, I told Kon I'd fallen in love with you, and planned to resign my commission after our mission so I could marry you."

With a moan of joy she climbed out of bed and ran to him, throwing her arms around his neck.

He crushed her to him, scattering kisses over her face and hair. "Forgive me for being so horrible to you. You're the most precious thing in my life."

"There was never anything to forgive. Let's not talk anymore, darling. We've said everything there is to say. I want to make love all night, and the same thing every night for the rest of our lives. You have no understanding of how much I love you."

Nikos gripped her shoulders. His black eyes blazed with desire. "Actually, I'm one man who *does* know. And one day soon, I'm going to do everything in my power to help you find your own father. He deserves to know he has the most wonderful daughter a man could ever be blessed with. I adore you."

"And I, you. Love me, darling. Love me."

They were on fire for each other to a degree they hadn't known in the Caribbean.

As he picked her up and followed her body down on the bed, he spoke the Greek words she'd been yearning to hear him say. Over and over again he whispered, *"Agape mou."* My love, my love.

April 26

"Stephanie? Are you ready?" Nikos walked into the nursery they'd made aboard the *Diomedes*. He was so gorgeous, she almost fainted as he approached in a formal gray suit and white shirt.

"We are!" She looked down at their precious four-month-old Alex, who was so excited to see his daddy he kept smiling and lifting his arms. The two were so handsome it brought tears to her eyes to see them together. "Guess what, big boy? Today you're going to get christened."

She expected Nikos to pick him up, but he fooled her and swept her into his arms first. "I need this before we go anywhere." Catching her to him, he gave her a long, passionate kiss reminiscent of their lovemaking earlier that morning, before the baby was awake. It was a good thing her eggshell-colored suit with lace trim was wrinkle proof.

After thinking it over, she and Nikos had decided the ceremony at the church would take place on the date of their baby's conception. It was a secret between the two of them. Knowing Alex was their miracle child, they'd chosen this particular date to commemorate the sacred occasion.

They'd asked Tassos and Elianna to be godparents. Except for the addition of Nikos's mother waiting for them at the church where they'd been married, it was like déjà vu to travel there with Yannis and join their closest friends for the baptism.

Tassos hugged Stephanie before speaking on behalf of their child, then they followed the priest to the font, where Nikos's mother took Alex to undress him and wrap him in a large towel. Stephanie watched in wonder and fascination as they went through the sacrament of baptism.

After the priest gave him the name Alexandros and anointed him, Tassos wrapped the baby in a white sheet and towel. Then Nikos's mother dressed him in his christening clothes, but as she did so, Nikos's father suddenly appeared in their circle. He handed the priest a gold cross and chain to give their baby, the first olive branch toward a reconciliation with his son. At that same moment Tassos lit a candle.

Stephanie slid a covert glance to her husband, whose black eyes filled with liquid. She grasped his hand before they walked around the font three times. Earlier, Nikos had told her it symbolized the dance of joy.

With the circle complete except for Stephanie's mother, who Stephanie felt was watching from heaven, they witnessed their adorable son's first communion. Stephanie followed Nikos's lead and kissed Tassos's hand before he handed her the baby. Everyone murmured, *"Na sas zizi,"* which meant "life to Alexandros."

They'd planned a party back on the yacht afterward, but for Stephanie the real celebrating was going on right here, seeing the beginning of peace for both families after years of turmoil.

On the drive back to the yacht, Nikos pulled her tight against him. "I have two presents for you, my love. One is a home I've bought for us on Oinoussa. Now that we have a son, he needs a place to play besides the deck of the *Diomedes.*"

She hugged him hard. "I agree."

"Your other gift is in my pocket. I was planning to show it to you tonight, but after seeing my father show up, I've decided I can't wait."

Nikos sounded exceptionally excited. "What is it?" she whispered against his lips.

"The private investigator I hired has found your father."

"Nikos!"

"This is a picture of him." He reached in his breast pocket and pulled out a small photo. The second she saw the dark blond man, she knew it was her father. "We look so much alike!"

Nikos nodded. "He works at a bank in Cheyenne, Wyoming, where he was born. He's married with a son and daughter, who are both in college. When he met your mother, he was on leave from the army. Like me, he had to go back and serve another tour of duty. Four years later he got out of the army and married."

"D-does he know about me?"

"No."

"Thank heaven!"

A look of confusion entered Nikos's eyes before he kissed her. "Why do you say that?"

"Because he's an honorable man who made a good life for himself." Her voice shook. "I don't want to disrupt it. Since Mother chose not to find him, I want to leave things alone." She grasped Nikos's face in her hands. "It's enough to know what he looks like and who he is."

She crushed her husband in her arms. "Thank you, darling, for such a precious gift. What really matters now is our family, our son. I married the most wonderful man alive and I'm going to spend the rest of my life showing you what you mean to me. I love you, Nikos. *I love you.*"

* * * * *

Join the Mills & Boon Book Club

Subscribe to **Cherish™** today for 3, 6 or 12 months and you could **save over £40!**

We'll also treat you to these fabulous extras:

- 🌹 **FREE L'Occitane gift set worth £10**
- 🌹 **FREE home delivery**
- 🌹 **Rewards scheme, exclusive offers…and much more!**

Subscribe now and save over £40!
www.millsandboon.co.uk/subscribeme

The World of Mills & Boon®

There's a Mills & Boon® series that's perfect for you. We publish ten series and, with new titles every month, you never have to wait long for your favourite to come along.

Blaze®
Scorching hot, sexy reads
4 new stories every month

By Request
Relive the romance with the best of the best
9 new stories every month

Cherish™
Romance to melt the heart every time
12 new stories every month

Desire®
Passionate and dramatic love stories
8 new stories every month